*He needed her to be
the lady of his castle.
She wanted him to be
lord of her heart . . .*

A shaft of moonlight fell between the bed curtains, illuminating Brec's face for Honora. Curious about the tender expression she discovered there, she reached out to touch his cheek. He allowed the touch, then took her hand and kissed it, resting her fingertips against his gently moving lips. Honora gasped with the pleasure, the breathy warmth.

"Do we go too fast for you, sweet soul?" he asked. When she didn't answer, he sat up and began to pull once more at the straps of her shift. As he removed each, he drew his hand down the full length of her arm, a warm caress.

Honora's fears dwindled. She closed her eyes and took pleasure in the firm feel of Brec's fingers moving over her skin. She let him slip the straps over her hands and down to her hips.

"Don't stop," Honora managed to say.

"I'm not stopping," Brec whispered. "Just trying a new way to please you." Gently he stroked her belly and down each thigh. All the time he held her gaze, his eyes black and glittering in the moonlight. A slight smile curved on his lips—a knowing smile, not mocking, but tender and welcoming. Honora had no fear of that smile. She closed her eyes, savoring each stroke of his fingers . . .

Books by Linda Madl

Speak of Love
Sunny
Sweet Ransom

Published by POCKET BOOKS

SPEAK OF LOVE

LINDA MADL

POCKET BOOKS

New York   London   Toronto   Sydney   Tokyo   Singapore

An *Original* Publication of POCKET BOOKS

POCKET BOOKS, a division of Simon & Schuster Inc.
1230 Avenue of the Americas, New York, NY 10020

Copyright © 1991 by Linda Madl

ISBN: 0-671-73390-7

First Pocket Books printing December 1991

10 9 8 7 6 5 4 3 2 1

POCKET and colophon are registered trademarks of
Simon & Schuster Inc.

Cover art by Lina Levy

Printed in the U.S.A.

MARIA LUISA YEÉ

To my husband, Ron,
who always remembers to speak of love

ACKNOWLEDGMENTS

I'd like to thank the librarians of the St. Louis County Public Library and the St. Louis City Public Library for so willingly sharing their time, resources, and knowledge.

To Lillian and Don Seese, thanks for the sailing lesson aboard the *Midnight Pass*.

And a warm word of gratitude to Karyn Witmer-Gow, whose fine work, generous support, and honesty have served as guidance and encouragement in my own writing.

And a special "thank you" to my editor, Caroline Tolley, for her enthusiasm for this project.

From the Gaelic—

> Woe! woe! son of the Lowlander,
> Why wilt thou leave thine own bonny Border?
> Why comest thou hither, disturbing the Highlander,
> Wasting the glen that was once in fair order?

Sir Walter Scott
from the Introduction to
A Legend of Montrose

1

Edinburgh, Scotland
Spring 1644

Outside the Duke of Rosslyn's town house the fury of the storm swelled to match Honora's mounting anger. Raindrops beat a stinging tattoo against the library's diamond-pane window. Thunder rumbled across the heavens. Wind wailed like a banshee through chimney tops and howled along the city's dark wynds.

Honora stood by the window, listening to the tempest, drawing strength from its passion. She preferred the storm's rage to the emptiness that Lanie's betrayal had just hollowed out in her belly. She could hardly believe that halfway across the room her own serving woman—the same woman who had kept all of Honora's and her sisters' childhood secrets for years—stood confessing everything to Uncle James and Uncle Malcolm.

Lanie's sobs splintered the tense silence inside the library. "Aye, yer grace, I carried the notes across town for Lady Honora, and I accompanied her when she met with Mister Parrish in secret. She made me promise to tell no one."

Honora regarded her uncles' faces as they considered Lanie's words. Their deepening frowns told her there would be no talking her way out of this one. She wouldn't even try. After all, she had done no wrong. With a defiant lift of her chin, Honora set her shoulders and waited for her uncles to speak.

"I'm so sorry, milady," Lanie whimpered. She bowed her gray-streaked head covering before Honora and the two scowling Scotsmen who sat by the fire. "I didna want to tell of yer secret meetings, but yer uncles insisted. They reminded me that they are now like yer father, the first duke. God rest his soul. I had to tell."

The serving woman sniffled again and wiped away her copious tears with the corner of her brown wool shawl. Out of pity and exasperation Honora thrust her own handkerchief at the poor woman. She knew her uncles had given Lanie no choice.

"You did the right thing, Lanie," Uncle Malcolm said. "Now, tell me, was Lady Honora ever alone with Mister Alexander?"

"Of course I wasn't," Honora replied, her words short and terse. "Lanie was always present. Alexander and I never do any more than read poetry and sing lyrics."

"Then why did you keep the meetings secret?" James demanded.

"Because I know how you feel about the Parrishes," Honora retorted. And because she had no intention of dangling after every suitor her uncles chose for her, she thought. As far as she was concerned, there wasn't a suitable man in the whole of Edinburgh.

"You may go now, Lanie." Malcolm rose from his fireside chair and paced to the door as a signal of dismissal.

Everyone remained silent until the serving woman had left. Malcolm's footsteps rang firm and solid on the wood floor; his sharp shadow angled across the bookshelves filled with gold-imprinted, leather-bound volumes. His golf clubs leaned in the corner by the door. On the mantel, the brass-faced lantern clock, a favorite of Honora's, ticked on steadfastly.

Honora's other uncle, James, the second-born Maitland son who had inherited her father's title, remained seated, his white hair shining in the firelight. The wood fire crackled, spewing bright sparks across the stone hearth. Uncle James preferred wood fires to coal and willingly paid the difference. He stared at the burning logs and puffed on his long-stemmed clay pipe.

"You understand, Honora, that Lanie told us about these assignations with the Parrish lad for your own good," Uncle Malcolm said. He stopped at his writing desk and toyed with a leather golf ball. "Alexander is completely unsuitable. The Parrishes are little more than rich horse traders. Besides that, the lad is a fourth son. He has absolutely no prospects."

"Not to mention that he pales at the sight of a sword, and despite what he prattles, he's a poor poet," Uncle James added without turning away from the fire.

"Are we seeking a husband for me or a warrior for your Covenantors' army?" Honora demanded. Tense and angry, she clasped her trembling hands before her and put on her bravest face. But inside she feared that those wonderful hours with Alexander were lost to her forever.

"My dear niece," Malcolm implored, his voice lowering to a kindly note, "you are nineteen and without your mother and father, God rest their souls. You've been seeing to your own household for five years now, and you've cared for your sisters most admirably.

"I can't deny that your Uncle James and I have been remiss. We should have tended to your marriage sooner. But now Scotland has joined the war between Parliament and King Charles. Honora, you're a practical lass. Surely you see the necessity of making a suitable match soon—for your sake and your sisters' as well."

Honora looked away from Uncle Malcolm, unable to meet his gentle blue eyes. Of her two uncles, he was her favorite. He was most like her father—straight and thin, kind and generous. She liked dour Uncle James, too, but his cold, harsh outlook on the world was more difficult to love. They were compassionate men who in their own way always meant well. But she knew they would never tolerate an alliance with Alexander Parrish.

And she did pride herself on being a practical person. She had always known that her marriage would be arranged for the benefit of the Maitlands as well as for the bridegroom's family. But she was wary of this sudden insistence on making a match. Honora looked at her uncles again. With great effort and an audible sigh, she attempted to lay aside her anger.

"Have you found a more suitable candidate, then?" A note of unintended challenge slipped into her voice.

"I'm losing my patience, lass." Uncle James snatched

his pipe from his mouth and pointed the stem at her. "David Ramsay has made no secret of his admiration for you. He's a fine gentleman of good standing. You will not drive him away as you have other gentlemen for a fool like Parrish.

"Finding you a husband has been the bane of our existence for the last three months. You have turned away nearly every eligible man in Edinburgh."

Honora's control broke. "I am no more taken with the Earl of Rothwell's suit than you are with Alexander Parrish's poetry. Don't you see? Laird Ramsay wants a nursemaid to curb his wild, motherless children. And he wants the prestige of an alliance with the Maitlands, not to mention the benefit of my dowry to fill his empty coffers."

Her uncles glanced at each other like two guilty children. Outside, the storm raged on. Silent moments ticked away, confirming Honora's accusation.

At last Malcolm tried again. "At your age the burden of six, ah, *spirited* children must seem grave, Honora. But you're a canny female. You'll learn to care for the wee ones. Think of the advantages. Laird Ramsay's family wields Scottish and English influence. He is well-thought-of in high places. And remember, he owns a number of fine homes where you would be mistress."

Honora almost gave an ill-bred snort.

Uncle James picked up the theme. "Mind you, we would negotiate an agreement that would ensure the future of you and your children." He cast a sincere look in Honora's direction before he put his pipe back into his mouth and turned once more to the fire. "And it would be a worthy alliance—for the Maitlands and the Ramsays."

"And for your cause," Honora accused. "I will not marry that bowlegged, hawk-nosed man. Not even if you think it's going to help win your war."

The fire popped and spewed fiery embers at Uncle James. He sprang from his chair and hastily stamped out the live coals. Uncle Malcolm joined him. The clatter of their stomping filled the room, and the scent of singed leather reached Honora.

She decided to take this opportunity to end the unpleasant interview. Drawing herself up to her full height, which

4

was almost an inch taller than Uncle Malcolm's, she marched to the library door. Carefully aiming a parting rejoinder, she turned to face the men. Uncle James stomped on, but Uncle Malcolm stopped long enough to meet her gaze searchingly.

"Perhaps Alexander Parrish doesn't suit you," Honora declared with her hand on the door latch. "Well, David Ramsay doesn't suit me. I'd rather marry the devil himself."

Lightning flashed. Thunder rolled overhead.

Satisfied with that final remark—and intent on finding Lanie—Honora yanked open the door and stalked out into a warm, solid blackness.

Her nose abruptly met with the smell of damp wool and soft, well-oiled leather. Frantically she reached out to halt her headlong rush, inadvertently striking an icy-cold sword hilt and catching at the scratchy folds of a wool plaid.

"At your service, mistress," the impenetrable blackness announced in a deep masculine voice. Hands with an iron grip seized Honora's upper arms to steady her, holding her in his shadow and pressing her so close that she could feel the warm rumble of his words.

Confused and embarrassed, Honora tipped her head back to get a better look at the colossal creature's face. Slowly she tried to push herself away, but his grip remained unyielding, the heat of his fingers searing through her gown.

"Who are you?" she demanded in a quavering voice. She pressed her hands more desperately against him and struggled to free herself.

A blaze of lightning lit the hallway, and thunder boomed through the house. Timbers shook and window panes rattled.

"I believe I heard you call for the devil?" he replied with a mocking smile. Even white teeth flashed against his woolly black beard and long, untamed locks. His cheeks were ruddy with good cheer and wind burn—it was wind burn, wasn't it? And his glittering black eyes peered from beneath quizzically arched brows. Entranced, Honora ceased her struggle. He released her.

Swiftly she put several steps between them but remained unable to take her gaze from his black, faceted eyes. He waited, watching her with that fiendish smile. She shook

5

her head to free herself from him, but he held her mesmerized.

" 'Tis just—you know—a manner of speaking, to call on the devil.'' Her hands fluttered in a gesture of innocence. She babbled on, vexed with herself for being flustered by this unkempt stranger, yet unable to stop defending herself. "I mean, doesn't a true summons require six dead cats or some such vile thing?"

Soft thunder rumbled overhead once more. Guiltily Honora glanced upward. A cold draft tugged at her skirts. A whiff of sulfur tickled her nose.

"To be exact, you must burn six black cats, one each night for six nights in a row on a sandy beach,'' the giant corrected. Then he added with a shrug, "But I believe other invocations can be negotiated.''

"Oh,'' was all Honora could think to mutter as she continued to stare at the black-clad Goliath.

" 'Tis a regret to learn that your charming declaration was merely a manner of speaking,'' he added, his flashing white smile fading into his ebony beard.

He continued to hold her gaze in a bold way that both flattered and frightened Honora.

"McCloud—Laird McCloud?'' Uncle James appeared in the library doorway with Uncle Malcolm peering over his shoulder. "We never expected you near so soon.''

The huge ruffian said nothing, just idled there, dark power and restless energy restrained in the easy shifting of his weight. He wore black leather breeks and boots, and a raven-colored linen shirt. Only his wool plaid—dark blue and green threaded with red and yellow—relieved the sinister bleakness of his costume.

Honora was unable to place the tartan. But her uncle's use of a title told her that despite his rough appearance, this man belonged in a clan chief's chair in the great hall of a lofty castle.

"Allow me to make introductions,'' Uncle James said, stepping to the laird's side. "Our niece, Lady Honora Maitland.''

Powerless to look away, Honora continued to stare at the black-bearded hulk, fascinated by the mocking smile that had returned to his lips. She knew that her Uncle

James detested bad manners, but she was so unnerved that she could hardly bring herself to sketch a curtsy or even to offer a hand in greeting.

"Honora was just retiring for the evening, weren't you, my dear," James cued her.

"Milady," McCloud said, honoring her with a slight bow while his devilish smile grew broader.

Honora opened her mouth to speak, but no words came forth. She barely managed a nod, then with trepidation she began to edge her way around the perimeter of the entry hall. She told herself that he couldn't be the devil, not if her uncles knew him, not if he had a name—a good Scots name.

"Sir, Malcolm and I will see you now," James stepped between Honora and the dark giant.

"Aye," McCloud said, without so much as a look in the little man's direction. "I'll be right there."

Honora sidled a few more steps, in and out of the man's shadow and toward the stairway, hoping the giant McCloud would forget her. But to her discomfiture he turned to her again, that infernal grin still curving his lips. His riveting gaze halted her. For a long moment his heated coal-black eyes moved across her face, consuming her expression, even her thoughts.

Honora went cold, then hot. What did he see? What did he want of her?

When he was apparently satisfied, the ruffian turned away and followed James and Malcolm into the library. Baffled, Honora stared after him. Just before he ducked beneath the library lintel, the dark laird stopped to throw her a quick, conspiratorial smile, then shut the door softly.

For a moment Honora gaped at the closed portal, then released a sigh of relief. She hadn't realized until that moment how much the man had disturbed her. And that look—what was that all about? she wondered. Feeling a little foolish, she peeked at the hem of her skirt to see if her petticoat showed. No. Had he seen something in her eyes? In her mind?

Suddenly sensing that she wasn't alone, Honora whirled around to discover Uncle Malcolm's steward, Francis near the door, as well as a square-built man wearing a kilted plaid and trews of the same tartan as the laird's.

The stranger's beard gleamed orange, and his ears stuck out from a thick crop of red hair. His arms hung long at his sides. When he caught Honora's eye, he frowned in disapproval. One of the laird's kinsmen or a retainer, Honora thought, and the man no doubt considered her behavior toward his laird disrespectful.

"Francis?" she called softly. The old steward still stared after the giant as she had. "My uncles know the Laird McCloud?"

"Aye, milady." Francis replied. "He is the new Laird of the Isle of Myst in the west. He's come to see yer uncles about the Covenantors' cause."

"Oh," Honora said, without feeling particularly enlightened. Islemen rarely visited Edinburgh, and little was known of them—except that they were rough and wild, and mostly papists.

But surely not devils, Honora thought. The dark man had merely taunted her. He had overheard her hasty declaration, then baited her with it. A bold move for a man who didn't even know her name or why she would say such an outrageous thing. But the big man was no devil. Just a laird from the isles who possessed an odd-looking retainer, Honora decided. Nonetheless the red-haired man was a guest. "Francis, see to our guest's comfort."

"Aye, milady." Francis turned to the retainer. "And ye are sir?"

"Kenneth Dunbar," the man replied with a thick western accent and a proud lift to his chin. "I be master at arms to the McCloud."

The McCloud. Honora smiled at the old-fashioned title. She suspected this red-haired man served as the laird's man of the chamber, groom, and bodyguard—as if that giant needed one. The Islemen and Highlanders seldom traveled with a showy retinue of servants as Lowlanders often did. "Welcome, Kenneth Dunbar," Honora said. "Francis will see you served with refreshment."

The two men were halfway down the hall to the kitchen, when Honora suddenly recalled the unpleasant scene with her uncles and Lanie. The giant was forgotten and her indignation returned.

"Francis," she called after them. "Tell Lanie I want to see her in my chamber right away."

"You mean Lanie told Uncle Malcolm about your meetings with Alexander?" Rosemary exclaimed. Honora's youngest sister sat on a fireside stool with her clubfoot tucked under her and a leather-hinged casket of rocks open on her lap. Firelight shimmered off her chin-length, red-gold curls. Her green eyes grew wide and her pretty pink lips parted in disbelief. "But Lanie has always kept our secrets."

"I know. I could hardly believe it myself," Honora admitted sadly, her anger fading. She threw herself down in a chair across from Rosemary and stared into the fire. That hollow feeling of betrayal recurred as an ache in the pit of her stomach. She could not dismiss the sense that Lanie's confession, however unintentional, had robbed them of something of great value—an implicit trust—a thing solid and precious because of its invisible nature; an unacknowledged bond ruptured in a moment of weakness and deception.

"Well, you know how our uncles work," Beatrix said from across the room. The golden-haired beauty of the Maitland family bent over Honora's black-lacquered jewelry box to examine a brooch. Turning to the mirror, she held the silver piece to her throat, admiring the effect against her ivory, heart-shaped face.

"They probably heard some rumor," Beatrix said when she was satisfied with her reflection. "Then they called Lanie into the library and offered her an extra penny. Of course, she refused it. So Uncle James preached a few words about his responsibility to us and the fate of her soul. Then the poor woman sobbed out everything she knows."

"Surely Lanie's been with us too long for that," Honora said. "Loyalty isn't a thing to be sold for a few coins or given up for a sermon."

With a disarming and indulgent laugh, Beatrix turned away from the mirror and walked to Honora's side.

"You may be practical, Sister. But you're not very realistic. I'm sure Lanie thought she was doing her duty.

9

Besides, we all knew it was only a matter of time before you and Alexander were found out."

Beatrix turned back to the mirror. "Do you mind if I wear this brooch tomorrow when William and I play cards with Lady Elizabeth? I think it would set off my wine-colored gown."

"Of course," Honora replied, hardly noticing the silver pin. "Perhaps you're right. Perhaps it's just as well that everything is out in the open. But what now? How am I ever going to find a husband acceptable to Uncle James and Uncle Malcolm? What about Alexander?"

Rosemary closed the casket on her favorite rock collection. "Are they going to forbid your seeing Alexander?"

"Probably," Honora said, staring distractedly into the fire. "They haven't said so, but I'm sure they will. They may even bring their influence to bear on Alexander's family."

"What are you going to do?" Rosemary asked. But before Honora could answer, her little sister's face took on a faraway look, the aspect of a dream spinner. "Steal away? Ride off together into the night. You could pledge a handfast marriage, consummate your love, and challenge the world in the light of dawn to put the two of you asunder. That's what I'd do!"

"Rosemary!" Beatrix exclaimed with a giggle. "What do you know about consummating love and handfasting? Your Uncle Malcolm would have apoplexy if he heard you."

"Aye," Honora chimed in. She sat up straight in her chair and peered at her fifteen-year-old sister. "What do you know about, uh, those things?"

"Oh, I heard one of the kitchen maids talking," Rosemary said with a toss of her red-gold curls.

Honora knew that Rosemary often loitered about the kitchen because she felt more comfortable with the servants. They took little notice of her hobble.

"When Mary talked she made the touching and the kissing seem so beautiful. Remember how Mother and Father kissed? I want that kind of marriage. True love and respect, forever and always. Isn't that what you're looking for, Honora?"

Dismayed, Honora sat back in her chair and rested her

elbows on the arms. Yes, she wanted that too. And she especially wanted a loving marriage for Rosemary—the sweetest and the most loving of the three of them. Honora had no doubt that her little sister would make a fine wife and mother. She also knew that her uncles considered Rosemary's prospects dim. Few noble families would accept a daughter-in-law with a clubfoot.

"Mother and Father's love match was exceptional," Honora said. "They were a perfect alliance in family standing and temperament. That was unusual, even these days. Most marriages are arranged between suitable families with two people who like each other well enough to . . ."

"Well enough for what?" Rosemary prompted, her smile bright and curious.

"Well enough to live their lives together amicably," Honora finished. She avoided Rosemary's gaze and reached for the fire iron to stir the coals.

"She means well enough to sleep together," Beatrix hissed in a mock whisper from across the room. She was digging through Honora's jewelry box again.

"I know," Rosemary said. "But you want more than amicable, don't you, Honora? Isn't that why you've been so difficult? You've turned away more suitors than Beatrix."

Beatrix laughed and left the jewelry box to sit on the foot of the four-poster bed hung in blue brocade and red velvet. " 'Tis true, Honora. Admit it. You have run off more men than I have. Remember how clumsily you danced with Robert Gordon?"

"And don't forget the plate of food you dumped in his lap," Rosemary added gleefully.

"You make it sound as if those unfortunate events were intentional," Honora complained. "Robert was the poor dancer, not I. And I'm sorry if that spill ruined his red satin suit. More's the pity."

The girls giggled.

"With John Murray you feigned illness," Beatrix continued.

"I was not ill," Honora corrected. "But whenever I was near that man, I couldn't stop sneezing. John took offense."

"And what was it you did to George Nisbet?" Beatrix

asked with a grin that disclosed she remembered well enough.

"I did nothing to George," Honora replied. "But I think I may have offended his mother with a remark about her gown."

This time Honora joined her sisters in laughter. Even Uncle Malcolm disliked Lady Nisbet.

"There, see, Honora," Beatrix said, recovering first. "If you have no suitors now but Laird Ramsay, whom you dislike, and Alexander, whom Uncle James cannot tolerate, 'tis your own fault."

"Beatrix, don't be unfair," Rosemary protested. "Just because you have found your true love already. It may not be so easy for the rest of us."

"True, 'twas easy. I knew William was the love of my heart the day I saw him at the sweetmeat shop," Beatrix said matter-of-factly. "He was ordering sugared gillyflowers to be sent to Flora Selkirk. Something about his earnest face touched me. I knew there'd never be anyone else. Then he contrived to meet me at the Earl of Lothian's birthday party."

"Is he going to offer marriage soon?" Rosemary asked.

"We have not talked of it yet," Beatrix said, "but I hope we will soon. There is no other I wish to offer for me. No one else I would accept. I don't think even Uncle James would dare to object to marriage with the Cassilis family, do you?"

Honora shook her head and smiled, genuinely pleased for Beatrix—glad that her sister knew who was right for her. The Cassilis family gave lavish parties, appreciated stylish clothes and well-appointed homes, and played the most fashionable games. Beatrix would shine among them.

"Oh, I'm so happy for you," Rosemary squealed. She set aside her rock casket and hobbled across the room to embrace Beatrix. Honora, too, rose to hug her sister.

A hesitant knock at the door interrupted their joy. Honora turned from her sisters. "That's probably Lanie. I must see her alone. Along you go."

Rosemary and Beatrix filed past Lanie with their heads together, chattering about wedding parties, dresses, and guests.

With her sisters gone, Honora seated herself by the fire again and motioned for her serving woman to enter.

Lanie stepped into the room and closed the door carefully behind her. She hesitated for a moment, her fingers trembling so that she had difficulty with the door latch.

"Sit down, Lanie," Lady Honora said and pointed to the fireside stool.

"Aye, milady." Lanie replied, but she walked quickly to the poster bed instead. She began to turn down the coverings. "Just let me take care of this for ye, milady. 'Tis getting late."

"I want you to sit down here," Lady Honora repeated in a low, firm voice. She pointed to the stool once more.

Lanie straightened from fluffing the pillows. There was little else she could do to avoid facing her mistress. Reluctantly, she stepped out from the shadow of the bed and noted the angry flush in her lady's cheeks. A frown furrowed Honora's high, clear brow, and anger thinned her generous mouth.

Lanie still remembered clearly the morning nearly five years ago when young Honora had set aside her white linen cap—the one she had worn as a child in the nursery. The day after the funeral of Honora's parents—the Lord and Lady Maitland, the Duke and Duchess of Rosslyn, who had died in an unfortunate carriage accident—the young Honora solemnly bade Lanie to help her twist her thick hair into a coil at the back of her head like the lady of the manor.

"I have two sisters to raise," Honora had said when Lanie asked why she'd set her linen cap aside. "I must take charge of the household now."

And indeed the girl had. From that day forward, Lady Honora had been a firm, fair mistress. Lanie loved and respected her for that. But now, because of her lady's meddlesome uncles, Lanie feared their relationship was about to come to an end.

With the sigh of a condemned man, she sank onto the stool and wrung her hands. She wished she had foreseen the trick the new duke had played on her, but she hadn't, and now she had to suffer her mistress's displeasure.

"I'm truly sorry, milady," she began before any accusation could be uttered. "Yer uncles told me they already knew about the secret meetings. They tricked me. I'd near told them everything before I saw 'twere a trick. Then I couldna lie, milady. Ye've always said yerself, be honest."

"Aye, enough." Lady Honora held up her hands as if to ward off more excuses. "When did they first ask you about Alexander and me?"

"Yesterday, when we returned from our outing," Lanie said. She plucked at a spot of dried porridge on her brown skirt and wondered whether Honora would send her away. "They didna tell me anything. But they talked between themselves. They said that Laird Ramsay has hinted that he would like to offer for ye, and they no' want to have a scandal that would alter that."

" 'Tis gone that far then?" Lady Honora said, leaning back in her chair. Palm to palm she pressed her hands to her lips.

"Aye, I thought ye'd want to know," Lanie said. "I've no desire to move into a household where we'll have to tame six wild bairns. Laird Ramsay be an impressive gentleman and all, but he's too old for ye, milady. He's all . . ."

To Lanie's dismay, Lady Honora caught the hesitation and focused on her again. Without moving her hands, she prompted, "He's all what? Lanie. Out with it."

"Well, he's all fancy brass buckles. All shine and no gold, if ye take my meaning."

Behind her hands Lady Honora began to chuckle.

"Well, ye ken what I mean," Lanie said with a shrug.

"Aye," Lady Honora agreed, a smile coming to her lips. "I ken."

"Are ye going to marry the man?" Lanie asked finally in low tones, unable to resist looking into the shadows. Someone might be spying for the duke.

"The earl? Nay, never," Honora said. She went to her writing desk and bent over it. "Tonight send one of the stable boys with this note to Alexander. Not a word to my uncles."

"But be that wise?" Lanie asked, rising from the stool.

"It will be our last meeting." Honora continued to write.

"You will do this for me without telling my uncles, won't you?"

"Aye, of course." Lanie replied with a nod. She would gladly see to the note if it were her only penalty. She turned to the fire to stir the glowing coals, listening to Honora's quill scratch across the paper. Lady Honora was the most learned female she knew of. Soberly she wondered whether her lady now wrote to her poet-lover of elopement. But with a shake of her head, Lanie decided that she had no desire to know. What she didn't know, she couldn't tattle.

"There," Honora said, sprinkling sand across the paper to dry the ink. She folded the note and handed it to Lanie. "Alexander must have this by tonight. You and I will be off early in the morning to church services."

"Aye," Lanie said with a quick curtsy. "I'll see to it right away. Ye have me word. I'll no' disappoint you again."

"Good," Lady Honora said. "Good night."

Outside the door, Lanie sighed in relief, then turned over the note in her hand. Although Lady Honora had folded it carefully, in her haste, she had forgotten to seal it with wax. But that didn't matter. Lanie couldn't read.

"Lady Honora, 'tis Francis."

Honora had just pulled off her hair net and shaken loose her curls, when she heard the steward's soft knock at her door. Startled, she hesitated, wondering what he wanted at this time of night. He seldom ventured upstairs except to direct the servants.

"Yer uncles wish to see ye in the library right away."

"At this hour?" Puzzled, Honora opened the door.

"Aye, in the library," Francis repeated. "They say 'tis important. Must be tended to tonight."

"I'll be right there," Honora replied. She brushed out her hair quickly and tied it away from her face with a blue ribbon before following Francis down the stairs.

She had tread only a few steps downward when she spied the black boots on the hallway flagstones. Hands on the rail, she halted. Why was the Laird of the Isle of Myst still here?

Honora was in no mood to meet that strange man again

15

with her hair tousled about her shoulders like a girl fresh
from the nursery. Yet, she couldn't turn back, either.

Taking a deep breath, Honora continued down the stairs,
watching the black boots shift impatiently on the entry
flags.

2

Black Spanish leather boots, but no cloven hooves, Honora
observed. Unaware of her, the laird stood with his left side
to the stairway. She took another step, allowing her gaze
to follow the line of the giant's boot, up his shin. Supple
leather stretched around his long, lean thigh and over narrow hips to contour a firm flank. No room to tuck a tail in
those snug breeks. Heat flooded into Honora's cheeks.

She shook herself. He was no devil. Just a big Isleman
with broad shoulders that made him seem to fill any room
he entered and a taut belly that she had already been
smashed against.

Honora forced herself to look down at the stairs, taking
three more, but curiosity drew her to the laird again. She
longed to see his face once more. Were his eyes really as
black as she first thought? Did his brows really arch so
eloquently?

Before she reached the last step, the laird cast his gaze
on her. His eyes were indeed black, and keen and sharp.
Then he lowered his eyelids as if he wished to hide something from her.

Disconcerted by her unreasonable fascination with the
man, Honora quickly descended the remaining steps and
forced herself to approach him.

"Laird McCloud?"

"Milady Honora." The laird smiled at her now, a guile-

16

less smile. Yet, she felt his eyes caress her loose hair and touch her face. A feeling of unexpected intimacy swept over her, causing her to shiver and look away.

"Have my uncles not offered you their hospitality?" she asked, noticing for the first time that Kenneth Dunbar lingered in the shadows. She tried to ignore her growing discomfort in the laird's presence.

"Your uncles have been most kind, milady," the McCloud replied. "Kenneth and I but await their answer to a request."

"Oh, I see," Honora said, wondering why her uncles wanted to talk to her, when they obviously had more pressing business.

"Your uncles await you, I believe," the McCloud said. He gestured toward the library and smiled conspiratorially again.

She wanted to ask him what he knew that she didn't. But she turned and walked into her uncles' library. Her uncles rose from their fireside chairs in a show of respect that startled Honora. Adding to her surprise was Laird McCloud's entrance and the closing of the door with a quiet, final click.

"Honora, my dear," Malcolm greeted her. "Sit down."

"What is it that you want?" Honora asked. She glanced uncertainly at the laird. He remained near the door, the top of his head just clearing the painted ceiling beams, his eyes still hooded.

Uncle Malcolm cleared his throat. "Well . . . my dear, it seems that Laird McCloud is in Edinburgh to affirm his lordship over the Isle of Myst."

" 'Tis a journey the lairds of the isles are obligated to make each year," Uncle James added. He and Malcolm exchanged an uneasy look.

"And 'tis a long way," Malcolm continued.

"Aye, a very long way and the weather has been . . ."

"I see," Honora said, interrupting James. But she didn't see at all. Why should this matter to her? Mystified, she gave the laird a polite smile. He returned a smile as innocent as an altar boy's. That's when she knew she might not like what her uncles were going to say.

"Tell her what I want, your grace," the McCloud

ordered, without releasing Honora's gaze. He cast her that mocking smile once more. His jet-black eyes made her forget the shaggy beard, the flowing locks that glistened with raindrops, and the smell of peat fire smoke that drifted about him like a sulfurous cloud.

Uncle James' face reddened and his lips twisted in annoyance. He disliked being prompted. "The laird has asked permission to pay you suit, my dear."

"What? Me?" Honora wrested her gaze from the McCloud's face and stared at her uncles in disbelief. "But you are so set on David Ramsay's suit!"

"Laird McCloud is the new Laird of the Isle of Myst, and he is unmarried," Malcolm explained. "He says he is looking for a fitting wife."

"And just how am *I* fitting?" Honora challenged. She looked from her uncles to the laird.

"Well, it makes no sense to me." Uncle James threw up his hands in exasperation. "Apparently Laird McCloud finds what he has seen of you agreeable."

Expectantly, Honora turned on the black-clad giant for enlightenment, but he remained silent, his look of conspiracy now impassive.

Malcolm spoke first. "We really know very little about you, sir."

The McCloud stepped forward. "What do you need to know? The McClouds have held the Isle of Myst in its entirety for six centuries. We can trace our line back to Robert the Bruce and beyond to Viking kings. The McClouds' seat is Castle Dunrugis. The first stones of its foundation were laid before the time of St. Columba."

At his words, visions of a cold, primitive castle on a lonely, desolate isle flashed before Honora. She almost groaned aloud.

"What I intended to say, sir, is that we know very little about you as a man," Malcolm persisted.

"What is there you wish to know?" the laird asked with an indifferent shrug. "I am a Christian. My father was Laird Alec McCloud. I was educated like my brother at the University of Glasgow. I have been at sea for a number of years. Now I've succeeded Colin as Laird of the Isle of Myst."

18

Malcolm turned to Honora and spoke under his breath. "And you should know, lass, that the McClouds have not given up feuding."

" 'Tis true," the laird admitted, without any sign of embarrassment. "But feuding has not diminished the Mc-Cloud influence in the isles."

"Remember, Malcolm," James warned. "The McClouds trace their ancestry back to Robert the Bruce himself."

A glimmer of understanding flickered in the back of Honora's mind. Neither James nor Malcolm wished to offend the McClouds, for reasons that were certainly connected with the war. And she had little doubt that the McCloud intended to make the most of her uncles' weakness.

Ever since the Scots parliament under Argyll's influence had passed the Solemn League of the Covenant the previous fall, the Scots had been at war with King Charles. Despite the English parliament's promises to pay for the Scot army, funds were short. Honora's uncles labored day and night to raise additional support. And they fought—diplomatically—to maintain the loyalty of influential Scots. They had lost Montrose, who had gone over to the king's side. Now they were determined to lose no one else. Even if it meant marrying off their niece to seal the allegiance.

"You need not do anything you don't wish to do, lass," Malcolm said. "You don't have to accept the gentleman's suit. And the laird said himself he would abide by your answer."

"Aye, milady," the giant said. "But I insist on your decision tonight."

"Tonight?" Honora echoed. She understood now his look of connivance. Was it possible that he could have measured them all so well after hearing only a few bits of conversation? Had he heard enough to know what would tempt her uncles? Could he possibly understand her distaste for Laird Ramsay? But why should he care? For her dowry? For the prestige of an alliance with the Maitlands? Or merely to have a Maitland on his arm during his stay in Edinburgh? Whatever his reasons—which could also serve Honora well—and despite his rough appearance, the laird seemed a clever and discerning man. Even if he was not

19

Ol' Nick himself, he was at the least the devil's able apprentice.

"I accept Laird McCloud's suit," Honora said at last.

"Are you certain?" Uncle Malcolm asked, squinting uncertainly at Laird McCloud.

"I'm agreeing only to his suit," Honora pointed out. She couldn't imagine that unkempt giant persuading her to do more than sit with him in a public garden. But the devil's courting would keep Laird Ramsay at bay.

"We ask one more thing," James said. "That you'll continue to also accept Laird Ramsay's courtship. You must give him, as well as the McCloud, the opportunity to press his suit."

"Nor will I refuse Alexander, then," Honora said.

Both men frowned and glanced at each other before James spoke. "You might as well know now, lass. You will not see Alexander again."

Honora's heart skipped a beat, but she never let her fear show on her face. She knew her uncles were powerful men, capable of making things happen.

"You won't do anything to hurt him or the Parrishes, will you?" Honora asked.

"Of course not," Uncle James assured her, letting a moment of silence give his words weight. "Now, Laird McCloud is in Edinburgh for only a short time. When he leaves, we will entertain his offer of marriage, if he makes one, and Laird Ramsay's also."

Honora nodded, knowing that her reprieve was small. She noticed for the first time that the storm outside had ceased. At last the night was hushed, as if nature was satisfied to have spent its fury in a wild and wicked display of power.

Slowly she turned to look at the laird once more. One corner of his mouth turned up in a smile that told her he had known what her answer would be. His arrogance irritated her, and she wondered if she had made a mistake.

With only a brief glance at Honora's Uncle James, the laird crossed the library to stand before Honora.

"You'll court our niece as a gentleman would, sir," Uncle James was saying as he toyed with his pipe. "That is . . ."

"No schemes of a handfast wedding," Malcolm warned.

At those words, the laird's black brows came together. The white of his smile disappeared into his beard as he rounded on Malcolm and James. Sparks burst bright and hissing from the fire. Honora's uncles started.

"No more conditions," the giant thundered. "Milady agreed to the suit. I will not have you insult her with the suggestion of anything less than proper."

Honora's uncles stared wide-eyed and opened-mouthed at the giant.

"May milady and I speak in private?" the laird asked.

"Uh, yes," Uncle Malcolm stammered.

"No," James snapped, more decisively.

The laird ignored them. He loomed over Honora and held out his hand. Gratified by her uncles' uncertainty, Honora smiled at him, put her hand in his, and let him draw her into the corner.

"Milady with stormy sea-green eyes and the light of rubies in your hair," he said in a low, rumbling voice, his gaze roving over her face and loose curls. "I'm very pleased with your decision. I look forward to our meeting tomorrow."

He squeezed her hand, gave a nod of dismissal to her uncles, and with a flourish of his plaid disappeared out the door.

In Honora's dreams a black-bearded, horned devil pursued her. He trotted after her on cloven feet, his kilt flapping about knobby knees. A hairy tail bobbed behind. He pointed his clay pipe at her and shouted so that all passersby on High Street turned to stare at them. "Ye must marry soon," he boomed, "or all chance for happiness for yerself and yer sisters will be lost."

Honora awoke with her heart pounding, her face feverishly warm, her night dress twisted about her knees and damp with perspiration. She pulled her gown free, threw aside the brocade bed curtains, and climbed out, refusing to dwell on her dream, on the fact that her sisters' happiness rested on her shoulders.

A shaft of golden light fell between the window curtains. She drew the dimity draperies back to see that the storm had passed in the night and that, though misty, the morn promised to be bright and clear. She would meet Alexander today and then receive that devil from the isle at dinner. Laird Brec McCloud. What kind of conversation did one make with an untidy clan laird from a remote isle in the west?

When Lanie entered, Honora was already dressed in her shift and petticoats and was standing before her mirror, intent on examining a lock of hair that she had pulled over her shoulder.

"Good morning, milady," Lanie said.

"Lanie? Does my hair have the light of rubies?"

"What, milady?"

"Never mind. Rubies indeed," Honora muttered with a toss of her head. Silly flattery from such a rough-looking man, she thought. Impatiently she began to twist her hair into a coil. "Did you send the note to Alexander?"

"Aye. The boy told me he delivered it to the steward himself. And he said there were some commotion going on. A light burning in every room of the house. The Parrish's steward was no' too pleased to get the note, but he promised to give it to Mister Alexander."

"Oh, dear," Honora said. She frowned into the mirror. "So my uncles have been about their business already. *Please be there, Alexander*. Lanie, we must dress simply today so as to call no attention to ourselves. The green, I think. Walking shoes and my rust rabbit cloak."

Lanie helped her lady dress quickly, talking all the while. She chattered about the stranger in the kilt, Kenneth Dunbar, who had downed a whole plate of cold salmon, a loaf of white bread, and two mugs of ale in the kitchen the night before.

"What did he have to say for himself?" Honora asked.

"He had little to say, milady," Lanie said as she combed Honora's chestnut ringlets around her finger.

"But he told us they—he and the Laird of the Mc-Clouds—had just ridden into Edinburgh and had had no time to refresh themselves. He said his laird was in a great rush to finish his business and return to the Isle of Myst. I've heard 'tis said that the mist there never burns away. And the little people live still in a mound near a stone circle high in the hills. And ye must always wear something of iron to keep yerself safe from the evil ones," she continued. Then she stopped brushing a lock long enough to add, "And before ye die, ye see yer own ghost."

"Those are pagan tales," Honora chided with a smile into the mirror. "You know that, Lanie. What would Reverend Crawford say if he heard you?"

"Aye, but maybe the followers of the old religion know something we donna," Lanie said as she put the brush down. "Where there's smoke, there's fire. There be witches still."

"People tell tales of little people just to frighten the children and make them mind," Lady Honora said. She rose from the stool where she had been sitting while Lanie dressed her hair. "We must be on our way or we'll miss Alexander."

"Are ye sure we should do this?" Lanie asked. "What will yer uncles do if we are caught?"

"We won't get caught," Lady Honora said. "I only want to say good-bye to Alexander. Now, fetch our cloaks. We'll go down the back stairs."

At the end of the narrow wynd on the corner of High Street, Honora turned away from Cannongate, past the Tolbooth, and hurried past St. Giles, where she was supposed to be attending services. She hiked swiftly toward Castle Hill. Head down, Lanie followed close behind.

Honora had nearly forgotten her dream of the devil until the crowd—mostly servants doing the daily marketing—pressed close. She couldn't help but look over her shoulder for a giant, horned, black-bearded, pipe-smoking creature. Of course, she saw none, but once she thought she caught a glimpse of an orange beard and large ears. *Just imagination,* she told herself and pressed on.

She passed the shops of many craftsmen—tailors, jewelers, cabinet makers—who catered to the Scots peerage, old families like Honora's. She hurried on past the street market and turned into another wynd that took her toward the Nor' Loch below Castle Hill. She pulled her hood closer about her face and hoped no one recognized her.

The morning mist cleared. The sunlight sparkled on the dewy grass along the side of the Mound Road beyond the marketplace. The sun toasted Honora's back as she walked. The warmth eased the tension in her shoulders and softened the weight of her troubled mind. She turned to smile reassurance at Lanie. Once out of the crowd, Honora tossed her hood back and reveled in the fairness of the day. Only a few travelers strolled along the road. Several men fished the loch for eels while birds swooped across the water's glassy surface and sang from the trees.

Above them, Castle Hill basked in the golden light, its stone walls grown out of the mossy rock and its ramparts rising jagged against the clear blue sky.

Honora's heart sank when she saw no one near the gigantic boulder where she and Alexander usually met. "You're certain he received my message?"

"Aye, milady," Lanie said with an emphatic nod.

Honora turned to the road again; this time she spied Alexander loping toward her.

"Here I am, my sweet Honora," her poet called and waved. When he reached her, he seized her hand with a gallant sweep of his red cloak, and bent to kiss her fingers. His hat plume tickled Honora's nose and almost made her sneeze before she could brush it away.

"You didn't think I wouldn't answer your summons, did you?" he asked when he straightened.

His golden curls gleamed in the sunlight. From the pink flush in his cheeks Honora knew he'd been drinking spirits already, and it was only seven o'clock.

"Of course I knew you'd be here," Honora said, smiling at him, touched by his sweet face and vulnerability. "We must talk—Lanie, keep watch."

Lanie frowned her disapproval and walked away toward the road.

"I've written a poem for you." Alexander brandished a piece of paper from his sleeve and unrolled it with a flourish. As he read, Honora studied his long jaw, the soft full cheeks, large nose, and sensitive bow-shaped mouth. He was indeed intended to be a cavalier poet.

He read:

> "I love Honora not for her comely face,
> For her pleasing brow or grace,

Nor for her tiny hands or dainty pace,
For those virtues in time may diminish.
Therefore I keep a true lover's vision,
And love her for no reasons,
Save to favor her for all seasons.''

"Alexander, that's lovely," Honora said, touched by the
sentiment. She knew better poets, but no others who wrote
verse for her.

She had met her gentle Alexander more than a year ago
at a New Year's reception given by the Duke of Hamilton
at Holyrood Palace. Alexander had stayed at her side for
some time, saying little and avoiding her gaze. After the
reception, Uncle James scolded Honora for spending so
much time with Alexander Parrish. But the next day she
received the first of Alexander's poems. In return she sent
him a note of thanks and offered the loan of a book they
had discussed. That led to the first of their meetings. He
had never called at the Maitland town house. Without
speaking of it, both knew that open suit from Alexander
would not be accepted.

"You do like the poem? I'm so glad." The poet squeezed
her hand and squinted at her with earnest—if bloodshot—
pale blue eyes. The gentle smile faded from his face. "I
have sad news."

"I, too, have something to tell you," she began. A movement beyond Alexander's shoulder caught her eye. Lanie
was waving excitedly. Honora turned, expecting to see
Uncle James marching down on her.

Instead, the black-bearded giant strode forth from behind
the boulder. Kenneth followed.

"Milady Honora," Laird McCloud boomed, his greeting
echoing against Castle Hill. "Imagine meeting you on the
lonely shores of Nor' Loch at such an early hour."

He was dressed in the same black leather and wool as
he had worn the night before. Even in the daylight his eyes
were jet. His long, unruly hair shone pitch-black. In the
open air his movements were broader, yet easy and
smooth. Honora was struck again by the contradiction of
his shaggy appearance and his refined control. And if anything, he seemed even more massive than he had in the

hallway the night before. But what Honora found most curious was the sense of breathless haste about him, as if he had nearly missed something he felt was important.

"Laird McCloud," she greeted coolly.

"I have not met this gentleman," he reminded her with a nod toward Alexander. She thought she saw a hint of mischief twitch at the corner of his mouth, and she wondered what he thought he was up to.

"Laird McCloud, this is Alexander Parrish," Honora said.

"Truly? The gifted poet, Alexander Parrish?" Laird McCloud exclaimed and made a slight bow.

"You've heard of me?" Alexander replied. Innocent surprise shone on his poet's face.

Honora glared at the laird, aware that he was making sport of Alexander. He might play games with her uncles, but not with her gentle poet.

As if McCloud had heard her silent warning, he quirked a brow at her. She met his gaze boldly.

"Aye, Lady Honora has spoken of your work with great admiration."

Alexander beamed with pleasure. "Why, thank you, milady. And kind sir."

"I understand your family is leaving Edinburgh very soon," the laird commented.

The smile again faded from Alexander's face.

"Is that true?" Honora demanded, turning to her friend.

"Aye, 'tis what I came to tell you, Honora." The young poet took her hands once more. "We're going to London. Father has discovered military friends there who offer opportunities to become suppliers to the new cavalry. Cromwell is reorganizing the English army, you know. Father wants me to spend more time learning the horse business."

"But—but I thought you wanted to write poetry," Honora stammered. She looked from the McCloud to Alexander and back again. So her uncles had presumed to rearrange Alexander's life like this? And hers?

McCloud folded his arms across his chest; victory gleamed in his black eyes. Just what did the laird know about this matter? Honora wanted to know. How had he become so well informed? Angered, Honora turned her back in an effort to give Alexander her full attention. She hoped that McCloud would take the hint and leave.

" 'Tis best, Honora," her poet was saying, drawing her aside. "I care for you, but you know . . ." Alexander hesitated, his eyes straying in the laird's direction.

This time Honora whirled on the giant. "It was so nice to see you again, milaird. Now, if you'll excuse Alexander and me, we have private matters to discuss . . ."

The laird never moved a step. "I'll just wait here and see you home when you've finished."

"Please, sir," Alexander said. The lithe young man in fine cavalier dress drew himself up and faced the black-clad giant. With a quiet dignity that touched Honora, he made his appeal. "Lady Honora and I have farewells to say. You seem a man of some sensitivity and discretion, sir. Surely you understand that we desire a moment of privacy."

Laird McCloud studied Honora, the gleam of victory gone but a hard darkness remaining. With a nod, he relented and walked away. Honora almost gave a cheer for Alexander's victory.

"How do you know him?" Alexander asked in low tones.

"He's an acquaintance of my uncles'," Honora whispered in return.

"Is he a suitor?"

"Aye, but—"

"Honora, it's all right," Alexander interrupted. "I knew there was little hope for us from the beginning . . . from the moment I saw you at Holyrood, standing there dressed all in gold like a fairy queen. You have given me so much more than I ever hoped we could have in this last year. I love you, Honora. And if things were different . . ." Alexander touched her hair. "If our marriage would not bring you shame, I would ask you to elope with me. We would sleep in haystacks. Live a carefree life. Earn our living with our songs."

"But we would disappoint too many people," Honora whispered and smiled. "My sisters. Your father and mother."

"I don't care for myself anymore," Alexander said. He

took her hand and looked into her eyes. "But for you . . . I only want happiness for you. I wish you well, Honora."

"And I wish the same for you," Honora whispered. Her throat closed and tears brimmed in her eyes as she beheld Alexander's gentle sadness. Before she knew what was happening, he placed his hands on her shoulders and kissed her full on the mouth.

His lips moved over hers passionately. Honora closed her eyes and kissed him back. He had never ventured more than a light brushing of lips before. She had daydreamed of his kissing her, wondered how it would feel. She liked it. When he drew her closer, she spread her hands on his chest and leaned against him.

Sudden darkness enveloped them. A cold breeze dragged at Honora's cloak. When they separated, she expected to see the McCloud looming over them. He wasn't. He remained near Kenneth, watching them, his arms folded across his chest. He frowned, his brows forming a forbidding line.

A mighty thundercloud billowed and swelled behind him and over the city, blocking out the sun. Distant thunder rumbled.

"Farewell, Honora," Alexander whispered before Honora could say more. He turned quickly and strode toward the market.

Honora bit her lip to hold back the tears as she watched her poet walk out of her life. She would never see Alexander again.

All too quickly the market crowd swallowed him. He was gone, never to steal another hour to read poetry to her or compose lyrics for her guitar melodies. When Honora caught Laird McCloud eyeing her, her desolation turned to anger.

"Are you satisfied?" she demanded. "I suppose you are going to tell Uncle James about this meeting."

"I see no reason to trouble your uncles with this," Brec McCloud said, his expression bland.

Again Honora heard thunder roll across the heavens.

"But I have no intention of sharing you with a mere boy, one that even your uncles do not approve of," the laird added. "Kenneth, see the ladies home."

Honora remembered little of the walk. She still ached from her loss of Alexander, still simmered with anger over the McCloud's—as well as her uncles—highhandedness. When she reached the town house door, the warmth of the morning sunshine on her face made her glance up to see that the threatening thunderstorm had vanished.

"Oh, Beatrix, what am I going to do without Alexander?" Honora sighed as she and her sister sat in their dressing gowns in Honora's chamber, preparing for the evening. Lanie stood behind Honora, brush in hand, arranging her lady's hair for the dinner party. Beatrix sat on a stool near the window, waiting her turn.

Outside the room, purple and peach twilight lingered over the city. In the streets, occupied sedan chairs—the bearers puffing frosty plumes into the chill spring air—bobbed up the narrow wynds, hauling nobles and merchants to taverns and dinners with friends. Lantern-lit coaches rattled along Cowgate Street.

"As long as I could see Alexander, I could tolerate the earl's attentions," Honora said. "I kept thinking someone suitable would turn up." She waved her hands in frustration. "Now Uncle James and Uncle Malcolm have lost patience with me. And I can no longer see Alexander."

"Perhaps *you* should have patience," Beatrix said, leaning forward to rest her elbows on her knees. "This Laird of the Isle of Myst might be interesting. What do you know about him?"

"That he's a brute with no manners," Honora replied. "Our uncles are considering his suit because Uncle James wants him as a Covenantors' ally. But I know he's just like the earl, another man after my dowry."

Beatrix patted Honora's knee. "Well, moping for Alexander gains you nothing."

"I know. I must be practical about this," Honora said with a shake of her head. Lanie mumbled in consternation. Honora renewed her efforts to sit still.

"The winter is over and we're almost through the social season," Honora said, thinking out loud. She was desperate to find any escape. "Once the war heats up again,

Uncle James and Uncle Malcolm will turn to their maps and fund raising. We could retire to the country."

"Then I couldn't see William," Beatrix wailed.

"I forgot about that." Honora stared into the mirror, blind to her reflection, her mind once more snared by the memory of Brec McCloud, his simple clothing and shaggy beard. "What is it about him? . . . What can I do to discourage the laird?"

"Will Uncle James suspect what you're doing?" Beatrix asked.

"Perhaps, but 'tis worth a try." Honora rose, a spark of excitement flashing in her head as ideas formed into a plan. "Beatrix, tell Francis I want to see him. I want the dining table set as formally and lavishly as possible. I want him to bring out all the best silver, the porcelain, and even the Venetian glass. The menu will have to do. 'Tis too late to change that.

"Lanie, I will wear my best burgundy gown—the one with the expensive lace—and my best pearls and the pearl earrings with diamonds. Why didn't I think of this before? With an expensive show, I might be able to discourage the laird and the earl as well."

"But you said he practically introduced himself as the devil," Beatrix said. "What if the laird is truly from . . . ?"

"Well," Honora said, briefly considering the possibility, "then it wouldn't matter, whatever I do, would it?"

From the threshold of the blue room Honora stared at the back of a clean-shaven, black-clad gentleman standing at the garden doorway. She hesitated and turned back to Francis.

"I thought you said Laird McCloud had arrived."

" 'Tis Laird McCloud, milady," Francis replied, with a lift of his brow. "I nearly didna recognize him meself. I've put out all the best, as ye asked."

"Oh, thank you." Honora turned back into the room.

The laird stood at the window overlooking the garden, his hands clasped behind him. His hair had been trimmed to collar length and the beard was gone, exposing a firm jawline. His suit coat was fashionably tailored in black velvet and fitted at the waist. Raven satin slashed the full sleeves. Velvet hugged his long legs down to the top of his stylish bucket-top boots. Only a white lace collar relieved the austerity of his costume.

Before Honora could say anything, he heard her footstep and turned. With a smile he gave her a slight bow. She realized with an odd flutter in her belly that Laird McCloud was a darkly handsome man.

"Milady." His jet eyes sparkled.

Once more the power of his gaze overwhelmed Honora. A small sense of alarm tingled through her. Then a rush of resentment and irritation followed. The refined gentleman in raven satin standing before her would be welcome in any Edinburgh receiving room. She wanted him to present himself in his ruffian's beard, dressed in his rough Isleman's leather and plaid costume, and looking suspiciously like the devil. He was easier to dislike that way—and much more likely to offend her uncles.

"Milaird," she greeted.

"You are still angry," he observed, walking toward her.

"What did you expect?" Honora snapped. A servant lighting the candles of the wall sconces turned to look. She softened her voice. "I don't need you interfering in my life, milaird. Two uncles are quite enough."

"They needed my help. I'm afraid poor Parrish was very taken with you."

"And what about how I feel?" Honora demanded. She heard voices in the hallway. Uncle Malcom and David Ramsay, the Earl of Rothwell, walked into the blue receiving room.

To Honora's surprise, McCloud grabbed her hand. Before she could yank it from his grasp, he murmured, "You look lovely tonight," and brought her fingers to his mouth.

He regarded her with a diabolic smile on his expressive lips. She was uncertain whether the gesture was for her benefit or that of Laird Ramsay and her uncles. Nevertheless, the warmth of the McCloud's touch flooded through her, flushing her cheeks. Unwillingly she gave the devil a saucy smile.

"Burgundy velvet and pearls suit you," he added. "Brings the rubies to your hair and enhances the luster of your skin."

Honora heard the earl suck in his breath indignantly. Uncle Malcolm hurried to her side. "Laird McCloud, we are pleased to have you dine with us. Let me introduce you to our guest."

Honora stood back as Uncle Malcolm made hasty introductions. Despite the earl's avowed allegiance to the cause of the Covenantors, their sober colors and shorn locks were not for him. He wore a pale yellow satin suit with white hose and yellow leather shoes trimmed with shiny, out-of-fashion brass buckles. Beside the earl's glowing yellow garb, Laird McCloud's solemn ebony suit looked rich and dignified.

"Laird McCloud," the earl said as the two men shook hands coolly, "my sympathies on the death of your brother. I see you remain in mourning. A great tribute to him. I met Laird Colin a few years ago, during the Irish trouble. An admirable man and a great clan chief. I'm sure he is missed."

The line of Laird McCloud's jaw turned to stone. He swiftly withdrew his hand. His black brows inched together. "Aye, my brother is missed."

Uncle Malcolm stared at the two men, as surprised as Honora by the palpable dislike that suddenly flourished between them. Honora caught herself looking about for a thundercloud.

Light laughter tinkled through the doorway from the hall. Beatrix swept into the room arm in arm with William and his mother, Lady Elizabeth, their gaiety dispelling the tension that had gathered in the room.

Honora marshaled the earl to Lady Elizabeth's side and prayed that dinner would go more smoothly.

3

With half an ear Brec listened to James Maitland, the Duke of Rosslyn, outline why the lairds of the isles should join the Covenantors and the English parliament against the king: the old prayer book issue, the shipping restrictions, the influence of King Charles' French, papist queen.

Brec had heard it all before.

They were seated at a long table laid out with an elegant meal of fricassee of veal, a great board of a side of lamb, a platter of roasted pigeons, a bowl of eight lobsters, a dish of anchovies, and several sorts of good wine. No less than Brec expected from a duke's table.

While he ate, he knew he should give James Maitland more attention, but he was unable to resist watching Honora.

His hostess was seated at the other end of the table, with Ramsay on her right and Lady Elizabeth on her left. Brec sat at the right of the duke, a position of honor, he knew, but he really wanted to be near Honora. She toyed with the food on her plate and turned towards the earl, appearing to be courteously intent on the little man's conversation.

Brec caught her eye once, but she looked away. When her gaze darted back, she cast him a small, disapproving frown. He decided to ignore it.

He allowed himself to take pride and pleasure in the sight of her—the tendrils about her face, the glitter of gold in her chestnut hair, the soft pink luster of the pearls in her ear lobes—and at the pulsing hollow of her throat.

She was the exemplary hostess, politely dividing her time between Lady Elizabeth and the earl. Subtly she signaled the servants when more claret was to be poured or dishes were to be served or removed.

She was the perfect lady for Castle Dunrugis, and he silently congratulated himself on finding her so easily. When she'd vowed to marry the devil, he'd had the good fortune to be standing in the Maitland's hallway. Surely it was an omen, and he was not a man to dispute the wisdom of fate.

He'd meant every word of the compliment he'd paid her earlier when inspired by the square neckline of her burgundy gown—a fashion intended to give ladies a flat-chested silhouette. With pleasure Brec relished the dress's failure. There was no restraining the lush swells of Honora's confined breasts.

But most of all he admired her sensual lips. For an instant he imagined tasting her soft warmth and the lingering sweetness of the marchpane she was nibbling on. Then the sudden memory of Alexander Parrish putting his lips to hers soured Brec's vision. Annoyed, he turned back to the duke.

"You've been more than a clan chief," James was saying. He shook a fork at Brec. "You've been a sea captain and a man of commerce. You know this war is about more than religion. The English have made shipping and trade difficult for us for years."

"And if King Charles is defeated, what makes you think the English parliament will treat Scotland any better than before?" Brec asked, playing devil's advocate, which always amused him.

"They have signed the Solemn League and Covenant," James said. "It may be that Argyll is our bigger danger."

"Aye, Argyll, the Campbell chief." Malcolm nodded across the table. "Perhaps you've heard his title spoken in the streets—King Campbell. But you didn't hear that spoken here."

Brec's head came up in surprise. So that's how it was. Archibald Campbell, Marquis of Argyll, had emerged as a leader of the Scots' Covenantors cause, and he needed to unite the clans to support the English parliament. A difficult task. Over the centuries the Campbells had usurped the lands and feuded with more than a few clans, east and west. Islemen and Highlanders alike had long memories and short tempers. Brec could name several clans—McDonnells, McNeals, McGregors—who would rise up righteously and with pleasure against Argyll and the Campbells in the name of King Charles.

Brec looked down the table at the earl, David Ramsay. Ramsay had once been a close friend of James Graham, the Marquis of Montrose, and was now considered a close adviser to the Marquis of Argyll.

"Do you see? That's why we wanted to talk with you," Malcolm explained. "Think what Montrose would do to us if he were to use his Royalist influence with the Gordons, the Highlanders, and you of the isles. McDonald of Antrim is dead. We know he offered Montrose troops a year ago. But there are others."

"We've heard rumors that Alasdair mac Colkitto in Ireland wants to join Montrose," James said. "Montrose and Colkitto could open a second front at our back door while the king's forces under Prince Rupert marched on our front doorstep."

"Have you no faith in Leven and his army?" Brec asked, referring to the general of the Scot army who had begun his campaign against the Royalists at the first of the year.

"Leven is a good man," the duke said. "But even he can't be in two places at once. You know what we want, McCloud. We need your influence in the west."

He leaned toward Brec and began to outline a plan that Brec knew he could never agree to.

"My dear, Honora," Laird Ramsay said, his head inclined over his plate to share a confidence. The candle-light shone off his brown, curled locks and cast a shadow along his sharp nose. "The table looks lovely, but 'tis rather extravagant, don't you think? Such a display for a laird from the isles. This must be more luxury than he's accustomed to."

"I frequently have the best laid out for our guests," Honora said, peering down the table at Laird McCloud and her uncles. To her annoyance, the laird's table manners were flawless. She'd hoped he'd stare at his fork as if he'd never used one or wipe his mouth with the back of his hand like a common fisherman. Or an unseemly belch from him would have pleased her mightily—and offended her uncles.

But he dined like a gentleman, oblivious to the richness of his surroundings and speaking with her uncles in a low voice. She could hear that they were talking of the war in the south. Her uncles talked of little else—except her marriage.

"Laird McCloud seems to be a most refined gentleman," Lady Elizabeth commented, sweeping a look his way. "And such a sinister yet princely mien. Did you know, Honora, that the McClouds trace their lairdship back to Robert the Bruce and beyond? But we do hear such strange things about the goings-on in the western isles. Those people have such quaint and strange customs."

"Aye," Laird Ramsay agreed. "The death of the former laird, Colin McCloud, was very—sudden. From what I hear of their customs, I'm surprised they didn't lay his body in a galley, set it ablaze, and send it out to sea just like the heathen Vikings."

"Vikings?" Honora repeated, taking a moment to confirm and admire Brec's curiously fair skin and dark coloring.

Lady Elizabeth put down her fork and picked up her glass of claret. "Indeed, and they say the dead laird was tall and blond. Very well liked. Is that what you heard, my dear earl?"

With a quick glance down the table and a pursing of his bloodless lips, the earl cleared his throat.

"It wasn't just that Laird Colin's death was so sudden," Laird Ramsay began, "but it came unexpectedly, just after his brother Brec returned from the sea at Christmastime. Colin was a young man, healthy, well-liked, but he had no heirs. I understand the whole island was shocked by his death."

"Aye, I heard that too," Lady Elizabeth said, disappointment on her face. She had obviously hoped for a rumor she had not already heard.

"Of course, there's more to the story," the earl added, taking another bite from his plate.

Lady Elizabeth frowned at him for baiting her.

With deliberate slowness, the earl washed down his mouthful with claret, taking his time to begin his tale.

"Please don't keep us in such suspense," Honora prodded, amused by the way Lady Elizabeth leaned forward as the earl opened his mouth to speak.

"One wintry night just after the New Year, after Laird Colin and his brother had been closeted together for hours, the priest was called—the McClouds are still papist, you know. The priest found young Laird Colin dead, a bullet in his head. His brother claimed it was an accident. Laird Colin had shot himself while cleaning his own pistol. The priest refused to preside over the funeral. Another priest from a neighboring isle performed the rites. *And* there was a rumor that kirk records were altered."

"Ooh," Lady Elizabeth cooed, delighted with the tale's implications.

Laird Ramsay returned his attention to his meal. "Then there is the dog, a great black animal with blue eyes. It often accompanies Laird Brec, they say."

"Truly?" Lady Elizabeth exclaimed. She openly stared down the table at Brec McCloud. "Like Prince Rupert and his familiar, the dog named Boy? King's nephew or no, they say the prince is a warlock. That's why he wins his battles. Indeed, he has a pact with the devil."

"Much the same is said of Laird Brec," the earl said before draining his glass and motioning to the server for more. "His own people believe he's a warlock, and they say that he, too, has made a pact with old Nick. With that strange blue-eyed dog always at his side, 'tis easy to believe."

Irritated, Honora motioned to the servant to take away her plate. "Isn't this all a little fanciful?"

"But there's more, my dear," Lady Elizabeth whispered with a nervous giggle. "Have you heard the story about a fairy who married into the McCloud family centuries ago? They say she bore the McCloud laird a child. Just imagine! Blood of the little people in the McCloud's veins. Those devilish good looks *do* make him appear capable of anything—magic, murder. Of even seduction." Lady Elizabeth giggled again.

"Aye," Laird Ramsay agreed, ignoring the last. "If he's made a pact with the devil, he would indeed be capable of murdering his brother. Wearing mourning doesn't fool anyone."

"But something in all this doesn't fit," Honora said, unable to resist defending a guest at her table.

"What is that, my dear?" Laird Ramsay inspected her patronizingly, as if she were a willful child to be indulged.

"If Laird Brec was so ambitious for himself, why would he have waited until now to eliminate his brother as clan chief? He could have done it years ago. And why use a pistol? Why not something more subtle, like poison?"

The earl shrugged. "Only our Lord in heaven knows what dwells in the hearts of men."

"The Lord knows," Honora agreed. "Fools and gossips speculate." When she looked down the table at Laird Brec McCloud, she had to admit that the infernally handsome, black-haired man with a strong chin, rugged jaw, and straight nose looked quite capable of anything.

Unexpectedly, he turned his attention to Honora—his black brows arched and his dark eyes kindling with admiration. A small, private smile curved on his lips. Holding her gaze, he lifted his claret goblet up in the gesture of a toast. He drained the ruby liquid from the goblet, his eyes never leaving her face.

Honora shivered.

Not a soul at the table witnessed his silent tribute.

The ladies' conversation about fashion bored Honora, and she looked up, apprehension mixed with relief, when the men joined the ladies in the blue receiving room. The dinner had not gone as she had hoped. She'd heard enough stories about murder and Viking funerals to satisfy her for a lifetime. She needed no more secret toasts. The sooner these guests—particularly Brec McCloud—excused themselves, the better. But there was still the after-dinner entertainment.

"Beatrix, dear, please entertain us with a song," Uncle James proposed as he ushered his guests into the room. He gestured toward the virginal.

"Of course," Beatrix agreed, leaving William's side to go to the gilded instrument. " 'Twould be my pleasure."

"I understand Lady Honora plays the guitar also," Laird Brec said to his host. "Will you play for us, milady?"

"Just how do you know that?" Honora demanded with more obvious annoyance than she'd intended to display.

Her uncle cast her a disapproving frown.

The laird regarded Honora without the least bit of fluster. "I met a wee sprite named Rosemary in the hall. Perhaps you know her. Red-gold curls and green eyes. She carried a basket of rocks and told me you fancy the guitar."

"Aye, Honora, you must play for us too," the earl agreed as he joined them.

Laird Ramsay and the McCloud exchanged hostile glares. Without saying more, Honora sent Francis for her guitar.

Polite applause followed Beatrix's reedy performance of a popular love song. She joined William on the settle, where he leaned forward to whisper compliments in her ear. She blushed attractively.

When Francis brought in her guitar, Honora took it up and strummed. The singing strings made her think of Alexander. She was in no mood to please anyone—uncles, earl, or laird of the isle. She knew she would probably regret it later, but she chose to sing a song that she and Alexander had laughed over more than once. Dear Alexander, she thought. She could always count on him to make her laugh, to make her forget about her duties and her worries. With Alexander she had found freedom and comfort. And now that was gone.

A wood fire burned quietly in the brick hearth. The candlelight lit the sheen of the blue draperies and flickered against the polished wooden paneling as the duke's guests turned their attention toward Honora.

Brec had settled back in a damask-covered chair, prepared to enjoy Honora's singing. She played the guitar expertly and sang a ballad about a shepherdess and a cavalier. Her voice was mellow and clear, easy on the ear. But after a moment Brec saw Uncle Malcolm shift uncomfortably in his chair and squint sideways at the duke. As Honora sang on about the shepherdess and the cavalier's games in a haymow, the duke's brow twisted into a disapproving frown.

Brec carefully kept his amusement from his face. He had heard bawdier songs, but not in a polite receiving room. At the end of the lively ditty, the ballad's cavalier was forced to retreat with an unrequited love. The audience—especially Lady Elizabeth—applauded enthusiastically.

"What a delightfully shameful song, my dear!" Lady Elizabeth cried. "Wherever did you hear it?"

"It is delightful, isn't it?" Honora replied. Defiance smoldered in her eyes when she met Brec's scrutiny. "Laird McCloud taught it to me."

Brec never blinked. Truth was, he had to admire this surprising yet foolish attack, and he wondered where she intended to go with it.

"Oh, really," Lady Elizabeth exclaimed with a snicker.

Malcolm and James turned to stare at Brec in astonishment. The earl absolutely glared. With meticulous control Brec resisted the urge to sink lower in his chair, but he felt heat rise in his face.

"You taught Honora that song?" James demanded in cold tones.

Brec hesitated. Either he'd admit to the transgression and lose the uncles, or he'd deny it and lose the lady. "Aye, when we met by Nor' Loch this morning," Brec said, his gaze holding Honora's. He watched her smile in satisfaction.

"Honora, what were you doing at Nor' Loch this morning?" James asked. "You said you were going to services at St. Giles."

"I started to go there, but it was such a lovely morn that I decided to walk along the loch," she explained.

Brec watched her measure in an instant how much she wanted to tell about her last secret meeting with her poet lover. How far to go with the lie? With growing irritation, he realized that as much as she wanted to strike at him, she would protect Alexander Parrish at all costs.

"I happened upon Laird McCloud and his man there," Honora added, her eyes flickered uncertainly in Brec's direction. When he said nothing, she went on. "We walked for a few minutes, that's all. Don't you think it was a lovely day to walk, Lady Elizabeth? Beatrix, sing us that new French song you learned."

Beatrix willingly consented.

At the end of the evening, when the guests said their

thank yous and farewells, Brec made himself first in line. He took Honora's hand.

"My thanks for a delightful evening, Lady Honora. Tomorrow we shall enjoy this fine weather. No walk by the loch. We'll go riding instead."

"What?"

"You do ride, don't you?"

"Well, of course, but I don't—" she began.

The Earl of Rothwell jostled William and Lady Elizabeth aside to reach Honora. He stepped on Brec's toe and elbowed him in the ribs, but Brec held his ground. Only curiosity kept him from correcting the earl's manners.

"Honora, my dear, it was my hope that you'd join my hawking party tomorrow," the earl said. "Everyone will be there. Even your sister Beatrix and William."

With only a fraction of a moment's hesitation—a hesitation only Brec noticed—Honora's face fell in disappointment. "Oh, milaird, I'm so sorry. This is most unfortunate. You see, Laird Brec has already engaged my time tomorrow."

Ramsay stared at Brec, animosity deepening in the lines around his mouth. "I understand, my dear. Your uncles have apprised me of the situation. Have a pleasant outing."

With a grave bow to Honora and Brec, the earl disappeared out the door. Brec turned to Honora. "I feel honored to have my invitation accepted over the Earl of Rothwell's."

Honora pressed her lips together and shook her head. "You needn't. I quite detest hawking."

Rosemary's and Beatrix's eyes had grown wide when Honora repeated the story that the Earl of Rothwell had spun out about Laird McCloud at dinner: of mysterious death, an odd funeral, and a hypocritical mourning.

"Was the earl saying that the laird killed his own brother?" Beatrix asked. "How shocking! Do you believe him, Honora?"

"Oh, I don't believe all that," Rosemary said, dismissing the accusation with a wave of her hand. "I met Laird McCloud in the hallway. He seemed very interested in my rock collection and spoke quite charmingly to me."

41

"You showed your rock collection to the laird?" Honora asked, suddenly recalling Brec's mention of meeting a wee sprite. Yet, she had difficulty picturing the imperious McCloud taking any interest in her little sister's pastime.

"Aye, I didn't think he was a murderer," Rosemary declared. "In truth, I thought he was rather nice."

Honora and Beatrix exchanged understanding glances. Their little sister thought the best of everyone.

"If even half of what the earl said was true, perhaps you should beg off on the ride with Laird McCloud," Beatrix suggested. Anxiety creased her lovely brow. "Say you're ill."

"Nonsense," Honora said. "I'm sure the stories are exaggerated. I can't believe that Uncle James and Uncle Malcolm would entertain the suit of anyone they believed to be a murderer. They may want to see me married off to help their cause, but they wouldn't put me in danger. Besides, time spent with Laird McCloud is time I don't have to spend with the earl."

"Why don't I go with you?" Rosemary offered. "I make a better companion than Lanie. I love to ride. I don't understand why Uncle Malcolm discourages me. My foot doesn't prevent me from sitting a horse well."

"What a good idea!" Honora said, surprised at her sudden relief—anything to complicate the McCloud's plans. "I'd love to have you along. Beatrix, would you and William join us?"

"I can't." Beatrix shook her blond curls. "William and I are joining the earl's hawking party."

"Can we ride somewhere besides Arthur's Seat?" Rosemary asked. "I collected rocks there today."

"We'll ride wherever you like," Honora said, pleased with the thought of Rosemary's baskets of rocks. "And we'll collect whatever you want. Now, along with you to bed. No more tales of death and funerals."

In her dreams Honora found herself riding beside the horned, but now clean-shaven devil. They cantered along a barren beach under a sunless sky. The devil grinned at her and kept a tight rein on his high-strung mount—a great black kelpie—that wanted to bolt into the sea.

The mythical beastie snorted whiffs of steam and fought

furiously for its freedom. The smiling devil held a tight rein and appeared unconcerned. Honora longed to gallop away, but when her mare refused to leave the black beastie's side, she realized that when the devil gave the kelpie its head, the creature would dash into the sea—dragging them all along with him.

"Is that really your horse?" Honora demanded as she and Laird Brec rode side by side along the road beside the Firth of Forth. The sea breeze was light and invigorating on her face. The spring sun shone bright and warm. No clouds in the sky. No storm on the horizon.

When Honora had informed Laird Brec that her sister would join them, the laird heartily welcomed Rosemary to their party. His man, Kenneth, instantly became a conscientious groom. With startling courtesy, the rugged, orange-bearded man assisted Rosemary in mounting her gray pony, and they followed at a safe distance behind Honora and the laird.

"I mean, do you own that animal?" Honora repeated. "Is he the mount you rode across the Grampians?"

The laird regarded her from atop the snowy-white steed—a prancing, deep-chested animal—the sort of horse St. George must have ridden when he slew the dragon.

"Aye," Laird Brec replied. Once again he was dressed entirely in black, even down to the ink-colored shirt he wore beneath his leather doublet. The color suited him—highlighting his jet eyes, his black hair, and the healthy ruddiness in his complexion. The contrast between rider and horse was striking.

"Why do you ask? Did you think I'd ride a great black kelpie?" He grinned at her.

"Well, of course not," Honora said, but she could feel the heat of embarrassment rise into her cheeks. "What do you expect a lady to think after you practically introduced yourself as Ol' Nick himself?"

"And you think I'm not?" he asked, still smiling.

"Do you have horns?" Honora demanded.

He halted his horse and swept off his soft, wide-brimmed hat. Turning toward her, he bowed his head. "Do I?"

Honora stared at his dark hair, uncertain of what he wanted of her. "I don't see any."

He looked up from beneath his eloquent brows. "My hair may hide them. Search carefully."

Did he really expect her to touch him? Honora wondered.

" 'Tis the only way to be certain," he prompted. He remained bowed before her.

Reluctantly Honora pulled off her glove. Part of her thought that touching the laird was a ridiculous, improper thing to do. Part of her demanded that the mystery be solved. Part of her thought his hair looked thick and clean and inviting.

Honora reached for him. Like the night before, the instant she touched him, warmth flooded through her. She spread her fingers in his hair, first on one side of his head. Gently, she combed through the dark strands across his crown to the other side. She found his scalp clean and warm and his hair soft and fine-textured. She liked the feel of it and the scent—spicy and clean, no smell of smoke. She blushed when she saw how she had mussed his hair and carefully smoothed the dark locks.

"That's enough." Without warning, Brec grasped her wrist and pulled her hand away. He sat up abruptly and slapped his hat back on his head, a frown suddenly threatening his expression. "Well? What do you find?"

"No horns, milaird," Honora replied in confusion.

"There, you see," he said. "Are you satisfied?"

He urged his horse on, quickly outdistancing her.

Trembling and embarrassed, Honora concentrated on pulling on her glove. He acted as if the silly search had been her idea. She tapped Brownie with her crop and followed him down the road.

"Actually, I do have a kelpie in the stable on the isle," the laird called over his shoulder. "Isn't that right, Kenneth?"

The master of arms and Rosemary had reappeared over the crest of the hill behind them.

"What is it, milaird?" Kenneth asked, closing the distance.

"We have a kelpie in the stable on the isle, don't we?"

"Aye, ye could call him that," Kenneth said with a rare smile. "We ride him each St. Michael's Day."

Brec turned to wink in Rosemary's direction. "You must come to Castle Dunrugis and ride our kelpie one day."

"Oh, I'd love to," Rosemary cried. "Does he grant wishes?"

"Depending on your wish, lassie," Kenneth said. Genuine pleasure spread across the man's face, an expression Honora never expected to see on the big-eared man.

"Let's see. What shall I wish for?" Rosemary asked, so absorbed in her wishing that she stopped her pony. Kenneth halted beside her. Brec motioned to Honora to ride on with him.

"Your sister is a delight," he said.

"Aye. Beatrix may be the beauty. But Rosemary has the gentlest and sweetest disposition," Honora said. She looked over her shoulder once more to assure herself that her sister fared well in the company of the ungainly orange-haired man. She was sorry now that they had not brought along their own groom.

"She's safe with Kenneth," Laird Brec said, as if reading her thoughts.

"Of course," Honora said, a little embarrassed that her distrust showed, yet irritated by him for calling attention to it. This ride was going to make for a very long afternoon. "You know, it really was rude of you the other night to eavesdrop on our conversation in the library."

"Milady Honora," Laird Brec began, with a challenging lift of one brow. "That was no conversation. 'Twas a battle. And I'll not apologize for listening to what everyone in the house could hear. In fact, it seemed necessary in the name of peace to offer something to end the standoff."

Honora said nothing and looked straight ahead. Had they been as loud as that?

"You weren't satisfied with your uncles' choice, and they weren't satisfied with yours. I simply offered my services. Fact is, I've never asked permission to court a lady before."

"Am I to be flattered by that?" Honora glanced sideways at him, judging his age to be at least thirty years. She found his admission difficult to believe. "If you've not courted before, why should you begin now? Even in the name of peace."

45

"I didn't say I haven't courted before," he corrected. "I said I've never asked permission before."

"Oh? So you seduced poor girls from their families and homes without speaking with their fathers?" Honora concluded. She had no difficulty picturing this. It fit well with the picture Lady Elizabeth had painted.

"That's not how it was." Laird Brec's brows formed a threatening line. "I will not spend my time defending myself."

"As you wish." Honora gave a curt nod of her head. "Will you tell me why you've decided to bestow this honor on me?"

"I'm trying to remember." His white steed suddenly flung its head up and bounded forward only to be brought up short by the angry laird.

Honora repressed a smile of satisfaction. "This must be a difficult position for a proud man—to find yourself suddenly a laird and in need of a wife."

She had not forgotten his first bold appraisal in the hallway. She wasn't sure she'd liked it any more than the blatant assessment from the matrimonial candidates her uncles had chosen.

"I can assure you, milaird," Honora went on, "if you are in the marriage market, there are a number of ladies in Edinburgh who would be suitable and ever so willing to oblige you. I would be glad to introduce you to them."

"No doubt," the laird replied. "But I make it a policy to seek out and acquire only the best. It adds a certain challenge to life, don't you think?"

"Perhaps," Honora agreed. "But that's not very practical, especially if circumstances don't permit enough time to pursue a conventional suit."

"So, you admire the practical?" he asked. Honora caught the surprised lift of his brow.

"Of course. Don't you? It makes life so much simpler. Why clutter it up with silly, unrealistic notions?"

"So you never intended to do the impractical and run away with Parrish?" the laird asked. He made a sweeping gesture toward the empty road ahead of them. "You never intended to ride away pillion with your poet, your true love. Gallop down the road toward an idyllic life of love and poverty?''

"Of course not," Honora exclaimed, astonished that he would assume that she was so foolish. "I suppose a love match would be nice. But I've always known my marriage would be arranged. As dear to me as Alexander is—was, I've no desire to live in a haystack and steal food from market stalls. There'd be no happiness in that when the babies came. Don't tell me you thought Alexander and I were going to run away yesterday?''

"Your uncles had some concern," the laird said, giving a shrug of indifference without looking at her.

"Did they send you to find me?" Honora demanded. She pulled her mare to a halt and glared at the laird. She would have something to say to them if they had.

"No one sends me anywhere," Brec replied sharply, turning his horse toward hers. "I just happened along. Your uncles know nothing of yesterday except what you told them."

A grin spread across his face, taking the menace out of his words. "But they should lock you in your room for singing that disgraceful song. Hardly what a departed duke's daughter should be singing to her guests after dinner."

Honora grinned, unable to resist returning his smile.

"Over there," Rosemary called, startling Honora and the laird. They looked around at the riders behind them. Rosemary pointed toward the shore.

"I want to look at the stones and the shells on the bank just there," she called as Kenneth took the bridle of her pony and began to lead the way down to the shore of the firth.

4

"Lady Rosemary," Laird Brec said as he strode along the rocky sand beach, "just what are we looking for?"

Honora listened for impatience in his voice, ready to come to her sister's defense, but she detected none. Brec McCloud seemed as intent on the search as Rosemary was.

"Unusual shapes or colors," Rosemary told him. "I especially like rocks that sparkle. And blue ones with a hole are lucky."

"Like this?" the laird asked. Honora, who had walked farther down the beach, turned in time to see him present her sister with a slate-blue stone. Even from a distance she could see that the rock was pierced by a smooth, round hole.

"Aye, how lucky we are," Rosemary exclaimed. She held out her basket, and he dropped it in.

"What will you do with them?"

"I'll wash them off when I get home," Rosemary said, her head down already in her renewed search.

"Rosemary's wash basin is always full of stones," Honora added with a smile.

"When they are clean, I line them up along the window casement, and sometimes I arrange them in the garden."

"How about this?" With a quick flick of his wrist the laird opened his hand and offered Rosemary a beautiful salmon-colored, pockmarked stone.

Rosemary gasped.

Concerned, Honora hurried closer.

"That's not a firth stone," Rosemary said, staring at the specimen again and pulling her hand away as if she dared not touch it.

"True enough," the laird agreed. "This is coral from the New World. For you." He offered it again.

"Really?" Rosemary asked, wide-eyed and still not reaching for the bright coral. "You didn't find that on this shore."

"Nay, it just appeared here in my hand," he said with a grin. "A magic gift for the rock collector."

"Oh, 'tis so beautiful," Rosemary said, staring at the rock again. This time she took the coral in the palm of her small hand and examined it more closely.

As Rosemary inspected the gift, Honora studied the giver. She was startled by the gentleness in his expression as he explained to Rosemary about the coral, how it grew just below the surface of turquoise-blue seas of the New World. He talked of white sand beaches and of brightly colored fish as one who had seen and admired them all. Rosemary fell enthralled into his tale.

"See, Honora, what Laird Brec gave me," Rosemary cried as Honora joined them. "Isn't it beautiful? Kenneth?" The girl hobbled up the bank toward Kenneth Dunbar, who tended the horses.

"That was very kind of you," Honora said quietly, just a little ashamed of her uncharitable thought about him.

The laird's eyes were velvet dark. He merely smiled and offered his hand. " 'Twas a pleasure to offer your sister something new for her collection."

"You've made her very happy." Honora took his hand and relied on its strength to help her over a small cairn.

"And you?" he asked.

Honora snuck a glance up at him as he steadied her. She was surprised to see that his expression was guileless and innocent. "Me? Of course, I'm happy for her."

As soon as she was over the stones, she pulled her hand free. He released her reluctantly, a frown forming on his lips, but he said nothing. With mock gallantry he swept his hand in a gesture indicating she should lead the way.

She headed for the cover that had been spread on the grass, not far from the horses. Fruit, bread, and a bottle of claret had been placed in the middle. Kenneth and Rosemary were already seated on one corner, their heads bent together over the coral. All four shared the refreshments and sorted through the stones Rosemary had collected in her basket.

The laird's hand was broad and steady on the bottle as he poured claret for each of them. Rosemary asked more questions about the New World.

As Brec talked, he pulled a knife from inside his doublet and deftly sliced an apple—his fingers nimble, the movements of his wrist quick. He offered a slice to Honora first, the juicy fruit held between his thumb and finger. She looked to him as she took it, carefully avoiding his touch. His knowing smile annoyed her. She turned her back to him to watch the sea while she ate, but she found her ears intent on his every word.

"And what of your home, Laird Brec?" Rosemary asked. "Stories we hear in the lowlands make the isles sound like a faraway, magic place."

He laughed. "No magic," he said. "Only green hills and blue lochs full of fish. And there are seals, whales sometimes, and porpoises. Many birds—gulls, eagles, puffins, and falcons. The mountains, the Culdees, are often wrapped in a soft mist. But sometimes in the winter snow covers the peaks and they shine white in the sun, like they are covered in diamond dust. The forests are full of red deer, hares, and foxes. Some wolves. No different from the mainland."

"You've no fairy castles?" Rosemary asked.

"I've not seen any," Laird Brec said. "But the cottar folk prattle of little people. Brownies in the pastures to take care of the cattle. You know the old stories."

"And you have your kelpie," Rosemary reminded him.

"Aye, our water spirit," the laird agreed with a smile. "But Islemen are less isolated than some think. We sail between the isles to visit, hunt, and fish. Merchants and entertainers seek us out. 'Tis fine to live so close to the sea," he added, staring out across the waters. His fondness for his home colored his voice with a note of longing that enticed Honora into stealing a peek over her shoulder at his softly smiling face. He went on to point out the sails of a ship he had spotted, and their talk turned to various types of vessels sailing the firth.

The ride home was uneventful. In the stable mews of the

Cowgate, Honora and Rosemary took their leave. But not before Laird Brec helped Honora from her mare. Never before had she considered the opportunity to take liberties that riding offered a man. The earl had always left assisting her in dismounting to the Maitland groom. But the laird curtly dismissed the boy and reached for Honora. His hold was firm and strong, his hands lingering with the pressure of his thumbs just beneath her ribs and his long fingers splayed across her back. The stable master frowned at the laird, but the giant ignored him. A little flustered, Honora huffed, tugged at her jacket, and straightened her hat as soon as her feet touched the ground.

"This afternoon's outing has been a great pleasure, milady." The laird swept off his hat and bowed.

"Aye," Honora said. She leaned closer to speak in confidence. "I enjoyed the ride and the company. And thank you for your kindness to my sister. Rosemary is most pleased with the coral."

"But I also have something for you, Lady Honora." With a quick movement of his hand, the laird produced from thin air a bright, colorful arrangement of feathers.

A gasp of delight escaped Honora. "How did you do that?" She stared up at him surprised and captivated—uncertain of his intent.

"For your hat." He plucked the hat from her head and pulled off its royal blue ostrich plume. Then he tucked the spray of white, green, and blue feathers into the band.

"From the New World?" Honora asked.

"Aye." He adjusted the feathers to his satisfaction. "From a bright, graceful bird with a noisy cry. The natives covet his plumage. They believe it to be a strong charm against the advances of ambitious earls with designs on dukes' daughters."

Honora's laughter rang out before she could catch it. "Shame on you, milaird," she gasped. " 'Tis unfair of you to offer me magic when the earl can offer only houses." Honora admired the feathers. "Such a beautiful charm must be potent. I shall be pleased to wear it. But tell me, what do the natives wear to ward off the devil?"

"There is no charm against the devil," he replied with a mysterious smile.

Honora reached for her hat, but the laird set it on her head then tilted it to the angle he wanted. He leaned closer to adjust it properly.

"Tell me—if, as you say, Beatrix is the beauty in your family," he whispered, "and if Rosemary has the sweetest, gentlest disposition, what is your virtue?"

"My virtue?" Honora repeated, taken aback by the question. "I'm the eldest. I'm the practical one."

"Oh, I think not," he said with a shake of his head. "You're the one with a passionate soul and a romantic nature. And I will possess you, sweet soul."

He kissed her hand politely and was gone. Chilled, yet beguiled, Honora stared after the man in black who rode away on the great white horse.

The air in the room over the tavern hung close. Doublets, shirts, suit coats, belts, new boots, hats, and gloves—all in black—cluttered the hired lodging. Brec folded his arms across his chest and glared impatiently at his weary master at arms.

"Nay, I'll no' do more," Kenneth groaned. He sank onto a stool by the door and clutched his chest. "I canna do more." His breath came in gasps. With his shirt sleeve, the red-haired man wiped the sweat from his brow. "I'd rather follow ye onto a bloody battlefield than do more of this. Ye've become a madman, Brec McCloud."

Brec glanced across the room at the English valet, also slumped on a stool. The man had worn out an hour earlier. The harper he'd hired dripped with sweat and worked his fingers over the strings as if they were painful. In the middle of the room the dance master remained on his feet, his face drawn, his shoulders sagging with exhaustion.

"I want to be sure I've got this right," Brec said.

"Ye got it right enough to my thinking," Kenneth panted and shook his head. "I'll no' mince around this room like a dancing lassie again."

"What say you, dance master?" Brec demanded, turning on the sweating teacher.

The pale man with mousy brown curls started as if expecting to be attacked.

"Do I dance the current quadrilles well enough? No flattery now. I'll have the truth of it."

The dance master stammered while making a slight bow. "Milaird, you are a most adept student. Any lady in Edinburgh will take great pleasure in your dance performance."

Brec grinned. The last three hours of lessons hadn't drained his energy or his enthusiasm. In fact, his heart felt lighter than it had in all the months since Colin's death.

Another sharp rap from below made the men in the room cast each an inquiring look.

"Shall we give the innkeeper release from our stomping?" Brec asked. "Pay the master and the musician, Kenneth. And give them coin for a cool draft of ale. Thank you, gentlemen."

"Aye," Kenneth agreed. He took the purse and escorted the dance master, the harper, and the valet from the room.

Brec swung the window open wider and sat down on the casement. He gazed out at the drab spring sky. Rain had fallen off and on all afternoon. But Brec's mind was filled with the memory of the soft smile he had coaxed from Honora the day before. The only thing that troubled him about the lady was the reaction her touch had created in him the day she searched his hair for horns. True enough, he had invited her touch. The idea had been to put her more at ease with him. She had accepted the invitation, her sea-green eyes wide and her touch hesitant.

But her sober curiosity and the soft stroke of her fingers had unexpectedly kindled desire in him. If he had succeeded in putting the lady at ease as he had intended, he had also managed to forfeit his own composure. He'd had to pull her hands away before she stirred more in him than a little healthy lust. Brec shook his head. He could no longer deceive himself into believing he wanted the lady merely to fulfill his pledge.

"Are ye satisfied now?" Kenneth kicked the door to the room closed and handed Brec a tankard of ale that he had brought up from the tavern room below. "So, do ye think ye'll suit the lady at Balmoree's party?"

"That remains to be seen," Brec said. He took the tankard with thanks and drank from it. "I wish we had more time. The earl has a start on us."

"The lady has no fondness for the earl," Kenneth said. " 'Tis plain on her face when his name is spoken."

"But her uncles like Laird David Ramsay," Brec said. "And they know him better. He is a man of society. He has much to offer the lady and them."

"Do ye think that is what is important to her?"

"I'm not sure," Brec said with a shake of his head. "But I do know that when I stood outside that door and I heard her defying her uncles, invoking the devil—I never thought to meet a real lady with such passion. What man can resist a woman with fire in her eyes? And with a figure like that. A waist I can nearly put my hands around. And legs . . ."

"And just when did ye spy her legs?" Kenneth sputtered.

"I've recently discovered that horseback riding is a most rewarding pastime." Brec grinned over his tankard.

"Aye, she's desirable enough," Kenneth agreed. "But the lady has a reputation for thwarting her suitors."

"I know," Brec said with a laugh. "I never expected her to be easily won."

"There be plenty of fish in the sea. A sturdy Highland clan chief's daughter would do as well or better. A hearty lass who can thrive through the long, cold winters . . . and various other dangers."

Brec shook his head. "Nay. We've had enough of marrying our own kind. I pledged to bring a worthy lady to Castle Dunrugis. That's what I intend to do."

"Then, let's carry the lady off and be done with it," Kenneth said. "With the war on, her uncles couldna raise a hand against us. And ye wouldna be the first to claim his lady that way."

"Are you so eager to leave Edinburgh, Kenneth?" Brec turned to read his companion's face.

"Aye, I've no fondness for this city," he said. "The buildings block out the sun and the streets stink of cesspits, and that castle on the rock up there—it threatens us like an English fist."

Brec watched his friend drain his tankard.

"I long for home too. But she's the one, Kenneth. And if she is to be the true lady of Castle Dunrugis, she must come with me willingly." Brec turned back to the open window.

"And if she does," Kenneth said, "look at what ye'll be taking her into. There's no' a lass alive prepared for what awaits us on the Isle of Myst."

Brec continued to stare outside. Rain had started to fall again. "Perhaps. But the Lady Honora has the courage to face it. And more—much more."

The invitation to the Marquis of Balmoree's garden party had arrived early in the afternoon. Within the hour a request arrived from each of Honora's suitors seeking the privilege of escorting the lady to the event. Turmoil reigned in the Maitland library.

"What on earth are we going to do?" Malcolm almost wailed. "Honora can't go to Balmoree's party with both men."

"We'll think of something," Uncle James said, a finger pressed against his chin as he stared at the handwritten notes on his desk. With his other hand he finger-combed his white hair into disarray.

Honora was summoned to the library to watch Uncle James scribble an immediate reply. He wrote that there would be no favoritism; each man would receive his decision directly as to who would escort Honora.

"We simply can't afford to offend either man," Uncle James said. "The situation is too delicate."

"I don't think it would take much to make Laird Brec go over to Montrose," Malcolm agreed.

"Precisely," James said.

Honora listened, at first more exasperated than flattered. Then the humor of the situation dawned on her. Her uncles' machinations had gotten them all into a fine fix. For the moment, she was content to let them flounder with it.

Over the past two weeks the first chill of Brec McCloud's vow to possess her had faded. Even her memory of the devil in her dreams had dimmed. The tall, dark man had made himself a charming, courteous, and almost magical companion.

He walked with her in the garden, played cards—he had let her win once, then arrogantly taken the rest of the games—and they went riding again. He made no secret of his pleasure in her company. From thin air he produced another gift—a linen handkerchief embroidered with red roses and the letter "H." He even tried to tempt her into singing that bawdy song again.

"Oh, no. You won't be shocked this time," she told him. "That takes all the fun out of it."

He laughed. Instead she sang a traditional song for him. He joined in the singing with a deep, resonant voice.

Laird Ramsay had taken her hawking—she could find no excuse to avoid the second invitation. When they played cards, he chattered about his golf game, then turned sullen when Honora trumped his ace and won. Then, over dinner he had suggested she give up the guitar.

"The guitar is more fashionable for men, don't you think, my dear?" he advised. "You would do well to take up a lady's instrument, such as the virginal. And do use some discretion in your choice of songs."

She had nearly left the table without escusing herself. But for her uncles' sake, she had suppressed that urge and lied that she would consider the virginal.

This difficulty with the Marquis of Balmoree's party was exactly what her uncles deserved—and it might be just the opportunity she was looking for. All she had to do was persuade her uncles.

"I have the solution," Honora said. Her uncles turned to stare at her. " 'Tis really very simple."

"Really?" James said, his disbelief obvious. "You've worked out how to be with two people at one time?"

"Well, in a way," Honora said. "I will accompany one gentleman to half of the entertainments at the party. And the other gentleman to the other amusements."

James and Malcolm looked at each other to see what the other thought.

"I admit it would be a little awkward," Honora went on. "To be fair, I would be escorted by neither man. Instead I would arrive in our own carriage. Then I would divide my time equally between the gentlemen and depart with you."

"Don't you think they will be offended?" Malcolm asked.

" 'Tis unusual, but 'tis a practical solution," James admitted. "I've no doubt either gentleman would prefer to have

Honora all to himself, but I also know the earl understands the delicacy of the situation. And the laird has been cooperative.''

The discussion went on for a few more minutes, but Uncle James seemed to like Honora's suggestion. He and Uncle Malcolm would decide which entertainments she would attend and with whom, he told her and sent her away.

"That *is* a rather rude arrangement, don't you think?'' Beatrix asked when Honora told her sisters about the plan.

"Isn't that like arriving in the company of one gentleman and leaving with another?'' Rosemary asked.

"Precisely,'' Honora said. "But 'tis not my fault I'm in this position. Surely the gentlemen will understand about sharing my time and the party amusements equally.''

"Laird Brec will be offended,'' Rosemary prophesied with a regretful shake of her head.

Laird Brec smashed a fireside stool with a single blow of his fist. Wood screeched protest. Splinters skipped across the room. Voices in the tavern below ceased for a moment, then started up again, more softly this time.

Kenneth only blinked. "I've seen ye do worse.''

Brec cursed, ripped up the duke's note, and flung it into the fire.

"Equal time!'' He swore a seaman's curse. "If I can't have all of her, I won't go. Why share her with a man who curls his hair with a heated iron—a bellwether who switches alliances from Montrose to Argyll faster than a galley can come about?''

"Then leave the lady to him,'' Kenneth suggested with more hope in his voice than Brec liked to hear.

"Nay,'' Brec shook his head. The first wave of his anger subsided. "I'll not be defeated so easily.''

"I didna think so,'' Kenneth drawled.

5

Brec McCloud and David Ramsay faced each other across the entry hall of the Marquis of Balmoree's mansion as the Maitland carriage clattered up the drive.

"We're both to receive equal consideration from Lady Honora, McCloud," Ramsay said, regarding Brec with a cool expression of contempt. "I expect you to abide by the duke's decision."

"Umph," was Brec's only comment. He clasped his hands behind him and longed to be standing on the deck of the *Dal Riata*, where with a small gesture he could order the overdressed, hawk-nosed Lowlander thrown overboard and be done with the man.

The unsuspecting earl drew the note from his pocket and read aloud the schedule that the Duke of Rosslyn had drawn up. With Honora's consent, no doubt, Brec thought. This had to be her scheme. Every nuance of it bespoke of her sense of the practical and the outrageous.

"This selection was made at random," the earl read. "Lady Honora will participate in the garden sports, including bowls, view the entertainment—I believe there are to be jugglers and a contortionist—and have supper with Laird McCloud. With Laird Ramsay, Lady Honora will play cards, play billiards, and dance."

Dance with Laird Ramsay! Brec seethed.

A glowering, black-clad laird and a fawning earl in lime-green satin—which clashed with Honora's aquamarine silk—confronted the Maitlands at the door. Honora stood flanked by her uncles with Rosemary close behind. Beatrix had already arrived with the Cassilises.

58

"My dear Honora," the earl crooned, seizing her hand before she could offer it, "I've been waiting for you."

"As have I," Laird Brec said, suddenly looming over all of them. His glum shadow engulfed Honora, a frown and the grim line of his brow declaring his displeasure.

With her hand still held captive by the earl, Honora could only stare at the laird. He wore a well-fitted black wool suit coat trimmed in silk braid with his tartan kilt and shoulder sash. His handsome figure turned the head of every woman who passed by. For the first time since that day in her uncle's library, Honora regretted her scheme.

"The billiard table is free now," the earl said, steering Honora toward the billiard room. "Laird Brec, you can have the lady for the garden amusements when we've finished our games."

Honora looked back at Brec and touched the white, green, and blue feathers in her hair. He quirked a brow of indifference at her. To her bewilderment, he turned and sauntered toward the ballroom, where the dancing was about to begin.

Even though dancing and sumptuous display were now discouraged by Scotland's religious reformers, the people had proved more willing to give up the rich church decoration than the merriment of dance. Balmoree had provided good music and set aside a room for the activity.

In the billiard room Laird Ramsay annoyed Honora by being excessively lucky. In silent irritation she planned to annihilate him later at cards. During the second game, to her relief, William and Beatrix asked to join them. But Honora continued to play badly. Brec's look of displeasure had disturbed her concentration. She had wanted to annoy him, but not so much as the line of his dark brows had implied.

Once, during William's shot, Honora edged toward the doorway to peer across the hallway into the ballroom. There she saw the laird dancing with Janet Duncan, a most eligible lady. And he was laughing as if he were truly enjoying himself. Honora tapped her cue thoughtfully on the floor.

"Your shot, milady," the earl called from the far side of the billiard table.

They played three games. Laird Ramsay won all and scooped up Honora's wager and William's and Beatrix's as well.

"Are you well, my dear?" the earl asked as he handed their cues to the footman. "You don't seem your usual self. This affair," he waved his hand in a vague gesture, "this situation isn't distressing you too much, is it? I could talk to your uncles and the laird about it. This is a terrible strain to put on a young woman of your delicate sensibilities."

"I'm fine," Honora said, unable to keep the impatience from her voice. Laird Ramsay followed her to the doorway of the ballroom. She watched Brec dance an intricate quadrille with another attractive lady and wondered how she was going to let him know that it was time for him to take her from the earl.

She finally managed to catch his eye. He merely nodded. Honora waited. When the music ended, he escorted his partner back to her companion and asked the next lady to join him.

"Well," the earl said with a sniff. "Laird McCloud seems inclined to dance right now. Perhaps you'll allow me to escort you to the garden amusements."

"Aye," Honora agreed, confused and rankled.

She lost to the earl in her first game of bowls. The surprise of that brought her back to herself. Bowls was her favorite. She won the next two games. When the earl demanded an opportunity to recover, Honora granted it. A small crowd gathered to watch Honora defeat Laird Ramsay for the fourth time.

"So, my dear, you've won your billiards wager back," he said with a stiff-lipped smile. He guided Honora in the direction of the punch bowl. "Time for some refreshment, don't you think?"

So the day's amusements progressed with Honora only glimpsing Laird Brec. When she and the earl weren't involved in a game, the earl was talking politics with some of the gentlemen. To Honora's embarrassment for the rest of the day, the earl alternated between strutting with her on his arm and offering his pity for Brec's neglect.

She spoke briefly to Robert Gordon and to George Nisbet. But neither of her former suitors made an effort to join her.

The earl spent part of his time with the other men gathered around a stern, self-conscious man in Puritan brown—the Marquis of Argyll. The Campbell chief never joined in the dancing. One leg was enfeebled and one side of his sullen face sagged—the vestige of a childhood illness, doctors claimed. But the marquis had made no secret of his own belief that he was a victim of his stepmother's long-ago attempt to poison him. She'd wanted her own son to inherit the Campbell riches. Amid the festivities, struggles for power were not forgotten—a divided Scotland and the English parliament fought King Charles.

All the ladies commented on the undercurrent of expectation that ran through the gathering when they retired to the upstairs room to tidy their hair and rest their feet.

By the time Honora returned to the card table with the earl, she was thoroughly angry with Laird Brec. If he had not liked the idea of equal time, he could have informed them.

Her temper worsened when Rosemary and a young girlfriend appeared at their table and asked to join the game.

Before Honora could agree, the earl waved the girls away. "Young ladies should be cheering for the young men at archery."

Honora stopped mixing the cards and stared. Laird Ramsay shifted uncomfortably under her gaze. She had noted shortly after she was introduced to him that he seemed ill at ease in Rosemary's presence.

The girl turned uncertainly to Honora.

"I'm sure milaird would be pleased to play cards with two enchanting ladies, wouldn't you, sir?" Honora placed the cards on the table and smiled at her sister.

The earl fussed with his wheel ruff collar.

Rosemary's smile brightened. "That's very kind of you, Laird Ramsay, but Mary likes your idea about archery, don't you, Mary? We'll make a garland for the champion."

In her awkward gait Rosemary hobbled from the card room with her friend in tow.

"Well, my dear," the earl said, setting the deck of cards

61

aside. "I believe you were to sup with Laird McCloud, but under the circumstances, shall we?"

"Under the circumstances?" Laird Brec asked, seeming to materialize out of nowhere, casting a shadow over their card table. The earl started and so did Honora. "I believe the lady was to take supper with me."

Honora looked up to see a smile on Brec's lips, but a storm threatened on his brow. Tensely she waited for thunder and lightning to rattle the windowpanes—either from his anger or hers. Who did he think he was, this mere laird from some remote western isle who had the temerity to flaunt her uncles' wishes.

"Look here, McCloud," the earl protested, rising from his chair. "you're not abiding by the agreement. You can't just leave Lady Honora without an escort. The lady will sup with me if she wishes. You have neglected her all day."

" 'Tis true, she seems to be doing nicely in your company, sir," Brec said, bowing to Honora, a certain smugness in his smile. "but I would like to claim my supper if the lady will permit."

Laird Ramsay scraped back his chair and stood, his hands spread on the card table, his back rudely turned to the dark laird. "Honora, my dear, if you wish, I will take you to supper. I will settle things with the laird later."

Honora stared from one man to the other. Warmth rose in her cheeks as she realized that the three of them had become the center of some attention. At that moment she would have been content to sit at home alone, eating a supper of porridge and contemplating the prospect of becoming a spinster.

She rose slowly. *"I shall,* of course, abide by the agreement." She cast Brec a withering look of superiority which seemed to miss its mark.

The Laird of the Isle of Myst merely smiled, took her hand as if it were his due, and led the way to supper.

Meats—from venison steaks to shellfish—burdened the Marquis of Balmoree's table. Servants bustled to keep the shellfish platter filled. Savory pudding and vegetables complemented the meats. To top off the meal, the dessert table offered fresh strawberries, plum cakes, bread pudding flavored with orange juice, and colorful marchpanes in fanciful shapes. Honora couldn't resist taking a pink rose.

She and the laird were occupied during the meal by making conversation with a laird and lady from Aberdeen. But after dining, the kindly couple excused themselves to speak to friends across the room.

"I don't understand your actions, sir," Honora said the moment they had a chance for private conversation. She rose from the table and swept out through the garden doors and into the gathering twilight. She wondered whether he would follow. He did.

She stopped on the gravel path. He halted, so close that his bare knees brushed her silken skirts. "I thought you agreed to the equal time."

"I intended to," he said, leaning forward enough to make his breath felt on her bare shoulder. "Then I saw you with the earl. I thought, what a handsome couple. Perhaps I should not interfere. I thought to myself, perhaps Lady Honora is right. I should go at this in a practical manner. Why seek a lady of lofty station when I'm not even sure that she likes me or that I like her. As you said yourself, there are other eligible ladies to be had. I danced with several. After all, my time is short."

Warily, Honora stepped away from him, away from the disturbing effect of his nearness and his overwhelming size which could protect—or crush. She stared up at him, taking in his sober, seemingly honest expression. In her heart a sense of loss began to grow. Yet, a chill of suspicion tingled down her spine.

"Shall we walk in the garden?" he suggested, reaching for her elbow. "I feel the eyes of half of Balmoree's guests on us."

"Of course."

As they were about to turn the corner of the hedge into a more private spot, William and Beatrix hurried hand in hand from the shadows. William's lace cape collar was askew. Beatrix's coiffure was mussed and her blue taffeta skirt wrinkled. Embarrassment reddened William's face. Beatrix giggled. "Isn't it a wonderful party, sister?"

"Aye, indeed it is," Honora said. The couple hurried on past them. She glanced at the hedge. The thought of being secluded with the laird set off a warning. She pulled away from him and the shadows.

Until now all their time together had been carefully chaperoned and the laird had never failed to be a gentleman. Yet, Honora was unable to dismiss the sense that the man would take advantage of any situation that suited his purpose. Just the way he helped her from her horse—his hands always reaching a little beyond their proper place. The man was not to be trusted.

"Honora," Rosemary called, hobbling toward them. She stopped and clasped her hands before her. "Now don't you two look fine together, liked a sparkling jewel against black velvet. Oh, I wanted to warn you—the earl is looking for you. See, there he is. Quick! Behind the hedge. I'll tell him you're in the ballroom."

Before Honora could say a word, Rosemary limped away to head off Laird Ramsay. Brec tugged on Honora's arm. She hesitated.

"Are you ready to join the earl?" he whispered into her ear.

"You know I'm not," Honora snapped, vexed with how she seemed to be losing control of events. Brec grabbed her hand and pulled her around the hedge, into the evening shadows.

In the center of the garden retreat stood a sundial surrounded by a bed of bright yellow tulips. On either side of the sundial two white stone benches had purpled in the dusk. Distant voices from the outdoor entertainments floated to them over the tall hedge—taller than Brec.

Uneasily Honora realized that they were very much alone.

Brec released Honora's hand and sat down on a bench. She promptly seated herself on the other. He frowned at her.

"Well, you were saying, milaird," Honora began, determined to keep the conversation where she wanted it. She busied herself with arranging her skirts. "I believe you wanted to say that you are considering other ladies?"

"I'm simply taking your advice," he said. "Of course, besides a certain level of attractiveness, a man must find his prospective bride—shall we say—enticing, if you take my meaning. How can I say this tactfully? He must get children with her."

Honora ceased smoothing her silk skirt. She glanced over the sundial at Brec. The small smile on his lips belied the humility in the line of his brow.

She looked away and tried to ignore the warmth rising in her face. "Of course, I understand. 'Tis a wife's duty to bear children." She eyed him levelly. "Do you find it so difficult to be enticed by the charms of the ladies of Edinburgh?"

He laughed heartily. "Hardly. However, it seems that society has conspired to make it difficult—nearly impossible—for a man to be certain whether a woman is, shall we say, *adequately* enticing to be a good wife over time."

"Surely there is some way that a man knows," Honora stammered, then huffed in frustration. "Just what is it you are trying to say, sir?"

"Simply that kissing seems to be the only acceptable way for a man to know. The only practical way that society and the church permit," he said, serious now, without a twitch of his mouth or a glint in his eye.

Honora studied him across the tulips. "Kissing . . . is practical?"

"Let's just say that for a man, kissing is as practical as, for example, billing and cooing is for doves."

"Oh." As innocent as that sounded, Honora knew exactly what he meant. Heat flamed in her cheeks, and she was grateful for the gathering darkness. "Do you intend to kiss all the eligible ladies of Edinburgh? This party is a good place to start."

"I think there are a few I can eliminate without going that far," Brec replied before leaning forward. "Consider my request. All I ask from you is a kiss. You gave as much to Alexander Parrish a few weeks ago."

"Aye," Honora admitted. "But that was a farewell. And we were old friends."

"And the earl?" he asked, turning away. "You've kissed the earl, haven't you?"

"Well, yes," Honora said, recalling that she had kissed the earl once. It had been as exciting as kissing parchment, no comparison to brushing lips with a young romantic like

Alexander. She knew exactly what the laird meant by "entice." It was that warm tingling weakness that came into the limbs, making one feel helpless and desirous of being held close. Alexander had stirred some of that weakness in her and she suspected there was more. But she wasn't about to admit that to this man. "I can't imagine how a small kiss can tell you so much," she lied.

"Oh, it means more than you know," he replied and patted the stone bench next to him. "Come over here. We might be able to eliminate you just that quick." He waved his hands in the air as if to make something disappear.

The evening had grown even darker, and Honora could hardly see the laird's face. While she was glad he was unable to see hers, she longed to see his to measure his sincerity. There was a certain logic in what he said. And he asked only for a simple kiss. But he might be toying with her. Besides, she wasn't entirely certain she wanted to be eliminated. She rose from the bench. When she made no move toward him, he stood up. They faced each other over the sundial.

"If there is no enticement in the kiss, I will simply withdraw my suit," he added with an innocent shrug. "The field will be clear for the earl."

Honora froze, her embarrassment forgotten and the heat of anger rising through her. "You play an unfair game, sir. Threatening to leave me to the earl unless I . . . submit."

"Perhaps," he admitted, slowly beginning to walk around the sundial. "You've treated me so coolly I can only think that you prefer the earl."

"Really?!" Honora stalked away, keeping the sundial between them. "You know better than that."

Brec stopped. Honora halted when he did.

"All I ask for is a kiss, sweet soul," he implored with a humble bow of his head. He took a side step and seated himself where Honora had been sitting.

To see him settled so contritely instead of looming over her calmed Honora a bit. She began to reconsider his request. And he had only asked for a kiss. Not so much to give to keep Laird Ramsay at bay.

"All right, I grant you a kiss." With reluctant steps she

approached the bench. She leaned toward him, offered her lips, and closed her eyes.

"Oh, no," he said with a sinister chuckle. He gripped her wrist and tugged gently on her arm. "Not like that. Sit down."

Hesitant but obedient, Honora sat next to him. He leaned so near that all she could see in the darkness was his lips, surprisingly inviting, even tempting. She wanted to get this over with, so she licked her lips, leaned toward him once more, closed her eyes, and offered her mouth.

"Nay, not like that either," he said.

To her shock, his big hands descended on her shoulders, twisted her about on her bottom, and pulled her back across his lap. Honora felt the hardness of his thighs against her back and the heat—even through her whalebone bodice—of his broad hands spread across her belly.

At first Honora was too surprised to struggle. "What are you doing? Stop this." She pushed against his solid chest. She managed to get one foot on the stone bench so that she could put some real effort into her fight.

"You promised me a kiss," he reminded her with a grin, his face just above hers, his hand firm on her middle.

"But not like this," she gasped. "This is very ungentlemanly."

"I never promised gentlemanly," he said. "I'll leave that to poets."

Just as his lips descended on hers, footsteps crunched on the gravel path. Then she heard: "Honora, is that you?"

It was the earl's voice.

Horrified, Honora fought Brec's grip and tried again to sit up. To her growing embarrassment she succeeded only in kicking her skirt and petticoats above her knees.

"You've had your share of time with her, Rothwell," Brec countered without moving.

"What is this? Sir, I will not allow such liberties to be taken with my niece," another voice proclaimed. With a groan of dismay Honora recognized the cold tones of Uncle James. She tried to turn her head to see just who was standing there.

"You Islemen are barbaric," the earl stammered. He

stepped forward and reached for her. "Let me take you away, Honora."

"How dare you make a fool of me before my uncles," she hissed into Brec's face. "How dare you insult me this way!"

The laird released her but did not move. David helped Honora to her feet, her cheeks burning with shame.

"Make no mistake, sir, I consider your behavior most unbecoming a gentleman who would court my niece," Uncle James said. "Honora, get your things and find your sisters. We are leaving."

As she rounded the corner of the hedge, she turned to give Brec a scathing glare. He returned her gaze, his eyes dark and deep and his expression unreadable.

6

The carriage ride home from Balmoree's party was humiliating for Honora. Uncle James refused to speak to her. Uncle Malcolm didn't seem to know what had happened but was wise enough to remain silent. Rosemary squeezed Honora's hand. Beatrix petulantly complained about leaving early.

As soon as Honora reached her chamber, she yanked the feathers Brec had given her from her hair. She had needed no protection from the earl. She needed it from the devil, Brec McCloud, she thought as she flung the silken quills down on the dressing table. She stared at the iridescent feathers in silence while Lanie began to unlace her bodice.

"Were it a good party?" Lanie asked. "Jim, the footman, said everyone was there."

"Aye," Honora agreed. "Everyone." She had little inclination to share her humiliation with Lanie.

Beatrix burst breathlessly into the room. She still wore her rumpled party dress. "We must talk, Sister."

"Lanie, see to Rosemary," Honora ordered, relieved to be rid of the serving woman. "Beatrix and I can help each other."

Lanie curtsied and left the room. Without a word Beatrix took up the unlacing.

"I'm sorry we had to leave early," Honora said. "I'm afraid I was the cause."

"I know," Beatrix said. "Uncle James is furious." She helped Honora shrug out of the bodice. Honora began to loosen the laces at Beatrix's back.

"Honora," Beatrix began, "William asked for my hand in marriage at the party when we were in the garden."

Honora's fingers slowed a little, but she went on with the unlacing, glad that her sister could not see her face.

"He and his father will call tomorrow to make the formal marriage offer to Uncle James and Uncle Malcolm," Beatrix added.

Honora's fingers stopped.

"You know what our dear uncles will say?" Beatrix went on with a toss of her blond curls. "They will want to put off the betrothal and marriage until you, the eldest, are wed."

"Uncle James has told me as much," Honora said and resumed the unlacing, yanking angrily on each stubborn silken cord.

"Honora, do you think you will be accepting the earl or the laird soon?" Beatrix turned to her sister with her hands clasped before her in a gesture of pleading. "William and I love each other so. I know you don't care to marry just yet, but we want to be together now. If William and I aren't betrothed now, we'll all go to the country and another six months will go by . . . or longer. Who knows with the war and all?"

Honora sighed wearily. "I know." The doom settled on her shoulders and coiled itself about her. She was going to be forced make a choice.

"Honora, isn't the earl about to offer for you?" Beatrix asked. "And the laird? There is such fire in his eyes when he looks at you. Surely he would offer, if he knew how you felt."

"Me? And the laird?" Honora exclaimed. "I only agreed

to his suit because Uncle James insisted. After today, I don't ever want to see that man again."

"Did you quarrel?" Beatrix asked and waved the problem away. "William and I have had our disagreements too, but then we kiss and 'tis all over."

"I'm afraid it's not that simple. Come here." With a smile Honora embraced Beatrix. "I'm very happy for you, Sister, and I don't want to keep you and William apart. I'll do what I can."

"Oh, thank you," Beatrix cried. "May I tell Rosemary?"

"Of course." When her sister had left the room, Honora sat at her dressing table and began to take down her hair. For reasons known only to the laird, he had chosen to trifle with her. And the Earl of Rothwell wanted her only for selfish reasons. Her gaze fell on the shining feathers. As she brushed out her chestnut tresses, she wondered what she was going to do.

She slept dreamlessly and awoke to a rainy morn.

A chill crept over the house and Honora pulled her chair close to the fire in the blue receiving room. The sorrowful downpour suited her mood. With a book of poems open on her lap she contemplated the future. She didn't like what she saw in the orange glow of the coal fire.

She could be housekeeper, hostess, and stepmother to the earl's six children—take up the virginal and have her repertoire reviewed by Laird Ramsay, providing he would even offer marriage after yesterday. Or she could go off to the Isle of Myst to be mistress of a drafty, twelfth-century castle and live among people who probably didn't even speak English.

Honora groaned aloud.

Of course, that was assuming Laird Brec intended to ask for her hand. He had asked to pay proper suit, but in Balmoree's garden he had obviously mocked her equal time plan and taken the advantage of her naivete. She could no longer be certain what his intentions were.

What was even more confusing to Honora was the frightening weakness that had overcome her, melting through her limbs when the laird had pulled her across his lap—unlike what she had known with Alexander. Had she wanted the laird to kiss her, take her like that, helpless and at his mercy? Honora shivered. She tossed a few lumps of coal on the fire and pulled her chair closer to the hearth.

Her third choice was to run away. She had lied to the laird when he had asked her about running away with Alexander. She had no fear of sleeping in haystacks and stealing food if it meant being with the one she loved. But to run away would be to desert her sisters, and she would never do that.

From the hallway she heard the comings and goings of her uncles' acquaintances. From the front windows came the clatter of hooves on cobbles and the jingle of carriage traces.

Rosemary and Beatrix scurried into the blue room, all giggles, whispers, and swishing skirts. They put their fingers to their lips to warn Honora to silence and cracked open the window to look down on arriving carriages.

" 'Tis the earl," Beatrix whispered loud enough for Honora to hear. "Were you expecting him?"

"Nay, I was not." Honora sat up and wondered what had brought the earl to see her uncles. Book in hand, she hurried to the window in time to see the stern-faced earl march into the house. Pensively Honora returned to her chair. For once she was glad that she wasn't invited to hear Uncle James and the earl's discussion.

Beatrix and Rosemary were disappointed that the caller wasn't William Cassilis and his father. But their spirits were high; they had little patience with Honora's gloom. Soon they were off to Beatrix's dressing room to plan her trousseau.

The day grew darker and thunder rumbled deep in the heavens. Honora's spirits sank lower. She sat engrossed in the dismal future she saw for herself and her sisters. Heaven knew she had only herself to blame. She had eliminated every suitor except the Laird Ramsay—and he remained only because she dared not turn him away and disappoint her uncles. Was there no other choice for her but to marry him? She was so lost in bleak thought that she jumped when she heard the rap on the door.

"Aye, who is it?" she called out, praying it wasn't the

earl. She was unprepared to face him after yesterday's scene.

Jim, the footman, opened the door a crack. "Milady, there is a gentleman here to see you. Shall I show him in?"

"Who is it?" Honora asked.

"Me," Brec said as he brushed Jim aside. He invaded the room and shrank it with his size, his shoulders almost as broad as the doorway. He shoved the door closed on the servant.

Surprised, Honora stood up. Jim cracked the door again, a doubtful expression on his face.

" 'Tis all right, Jim," she assured the footman, but she didn't feel assured at all. A lady didn't see a man alone in a room with the door closed, especially if the man had been ungentlemanly the day before and was rude to one of the servants. Her anger returned.

She put her book on the table in a casual fashion, then asked, "Did you come to apologize for your behavior yesterday?"

He gazed at her for a long moment as if assessing her mood before removing his dripping hat and cloak.

"Nay. I came because I heard that the Earl of Rothwell has asked for your hand in marriage."

"He has?" Honora clamped her hand over her mouth, then chided herself for her lack of poise. Silently she willed herself to remain unruffled. "That's hard to believe, after that humiliating scene you subjected me to in the garden yesterday."

"Nothing has been said to you?" the laird asked. His dark-eyed gaze searched her face. "You have not accepted his offer?"

"I've heard nothing of it," Honora said, surprised by the importance he placed on this and still annoyed that he continued to evade the issue of Balmoree's party.

"Good," Laird Brec said. "I'll speak plainly then, milady. I'll ask you to put Balmoree's party behind us. Fate leaves little time for useless disputes. As laird, as clan chief, I must have a suitable bride—a lady for my castle. And I believe you have reasons to be in need of a suitable husband."

Honora forced herself to break away from his gaze and

turned to the window. A pounding began in her heart. She was going to have to make a choice. "I suppose that is a fair statement of our circumstances, sir. Go on."

"Before you accept any offer of marriage, I wish to put an offer for your hand before your uncles. Will you consider it?"

Honora remained at the window, her back turned to him.

It was hardly the kind of marriage proposal that moved a woman who had once—for all her practicality—secretly dreamed of true love. But she knew she had been a fool to hope for a love match like her parents. The laird's forthrightness had stolen the heat from her indignation and taken them straight to the heart of the matter. They were both in need of a suitable marriage arrangement.

"Honora!" The blue room door swung open, and Beatrix stood there, her face aglow with happiness. "William and his father are here at last. Rosemary and I saw them from the stairway. Oh, Honora, this is it. They are going to make the betrothal offer. Don't let Uncle James put it off. Honora, please."

Beatrix flung herself into Honora's arms. "Wish me happiness, Sister."

"Of course, I wish you happiness," Honora whispered. She held Beatrix tightly while joy and regret twisted in her heart. "I'm delighted for you. And I know that you and William will be very happy together."

"And let me be among the first to wish the newly betrothed happiness," Laird Brec said. He stepped forward.

Beatrix released Honora immediately. "Thank you, milaird." She glanced from the laird to Honora as understanding dawned in her eyes. Beatrix backed toward the door, fluttering her hands vaguely. "Well, don't let me disturb you. Goodbye, milaird."

The click of the door latch echoed through the blue room.

Brec spoke first. "So time has run out for me, and I see it has for you too."

Honora said nothing. The sense of smothering doom descended on her once more. What were her uncles telling Laird Ramsay right now? And Cassilis? She could imagine Uncle James at his desk, plowing his fingers through his white hair as he contemplated all the marriage proposals before him.

When she turned back to the windows, the laird paced restlessly across the room again. As he walked, he outlined each detail. She listened carefully.

"The marriage contract will specify that you are to be the McCloud's lady, the lady of Castle Dunrugis. I know you have seen to your own household and even your uncles' for years. So you are well qualified for this task. As is Scots custom, your dowry will be yours to do with as you wish. I will not interfere with it or make demands on it. Dower arrangements will be made. I will provide for all your needs.

"In exchange, you will see to the management of Dunrugis, be the hostess, bear the clan chief's children. Our issue will inherit the Isle of Myst."

With her finger to her lips Honora pondered the word. *Issue?* The laird spoke of a contract and of their issue. She would carry a *babe*. The historians would record McCloud offspring. She would nurse an *infant* at her breast. The bards would sing of McCloud heroes and descendants. She would comfort a *child* and shape a young mind. A McCloud would march off to war. She would stitch the body of her *son* into a burial shroud.

Was it any wonder, Honora thought, that men spoke of marriage contracts while women dreamed of love matches? For a man, matrimony was a bargain with the future, an arrangement to ensure a place in history. For a woman, marriage was a pact for her body, her heart and soul. She had no name to offer the generations, only her love.

"Lady Honora?" the laird broke in. He hovered uncertainly at her side, his hands clasped behind him as if he were afraid to chance touching her. "I would be glad to consider anything you might wish to add to the contract."

Honora shook herself and glanced up at him from the corner of her eye. She saw only grave concern in his expression. No mischief. No mockery. "No, milaird, I've nothing to add. All of your points make sense and are customary, as far as I know. But I don't understand why you offer this to me. Surely there are others more suitable than I. I know nothing of your isle or your castle or your people. I don't even speak Gaelic. And what of your family? Is there no one you must consult?"

"My mother is a gentle soul." The laird walked to the fire and warmed his hands before it. "She will accept my choice."

Honora sighed wearily and stared out the window at drooping rhododendron boughs in the garden. What sweet words of love and marriage had William whispered to Beatrix when he had proposed? she wondered. Was she never to hear a lover's tender declaration? Then she scolded herself for those unrealistic longings. She was a grown woman of nineteen years; she had more important things to consider.

The laird went on. "We'll take your horse and your serving woman. Your guitar and your chaplain, of course," he offered. "I will not ask you to give up your religion. We'll send for whatever else you need later."

Still Honora did not answer. Her mind churned with disappointment, uncertainty, despair. His words called up a vision of dozens of pack horses stretched along a dangerous trail that led to the end of the earth—only Ireland lay beyond the isles. The Isle of Myst seemed another world away.

"Perhaps you would rather stay here and marry the earl?"

Honora whirled on him. "Don't you threaten me with that! I thought you would have learned your lesson yesterday."

The laird raised his hands as if to ward off her wrath— the first mocking gesture Honora had seen him make since he had walked in. He went on. "Let me remind you that I have no motherless children for you to raise. I offer only one castle, but 'tis the oldest and the grandest among the isles. As the McCloud's lady you will be respected and protected. You will want for nothing."

Honora watched him, curious as to why he continued to talk of his assets. He had not said what she wanted to hear. She had dismissed more than one suitor for the absence of those words.

He caught her gaze and this time he refused to release her. With those lustrous jet eyes he searched her. What do you want? he queried, exacted, and probed. His soul-searing scrutiny stripped away her anger and prejudice, her pride and pretense, until Honora felt naked and defenseless before him.

Abruptly he turned back to the fire. Honora reached for the window casement to steady herself. Thunder rumbled overhead. The coal fire hissed softly.

"Would it help you to make your choice, sweet soul, if you knew that 'twould be no burden to have Rosemary with us?" he asked, without looking up from the glowing warmth before him. "Your sister will always be welcome at Dunrugis. Always. We'll add it to the contract, if you like. No kin of my bride shall ever be in need of a home."

Honora squeezed her eyes closed and turned away. She tried to resist the sudden flood of tears that threatened, tears of unexpected relief. She let her head rest against the cold windowpane and put a hand to her mouth to smother a sob. Had he really seen into her heart with those black eyes?

The man who accepted an alliance with Honora Maitland must accept her sister as well. She had shouldered that responsibility long ago. That's how she had always known when to turn a suitor away. So few saw beyond Rosemary's halting gait.

Honora sighed aloud this time and looked over her shoulder at the laird. "If I agree to your offer, will my uncles accede?"

"Accept and I will see that your uncles agree," he replied without hesitation, without looking up from the fire. "Do you accept?"

"I need time to think about it."

"There is no time," he said. Now he joined her at the window, looming over her, restless and watchful. "Remember, your sister wishes to accept her betrothal. I need to return to the isle soon. And I want to take you with me. If I speak to your uncles now, we can be wed tomorrow."

"Tomorrow!" Honora repeated in wonder and stared up at him. "I can't be ready to wed tomorrow. I haven't even accepted."

"But you are going to," he said, a pleased smile spreading across his dark face. Suddenly his expression sobered.

76

A look of surprise flashed across his face. He leaned closer, his gaze intent on her ear. Distracted, Honora touched her lobe.

"Wait," he whispered. "There is something behind your ear. I'll get it. Be still."

Before Honora could protest, he touched her temple and cupped his hand lightly over her ear. When he pulled away, he held an emerald ring. The polished green stone glittered atop a setting of diamonds and gold.

Honora stared at it, at the arrogant man before her, then at the ring again. "Where did that come from?"

"From behind your ear," he said with a smile. "Your betrothal ring, milady."

When Honora didn't move, he gently took her hand and slipped the ring on her finger. "An emerald, a poor imitation of the color of your eyes, sweet soul. But 'tis the best I can offer."

Honora shook her head, uncertain of her feelings. She found little joy in this moment. "We have agreed to a contract, milaird. There is no need for flattery."

"Nay, 'tis no flattery, milady," he said. "You are mistaken about Beatrix's being the beauty of the family. Your loveliness is one of your many assets."

"And what about my willfulness and my outspokenness . . . and my deceptions? Are those assets you wish in a wife?"

He kissed her hand formally, pressed it between his own large ones. "There are times when such liabilities can be used to an advantage, even for a woman."

There was a sound at the door.

"Laird Brec, I didn't know you were here."

Brec and Honora turned to see Uncle James in the doorway. Behind him stood the perpetually frowning Laird Ramsay.

"Your grace." Brec made a polite bow. "Milaird. Your appearance is most timely. Lady Honora has just accepted my offer of marriage."

"But—but you have said nothing to me, sir," Uncle James stammered. "And after your behavior yesterday . . . Did you know, Honora, my dear, the earl has also offered for you, just this hour? We've come to tell you. The laird cannot hold you to anything I have not accepted."

Brec held Honora's hand hidden in the folds of her skirt, and squeezed it. Her world tilted a little, just off center from reality. Had she really just accepted this man's offer so she could refuse the earl? If she had any doubts, now was the time to voice them.

She looked up at Brec, at the straight nose, at the long firm jaw and the eloquent brow, at the only man who had ever understood about Rosemary.

"I am decided," Honora said to her uncle. "I shall marry Laird Brec. See? I have accepted his bethrothal ring."

Anger twisted the earl's face as he made his way around Uncle James. "What have you done, McCloud? What promises did you make? What spell did you cast? You have no right to drag a woman of quality like Lady Honora off to your heathen isle."

Beside her, Brec stiffened. The implication stung Honora too. "Do you presume, sir, that I am incapable of deciding for myself?"

The earl appealed to Uncle James for support. "Jamie, surely you don't intend to let the lass make her own decision. I want only to save you from unhappiness, my dear. I wish you the best. These Islemen live in a different world."

"Malcolm and I are also concerned for Honora's welfare," James said. "We agreed that Honora could choose between her suitors. Other than Laird McCloud's questionable behavior yesterday, I have seen him use no foul means in winning my niece's affection. If the laird and I come to an agreement on the terms of the marriage contract, I can't stand in the way of Honora's choice."

"That's your decision?" the earl demanded. He moved to stand before James, disbelief on his face.

"Aye, and I hope this won't come between us as friends."

The earl studied Uncle James. "I thought we had an agreement, sir. Honora was to be mine in time. You have not heard the last of this."

7

The Maitland house brimmed with good cheer. Skirts rustled up and down the stairs, and laughter rang throughout the rooms. A wedding, a reception breakfast, a betrothal announcement, and a departure all had to be arranged in a day. Uncle James had insisted that the wedding take place the day after the next.

Francis sent for paper, ink, and quills. The girls scribbled invitations late into the night, and footmen, grooms, and stableboys were dispatched in the morning to deliver them. Food and hogsheads of wine were ordered, and extra chairs and china were hired. The wedding might be sudden and private—they arranged for a small ceremony to be performed in St. Giles—but Uncle James and Uncle Malcolm would spare no expense on the wedding and betrothal breakfast to follow.

Lanie pursed her lips as she listened to the giggles that floated from Lady Beatrix's chamber, where the sisters were sorting through their gowns. She worked in Lady Honora's chamber, carefully packing silken underclothes in a trunk.

Lanie wanted to be pleased about her lady's imminent marriage, but she wasn't. From the first day at Nor' Loch, that great dark devil Laird Brec had terrified her so that she couldn't meet his gaze. She was frightened, too, by the tales she had heard in the kitchen of his brother's death and the fantastic funeral. Who knew what a canny fiend like the laird might do to an innocent like Lady Honora. Anyone could see that the dark man would want strange things of her. Lanie didn't understand why Lady Honora's uncles and sisters were not also concerned.

Was no one going to tell Lady Honora of the stories?

Lanie wondered. Lady Honora disliked the carrying of tales. But someone had to say something.

The three sisters swept into the room, each bearing an armload of clothing.

"You'll need lots of warm things," Lady Beatrix was saying. "Take these warm undervests. I can get more made before winter. 'Tis a shame you don't have time to have a trousseau made."

"And warm hose," Rosemary added, spilling several pairs into the trunk Lanie had neatly arranged. "You'll need warm hose. You know how those old castles are. You'd be warmer in a shepherd's cottage."

"Sisters, sisters," Lady Honora said with a laugh. "I'll be all right. The Isle of Myst is not the end of the world."

Beatrix and Rosemary looked at each other in dismay.

"But 'tis so far away," Rosemary said.

"And so wild," Beatrix added.

That thought sent a chill over Lanie. She would be leaving behind her mum and her brothers too.

Beatrix nodded vigorously. "I can't believe that you won't be here to plan my wedding with Rosemary and me."

An awkward silence descended on the three. Lanie looked up from her packing to see the sisters staring at each other with sorrow on their faces.

"My thoughts will be with you, but you'll do fine without me," Honora replied. Her voice was light, and Lanie saw her lady put on her brave face. "Lady Elizabeth will be delighted to help you with the plans. Now, let's see that blue gown."

"Laird Brec really asked you to wear blue?" Beatrix asked, holding the blue damask gown up to Honora. "Why? I wonder."

"It was the color I was wearing the night I summoned him," Honora explained. She walked to her mirror with the gown.

"When you summoned him?" Rosemary repeated.

"He asked me to wear pearls too," Honora added.

"Oh, I think 'tis so romantic that you're going to be married twice," Rosemary crooned. She sat down on the stool by the fireplace and clasped her hands beneath her chin. "First in St. Giles, again on the Isle of Myst."

" 'Tis not meant to be romantic," Honora explained. " 'Tis to satisfy Uncle James and Uncle Malcolm, as well as Laird Brec's family. He said all the McCloud lairds have been married in the abbey on the Isle of Myst. What did he call it? St. Michael's, I believe. And besides, the islanders will feel left out if they are not permitted to join in the marriage *ceilidh*."

"I still think 'tis romantic," Rosemary said with a sigh. "I can see the tall arches and a spire reaching to the heavens."

" 'Tis a very old abbey," Honora said with a wry smile. "Laird Brec said that according to legend, it was founded by St. Columba himself. And 'tis probably small and squat and dark and smells of the dampness."

"And what will he wear tomorrow?" Beatrix joined her sister at the mirror. "Did you ask?"

"Will he wear his kilt, as he did to Balmoree's party?" Rosemary asked. "He has a fine pair of knees."

"Rosemary!" Beatrix began to giggle. "I'll prefer my groom in breeches."

"The laird said he wished to wear a black coat and the kilt," Honora said, turning to her giggling sisters with a mock frown. "He is still in mourning for his brother, and the kilt is traditional dress. So I agreed."

Lanie's sniff of disapproval went unheard. What man would wear black to his wedding? she thought. Only the devil himself. She continued to pack and listen to the girls carry on about the wedding gown.

Beatrix wanted to add white lace to the collar and to dress the bride's hair with pearls. Rosemary wanted Honora to wear the family's sapphire earrings. They drifted back to Beatrix's chamber to look for more pearls.

Later, Honora returned to oversee the packing. She approved Lanie's neat arrangement, and she began to dress for dinner. Lanie helped her step into an amber gold skirt, and then slip into her bodice.

"Has he told ye what the island is going to be like, milady?" Lanie asked, thinking to use her lady's curiosity to tell what she knew.

"Well, we won't have all the market stalls and tradesmen around the corner as we have here," Honora said.

"Have ye heard what they say about Castle Dunrugis?"

"What do they say?" Lady Honora asked.

"They say the castle has a hidden room and a secret dungeon," Lanie said, lowering her voice. She was certain that the dark laird would disapprove of her telling Lady Honora about Dunrugis. With the thought of Brec McCloud, Lanie glanced nervously over her shoulder at the shadows gathering in the room.

"Old castles frequently have hidden rooms," Lady Honora said, dismissing Lanie's concern with a smile. "Most likely, poor planning when new rooms are added."

"But this room has a purpose, Lady Honora," Lanie said, anxious to make her mistress understand. " 'Tis said that the McClouds hide a terrible secret there."

Honora sat down before the mirror, looked up at Lanie by way of the reflection, and smiled again. "So they hide the family's treasures and tell stories to keep thieves away."

"Nay, 'tis more than that," Lanie whispered.

"So what are the tabbies in the kitchen saying?" Lady Honora demanded, irritation in her voice, her eyes gone stormy green.

Lanie took a deep breath. "They say that centuries ago a fairy, one of the dark people, married into the family. She bore a child, a dark, humpbacked immortal monster that had to be hidden away. Only the laird of the McClouds knows the secret and has the key to the room where the terrible creature is kept. Before each laird dies, he passes the key and the secret of the room on to the new laird. Can ye no' see the dark fairy blood in Laird Brec himself?"

"Lanie, that is a terrible story," Lady Honora scolded in a low voice. She frowned. "Some wild tale like that has been told about nearly every clan in the Highlands. I don't want to hear a breath of it again."

"Donna ye see, milady?" Lanie pleaded. "The laird wants to marry ye because no Highland laird will allow their daughters to marry into the McCloud clan. And if he marries ye, he marries a Maitland, the daughter of a duke, and makes himself rich."

Lady Honora stared into the mirror at Lanie for a long, silent moment. Her full lips pressed tight in anger.

"That's true of nearly any man who marries me, Lanie. 'Tis no offense of Laird Brec's if he has considered those things in making his offer. I'll hear no more about this."

"Aye, milady," Lanie whispered and with trembling hands clasped a string of pearls around her mistress's neck.

Honora had her doubts, but she kept them to herself. The last thing she needed was to hear bizarre rumors about the man she was going to marry, a man about whom she knew almost nothing. She wondered about Lanie's tale that evening as she watched Brec across the dining table. He was talking with Uncle Malcolm about investing in the New World.

"But the English East India Company has a monopoly on all the shipping to the colonies," Malcolm pointed out. "There is no future there for Scot shipping trade."

"Aye, it seems so, but a resourceful ship captain can sidestep those problems," the laird said.

Suddenly, as if he felt Honora's gaze upon him, Brec turned to her and flashed her a seductive smile, his teeth white and even against a tanned face. She warmed inside and had to smile in return. She had no difficulty in believing that he might carry in him some magic blood. Often his eyes cast a spell making her long for that uncompleted kiss in the garden.

They were married in St. Giles Cathedral, beneath the newly crowned steeple and amid the four ancient pillars—with only Uncle James, Uncle Malcolm, Beatrix, Rosemary, Kenneth, and Lanie present. Reverend Crawford, Uncles James' chaplain who had agreed to accompany Honora to the Isle of Myst, officiated.

The first sight of Honora as she walked down the aisle on her Uncle James' arm touched Brec and made him eager to be done with the ceremony. Her face was pale, but she held her head high, composure evident in the set of her shoulders. A regal smile glowed on her lips. As Brec had requested, she wore the blue gown she had worn on the stormy night they met. And at her throat were the lustrous pearls—as she had worn them to the first supper they shared. The candlelight glittered in her hair. Her sea-green eyes were wide and a little dark with apprehension. As she stepped closer, once again Brec admired her delicate nose and her high, exotic cheekbones. He considered the feature he prized the most—her lips, full and generous, meant to be savored in passion.

When she took her place beside him and their gazes met, a lovely blush colored her cheeks.

Brec reached for her hands and pressed them between his own. They were small and cold and trembling just slightly. He ignored the look of reproach from Uncle James. Mentally he pushed aside all of Kenneth's warnings and admonitions that a Highland miss would do as well as Lady Honora. Brec had traveled the world over and met no woman who fascinated him as Honora did. No others had ever mattered.

She was worth every pact, fair or foul, he'd had to make. The dance lessons, the tailor's fittings, the barber's snippings. The bad will of the Earl of Rothwell. The hours of delicate negotiations with her uncles. Surely this lady was meant to be the lady of Dunrugis. All he had to do was to make her believe that too. He had miscalculated once—at Balmoree's party. He would not err again.

Her hands trembled in his as she said her vows. He repeated his. With her face cupped in his hands, he kissed her ardently, intent on convincing her that she belonged with him. Her hesitancy made him acutely aware that she could still change her mind.

Honora was proud of herself. She did not weep during the ceremony. She made all the correct responses. But she froze when the Reverend invited Brec to kiss his bride. She had not forgotten about that part of the ceremony, but she was uncertain what to expect from her bridegroom.

Amid St. Giles's towering cathedral columns and great glowing candles, Brec took her face between his hands and bent to kiss her. She was unprepared for the yearning his gentle smile stirred inside her, and for his tender, reverent touch. With only his lips he touched her deeply and stirred more than tingling and warmth in her limbs. His lips moved over her mouth, arousing feelings—longings to be caressed more thoroughly and kissed more deeply. When he drew away, Honora followed his lips, coming up on her toes, reluctant to be released.

Frustrated, she opened her eyes to find him smiling down at her with a secret smile of understanding—and promise—on his lips and shining in his eyes.

"When we get to the isle, sweet soul, when we're wed there," he whispered, "more then. Now we have guests to entertain and a long journey ahead."

They emerged from the cathedral into rain, but the wet weather didn't dampen the spirits of their breakfast guests. The Maitland girls and their uncles were well liked, and few had refused their invitation. Many wanted to meet this mysterious Laird of the Isle of Myst who had won the elusive Lady Honora Maitland. Of Edinburgh's social elite, only the Earl of Rothwell was absent.

Once at the breakfast, Brec and Honora were separated. A few minutes later, she was relieved when Brec returned to her.

"I missed you," she murmured lightly. Rosemary was at her side, sipping punch.

"I was detained," he replied. "By a Lady Nisbet, I believe. She said her son was someone named George. She gave me quite a thorough interview."

Rosemary choked on her claret punch. Honora frowned at her sister until the girl excused herself, hiding her giggles behind her hand.

When all the guests had left by early evening, Brec came to Honora with his hat in hand.

"Sleep well tonight, sweet soul," he murmured as he took her in his arms and kissed her lightly on the brow. "We leave early in the morning."

"Aye, husband, I'll be ready," Honora said, looking up at him. She knew they had planned all this before. Until after their marriage on the Isle of Myst, Brec and Kenneth would keep to their rooms, and Honora would remain with her family or her serving woman. But now, seeing him leave, she regretted agreeing to the plans.

She wanted to be with her husband as a bride should be. She wanted the promise she had tasted on his lips and had seen in his eyes to be fulfilled—on her wedding night. She longed to feel the heat of his hands on her bare skin, not through the whalebone of her bodice. Why postpone something that was inevitable?

"Patience," he whispered, his lips near her ear. "I wish to be with you too. Remember, we have a lifetime ahead of us."

So she was left by her guests and her bridegroom to sleep alone in her room, her once-familiar chamber now a clutter of trunks and boxes. The fireplace was cold and the drapes were drawn. She dismissed Lanie when the undressing was done.

Still too wide awake to sleep, she lay with her head propped up on an elbow and wondered what Brec's isle would be like. Would his mother accept Honora as readily as he seemed so certain that she would? What would his mother be like? And the castle?

A soft rap on her door startled her out of her reflections. "Come in!" She sat up, wondering who could still be awake.

Rosemary, in nightcap and gown, peeked into the room. "May I sleep in your bed, Sister? I had a bad dream."

"Of course." Honora smiled and quickly made room for her little sister. No sooner had they tucked the bed covers back into place and Rosemary settled herself in the great four-poster bed, than another rap came on the door.

"Aye?" Honora called, more perplexed than before.

Beatrix stuck her head in the door, her golden braid swung across her shoulder making a pendulum shadow against the wall. She, too, was in her nightcap and gown. "Honora?"

Honora was touched that her sisters were as reluctant to have her go as she was to leave them. "We've room for you too."

Beatrix tiptoed across the room, drew back the covers, and snuggled down into the bed on the other side of Honora. Rosemary blew out the candle, and they whispered and giggled about the events of the day—observations and opinions vital for sisters to share, but of no great consequence to the world. Eventually the laughter and conversation died away as the events of the long day overtook them and the girls drifted off to sleep. Regretfully Honora settled deeper into the feather bed listening to the peaceful, even breathing of her sisters.

This was their last night together as girls—without husbands and children to complicate their lives, making demands on them that would ever after have to come ahead of a sister's entreaty. With apprehension Honora wondered what lay ahead for them—she prayed for love and happiness. Beatrix had found it. Of herself she was not so sure. And Rosemary was another matter.

With a sigh Honora tucked the covers about all of them and smiled to herself in the darkness. She wondered where Brec was. In some tavern where he and Kenneth shared a comradely flagon of ale to celebrate the wedding? Silently she thanked him for giving her this night with Rosemary and Beatrix. Then she smiled to herself again. Surely she was the only bride in history who slept with her sisters on her wedding night.

The morning sun still hung low in the east. Far off a cock crowed, and in the eaves of the carriage house the birds had just begun to chatter. But the Cowgate mews already teemed with pack garrons, grooms, and riding horses.

"Honora?" Uncle Malcolm stood with the servants and Honora's sisters, who had lined up to say farewell. Carrying a brass-trimmed wooden box, he stepped up to her. He held the box forth with an uncertain smile on his lips. "This is a wedding gift from your Uncle James and me. We've had it packed and made ready to travel for you."

Astounded, Honora stared at the box he held. "But you've already given me table linens and so many other things."

"I know, I know," her uncle said. "But this is special. 'Tis the brass-faced lantern clock. The chiming clock from the library that has always been your favorite. We decided that you should take it with you. Something from home." He looked at Laird Brec, who was giving orders to some of the grooms and was out of hearing.

"And I wanted you to know that we would never have agreed to this match if we weren't certain that the laird would be good to you. He gave us his word." Uncle Malcolm hesitated before going on. "It serves many purposes, your marriage to the laird. But if there's any problem, anything that makes you unhappy—you must send word to us."

Speechless, Honora took the box from her uncle and agreed to his request with a nod.

"Goodbye, dear Honora." Uncle Malcolm took her by the shoulders and kissed her cheek.

She gave a quick kiss to Uncle James, who patted her hand and frowned but seemed too moved to speak.

Beatrix smiled sleepily at Honora. "I wish you happiness, Sister, and long life with your laird."

Rosemary, bright-eyed already, embraced Honora. "You are Lady McCloud, and soon Beatrix will be Lady Cassilis. I'm the only sister yet to find a husband," she chirped. "But I will find one soon. And I'll be Lady something too."

"You will, indeed, Rosemary," Honora assured her. "One day soon. Take care of Beatrix. She'll need help with the wedding."

Rosemary nodded.

Brec gave Honora a brief kiss of greeting as he helped her mount her brown mare and arrange the skirt of her riding habit. With waves of goodbye and only a few tears, they rode out of the mews and into the Cowgate.

Behind them trailed Kenneth, Lanie, Reverend Crawford, and a long baggage train of household goods and trunks.

Ahead of them lay the Isle of Myst.

8

Brec had offered to hire a litter for Honora because the roads west were too rough and narrow for carriage travel. But she'd declined.

"I'm a good rider," she said. "Horseback travel is faster."

Brec agreed.

During the long, exhausting days that followed, Brec pushed the baggage train from dawn into the dusk to make as many miles a day as possible. But he was thoughtful of Honora, making certain that she stayed in the most comfortable rooms at the inns where they stopped and that she was served the best food available.

Honora was prepared for the discomforts of the trip, but Lanie fretted at every stop.

"This room is filthy," Lanie complained. "And the linens—scratchy as wool. Not fine enough for ye, milady."

The serving woman slept on a pallet at the foot of Honora's bed. And, Honora noted, the farther from home they traveled, the more troubled Lanie's dreams seemed to become. Each day Honora watched Lanie's appetite shrink and the anxiety in her eyes grow.

Reverend Crawford seemed to pray overly much. He was a young man, not many years older than Honora, and unmellowed by the trials of life.

"I pray for the grooms and the horse handlers," he confided in Honora one day. "They make no secret of their sinful affairs with the local lassies. I despair for their souls."

In Glasgow the Maitland grooms insisted on returning to Edinburgh. They disliked being so far from home, they complained, respectfully. Honora gave them permission to return, but she felt oddly abandoned. Brec ordered Kenneth to tip the men generously. When Lanie forelornly waved goodbye to the grooms, Honora suspected that her serving woman, too, was more than a little homesick.

Brec's friends in Glasgow offered the services of their grooms. The new men were a rough-looking lot in tattered livery, with scraggly beards and little knowledge of English.

As the days went by, Brec became more remote and more absorbed in travel details. He took to wearing his black leather breeks again. And he let his beard grow. Daily Honora grew more exhausted, so that by the time they passed Loch Lomond and traveled on to Glen Mor, she had little energy to truly enjoy the glories of the Highlands in the spring. She decided Brec had been right, after all.

Their married life should begin only when they reached the isle.

A bitter wind whipped around Honora, Lanie, and Reverend Crawford as they stood on the stone quay and stared in dismay at the fog. Whitecaps beat against the rocks at their feet. Spray clung to their eyelashes and dampened their cloaks. Beyond the shrouded sea lay the Isle of Myst.

"I canna see a thing out there," Lanie whimpered as she pulled her cloak close about her. But she knew it was more than the wind that had given her the shivers. She shaded her eyes with her hand as if that would help her vision penetrate the gloom. " 'Tis a bad omen. We aren't meant to go to the isle."

"Nonsense. Laird Brec said you can see the mountains from here on a clear day," Honora reminded her serving woman. "He also said that the isle lies so near that the herdsmen swim the cattle across at market time. But our crossing will take longer. Castle Dunrugis is at the north end of the isle."

"Don't you think 'tis strange that there's no one here to meet us?" Reverend Crawford observed. The lanky man clutched at the brim of his hat to prevent the wind from carrying it away. "Didn't Laird Brec say he sent word ahead that we would be arriving today?"

Lanie nodded, also wondering. The Islemen must be eager to meet their laird and his new lady.

"I'm sure they're awaiting us on the isle," Honora said. "The ferryman said the weather has been bad for several days."

Now, wasn't that just like her lady, Lanie thought—to put the best face on things. Lady Honora would be a better wife than the black-bearded devil deserved.

The sound of footsteps on the rocks caught their attention, and the three turned to see Kenneth approaching.

"Milady. The ferryman's wife offers her hospitality," he said respectfully enough, but Lanie could read the disapproval in his eyes. "She has prepared a hot drink for you."

"Aye, and I would not offend by refusing her generosity," Lady Honora said. "Tell Laird Brec I will be right there."

"But how can ye abide the stench of fish?" Lanie asked. "Drove me right out of that hut, it did. I'd rather freeze in this wind."

"Laird Brec says the ferry will be here soon," Honora replied as she turned to follow Kenneth. "At least stand out of the weather so you won't take a chill."

Lanie and the Reverend walked from the quay to stand in the windbreak offered by the horses. Lanie stared at the bleak shoreline and shivered again.

"Do ye think there's really an isle over there?" she asked. She hugged herself beneath her woolen cloak and searched the Reverend's face for an answer. She wanted to know whether he was as unsettled by this strange country as she was.

"Of course," he said. "Why wouldn't there be?"

"I donna know," Lanie said, looking back at the quay where they had just stood watching the turbulent waters. Lanie knew she didn't dare tell the tale of the secret room. But she thought there were things the Reverend should know.

"Have ye no' heard the stories of the wee dark people of the isles? Have ye no' wondered? What if the laird be a kelpie himself and plans to drag us all into the sea to devour us?"

"I think he is a strange man," the hollow-cheeked Reverend admitted. "But what can you expect from these unreformed Islemen? They even speak a heathen tongue."

Lanie leaned closer to the Reverend and felt a blush spread into her cheeks. She was about to say something indiscreet, but she felt compelled for her lady's safety. "Aye, strange, indeed. What's even stranger is that he has no' touched her yet. Can ye believe it? A woman like Lady Honora his wife and he's hardly laid a finger on her. I tell you, 'tis unnatural."

"Aye," was the Reverend's only response. Lanie watched with satisfaction as a blush tinted the man's colorless cheeks. His eyes strayed toward the cottage doorway, where Lady Honora's elegant form had disappeared. "Aye, 'tis strange."

"Do ye think we can get her to return with us?" Lanie asked.

"Return?" the Reverend said, shock in his voice. He straightened his shoulders and peered down his long nose at Lanie. "Why would she return?"

"Ye canna see it? He has cast a spell over her. She doesna belong here with these people. He's been no sort of husband. What do ye think he intends to do with her?" Lanie leaned closer to the Reverend and spoke more plainly to the facts. "And what do ye think he intends to do with us?"

"Lady Honora is the laird's wife. Her duty is to be at his side, to obey him. She seems to follow him willingly enough. I see no fear in her eyes. Spell indeed."

"Didna ye know he introduced himself to her as the devil himself?" Lanie said with a sniff of disappointment. She had hoped to make the Reverend see things her way. "Didna ye know he pulled her betrothal ring right out of her ear?"

Startled at last, the Reverend turned to Lanie. "Did he hurt the lady?"

"Well, she smiled when she told her sisters of it," Lanie said, pleased to have captured the Reverend's attention at last. "But ye see, there would be no pain. 'Tis part of his spell."

"Aye." The Reverend agreed. "Of course."

Inspired, Lanie began to tell the Reverend of how she saw Castle Dunrugis, a looming black stone tower filled with little black-haired people—fairies, a strange and dangerous race. In the night, they would tiptoe up and down the spiral stairs to steal innocent babes from their cradles and to cast evil spells on innocent folk. Who knew what they might do to a stranger, a Lowlander. Lady Honora might never see her family again. Lanie shuddered and almost whimpered aloud. Her ol' mum had told her no good would come of leaving home.

Without warning, Laird Brec strode out of the ferryman's hut and down to the quay, interrupting Lanie in the telling of her tale. His black cloak billowed behind him and his leather breeks grew shiny with ocean spray. He was bareheaded; the wind blew his black locks wildly. His gaze never left the fog at the end of the landing. His stride was so confident, so masterful, that a chill slithered down Lanie's spine.

With a wave of his hand the laird hailed something beyond the vapor.

The hushed sound of oars slashing through the water reached Lanie and the Reverend. She stared as out of the fog floated the long, proud bow of a ship. The rest of the galley followed, materializing oar slot by oar slot from the cloud-covered sea.

Despite the rough water, the craft slid easily up to the quay where the laird stood. In silence the crew shipped oars. A gangplank was run out and the galley master disembarked. Behind him bound a great black wolfhound.

Lanie gasped at the sight. The enormous animal loped down the gangplank, wagging its wicked tail and lolling its evil pink tongue from its mouth. With a sonorous bark the dog greeted the laird, then turned its strange light-eyed gaze on Lanie. Its blue eyes struck her momentarily dumb.

Resolutely a black-clad woman with mannishly short hair and arms loaded with baskets trailed the hairy beast down the gangplank.

Lanie's heart stopped beating, but fear pounded in her ears.

"Do ye see that?" she managed to choke out to the Reverend. "Reverend, do ye see that? A black dog! With blue eyes! A black dog is a bad omen. And that woman. A witch. Or a fairy. I will no' go to that isle. Ye and Lady Honora shouldna go neither. Terrible things will happen. Me mum always told me I had the Sight. I see terrible things happening."

"Calm yourself, Mistress Lanie," the Reverend said. " 'Tis only a dog."

"But a black dog," Lanie screeched. "And a witch with him!"

"What are you screaming, woman?" the laird demanded as he marched toward her from the quay. Terror paralyzed Lanie, and she cowered behind the Reverend as the laird's black bulk descended on her. She would never allow the man to get near enough to her to pull anything from her ear.

"Be silent, woman. Cease your babbling," the laird ordered.

"Nay, nay," Lanie sobbed from behind the Reverend, burying her face in her hands to shut out the fiendish anger she saw in the laird's face. "The black dog is an evil omen."

"The cursed animal is only my dead brother's dog," the dark laird boomed in a voice that made Lanie shrink more. "The woman is just Oleen. She is a midwife."

The screaming and commotion brought Lady Honora from the ferryman's cottage. "Lanie. What is this? Calm yourself. Laird Brec said she is a healer. Every village has a healer."

"I'm more than a mere midwife, milady," the tiny Oleen announced with great haughtiness as she joined the group. Her deep, gravelly voice demanded attention. The two men and two women turned to look down at the miniature woman. "Sometimes the laird forgets that I'm of the family Beaton, the hereditary physicians of the Lairds of the Isles. We are read in the classic texts of the world's physicians."

Lady Honora appeared impressed, but the information meant nothing to Lanie. Sobbing, she sagged into her lady's arms. " 'Tis all an evil omen, milady. I know 'tis."

"I know 'tis frightening," Lady Honora comforted. "But when we get settled, everything will be all right. You'll see."

"Nay." Lanie took no comfort from Lady Honora's arm around her shoulders. "I'm sorry, milady. I canna go. And I donna think you should go either. This is no place for us. This be no place for anybody. The dog tells us so."

"Lanie, you are exhausted," Lady Honora said. "You need a good night's rest, and all will seem better tomorrow. I need you, Lanie, to help me with the wedding on the isle."

"I canna, milady," Lanie gulped between sobs. She glanced up long enough to catch the wee woman staring at her. Her head was large for such a tiny woman—a long jaw, squared chin, a small, nearly lipless mouth, a nub of a nose, and sharp dark eyes that darted about constantly, missing nothing. Lanie gasped. She was surely staring into the eyes of a witch.

"Do you wish something to calm her?" the wee woman offered.

"Nay, nay, nothing from you. I want to go home," Lanie cried. Her cheeks stung where tears had fallen. She shrank away from the deep-voiced witch, dragging Lady Honora with her.

"Well, if I can do nothing here, I must be on my way," Oleen said, impatience in her voice. "I have a baby to deliver."

"Kenneth, see Oleen to her destination," Laird Brec ordered.

"Please release me to go back to Edinburgh, Lady Honora," Lanie pleaded, clutching her mistress's hands. She took hope in the uncertainty she read in her lady's face. "Donna make me cross the water to that Godforsaken island, milady, please."

"Is that what you truly want?"

"Aye, 'tis."

"Umph," the laird said. " 'Tis just hysterics." He leaned toward Lanie, so close that she could feel the heat of his breath in her face, see the devilish lines of his anger around his mouth and evil furrowed on his brow. Lanie shrank from him.

"You aren't going to leave your lady now, are you? What kind of loyalty is that?" he demanded.

"Lanie and I have been together for many years," Lady Honora reminded the laird. Still she rubbed Lanie's back comfortingly. "Since before my parents died. But I can't force my woman to go with me."

The Reverend stepped closer. "Surely, Laird McCloud, you don't intend to force the poor soul to go on if she is this afraid?"

Lanie buried her face against Lady Honora's shoulder when the laird turned to her again. Those diabolic black eyes bore deep. "Please come with me, milady," she pleaded in a whisper.

Lady Honora hesitated and Lanie's hope grew.

"And you, Honora?" The laird's voice challenged. "Have you as little courage as your serving woman?"

Lanie felt Lady Honora's back stiffen. "I'm going with you, of course, milaird."

Another "umph" erupted from him before he added, "If she returns, someone must go with her. She can't travel alone."

"Come with me, Lady Honora," Lanie pleaded again, certain that some evil spell ruled her lady. "Donna go to the island with him. Please donna go with him."

"What is she saying?" the laird demanded. Lanie bit her lip, terrified that the infernal giant would hear her and curse her with some dire torment.

"Nothing," Lady Honora said. "She's just concerned about how she is going to return to Edinburgh. Please compose yourself, Lanie."

"Who can I spare now to take her back?" Laird Brec asked, turning to look at the cluster of grooms and handlers that had built a fire on the hillside to warm themselves.

"Perhaps I should go," the Reverend offered. "I mean . . . you are strong enough, Lady Honora, to hold your faith until I can return. We can't send Mistress Lanie away with these grooms who speak no English, nor can they be trusted with a lady of virtue."

"Is that what you want, Lanie?" Lady Honora asked.

Lanie looked up at her lady, at the sober, composed expression Honora gave the Reverend.

"Aye, 'tis, milady," Lanie admitted. She was unsure at the moment which emotion made her begin to weep once more—the joy of going home or the despair of losing her lady, this time forever.

" 'Tis settled then?" Brec asked. "Reverend, you'll take Mistress Lanie back to Edinburgh. I'll give you funds and see that you have good mounts. You may as well start back today."

The Reverend agreed and followed the laird to select fresh mounts. Before long preparations were complete.

"I'm sorry, milady," Lanie sobbed when she and the Reverend were mounted and ready to go. "I donna want to leave ye alone, but I canna help it. Ye understand? I pray ye'll be all right."

"I understand. Goodbye, Lanie," Honora said, patting the hand Lanie extended. "I'll be fine. I'm with my husband and soon will be with his family. Don't fret. Beatrix will be glad to have you with her on her wedding day."

The Reverend rode ahead, leading the way into the hills south towards the Lowlands. At the crest in the road, Lanie twisted around in the saddle to catch one last glimpse of her lady.

Lady Honora was standing alone on the quay, watching the baggage being carried aboard the peculiar long-necked galley. Mist still shrouded the sea beyond. At the lady's side sat the ominous black dog.

9

Honora clutched the railing to steady herself as the deck of the galley rolled beneath her feet. The oarsmen leaned into the oars in unison and began to sing in a language she didn't understand—rowing into the mist toward an unseen destination. Honora glanced around to see the fog obliterate the village on the shore. Lanie and the Reverend had long ago vanished.

Her sea legs came to her quickly. She hugged herself against the cold.

The shaggy black cur sat down at her feet. Eagerly he pressed a wet nose against her hand to claim her friendship. When she looked down at him, he stared back with remarkably friendly blue eyes. His tail thumped the deck. If he were an omen, Honora decided, he was a comforting one.

She scratched the dog's ears and tried to push away the niggling doubts Lanie's hysteria had stirred. She peered forward through the fog to find Brec, a tall, mist-shrouded shadow in the bow. She longed for a smile or for some reassurance from him, but as the craft slipped through the murk, her husband never acknowledged her. He leaned over the railing and gazed ahead into the grayness, impatient for the first sight of his home.

Sometimes the dark hump of a tiny island would loom beyond the bow, then slip by.

Darkness crept over the water. The crew ceased their singing. Finally the galley master lit a lantern and hung it from the mast.

Fingers of cold stole into Honora's boots. Her toes became numb. The wind died with the darkness, but a chill settled over her and she shivered from time to time. Just as she was wondering how much longer they would be sailing, the galley master called out orders. The oarsmen leaned back, heaving blades against the water. The galley lurched, and again Honora grabbed the railing to regain her balance.

Ahead she spied the orange glow of torches—two rows, one floating above the other. The flames reddened the fog, then blazed against the darkness. Dunrugis loomed out of the nebulous night. Men with torches walked the walls above, and two men stood below at the torchlit sea gate. Water lapped at their feet.

Panic fluttered in Honora's belly. For the first time since the trip began, her courage deserted her. This arrival wasn't at all what she'd imagined. In her musings Dunrugis gleamed white in the sun, a neat, square castle with festive flags flapping from the towers. On the landing a gaily dressed, merry crowd awaited them. The clan piper and the trumpeters blared a fanfare. In her daydreams she smiled at the welcomers and disembarked regally with her hand on her husband's arm. She wore the blue gown she had been married in—not a rumpled riding habit—and her hair was smooth and tidy, not damp and falling loose about her ears. A smiling little girl stepped forward from the crowd to offer her an armful of fresh flowers. Honora thanked the child with a kiss on the cheek, and castle guards threw their bonnets in the air and cheered. The music played on and the islanders danced with joy.

Cold reality washed over Honora at the galley rail when the ship master shouted a command. The oarsmen shipped oars. She stared up at the glittering damp walls of Castle Dunrugis and wished this were a bad dream.

She put her hand to her ruined hair. Her clothes were damp and her feet ached with cold. She had eaten only a little bannock since breakfast. While she wanted to meet her husband's mother and win the approval of the folks of the Isle of Myst, suddenly she was more eager to sit before a bright fire and eat a hot meal. She wanted to smooth her skirts and repair her hair. She longed for a reprieve to thaw her hands—to gather her wits—and recover her courage.

Without hesitation the galley slipped up to the landing at the foot of the castle rock. Honora looked up at Dunrugis again. The tower soared five stories into the night to give castle defenders a view of the loch and the headlands they protected. Two smaller stone structures flanked the main one. The fortress walls were broken only by small mullioned windows. All save one were dark. Honora prayed that one chamber would offer a hot fire and a comfortable bed.

From the bow Brec hailed the two men on the landing shortly before the galley nudged the quay. A moment later the deck swarmed with activity. Baggage handlers seized trunks and boxes and clambered ashore.

Honora hesitated as she looked back to the sea gate. She noticed that Brec, too, watched the gate. No one else appeared to greet them.

She started forward to join her husband. When she saw him turn back to her, she waited for him. Without haste he wove his way among the oarsmen and the baggage handlers to the stern deck where she stood. He approached her with an apologetic smile.

"Milady," he said, giving her a little formal bow. "I've not landed at Dunrugis with a bride before. Forgive my manners."

He offered his hand. Honora tried to smile as she put her cold one in his. With a firm grip he steadied her on the deck steps and led her across the narrow gangplank. The dog followed.

On the landing Brec made introductions to the two men who stood at the sea gate.

"This is Wallace, Dunrugis's master of the guard." Brec waved toward the tall, beefy faced man.

Wallace bowed. His golden-brown curls gleamed in the torchlight. The plaid draped around him hinted at broad shoulders to match his great height. He was nearly as tall and broad as Brec, but younger. When he straightened, he continued to eye the dog at Honora's side. "So this is where Colin's hound got to. I see he has befriended you, milady. An honor. The cur doesn't take to most women."

The man's tone was cordial enough, but Honora was curious about how he assessed her, his pale gray eyes moving over her not admiringly, as a man appraises a woman, but with calculation, as a warrior measures a foe. He was a man to form quick opinions, she decided, and she wondered what he'd concluded about her.

"This is Fergus, Kenneth's drinking partner." Brec laughed and indicated the man beside Wallace. The shorter man gawked in awe at his laird and even took a step backward when Brec spoke. "Fergus is keeper of our boats."

But wide-eyed, sober Fergus said nothing. He nodded in Honora's direction without closing his mouth or taking his gaze from his laird.

With a smug smile, Wallace stepped aside and waved toward the sea gate. "Welcome to Dunrugis, milaird . . . and lady."

The entrance to Dunrugis was no grand gate with a drawbridge and portcullis but a low, narrow, unwelcoming doorway with a woven iron grill gate, a yett.

Honora hesitated at the sight of it, but Brec took her hand and led her through the doorway into a narrow, curving, stone passage open to the sky and ramparts. Honora took only a few steps before she looked up to see armed men standing on the entrance walls above their heads. Dark, bearded faces arched over them. Gleaming eyes stared down in silence. Terrified, Honora shrank back from the sky full of faces. She resisted Brec's tug on her arm. What kind of welcome was this?

Metal grated against stone behind her. She whirled around to see Wallace lock the iron yett. He turned, blocking the only way out, legs apart and arms folded across his chest. He gave her a canny smile.

Honora shivered—with cold and fear—and her heart thumped. "Brec?" Was this how the island people greeted their laird? she wanted to ask.

Brec tugged on her hand again. " 'Tis all right, sweet soul. Have courage." He spoke under his breath and over his shoulder so that only she could hear. "Keep walking.

Hold your head high and smile. Just as you did when you walked out of Balmoree's party. I will do all the talking."

Honora had little choice. She took a deep breath, stepped forward, and concentrated on the warm strength of Brec's hand. With great effort she smiled up at the hushed visages staring down on them. Torchlight glittered off the warriors' sword hilts and the iron studs of their leather shields. The sound of her own footsteps echoed in her ears.

At the end of the passage Brec and Honora ascended stone steps into a courtyard. To her surprise the armed men melted away before her husband's advance. They seemed bent on keeping a certain distance between themselves and their laird.

Brec stopped to face them. Honora let him draw her to his side, her hand still safe in his. She hoped her smile endured as she turned to the warriors.

Brec began to speak so that all could hear.

"Thank you for your welcome." His voice was full of warmth as if flower petals had been strewn at their feet and the men before them had just cheered. "King Charles and his agent in Edinburgh send their regards to the people of the Isle of Myst."

Reluctant cheers rippled through the ranks.

"And I'm pleased and honored to bring with me Lady Honora Maitland, my wife and your new Lady McCloud."

A smile still frozen on her face, Honora nodded. She was greeted with a muttering of cheers and a restless shuffling of feet.

"You'll have an opportunity to properly greet her soon, when we celebrate the wedding," Brec told the men. He gave a quick salute, then turned away to the castle door, where a manservant bearing a torch met them and led the way into the castle.

Inside the door, Honora wanted to pause to catch her breath. But to her horror, just beyond the door stood another cluster of solemn faced people—men and women. She almost groaned.

Brec squeezed her hand reassuringly. "Ian is the castle steward."

The unassuming, gray-haired man bowed to Honora.

"Lady Honora's serving woman was unable to accompany us, Ian, so she will need a woman to wait on her—one who can speak some English. Send someone up right away."

"Aye, milaird," Ian said, then the man spoke in Gaelic. Brec's response was low and rapid. Ian frowned when they finished. Brec led Honora up the stairs.

"Ian tells me Mother has retired for the evening," Brec said. "I know the journey from Edinburgh has been exhausting. I thought you would prefer to rest before you meet her."

"Aye, that's fine," she agreed, thankful to be relieved of that obligation for the evening. She was unsure of how to ask all she wanted to ask about the indifferent greeting they had received. "I was a little frightened out there in the courtyard," she ventured.

"You did well," he said with an unconcerned air as he led her up the steps. "Don't let the men's looks frighten you. They are merely curious."

Curious? Was that all? Honora wanted to ask. But she was weary and had no desire to relive that moment when the clang of the iron grill door had sounded like the cold snap of a trap. When the wintry smile on Wallace's face looked more like that of an assassin's than an ally's.

Before she could say anything more, Brec went on. "Colin's death was sudden. My brother was a good leader and popular. The men are unaccustomed to my ways. But they'll learn."

He led Honora up the central stairway. When they halted beneath a torch on the wide landing, Honora felt a draft and looked up the stairs to see the play of shadows ahead of them. The tapestry hanging against the stairway wall fluttered. Honora thought she heard the whisper of skirts on stone steps above them. The dog at her side looked up the stairs and growled.

"What was that?" she asked.

"Old castles have drafts," Brec said, speaking more rapidly than Honora thought was necessary. She wondered whether he was trying to cover up something. He grasped her arm and hurried her up the stairs. "Mother hasn't been well. She may not be up to helping you with the wedding. But Ian will know what arrangements to make.

102

"Here's the chamber that has been readied for you."
Brec opened the door of a cozy, wood-paneled room.
Beyond the four-poster bed that filled the room, a fire
burned in the grate.

Honora rushed to the fire. Relief must have shown on
her face as she thrust her hands toward the heat. Hastily
Brec took the damp cloak from her shoulders.

"Sit," he ordered, drawing a chair to the fireside for her.
"Warm yourself. Food is coming."

Gratefully, Honora sank into the chair and rubbed her
hands together before the fire. With a sigh, the black dog
stretched out on the hearth. Honora heard Brec throw her
cloak on a chair behind her and walk to the door. For a
moment she thought he was leaving, but soon he returned,
and the smile he gave her was more relaxed than the one
in the courtyard.

"Is the fire hot enough?" He threw two more bricks of
peat on the flames. He brushed off his hands and turned to
kneel at her feet. Before she realized what he was doing,
he turned back the hem of her riding habit and grasped her
ankle. His grip was firm and his hands were warm.

"Milaird, what are you doing?" Honora gasped.

"I'm taking off your boots so that you can warm your
feet," he said matter of factly. He had already pulled off
one boot and begun to tug on the other.

"Sir!" Honora clamped her hands down on his. " 'Tis
not proper."

"I'm merely trying to make you comfortable, wife," he
said, grinning up at her, a devilish glint of hope in his eyes.
"And you have no woman to help you. No one but me."

A knock on the door interrupted them.

"Brec?" Honora hissed and leaned forward. "Release
me. Please, not in front of the servants."

Brec's wicked smile broadened and for a moment Honora
thought he would refuse her.

"Come in," he called as he rose.

Honora hastily removed her other boot and wrapped the
shawl she found on the footstool around her frozen feet.

Ian entered, carrying a tray of steaming soup, hot bread,
cold venison, and warm milk. He set it on the table by the
fire and disappeared without a word.

"What's the dog's name?" Honora asked after she had greedily drunk half of her warm milk. The cur had risen from his place on the hearth and come to rest his head on her knee—begging.

"I think Colin named him *Dubh*."

The dog flopped his tail in answer to the sound of his name.

"Blackie?" Honora said. She gave the dog a bread crust.

"So, you do know a little Gaelic."

"Very little," Honora said with a laugh. The tightness that had grown inside her all through the voyage and during the arrival eased a little. She noted when Brec smiled that tension had eased from the lines in his face. He seemed more like the man she had come to know in Edinburgh. He drew a chair up to the fireside table and joined her in the meal.

Readily he answered her questions about the village, the castle, and the names of the servants.

They were interrupted by another knock on the door.

A brown-haired girl with a pinched face and dressed in black entered and bobbed a curtsy. "If ye please, milaird. I'm Ellen, and Master Ian said I'm to wait on her." The girl glared resentfully at Honora.

With a suddenness that made Honora start, Brec stood up. "Nay, not you. You won't do at all. Where's Ian? He knows better than this. You have a lady to serve already."

Brec grabbed the girl's arm and hauled her from the room. Honora watched and wondered why he was so vehement in rejecting the servant, but she was glad he didn't approve of the obviously disgruntled girl. The warmth of the fire crept into her limbs. Her hunger appeased, she drowsed in her chair.

She was unaware of how much time passed before Brec's voice awakened her. "This is Brenda. She will serve you."

Beside Brec stood a tiny redheaded girl. She wore a drab but neat plaid gown and a ruddy scrubbed appearance that Honora liked instantly. But on closer inspection she was disappointed in the way Brenda sullenly pursed her lips and clasped her hands before her.

"You speak English, don't you?" Brec demanded. "Good. Have you ever served as woman of the chamber before?"

"Nay," the girl snapped.

"Then you'll learn to serve the new lady of Dunrugis well?"

With a frown, the girl gave a nod.

Honora stared at Brec, confused as to why the lass's cold expression and lack of experience made her more satisfactory than the first girl.

Brec gave Brenda additional instruction in rapid Gaelic.

After bestowing a brief goodnight kiss on Honora's cheek, he left the two women alone. Dubh made no move to follow the laird. Indifferently he sniffed Brenda's skirt, then settled himself on the hearth again.

"Brenda, is it?" Honora asked.

"Aye, milady, Brenda be my name." The girl drew a deep breath and announced, "I'm no' used to waiting on ladies. And I donna speak good. I donna know about fine dresses and jewels. I only come to the castle when they need extra help. I'm the blacksmith's daughter."

"I see," Honora said. She could only hope that in time the mutinous girl would mellow. After her experience with Lanie, Honora had little hope of finding a serving woman from Edinburgh who would stay in her service.

"Well, Brenda, the truth is I've never been the lady of an island castle. And I don't know much Gaelic. So we will be learning new things together, won't we?"

"Aye, 'twould seem so," Brenda admitted without a blink or a smile.

The turmoil of the day suddenly overwhelmed Honora. She had no more energy to placate hostile servants. With a shrug she decided she would have to make the best of it—for a while, at least. She turned to the luggage stacked next to the door.

"Well then, Brenda, please help me learn where to find my nightgown. I need to get out of this damp riding habit."

When Honora had dressed in her night clothes and had climbed into the four-poster bed, Brenda helped her pull the curtains closed. Honora yawned and settled herself beneath the downy comforter and counterpane. Beyond the curtains a candle still burned, and she could hear Brenda moving about. Finally she peeked between the bed curtains.

"What are you doing? You're not going to sleep there by the door, are you? 'Tis so drafty."

"Laird Brec said to let no one in the room until morning," Brenda said as she arranged her pallet in front of the chamber door. "No one will get by me. And Dubh is a good watchdog."

"But why?" Honora asked as Brenda crawled between the covers. Brec had never hinted at such precautions during their journey. Why would he post a guard with her now, here in his own castle? "Is there some danger?"

"I'm just doing what I'm told, milady," Brenda replied and blew out the candle. "I suppose milaird wants no hint of impropriety before yer wedding."

In the darkness, Honora settled back amid the down-filled covers. The canny look on Wallace's face as he locked them in Castle Dunrugis haunted her.

"Brenda, who is Wallace? I mean, is he loyal to Laird Brec?"

"Wallace is the master of the guard and successor—or he *was* successor. And he is Laird Brec's cousin."

Honora heard the serving woman shift her position on the pallet. She knew there had to be more to the story. "And what else? What does successor mean?"

"Wallace was Laird Colin's successor as clan chief until Laird Brec returned from the sea. Then Colin named his brother successor in place of his cousin. A week later Laird Colin was dead and Laird Brec became chief. Some say Wallace was a wee bit disappointed."

Honora clearly recalled the curly-haired man's keen-eyed assessment of her at the sea gate. Was it possible that he wasn't inspecting his laird's new lady, but summing up the mettle of his foe's wife? Honora shook her head over her folly and she let herself ease back into the soft pillows. She had no reason to jump to conclusions about the loyalty of her husband's retainers. She was overly tired, she decided. Things would look better in the morning. She was asleep almost as soon as she closed her eyes.

10

" 'Tis Lady McCloud's garden," Brenda explained, closing the courtyard door behind them. Honora stared about at the saddest-looking walled garden she had ever seen.

In the morning light faded rose petals littered the ragged grass of the pathway. Thriving weeds clogged the herb bed. Bees hummed around feeble rose blossoms, and butterflies flitted from overgrown fuchsia to undisciplined honeysuckle vines.

"Laird Brec wanted us to meet him here?" Honora asked, looking to Brenda for her reaction to the forlorn surroundings.

"This were the pride of Dunrugis." Brenda walked to Honora's side, where the girl folded her arms across her breast and tucked her hands into her shawl. She went on in the tone of one who would take mean pleasure in shocking her audience.

"Lady Margaret planted and tended it herself. Since Laird Colin died, she has neglected it. Anne, her woman, says that when the lady comes here now, she sits and stares at nothing.

"For a week after Laird Colin's funeral she denied his death. They say that Laird Brec refused to allow her to sew her son into his burial shroud—'tis a mother's right, ye know, if the man's wife willna do it."

A look of distaste crossed the lass's face before she went on. "But Laird Brec would no' have his mother do it. The poor lady never had a chance to say farewell to her first-born," Brenda finished with an indignant sniff.

"But why would he do that?" Honora asked, shocked to think that Brec would deny his mother the comfort of such a time-honored tradition. After another moment's thought, she asked, "How did Laird Colin die?"

Brenda shrugged. "Laird Brec said his brother was cleaning a pistol and accidentally shot himself. He allowed no one but himself and the priest to see the body."

"Perhaps Laird Brec thought only to protect his mother," Honora suggested.

"Perhaps," Brenda said, but the word lacked conviction. "Laird Colin was a good clan chief. He was fair and just. Slow to anger. Generous. He always had a kind word to offer. Everyone liked *him*."

Honora heard Brenda's unspoken implications. Laird Brec was not liked. And people of the isle suspected there was more to Colin's death than Brec's explanation provided.

"Good morning, milady," Brec called.

Both women started at the sound of his voice. Honora's smile of greeting broadened when she saw a clean-shaven Brec walking toward her. He appeared fresh and rested, dressed in a black doublet, clean shirt, and kilted plaid— once again the man she knew in Edinburgh.

"Milaird," she responded, strangely stirred by the sight of him and glad to put aside talk of Colin's death.

"You slept well?" He glanced at Brenda for confirmation.

"Of course I slept well." Honora offered her hands. " 'Twas so good to sleep in a feather bed again."

With an answering smile, he took her hands in his, holding them down at their sides and bending slightly to kiss her with the light, proper kiss a husband gives his wife in the presence of others. Their bodies never touched except hands and lips. But Honora liked the contact—his strong hands covering hers, his warm lips brushing across her mouth, his body sheltering hers. When he touched her so, her breath always quickened, and a sweet weakness uncurled in her belly.

Abruptly he broke away. Honora opened her eyes, wondering when he would kiss her again as he had in St. Giles—with true warmth and genuine ardor.

"Mother is on her way," he said before turning away, and Honora glimpsed an expression of misgiving on his face. "Did Brenda tell you? The garden is her own creation. I remember that before I went to sea, it was always fragrant and bright with colors.''

He went on to tell how his father, Laird Alec, had ordered the wall built to capture the warmth of the sun and to keep the sea spray from his new bride's flowers. As children, Colin and Brec had played there on the grass while their mother planted her flowers, herbs, and shrubs.

Those memories settled softly on Brec's face as he and Honora strolled through the garden. He pointed out the plantings that he'd helped his mother with. But the moment ladies' voices drifted to them from the doorway, Honora saw the line of Brec's jaw tighten. A guarded demeanor slipped over his visage—the cool distancing look Honora had seen him take on just before Wallace locked them in the castle. With a growing sense of dread, Honora turned to the garden door.

Brenda stood aside.

A small, delicate woman trod timidly across the threshold, followed by a pale, spindly serving woman. The lady greeted Brenda with a nod, then squinted at the sunlit garden. She stepped hesitantly onto the grass and shaded her eyes with her hand.

"There you are, my son, my boy!" Lady Margaret started across the grass toward Brec, her arms outstretched. A welcoming smile spread across her face and joy shone in her eyes. Brec met her halfway. They embraced, the big dark man bent over his fragile, fair mother, cradling her warily against him. Lady Margaret's pleasure in seeing Brec was so truly genuine that Honora's apprehension vanished and tears threatened. She brushed them away and thought Brec's caution strange.

"Your journey was safe?" Lady Margaret asked, her head tipped back to peer into her son's face. She caressed his cheek with the back of her hand. "But Colin, where is your beard? You look so like Brec with that beard."

Honora's breath caught in her throat.

Brenda coughed in the awkward silence.

Brec's calm never wavered, the tone of his voice never changed, but Honora saw a subtle mask mold over his face—over his feelings. Gently he took his mother's hand from his face and spoke softly. "I *am* Brec, Mother. Colin never wore a beard."

"Oh, aye, Colin never wore a beard," Lady Margaret echoed vaguely. She gazed up at her son with a lost look. "Brec?"

"Aye, I'm Brec, just returned from Edinburgh," he continued in a soothing tone.

Honora marveled at his control. Surely he suffered to see his mother so confused that she mistook him for his dead brother.

"Kenneth has returned with me. He complained that Edinburgh was noisy and smelly as ever."

"Kenneth? Aye, loyal Kenneth." Lady Margaret studied her dark son, eagerly anticipating each word, the confusion clearing from her eyes. "He saw that you ate well and got your rest?"

"Aye, Mother," Brec said. "Kenneth followed your orders and took good care of me."

"That old goat? I can imagine he grumbled the whole time you were in the city." Lady Margaret released her son and turned to Honora. "Anne told me you brought someone back with you, Brec."

"Aye." He reached for Honora's hand and she stepped to his side. "Mother, this is Lady Honora Maitland. She has done me and the McClouds the honor of consenting to be my wife."

Honora glanced at Brec, but he gave her no clue as to what he expected of her.

Lady Margaret peered up at Honora with watery blue eyes. She cocked her head to one side, then to the other. Honora glanced at Brec again, but his gaze remained on his mother's gentle face.

"Step closer, my dear," Lady Margaret said. "My sight fails me these days. You are lovely. Your hair so dark and warm. Not at all like Lilias. How brave you must be to come all this way with Brec! His dark scowl has frightened off many a lass. Welcome to Dunrugis, Lady Honora." Brec's mother opened her arms wide.

The embrace was warm and genuine; Honora returned it without reserve. And she wondered who Lilias was.

"But have you been wed in the St. Michael's abbey!"

110

Lady Margaret exclaimed in Honora's ear. She stepped back from Honora without releasing her. "Nay? I'd remember that, wouldn't I?"

"We've been wed in St. Giles Kirk, Mother," Brec said. "And we celebrated with Honora's uncles, sisters, and friends in Edinburgh. Of course, now we want to invite everyone on the Isle of Myst to celebrate with us at St. Michael's."

"Brec is to wed," Lady Margaret said with a smile and a clap of her hands. Color flooded into her face, and the soft blue of her eyes cleared. "This truly is great news. We must plan a magnificent *ceilidh*. We will put our mourning aside for that. Colin would understand. And tonight a welcoming supper. Anne, let's go to the kitchen and talk to the cooks and send out the grooms and ghillies with invitations . . . where is Ian? He will give the orders."

The swish of satin skirts silenced Lady Margaret, banishing the happiness from her face. The clarity that had come momentarily into her expression faded. Without looking toward the door her hands began to tremble. She gave her son a defenseless look of appeal. But Brec had already turned to the garden door.

Curious, Honora followed his gaze to see a tall, haughty woman in black standing just inside the garden.

"I asked Lady Lilias to join us to meet Honora," Brec explained. "Please go on with your plans, Mother. Find Ian and make him admit he still has some excellent Madeira in the wine cellar. Bring it out for the wedding."

The newcomer's black satin skirts whispered again as she stepped aside to allow Lady Margaret and Anne to pass her. The sound reminded Honora of hearing the hiss of skirts on the stairs the night before. Was it this woman who had spied on them? Honora wondered.

Lady Lilias fixed her blue-eyed gaze on Brec, offering him a knowing, assured look that instantly unsettled Honora.

The lady glided forward, carrying herself like the undeniable beauty she knew herself to be. Her hair was light, so light that it shone white beneath the black lace cap she wore. Her skin was flawless and ivory pale. Her smooth brow was high and her neck gracefully long and elegant.

When she glanced momentarily at Honora, her eyes were cool and disdainful—faintly slanted, adorned with thick, dark lashes.

Black—the color of mourning—more than suited the woman, it magnified her beauty, setting it off with a glow like the frosty moon against a night sky.

When Lady Lilias offered Brec her hand, he took it briefly, but gave her no other greeting. The look of covetous admiration that the woman gave Brec sent a stab of jealousy slicing through Honora. This Lilias wanted Honora's husband. But if Brec knew of the woman's desire, he never acknowledged it. In fact, Honora realized with a second glance, Brec's face had grown harsh and forbidding.

"Lady Lilias is my brother's widow," he stated.

Honora suppressed her astonishment. Of course Colin would have a widow. Why had Brec never told her? Why had she never thought to ask?

Smug supremacy sparked in Lady Lilias's slanted blue eyes and pleasure formed a superior smile on her lips. She had a claim on the McClouds and Dunrugis that far exceeded any that Honora could exact, and the lady took obvious satisfaction in that.

"Welcome to Dunrugis, Lady Honora," Lilias said with no welcome in her voice, or offer of hand or embrace in greeting. "I can't imagine what possessed Brec to bring a Lowlander bride to Dunrugis. You must be accustomed to so much more refinement. You may find our ways rustic after living in Edinburgh."

"Honora will do well here, Lilias," Brec interrupted. "I would like for you to give her the castle keys now."

"What?" Shock instantly wiped the self-assured smile from Lilia's face. She reared back. "What did you say?"

"You heard me," Brec said, his severe expression unchanged.

"She is not your wife yet," Lilias declared, her mouth twisted in belligerence. "Not until you are wed in the abbey."

"As far as you are concerned," Brec said, his voice deadly quiet, even, and controlled, "Honora is my wife and the lady of Dunrugis. Give her the keys. Now."

"You are making a terrible mistake, Brec. I'm a McDonnell. Your brother's widow. Do you forget that? You can't snub me like this."

"You have not been snubbed, Lilias," Brec replied, obviously unshaken. "Your dower rights have been honored. Give Lady Honora the keys."

The McCloud and the McDonnell glared at each other, the current between them charged with hatred. Honora stepped away from them.

With malice contorting her face, Lilias pulled a jingling brass circlet of keys from the sash at her waist and held them clenched in one hand. She glowered at Honora, her odd blue eyes spitting icy spite. Honora winced, certain that the woman was going to throw the keys at her. Suddenly Lilias whirled on Brec and flung the keys in his face.

Without blinking, he caught them in one hand. "Good day, Lilias."

The elegant lady snorted. With a snap of satin skirts she spun around and stalked from the garden.

Honora waited for the garden door to shut before she turned on Brec. "Why didn't you tell me Colin had a widow?"

"What difference does it make?"

"You know what difference it makes," Honora declared. "Lilias is the rightful lady of the castle. 'Tis your obligation to marry her—your brother's wife—especially if she is a McDonnell. Your clans have been feuding for centuries, haven't they?"

"Don't concern yourself about my obligations," Brec said with a shrug as he examined the keys in his hand.

"But how can you take that risk?"

"Do not concern yourself, milady." He turned to her, his face still and hard. Deliberately he took Honora's hand and put the keys in it, his touch cool as a stranger's. "You are the lady of Castle Dunrugis now. You have the keys. Your duty is to manage the castle and care for the people who reside here. See to it."

He left the garden. Honora and Brenda stood silent amid the buzzing of bees and the fluttering of butterflies.

Honora stared gloomily at the ring in her hand, the brass skeleton keys shining in the sunlight. There was no reason to despair, she told herself. That was their marriage agreement, after all. He was to provide and govern the clan. She was to be lady of the castle.

It was as simple as that. Yet, she could not dismiss the notion that was beginning to form that she was being used for a purpose that she did not understand.

Pipe music filled the Great Hall, drowning out the sound of voices and the clatter of dishes. The restraint of the gathering—Honora's welcoming supper—disappointed Brec. He could remember when the pipes could barely be heard over the shouts of laughter and rowdy choruses of song.

Honora sat at his side, lovely this evening as ever. He smiled with pride at the way she had put a hush on the hall when she appeared in the doorway. Simple pearls dangled from her ear lobes. She hesitated, then smiled when he caught her eye. Without taking her gaze from his, she walked toward him, followed by Brenda.

When she had reached the head of the table where he stood, she had given him a blushing smile of pleasure when he complimented her on the forest-green gown she had selected.

"Of course, I must show my best for you, milaird," she said as she sat down beside him, smiling greetings down the table at his mother, at Kenneth, and across at Wallace. Brec wondered whether Honora noticed Lilias's absence. The widow had refused to appear for supper, which suited Brec fine. He had found their meeting in the garden most satisfying. If Lilias wanted to sulk about giving up the castle keys, Brec wished her the best of sulks. He wanted Honora reigning here.

The pipes had begun then, and the meal had been served. Now Brec leaned toward Honora and put an arm across the back of her chair.

"Have you no appetite, sweet soul?" he whispered and nodded toward the silver plate of red deer venison pasty that Brenda had set before her. Honora smiled and shook her head.

"What Lady Honora needs is a little more claret," Wallace said, picking up the decanter and filling Honora's silver cup.

Anger at his cousin's presumption flared in Brec. "I'll decide what Lady Honora needs."

Brec seized the goblet from Honora's hand. Red wine sloshed onto the table top, and he and his curly-haired cousin locked gazes over the goblet. With great deliberation Brec took a sip from the vessel, slowly rolling the dark rich liquor over his tongue and around his mouth in search of bitterness or metallic flavor. Satisfied that there was none, that the drink was safe, he swallowed the sip.

Warily, Wallace set the decanter down on the table. "I was but being hospitable, milaird."

Brec removed his arm from across the back of Honora's chair and set the drink before her. He could feel her bewildered eyes move from his face to Wallace. He hoped for now she would demand no explanations.

"Pour for me," he demanded of Wallace without looking up.

Voices along the table died. Faces turned to stare at Wallace and Brec.

He could feel Wallace's attention fixed on him. The younger man never moved. Brec met Wallace's stare, challenging him. Without looking away, Wallace signaled to Ian.

"Fill Laird Brec's cup and mine," Wallace ordered.

Ian cast Brec an inquiring look. Brec made no move. With unsteady hands, the gray-haired steward reached for the decanter and filled first Brec's cup, then Wallace's.

"Wallace, won't you toast the new bride?" Lady Margaret called across the table to the former successor.

"If Laird Brec will allow," Wallace said with a wary look of inquiry in his laird's direction.

Brec raised his own goblet in silent permission.

"To the new Lady McCloud," Wallace said.

"Aye," Margaret chimed in. "To Lady Honora."

Agreement was murmured along the table, and cups flashed in the candlelight as claret and ale were downed.

"And I think another toast is called for," Wallace continued, obviously encouraged by the acceptance of his first salute. "To Laird Brec's successful interview with the king's agent in Edinburgh and to King Charles."

This toast met with more enthusiasm than the first.

Cup bottoms flashed, and someone at Kenneth's end of the table began to sing. Others took up the song. The piper had left the gallery, but the harper plucked out the tune, and soon the chorus was echoing through the hall and filled the silence at the head table.

Honora watched Wallace dally with his cup, obviously contemplating his words before he spoke. Brec also seemed to find something fascinating about his goblet. The tension between them made her uneasy.

"I heard rumors that you were pressured in Edinburgh to join with the Scot parliament—Argyll's cause—against King Charles. Is that so?" Wallace asked.

"Aye," Brec said.

Honora guessed that the pressure Wallace spoke of had come from her uncles.

Brec added, "It has come down to Montrose and the king against Argyll and the parliament."

A look of surprise crossed Wallace's face, and he hunched forward in his chair. "You have no sympathy with Argyll and his Campbell clan, have you? They've done us wrong and the McDonnells too. Why should we join them?"

"There are few in the isles and along the coast that the Campbells haven't stepped on," Kenneth agreed. He had drawn up a chair beside Wallace.

"But think you on what would happen to the isles if the Scot parliament and Cromwell and his English parliament defeat the king," Brec said without looking at either man. "The English merchants are no more likely to allow us free sailing with our galleys than the king does now. And if we side with the defeated, we could forfeit the McCloud charter to the Isle of Myst."

"What matters a charter?" Wallace said with a wave of his hands. "McClouds have held the Isle of Myst forever, against the Norse and against the Picts. 'Tis ours. We'll hold it against the English too, if we have to."

"But a king's charter cannot be ignored," Brec declared. "I have no desire to risk losing the isle for any man's cause but our own."

Honora listened. She had heard many discussions about Montrose and Argyll, but she had never considered how

116

the leaders of the isles might view the conflict. She realized that Brec spoke of things that he and her uncles must have discussed.

"Colin said we support the king," Wallace said. "Before he died, Colin and I talked of this. We must support Montrose."

"Aye, the Marquis of Montrose is a good general," Kenneth agreed. "They say that as a youth he studied warfare in France."

"Surely the good marquis with Scot forces like ours and the king's men can defeat the British parliament," Wallace said.

"And if they lose?" Brec asked. "We lose. What happens to the clans that fight along with Montrose? What happens when the victorious English and Campbells come to take the spoils of war?"

Honora watched Wallace and Kenneth turn to each other.

"The war will be fought in the borderlands," Kenneth said. "Neither the king nor the Lowlanders can touch us here."

"We would never give up the isle," Wallace said, pounding his fist on the table for emphasis and looking about the hall for agreement from the others. "Colin wanted to support our good king. I can never agree to anything less."

"Perhaps the greatest danger this war presents is to divide us against ourselves," Brec suggested, his voice calm, but Honora noted that his expression had become guarded.

"I see no division here," Wallace said, his voice rising with surprise and anger. "We are all willing to fight for our king. But I'll never fight beside Lowlanders for some misbegotten Campbells. Your brother wouldn't either."

"How do you know what my brother would do?" Brec challenged, his tone carrying a low, forbidding note.

Slightly alarmed by the growing hostility Honora detected in each man's expression, she looked anxiously from her husband to his curly haired cousin. This discussion—like the difference over the wine decanter—was rapidly becoming more than a disagreement between kinsmen.

Brec began to rise, his fists planted on the table. He

leaned toward Wallace. "Tell me, what do you know about what my brother wanted?"

"He told me we would fight for the king." Wallace also began to rise from his chair, his face, heated red with anger, only inches from Brec's. "I was his successor. He told me what he wanted."

"Not after I arrived at Dunrugis."

"Of course not. You never let me see him again once you set foot on the isle. Strange, isn't it, how you became successor and I was never allowed to speak to Colin alone again."

"That was Colin's choosing." Unlike his cousin's, Brec's face paled with hatred, and his voice iced cold. "But you are right, Cousin, I would have refused you the privilege if he had not."

Brec spoke the word *cousin* with a bitter, insulting twist to his lips and in his voice.

Honora and the others in the hall turned to Wallace for his reaction.

Glowering, the younger man straightened and reached for the sword at his side.

Kenneth's hand lashed out to stay the angry master of the guard from drawing a weapon.

"Gentlemen, please," Honora beseeched in her most soothing and ladylike voice, without betraying the sudden fear that fluttered in her belly. She did not understand who was accusing whom of what, but she put a restraining hand on Brec's fist.

Belligerently he shook off her touch. But she caught his hand again, along with his gaze and held both.

"Sir, I prefer no roistering at the supper table where I preside. I would rather hear the harper's song. 'Tis most sweet, sweeter than this noisome quarrel between kinsmen. Please be seated, Master Wallace. Let us enjoy the entertainment."

The two cousins glared warily at each other a moment longer before Wallace turned on his heel and marched from the hall, his sword clanking at his side. Brec watched him go, then sat down, black anger still shadowing his face. He turned to Honora.

"I trust you are finding your welcoming supper amusing,

milady.'' He drank from his cup, and when he thumped the empty vessel down on the table, Honora saw with regret that the pleasure and pride that he had smiled at her when she'd first entered the hall had been replaced by the brooding look of resentment and anger.

Laird Brec insisted that the wedding take place in four days' time, then locked himself into his book room and left everyone else to carry out his orders. Just like a man, Brenda thought.

With a flurry of activity Lady Margaret set about making plans. Invitations were issued to all the people of Myst and to the neighboring isles. She fussed over the wedding delicacies to be prepared and the wine stock and ale to be served. Sometimes her energies flagged and her thoughts wandered—which, Brenda noted, most often happened after Lady Margaret was faced with Lady Lilias.

"Them two never liked each other," Cook whispered to Brenda. And now it seemed Colin's widow, gowned in black and swooping down the castle passages like an evil raven, served as a painful reminder to Lady Margaret of her son's sudden, violent death. She had only to pass her daughter-in-law on the stairs to the garden for confusion and grief to overwhelm her. When it did, Anne and Ian took over the wedding preparations.

The women in the kitchen grumbled, unwilling to trouble themselves for this newcomer, a Lowlander. Not for Laird Brec's betrothed, they told Ian. Brenda saw the steward's backbone stiffen with McCloud pride and clan devotion. He snapped a few sharp words and issued sage, no-more-nonsense threats that set the women to work again. So it was that wedding plans grudgingly took shape.

After the interview with Lady Honora in the garden, Lady Lilias remained secluded in her rooms, except for meals and to take the fresh air in the garden, which was fine with Brenda. She disliked the McDonnell woman almost as much as she disliked Laird Brec.

When Brenda's father owed service on rents to the McClouds, she'd always performed her service in the Castle Dunrugis kitchen without complaint. She'd taken little interest in great ladies or clan intrigues. So waiting on Lady

Honora was a new experience. She had no intention of liking the lady. Despite that, Brenda found herself developing a respect for the Lowlander, a woman who had the courage to come between huge, quarreling men and set them straight at the supper table. But Brenda could not bring herself to change her feelings toward the laird.

He escorted Lady Honora to supper every evening, seated her properly, and saw that she was served the most succulent portions of the meal. At the end of the evening, he kissed her in that light, quick way that the lady always seemed to eagerly anticipate. But for some reason the laird always ended the kisses abruptly.

"Surely he finds her appealing," Brenda said to Kenneth one day when the laird's master of arms came to the kitchen for some ale. Brenda liked Kenneth's easy, quiet ways and always sneaked him an extra measure if she could.

"I think he finds her appealing enough," Kenneth muttered over his flagon. "Did ye never think that might be the problem?"

"And how could that be the problem?" Brenda asked with her hand on her hip.

Kenneth shook his head and gave her one of his slow smiles. "And how does the Lady Honora take all this?"

"You never hear a complaint from that one." Brenda stopped speaking long enough to peer at Kenneth seriously for a moment. "Ye donna like her, do ye?"

" 'Tis no' for me to like or dislike." Kenneth gave a shrug.

"Well, ye can understand, I think she's a little bewildered by all this. That doesna stop her, though. She's been at Ian already. Wants him to show her the castle and present her with an inventory of all the furnishings and of the storerooms. And what's our great laird doing?"

When Kenneth was hesitant to speak, Brenda answered her own question. "He's starting fights with Wallace. I thought they were going to draw swords over the table the night of the welcoming supper. All this over some fools—Argyll and Montrose—whoever they be. No wonder Lady Honora has lost her appetite.

"Then the laird locks himself up in his book room. What

does he do in there? Tell me that. Does he cast spells? That's what the servants say. And Fergus told us he saw Laird Brec sailing in the moonlight again. And one of the village boys saw him standing over the grave of Laird Colin—God rest his soul.'' Brenda crossed herself. ''Talking to it, Laird Brec was.''

''He wanted to be sure the stone was set as he wished it,'' Kenneth said and took another swallow of ale.

Brenda shook her head. ''But he was talking to it—the grave, I mean. Have ye ever heard of the like? There have always been stories about him in the village. How he made trouble. How he stole the fishermen's boats. He almost murdered one man in a fit of black temper. Our laird is a strange one, he is. 'Tis no' hard to see how he earned the reputation for being the devil's own. And his brother Colin was so good and generous.''

''The man he nearly killed had lied to Laird Brec, and he hates liars,'' Kenneth said, a hint of defense in his voice. He handed Brenda the empty flagon, and she wondered whether he was angry with her. ''Brec always returned those boats and in good condition. I've sailed the world over, lass. And I learned that everything is no' as it seems. Or what folks think 'tis.''

''So can ye prove anything different about the laird?'' Brenda flounced around, purposely turning her back on the man, certain he had no proof. She didn't dare bring up to Kenneth that everyone thought Laird Brec had murdered his own brother. ''Can ye prove he's no' the devil's own?''

With a wink of an eye and a lightning reach, Kenneth pinched her bottom.

''Ow!'' Brenda screeched, whirling around. She frowned at him as she rubbed the injured portion of her backside.

''Well now, I know ye are real enough,'' Kenneth said with a slow grin. He saluted her and disappeared out of the doorway.

''See if I have any ale for ye next time,'' Brenda called after him. But she knew she would if he came back.

11

Honora's second wedding day dawned gray and quiet, with just the hint of a storm on the wind. She awoke depressed, yet relieved that she wouldn't have to struggle through another four days like the last.

The tension in Dunrugis had taken its toll on her—the servants' hostility, Lady Margaret's distraction, Lady Lilias's contempt, and Laird Brec's neglect. Hollow and exhausted, she longed to put this wedding behind her and get on with her duties.

She had been nurtured in the warm embrace of love: that of her parents, her sisters, even her irascible uncles. When she had agreed to this marriage arrangement with Brec McCloud, she had never bargained for how difficult a loveless future might be.

"Ye look lovely in this sea-green silk, milady," Brenda said as she smoothed the skirt and reached for the sapphire-and-emerald necklace to place around Honora's throat. "None of us knew any stones as beautiful as these were among the McCloud jewels. Lady Lilias never wore them. Laird Brec made a perfect choice for ye."

Silently, Honora blessed the girl for trying to cheer her.

"Here are the earrings." Even in the indifferent daylight the blue and green gems sparkled and glowed as Brenda helped Honora put them on.

"And have ye heard who has come for the wedding?" the lass asked as she met Honora's look in the mirror.

The day before, galleys and birlins of clan representatives and chiefs had begun to sail into Loch Dunrugis, their brightly painted sails proclaiming the identity of each. To Honora it appeared as if every little loch and headland of the Hebrides were represented at the Maitland-McCloud wedding *ceilidh*.

But before Honora could open her mouth to answer, Brenda went on. "The pirates sailed in during the night."

"Who?"

"Laird Brec's friends, the pirates."

"Actual pirates?" Faced with this unexpected development, Honora's depression dimmed. "Brec invited pirates?"

"Come see," Brenda said, gesturing for Honora to join her at the chamber window.

They peered out at a large, three-masted man-of-war riding at anchor on Loch Dunrugis. Its sails were neatly furled, and no flag flapped from the main mast.

"How do you know they're pirates?" Honora asked. She watched a sailor aboard the ship swing down from the rigging, his movements lively and agile.

"I know. We all know," Brenda said. Any other explanation seemed unnecessary and impossible.

As the sailor shrugged into a purple coat, he spied them. He waved, then cupped his hand around his mouth. "Ahoy, my pretties. Will ye be at the wedding?"

Hastily the two women flattened themselves against the wall on either side of the window. They looked at each other and giggled nervously.

"I don't want any brawling at the wedding," Honora said, suddenly recalling the confrontation between Brec and Wallace. "The pirates won't make trouble will they?"

"Probably." Brenda shrugged, then laughed. "But donna fret about it. I'll wager ye didna have anything this exciting happen at yer fancy Edinburgh wedding."

With her first smile of the day, Honora shook her head. "I shall write my sisters about it. How do you think this will sound? 'Dear Sisters, Among our esteemed wedding guests were the renowned pirates of the isles, Captain Cutthroat and Mister Swashbuckler . . .' "

Brenda giggled. "And what will they think?"

"Beatrix's eyes will grow big, and her cheeks will pale with the humiliation of it. Rosemary will squeal with delight and clap her hands over the novelty."

"I'd like to meet yer sisters," Brenda said.

Surprised and touched, Honora turned to her once-sullen

serving woman. "Perhaps you will soon. Rosemary may join me before long. She would like you."

Brenda smiled and nodded. "I look forward to it. Now, ye know every man will expect a kiss from the bride."

Honora had willingly kissed the men at her wedding breakfast in Edinburgh. But those were men she knew, many since she was a child. Visions of bearded oarsmen and swarthy pirates danced through her mind. She groaned. "Every man!?"

"Aye, but I think they'll mind their manners today," Brenda said. "Out of respect to Laird Brec. They were cautious with Lady Lilias, too, five years ago. But that was because no man was eager to kiss a McDonnell."

"What else should I know about the wedding?" Honora asked.

"Well," Brenda grinned impishly, "Laird Brec has forbidden the ladies to dress ye for the wedding night. Seems he intends to do it himself. Ye should hear what they're saying in the kitchen."

"Oh, nay," Honora said, rosy embarrassment warming her face.

" 'Tis all part of the fun, milady." Brenda chuckled and patted Honora on the shoulder. " 'Tis no kind of celebration without bawdy stories. Here, drink this glass of claret I brought for you, and donna mind what they say. And one more thing. Donna be surprised if some folks seem a little— woeful. Some still mourn Laird Colin, and even the wedding of their new laird will no' cheer them."

A blast of pipe music shook Honora when she appeared in the sea gate courtyard. The piper on the quay across the water had been watching for the bride to make an appearance, and as soon as she did, he puffed up his pipes and blasted the crowd with a processional. Honora steadied herself with a deep breath.

Brec awaited her at the gate, smiling, with the rest of the wedding party behind him: his mother, Lady Lilias, Wallace, and even Dubh. They all smiled at Honora, except Lilias. With a flutter of self-consciousness Honora realized that Lilias was glaring with great envy at the sapphires and emeralds that Brenda had fastened at her throat.

Before she could think any more of it, Brec stepped toward her, his large hand extended to take hers. He was dressed in his kilt, black velvet coat, and tartan sash. He grinned down at her—the first smile she had seen on his face since the evening of her welcoming supper. Since then she had seen him only at supper time, and often he seemed distracted and distant. She had wondered whether he was having second thoughts about the marriage too.

But now, with an air of pride he took her hand and tucked her cold fingers around his arm, warming them with his large hand. Under his approving gaze Honora forgot her misgivings and her irritation over his neglect. Did he cast some kind of spell over her with those faceted eyes of his, she wondered.

"You look lovely, milady, even lovelier than on our wedding day in St. Giles, if that is possible," he whispered so that no one else could hear. His black eyes sparkled. "But I promise you that tonight you won't be sleeping with your sisters."

Honora found herself staring up at Brec, intensely aware of his wicked good looks, the bulk of his body, his warmth and strength. "I'm sorry I told you about that," she replied, a furious blush flaming to her cheeks, but a smile tugging at the corners of her mouth. "Oh, I hope the villagers on the landing can't see my face. Those aren't the words of encouragement I needed to hear from you, milaird."

Brec glanced across the water. With an arrogant smile he squeezed her hand. "Don't let the people's curious looks and long faces trouble you, milady."

Brec handed Honora into a flower-bedecked boat that Fergus rowed to the village quay. The clan piper played them across the water. The drone of his lively processional filled the silence as the bridal couple climbed from the boat. They were greeted with no cheers, no songs.

A dark-haired little girl dressed in her best tartan and lace stumbled forth—shoved by someone in the crowd—to present the bride with a bouquet of wilted flowers. Honora thanked the child with a kiss on the cheek. After a hasty curtsy the little girl scampered back to her mother.

With an open grin, Brec took Honora's arm and led the

way up the hill toward the abbey. Lady Margaret, Lady Lilias, Wallace, and visiting dignitaries followed. Servants trailed behind. The hushed crowd of villagers parted to make way for them. Face after face stared back at Honora, solemn, sober, and stoic.

She quickened her step to match Brec's stride. "Is a wedding on the isle a solemn affair?"

Brec cast her a look of surprise. "Of course not. But I think Colin's memory is still fresh for some of these people. Have no fear. When the time for dancing comes, they will forget their frowns."

St. Michael's abbey, squat and solid—curiously like a Norman structure—drowsed in a hillside glade beneath the gray sky. Ragged ruins of a larger structure spread across the grassy meadow. At the kirk's side lay the cemetery, ancient and unkept. When Honora looked over treetops beyond the glade, she could see the Castle Dunrugis below and the sea. St. Columba had chosen a fitting site for his Christian abbey.

Without hesitation Brec pulled Honora up the stone steps of the squat, little kirk with narrow windows. At the doorway Honora paused to prepare herself to step into the cool, dank abbey.

At the tug of her hand, Brec turned back to her. Honora glimpsed the look of anxiety on his face and wondered why he would be concerned now.

"I just need to catch my breath," she assured him.

He nodded and turned away, observing the crowd that had followed them through the forest and up the hill.

When Brec turned back to her, he spoke softly. "My mother and father were wed in this abbey and most of the McCloud chiefs before them as well."

Honora nodded.

"This is where Colin and I were christened, and his funeral Mass was said here," he added, as if those details were vital to make her understand the significance of the place. "The storytellers say there's been an altar on this spot since druid times."

"Aye, I can feel the weight of the ages here," Honora said, watching Brec's face and willing him to know that she understood.

His ebony gaze captured hers, bore into her. "This is your last opportunity, sweet soul, to gainsay me and the McClouds. You have seen the isle and slept in the castle. You have met my family. You know what the bargain is. The final vows are yet unsaid."

Honora saw the earnest appeal in his dark eyes and knew that he understood how much he asked of her. She wondered again whether he had misgivings. Did he want her to beg off? Or was he truly offering her an opportunity to say no? Whichever it was, Honora decided, she had come too far to turn back now. Her uncles had turned to the war. Beatrix would soon be married. There was no place for her in Edinburgh, and soon there would be no place for Rosemary, either.

"I stand by the agreement we made in Edinburgh," Honora said. "Do you?"

"Aye," he declared without blinking, without hesitation.

Honora swallowed a lump of fear that threatened to choke her. "I am honored to wed you, milaird, in the tradition of the McCloud lairds and ladies of the Isle of Myst."

When she was ready to enter the shadowy abbey, she touched his arm and stepped across the stone threshold. Mustiness mingled with a spicy fragrance of incense. Shafts of daylight fell from the narrow window to the floor at Honora's feet. Silvery motes of dust drifted in the rays. Delicately carved stone Celtic designs vined up the columns and stretched across the archway over the bluestone altar. A golden cross on a white satin cloth gleamed in the candlelight. Near the altar Father Andrew awaited them, his white hair shining like polished silver. Slowly, with Brec at her side, Honora walked across the flagstones followed by the crowd—Lady Margaret and Lady Lilias first, then Wallace, notable guests, Brenda, and the villagers.

In the silence between their footsteps Honora heard a cuckoo call from the forest beyond. Despite all the people gathered about, Honora felt as if she and Brec alone stood before some higher power that dwelled here.

Brec's grip on her hand became suddenly painful. Honora could not see his face as he turned away and signaled for Father Andrew to begin.

The ceremony was brief, as it had been in Edinburgh.

127

Before Honora knew what had happened, Brec gave her a sound kiss and they were outside on the church steps in the daylight.

The piper piped away. Brenda came forward and pulled a round shortbread cake from behind her skirt.

"Who will break the cake with me?" she called, a challenge to the wedding guests.

Silence hovered. Two village girls in white caps twittered, squealed, and scurried forward to lurch to a stop beside Brenda. Grinning, Brec released Honora's hand and backed away.

"What? . . ." Honora spun around, looking from Brec to Brenda for help. She didn't understand a word of the girls' prattle.

"We break the cake over yer head, milady," Brenda explained. She had to shout over the chatterings of the girls who joined the circle. "The lass who gets the largest piece will be the next to wed."

Honora looked at Brec. Still laughing, he nodded reassuringly. Lady Margaret stepped to his side and waved encouragement also.

Brenda gestured for Honora to lean down. Closing her eyes, Honora bowed her head so that the diminutive Brenda could hold the cake over her.

A silence of anticipation fell. Then squealing shrilled in Honora's ear. Crumbs tickled into her hair, atop her tiny lace cap, and down her face and neck. More screams. Another shower of cake crumbs. Girls lunged around her, jostling her to and fro. Brenda screeched and danced away.

"I've got it," she shouted to the crowd. "I've got it. I'll be the next to marry."

"Well, 'tis about time, lass," someone from the back of the crowd shouted. To her surprise Honora understood the Gaelic. She stood up to peer over the heads of her guests at the speaker, a red-bearded man with a broad toothless grin and bright blue eyes. He could only be Brenda's father.

Brenda blushed. The crowd laughed, the first laughter of the day. With pride, Brenda thrust the piece of cake, her trophy, into the air. The villagers applauded.

The harper plucked away at a lilting dance tune. The wedding guests remained subdued, but smiles lingered.

With no hint of concern or embarrassment, Brec drew Honora into the center of the glade amid the abbey ruins.

"At last our first dance, sweet soul," Brec whispered as he awaited the proper beat to begin the steps. Honora wondered at the easy expression on his face, how he could take no notice of the villagers who drew away from them. "I've waited for this dance longer than you know."

When the time came, Brec whirled her around with enthusiasm, his hand spread firmly across her back, his enthusiasm evident in his quick, light step. Honora tossed her head and laughed, regretting only that they had never danced like this before.

At first no one joined them. Brec danced on undaunted, but Honora began to feel ill at ease.

As the daughter of a duke, she had been brought up to understand her responsibility in leading the common folk. But she felt uncomfortable being the center of curiosity on the Isle of Myst and was grateful when Brenda and Kenneth joined them. Then, to Honora's delight, a pirate in a purple coat and red hat grabbed Lilias about the waist and whirled her, protesting, out into the dancing. Soon others followed.

When at last the bride and bridegroom took a rest, Lady Margaret embraced Honora. A confused, but gentle smile lit her rumpled face. "Welcome to the Clan McCloud, my dear. I know you and Colin will be very happy."

" 'Tis Brec and I who will be happy," Honora corrected gently. She glanced at Brec and was relieved to see that he hadn't heard his mother use his brother's name.

Brec was well pleased with the wedding. He had fulfilled two important obligations now. He'd become clan chief and acquired a proper woman for his wife and lady of the castle. He gladly accepted the respects paid by isle folk—each humbly shaking his hand.

As he proudly watched Honora accept the quick, shy kisses of the village craftsmen and fishermen, he let his dreams drift ahead to the future, when they would celebrate the christenings of McCloud babes. One day soon he would watch Honora slip her gown from her shoulder and put their babe to her generous breast. She would make a fine mother. He would catch her smile, gentle and soft with love. And he would admire her long, delicate fingers as she stroked their nursing babe's head.

The tightening in his loins brought him back to the present. He hadn't even bedded her yet. He grew impatient with the thought of the long celebration that lay ahead. They couldn't slip away before darkness fell. Besides that, he had certain wedding guests who must be well occupied for the evening to prevent untimely interruptions.

"Milaird," Honora whispered in his ear.

"Aye?" Brec took the opportunity to lean closer to her, to inhale her scent and touch the fabric of her gown.

"My face is stiff from smiling," she whispered and rubbed the side of her face. "My cheek is chafed with so many kisses."

Brec laughed and caressed the spot with his knuckles. " 'Tis true, I don't think a man in the isles has missed his chance to kiss the bride."

He savored the softness of her skin beneath his fingers and lost himself in the sea-green depths of her eyes. Briefly he thought about ordering everyone to go home. After all, he was clan chief, and he wanted to be alone with his bride. But he also knew the privilege and responsibilities of his title didn't permit that. With power came obligation to the people. For a moment he regretted becoming enslaved with Colin's burden of clan chief.

"Ahoy, Brec, ol' friend."

At the sound of a familiar voice Brec turned. The man dressed in the purple velvet coat shouted and pushed aside the isle folk to make his way toward Brec and Honora. He waved a broad-brimmed red felt hat with its flopping peacock feather.

"Simon!" A measure of relief washed over Brec. He'd seen the *Sea Gull* sail into the loch but had been unable to slip away to greet the captain, his friend.

"You ol' sea dog," Simon shouted, even though he stood face to face with Brec. A grin split his bronzed face. His sun-streaked brown hair was pulled back in an unfashionable queue that enhanced his blue eyes and high cheekbones. He slapped Brec on the back then embraced him.

"Ye swore ye'd never take a wife. Remember! Now look at ye. Well, let's have a look at her."

"Simon—"

Before Brec could warn the pirate, Simon grabbed Honora by the shoulders and turned her so that daylight fell on her face. With a practiced squint, Simon eyed her.

Brec saw Honora's anger flash. He knew she hated appraisals and would not welcome one from a man like Simon, who wore glistening gold chains around his neck and a golden hoop dangling from his left ear.

"Do I meet with your approval, sir?" Honora demanded, crossing her eyes and wrinkling her nose in the pirate's face. "Perhaps you would like to see my teeth?"

Simon threw back his head and laughed. "So ye gave up a peaceful life at sea for a sharp-tongued wench in fancy rigging?"

With a sardonic smile Brec peeled Simon's hands off Honora's shoulders. "As you well know, even at sea a man has to weather a storm now and then."

Simon laughed once more and winked. "And Brec, me lad, I never saw a storm ye couldna weather. Ye'll fare well enough with him, milady."

Honora frowned at him. "Are we about to have a storm?"

"Ignore him, Honora," Brec advised and cast the pirate a look of warning. "The old goat is trying to sow the seeds of discontent."

"I know what ye'll be sowing soon enough." Simon gave another hearty laugh and pounded Brec on the back.

"Enough, Simon." Brec put himself between Honora and the pirate, lest the conversation turn more lewd and his bride become embarrassed.

"Now donna lose that foul temper of yers," Simon warned with a wave of his hands. "So who is it ye want me to entertain tonight?"

Brec was about to draw the pirate away from Honora to explain his plan, when he spotted Wallace approaching them. His cousin wore no weapon, but his face was already flushed with drink. Although all of Brec's senses became alert, he gave no sign of it and waited for Wallace to make the first move.

"I would have my kiss from the bride," Wallace proposed when he stopped before the bride and groom. Like the other merrymakers at the celebration, the former successor was trimmed, brushed, and wore a clean plaid. He turned to rake his gaze over Honora.

Brec felt the weight of Simon's restraining hand on his shoulder. With great effort he kept the hatred from his face. " 'Tis all right," Brec said when Honora cast him an uneasy look.

Wallace's kiss was polite enough. "I wish you long life and happiness together, milady."

"Thank you, sir," Honora replied with a smile befitting a new bride and a lady.

Brec could not resist drawing her back against him.

"I congratulate you, Brec, on securing your place as clan chief. Handily done. A beautiful wife, the daughter of a duke and wealthy in her own right. All you need now is a son, which I'm sure you've been working on." Wallace grinned at Honora obscenely.

Brec strained against Simon's grip on his shoulder.

"Don't judge me by your standards," Brec muttered between his teeth, unsure of how much longer he could resist the urge to smash Wallace's face in.

"But you must tell me," Wallace began, his tone light and giving a brief shrug of his shoulders, as if Brec's answer mattered little to him. "How, after years of silence—as I recall you didn't even return for Laird Alec's funeral did you? Your own father's funeral, God rest his soul, and you never sent word or anything—how did you manage to sail into Loch Dunrugis with your pirate friend and have Colin greet you with open arms? 'Twas just short of a miracle.

"I was only a lad when you left, but I remember that day. You vowed you'd never return. Your father was glad to be rid of you. Brought out ale and declared a celebration."

Brec took a deep breath, refusing to allow the first words that came to him to escape his lips.

Honora stared from Brec to Wallace, obviously bewildered by the threat of violence that hovered between them.

Brec longed to reassure her, but could not. He wanted to go for Wallace's throat.

"Just what are you trying to say, Wallace?" Brec finally growled, old insults now stirring and smarting under his cousin's unspoken insinuations. There was no keeping the bitterness from his voice. "If 'tis how you say, that my father was glad to be rid of me, why should I have returned for his funeral? I was never his fair-haired son. I was never the one he doted over and bragged on."

"Enough, lads, enough. 'Tis a day to be joyous." Simon elbowed Brec away, edged Honora aside, and faced Wallace.

Brec almost swung at Simon, then contained himself. He knew that someday he'd be grateful to his friend for having separated them, but at the moment, he could barely resist the urge to shove Simon away and bash in Wallace's drunken face.

"Ye made yer moves, Wallace, and ye lost the game," Simon warned. "Donna be a bad loser and a fool, to boot."

"Did you invite this pirate here to kill me?" Wallace demanded, looking to Brec and pointing to Simon.

"I don't hire someone else to do my murdering," Brec said. "If I wanted you dead, Wallace, you'd be rotting at the bottom of the sea now. But you're free to leave the isle any time you want."

"True enough. I'd be rotting just like your brother. Nay," Wallace said with an ironic laugh. "I'll stay at Dunrugis like a silly lass putting scraps of cake under my pillow, dreaming of a future that will never be."

"Sleep!?" Simon exclaimed, claiming their attention once more. "Now there's a grand idea. I think it'd be a fine thing to sleep off some of that ale now, lad."

The pirate draped a friendly arm around Wallace's broad shoulders and guided the drunken man toward the trees. With a hateful glare, Wallace shook off Simon's embrace and marched alone into the forest.

"So that one is who ye wanted me to entertain?"

Brec nodded.

"Charming," Simon said with a wry twist to his mouth. "Well, me lad, I'll get to it as soon as I've eaten me fill, if ye donna mind."

Brec and Honora watched the pirate make his way through the crowd of dancers, his gaze on the forest where Wallace had disappeared. Brec scanned the dancers quickly and caught Kenneth's eye. When he saw that the master at arms danced with Lady Lilias, he nodded his approval.

"Do you expect more trouble from Wallace?" Honora asked.

Brec turned to his bride and was disappointed to see that the light of happiness had disappeared from the depths of her eyes and a furrow of worry puckered her brow.

"Nay, don't bother yourself about Wallace's bad manners," Brec said with confidence and a careless smile. "Let's dance." As he led Honora into the crowd of dancers, he silently prayed that Simon would remember why he had been invited.

Overhead the clouds had cleared and the moon rode high in the sky, spilling silver light down on Loch Dunrugis. Distant pipe music filled the air; the bonfire still glowed bright on the hill.

"Surely they have missed us by now," Honora whispered in the dark. She looked back toward the village and up at the fire-lit glade where wedding guests danced. "I feel like a naughty child sneaking away from my own party."

Brec untied Fergus's boat as Honora spoke. With easy grace he leaped aboard the bobbing craft and reached for her. "No one expects the bridal couple to dance all night. 'Tis time for us to sail away, milady."

Honora smiled uncertainly at her husband, then took his hand and climbed aboard. Brec shrugged off his velvet jacket before taking up the oars and deftly eased Fergus's boat away from the landing. His white shirt glowed in the moonlight; Honora was glad he had chosen not to wear all black to their wedding.

With his knees spread and his feet braced against the bottom of the boat, he leaned into the oars, stretching the white linen taut across his shoulders and sending the boat skimming across the water. Honora was suddenly reminded that she would soon be embraced by those strong arms. And those knees would . . . She swallowed and looked out over the shining loch.

Torches burned for them at Dunrugis's sea gate—a sight not nearly so frightening in the moonlight as it had been only a few nights before. The guard who tied up the boat gave them a quiet greeting and a secretive smile.

In the castle passage Honora became painfully aware of the ring of Brec's leather shoes over the sound of her slippered footsteps. Dunrugis was empty—theirs alone. When they reached the stairs, without thinking, Honora turned down the passage to her chamber.

"Where are you going, milady?" Brec tugged on her hand. She heard an unfamiliar huskiness in his voice.

Honora stopped.

No words would come to her lips. The rush light that Brec carried cast dark shadows across his face. But the mocking arch of his brow and the desire in his expression were plain. It was enough to make Honora think of retreat. What did she really know about this man? That he was the McCloud clan chief and took delight in being considered something of a devil. Saying vows before the priest was one thing, but giving up her body to this unconventional man was something else—something she was suddenly reluctant to do.

"Oh, no, milady. You're not returning to your maiden's bed. I'm taking you to the laird's chamber. 'Tis time you learned the way."

12

Honora planted her feet and refused to follow Brec down the darkened passage. Her hand at her throat, she watched Brec turn to her, his dark eyes glittering again.

"The laird's chamber?" she asked breathlessly. "I don't remember hearing of the laird's chamber."

She was stalling, but she needed a few moments to come

to terms with reality—that at last she was to sleep with this man. She had wanted this, didn't she? That was what she had agreed to. Since she had walked into his arms at her uncles' house, encountered his solid warmth and caught the scent of peat smoke on him, since he had gripped her by the shoulders and grinned that devilish grin. This moment had been inevitable.

She had longed to feel his hand on her bare skin, to taste his mouth again as he had offered it on their wedding day in St. Giles. Now that moment was upon her.

But she had no experience in these matters. How did she walk into his bedchamber and begin to act as a wife? By tradition, her mother and sisters and friends should help her. Should she peel off her clothes while he watched? Should she crawl into bed first or wait for him? How did a lady do this? What if there was some part of her he didn't find enticing?

Once again, Honora tried to tug free. With a look of mystification, Brec refused to release her. "What is it, sweet soul? Are you frightened?"

"Of course not," Honora snapped, vexed with herself for hesitating and with him for thinking her afraid. "The bedding, 'tis a bride's duty—my duty." She paused. "Are you afraid?"

A look of surprise flashed across Brec's face. Honora smiled at him sweetly and prayed she hadn't offended him.

He shook his head as if bemused. When he turned to her once more, she found humor in his dark smile. And honesty too.

"Sometimes. But not tonight, not of this. And I wouldn't have you frightened, either." He squeezed her hand. "I think for all your bawdy songs and your poet lover, you haven't had much experience in these matters."

His honesty deserved honesty. Honora nodded.

"Do you want me to send for Brenda?" he asked. "Would that make you feel better?"

Honora gulped and shook her head. "You will assist me, if you like, milaird. As you did the night I arrived at Dunrugis. Remember? When you removed my boots?"

" 'Twill be my pleasure to assist you."

The shared memory eased the awkwardness between them.

Honora allowed Brec to lead her up the spiral stairs to another floor, then down a passage. Brec flung open the door to a cavernous chamber. In the center of the vaulted room stood a huge bed bedecked with blue and yellow plumes.

"Milady, the laird's chamber." With a knowing smile, he stood back for Honora to enter.

Candlelight danced in the draft from the door, yet the room glowed warm with a low fire on the hearth.

"Brenda's been here," Honora said with a gentle laugh.

Sweet, flowering garlands draped the great bed and scented the room. Across the bed covers lay a piece of blue silk embroidered with a yellow scrawling design. Trembling light shimmered over its rich, textured surface. Honora went to it.

"This is beautiful," she said, fingering the stuff. "What is it?"

"A banner," Brec said, closing the door behind them. "You've probably heard that a fairy married into the family long ago?"

"Aye," Honora said, remembering the stories Lanie had told her of humpbacks, fairies, and secret rooms.

"They say that when the fairy bride left her baby son, she wrapped him in this. Through the centuries the banner has protected McClouds on the battlefield."

Honora continued to admire the fabric. She heard Brec walk up behind her. He slipped his arms around her waist and pulled her against him. For the first time she allowed herself to rest against him. His embrace tightened, pressing her whalebone bodice against her breast.

"What is not so well known is that when unfurled, it multiplies the McCloud men on the field of battle. It also makes McCloud brides fruitful." Brec kissed her ear.

Unexpectedly the warmth tingled and slithered down her neck and into her belly.

"Fruitful?" Honora's face grew hot. Of course, there was no sense in being fainthearted or coy; she must bear an heir. It was her duty. And with a little stab of disappointment, she realized that the laird knew his duty also.

She pulled free of Brec and turned to him. "But I should think the performance of the McCloud bridegroom would have more effect on the bride's productivity than a mere banner."

Brec laughed. He took her by the shoulders and gave her a sound kiss. "No doubt you are right. Perhaps we both should wear it. Wrap ourselves up together in this silken stuff. Surely that would ensure the best possible results."

As Honora watched, he shook out the banner so that the scented air of the bedchamber swelled the fabric. Just as the billowed fabric began to settle, he pulled it over them.

Satiny blue fell about them. Honora giggled. Brec's lips brushed against her temple. Burying his face against her neck, he kissed her, nuzzled her, tasted her ear lobe once more. Something about the privacy of the silken cocoon allowed Honora to relish the sensations stirred by his body pressing against hers. His contours were unfamiliar to her. She slipped her arms around his waist and began to explore the hardness of his back—the two cords and the valley between.

Honora wanted to learn more. She offered him access to the most sensitive places below her ear while she sought to slide her hands down his back. She pressed against him and felt the rich rumble of a chuckle deep inside him.

He caught her questing hands and kissed them. "Didn't I tell you that you are a passionate soul?"

Honora blushed but looked up at him bravely. "I want to touch you and I want you to touch me. Is that what you want too?"

"Aye," he said with a captivating smile. "I promise you I'm more impatient than you. But this is no time to rush. Turn around. We'll start with your gown."

Inside the silken tent she turned her back so that he could begin to unfasten the laces.

"Tell me more about the fairy bride," she said, genuinely curious about the banner draped over them.

"She is said to have been dark-haired and fair of face."

"Like you?"

Brec paused. "Aye, I suppose. Dark like me. They say she fell in love with and married a McCloud and bore him a son."

SPEAK OF LOVE

Honora could feel his fingers skillfully pulling the laces free, moving faster than Brenda ever could.

"And what happened? Is there more to the story?" she asked, praying that there was. Anything to delay that inevitable moment when she would be naked before him.

"Aye, the fairy folk had given her only a short while to live in this land of mortals," he said. "And when that time came to an end, they called her back to their underground world. Because she didn't want to leave her son unprotected, she wrapped him in this banner. Then she bade a sad farewell to her husband and returned to the fairy world." Brec paused. "At least, that's the story. The child's nurse claimed that when she left the room, she could hear the fairies singing to quiet the fussy babe. As soon as she rushed back into the nursery, he was always smiling, safe, and happy."

"What a delightful tale!" Honora said, buying time as she clasped her loosened bodice against her breasts. She could almost hear the fairies singing and see the wee babe smiling.

"Enough of stories," Brec whispered. "Off with that bodice."

"Milaird, you are too adept at this," Honora protested. "I'll not undress more, sir, while you still have on your shirt."

Brec gave her a look of suspicion.

Honora grinned. "Off with it, I say."

Without further delay, he unbuttoned his shirt, shrugged it from his arms, and flung it to the floor. The muscles of his chest and upper arms moved sinuously beneath tanned skin and crisp chest hair. Honora leaned close to gain the scent of him, warm and musky. She touched him, spread one hand across his rib cage to feel his sudden intake of breath. She liked their silken tent and the soft blue light it cast on his face.

"Now your gown, milady," he demanded, his voice grown huskier.

With haste he yanked Honora's bodice from her arms and pulled her skirt and petticoats down over her hips.

Honora immediately grabbed the banner. She whipped it from their heads and wrapped it around herself.

A shoulder strap of her shift slipped off one shoulder. Brec's brow lowered, a dark, hungry look flashing in his eyes. Honora pulled the banner tighter and tried to smile.

That brought the humor and exasperation into Brec's eyes. "And you were so willing only a moment ago."

"I was—well, I'm just not ready yet. And you seem so greedy sometimes."

" 'Tis getting beyond greedy, milady," he rasped.

Before she could reply, he seized her with one hand behind her neck and planted his lips on hers. He kissed her long and hard, as Honora knew he had intended to do at the garden party when he pulled her across his lap.

After the initial shock of his mouth against hers, she liked it. She liked the probing of his tongue, the hard, ravenous movement of his lips over hers and the feel of his hand on her neck as the other stroked her banner-covered back.

Brec pulled away first, his black eyes hungrier than ever.

"Sir," Honora gasped, trying to catch her breath. Her hair had come loose, and the other strap of her shift had slipped off her shoulder. Brec's gaze locked on that errant strap.

"Someone must snuff the candles," she reminded him, desperate to distract him now.

"To hell with the candles," he muttered. He began to pull at the straps of her shift.

"At least allow me the privacy of the bed curtains," Honora begged, edging her way around him, toward the bed.

"To hell with the bed curtains." He reached for her as she scrambled onto the bed. "We'll make love in the light, wife. 'Tis the best way."

When he began to unbuckle the belt to his kilt, Honora retreated to the shadows of the curtains and pulled the banner about her. She didn't want to watch Brec. Her thoughts were a tumble of desires and doubts. She wanted to do her duty as a wife. She wanted to please him as a woman. But nothing in her life had prepared her for responding to a passionate man like Brec. A true lover would be gentle and tender. Brec looked big and hungry.

She heard him snuffing the candles and smiled to herself, touched by this concession. The shadows of the bed deepened. The bed curtains parted, and Brec's lean silhouette appeared against the moonlight. The silvery light sculptured his taut flank and long thigh, and rippled along his ribs. Moonbeams mantled his shoulders and back, but shadows hid his lower body.

"I have your share of the banner here," Honora said, holding out a silken corner with trembling fingers.

Slowly Brec crawled across the bed. He lay down next to Honora, took the banner, and laid it over his hips.

A shaft of moonlight fell between the bed curtains, illuminating his face for Honora. Curious about the tender expression she discovered there, she reached out to touch his cheek. He allowed the touch, then took her hand and kissed it, resting her fingertips against his gently moving lips.

Honora gasped with the pleasure, the breathy warmth.

"Do we go too fast for you, sweet soul?" he asked. When she didn't answer, he sat up and began to pull once more at the straps of her shift.

As he removed each, he drew his hand down the full length of her arm, a warm caress.

Honora's fears dwindled. She closed her eyes and took pleasure in the firm feel of Brec's fingers moving over her skin. She let him slip the straps over her hands and down to her hips. With a little urging, she lay down beside him to allow him to pull off her shift. She felt his breath as he kissed her brow. With a finger he lifted her face to kiss her nose, her cheeks, her lips, her chin, her throat. Her eyes fluttered open when he began to trail kisses along her collar bone and to tickle the hollow of her throat with his tongue.

But her fears had deserted her, leaving her weak and needful. She traced Brec's ear with her fingers as his mouth moved over her skin, down her throat to the valley between her breasts. She was aware of sensitive, puckered nipples abraded by the silk and of warm, flowing sensations. He drew his tongue around one silk-covered nipple, then across it. Honora shivered and bit her lip against the moan that threatened to escape her.

She offered her breast to him again, but he ignored it this time, kissing each rib and her navel. His hand slipped down her back and spread across her bottom as he kissed one thigh, then the other. To feel only his warmth through the silken fabric was frustrating, but before Honora could pull away the banner, Brec rose to his knees and straddled her legs. His hand came to cover hers, and he stripped the banner free.

Pale moonlight fell between the bed curtains to caress their bodies, shaping the mounds of Honora's breasts, pooling a shadow in her navel and highlighting the tender whiteness of her belly—limning the length of Brec's thigh and contouring the muscles of his shoulders.

Honora reached for those muscular shoulders, but Brec took her arms and stretched them above her head, whispering for her to let them rest there. Then he put his hands on her shoulders and began to stroke downward, gently kneading each breast, around the nipple, molding the flesh gently in his hands. Over and over again he massaged and cuddled each breast, sharing the warmth and strength of his hands with her.

A lock of black hair dropped over Brec's brow. His face was shadowed, his expression hidden from her. She could only hope that he derived as much pleasure from what he was doing as she did. His hands worked around to the sides of her breasts, then to the tender areas at the base and up between—never touching her nipples, now tight and aching for his caress.

Slowly she became aware of other needs, of the need to open to his touch. But Brec straddled her, his swollen manhood cradled in the valley between her thighs—teasing the part of her that would hold him.

Finally he leaned over and took her nipple into his mouth. Honora sighed with relief and pleasure, delighted with the feel of the wet roughness of his tongue. She wrapped her arms around his neck and moved against him, abandoning herself to the delightful sensation his lips stirred in her. He took the other breast and slipped his hands beneath her shoulders.

Slowly his head came up. "Are we going too fast now?"

"Nay," Honora managed to say. "Don't stop."

Brec moved off her. Honora reached for him to draw him back to her breasts, but he would not return to her embrace.

"Patience," Brec whispered. "Just trying a new way to

please you." Gently he stroked her belly and down each thigh, encouraging her to open for him. All the time he held her gaze, his eyes black and glittering in the moonlight. A slight smile curved on his lips—a knowing smile, not mocking, but tender and welcoming. Honora had no fear of that smile. She closed her eyes, savoring each stroke of his fingers.

His first touch in that most private of places made her cry out, and she was surprised at how moist she was. Her eyes fluttered open in alarm. Brec was still smiling at her and seemed very pleased.

"That's the way it should be, Honora," he murmured. His probing continued slow and gentle. Reassured, Honora closed her eyes and gave way to the divine sensations his fingers brought.

Moonbeams danced between the parted curtains, creating a magical bower and dusting the lovers with silvery splendor.

Tenderly Brec bent over Honora, studying her face, smooth and lovely in the moonlight, soft with pleasure, her lips parted and her breath coming quick and sweet. As he explored her delicate depths and fostered her desire for him, he knew he had found what he needed.

Despite all the obstacles to be overcome and the things he had given up, possessing Honora was the most important thing he had done in his life. She was the key to his future and to the clan's. He had no regrets.

Possessively he covered her. With a sigh she slipped her arms around his neck. He held her tightly, then made his first thrust, swift and purposeful so that the discomfort of her loss was quick.

He saw Honora's eyes widen with pain, but she didn't cry out. She tensed for a moment and gasped. But she didn't shrink from him. He held her all the more tenderly for that.

"That's all, sweet soul," Brec reassured her. "The best is yet to come."

He stroked damp hair away from her temples. Despite his own aching need, he did not move for some time. He wanted her to become used to the feel of him. He would take his cue from her. When she moved again, she stroked the small of his back and kissed his cheek.

"Is this how a husband and wife embrace one another?" she whispered against his neck.

"Aye, and this is only the beginning." He moved again, this time to finish her initiation.

Instinctively Honora joined Brec's rhythm, her mind and body full of him, his hardness, his scent, his passion—and of a yearning to reach some destination, some Eden sweeter, more glorious than the one she now enjoyed. Another thrust and the summit was breached. Honora clung to him, longing to take him with her. She soared and fell, weightless in shimmering joy. She drifted through bliss. With a final thrust Brec tensed in her arms, filling her with his seed, his sigh hot and passionate in her ear.

When Brec started to leave her, she refused to release him. He spoke quiet words to her and wrapped her in something soft and silky. She remembered that he kissed her before she slept.

In the morning light she awoke alone, sheathed in the silk banner. She sat up in the big bed and whipped back the curtains. The window was shuttered against the morning cold and a low peat fire burned in the fireplace. Disappointment settled over her. She was alone. The cavernous laird's chamber bore no sign of Brec.

13

Honora followed Lady Lilias down the passage on the last part of their tour of the castle. Dubh trotted at her heels.

The message that Brec would be with Simon and Wallace all day had arrived with Honora's breakfast tray. So when Lady Lilias had sent an invitation to show Honora the castle, she had accepted—partly to avoid offending the lady and partly because she wanted to learn her way around.

Before her in the passage she could hear the rustle of Lady Lilias's black satin skirts. Behind her she heard Brenda's snorting and sniffing.

Honora stopped short, her patience worn thin. Brenda almost walked into her. "What *is* the matter with you? You've been carrying on like this all day."

" 'Tis a wonder that woman is up and about today," Brenda muttered with a look of murder at Lady Lilias. "She was a-drinking and dancing all night."

"Did she stay late at the *ceilidh?*" Honora asked, surprised.

"Danced into the wee hours like a fool, then disappeared into the woods like a common—"

"Brenda," Honora warned. "I don't care for that kind of talk in my household."

"Lady Honora, where are you?" Lilias called from the doorway at the end of the passage. "I thought you would like to see the portrait of Laird Colin in the Great Hall."

"Aye, indeed I would," Honora replied. "I'll be right there."

Honora's curiosity got the better of her, and she turned back to Brenda. "Who was Lady Lilias with?"

"Kenneth," Brenda bit off.

"Oh, I see." Honora understood Brenda's pique. She had witnessed the bantering exchanges between Brenda and Kenneth in the Great Hall at supper times. She had also seen Kenneth dancing with the Lady Lilias at the wedding celebration and had been unable to imagine why the man would prefer the cool, haughty lady over the lively, warm Brenda. "Perhaps Kenneth was being kind. 'Tis almost time for the lady to come out of mourning."

"Mourning, indeed," Brenda exclaimed. "That lady never mourned Laird Colin. Not one bit. She danced at his wake as if she had been set free."

"Really?" Honora drew back in surprise.

"Aye, and Laird Brec shouted at the priest. Reached across the table and grabbed poor Father McGregor by the throat, he did. Would have done him in right then and there if Kenneth hadna put a stop to it. And all the while, Lady Lilias was singing like a banshee. Lady Margaret locked herself in her chamber and wept. 'Twas a strange wake.

145

Laird Colin, God rest his soul, was probably glad to be laid to rest in a peaceful grave.''

Honora shivered. Brenda painted a disturbing picture of Colin's wake.

"I told you that you didn't have to come on the tour with Lady Lilias if you didn't want to," Honora reminded Brenda.

The blacksmith's daughter shook her head vehemently. "Laird Brec said to never let ye out of me sight and to always watch yer food. The truth be I have no fondness for yer husband, milady, but I'll do as I'm bid."

Astonished, Honora stared at the irate redhead who reared back to regard her with a stubborn set of her chin. "Brenda? What do you mean he told you to never let me out of your sight?"

Brenda only shook her head and sniffed.

"Are you coming, Lady Honora?" Lilias waited for them at the end of the passage looking something like a strutting raven. Ellen, her serving woman—the one Brec had rejected on the night of their arrival—lurked in Lilias's shadow.

At Honora's feet, Dubh growled at the ladies, hackles prickling on his neck. Honora gave the dog a restraining pat and wondered what Lilias had done to offend him.

When Brenda and Dubh seemed mollified, Honora followed Lady Lilias into the Great Hall, where they supped nightly. Ellen and Brenda remained near the door. Lilias and Honora stood back to view the portrait. Ian brought in a ladder, scaled it, and reached for the white linen mourning drapery.

The life-size portrait hung against the inside wall opposite the high diamond-paned windows. Honora had never seen it undraped, and she was eager to come face to face with Colin at last. The stories she had heard about his death made her increasingly curious about the man. She knew that if the portrait painter had done his job well, had captured the likeness and character of Colin, she would learn something more about Brec as well.

Lilias stood close at her side as the mourning drapery fell away. Honora studied the painting, surprised and excited to find that it pictured both brothers.

Colin, the young clan chief-to-be immediately captivated

the viewer—blond, blue-eyed, and bold. He wore a kilted-plaid, a green velvet coat, and a jaunty blue bonnet decorated with an eagle feather. He stood straight, a boy of perhaps only ten years, yet already blessed with the knowledge of who he was, of what the future would hold for him. His gaze pierced. His demeanor commanded. His smile warmed. His features so like Brec's—the high, eloquent brows, the straight nose, and the firm, expressive mouth.

Honora's heart fluttered. A religious painter would have painted Colin's golden visage on an archangel—courageous, compassionate, and powerful. No wonder the man was not forgotten. No wonder grief had unhinged his mother's mind. And his wife's? Could a man like that go unloved and unmourned by any woman?

"That is the McCloud I married." The pride in Lilias's voice was unmistakable. "The man who brought peace to the McDonnells and the McClouds. There will never be another like him. And I was his wife, lady of the grandest castle in all the isles."

"He is a handsome man," Honora agreed. The light of understanding glimmered inside her. If the woman didn't mourn her husband, she certainly mourned the loss of her place as his wife.

Apprehensively, Honora turned to study the youth at Colin's side. In the shadow of his brother stood a black-haired boy, his shoulder turned slightly to the viewer. He, too, wore the traditional tartan kilt and the green velvet coat. He did not look out of the painting as his brother did but was distracted by the toy in his hand—a miniature galley, oars readied and sails unfurled.

Honora's breath caught in her throat. She recalled their courting days in Edinburgh—the rapt expression on Brec's face as he pointed out the great sailing ships on the Firth of Forth. "Has Brec always loved to sail?"

"Well enough to desert his clan," Lilias accused. "And, I tell you, Colin was glad enough when Brec sailed away for the New World. He was just trouble here. His father wanted no traffic with the pirates that Brec always seemed to bring home. Like that one with the purple coat."

Honora could only nod. She had a new picture of Brec to contemplate now. No devil, but a black-bearded Viking in a horned helmet. A man of courage and passion, of restless energies and aspirations.

"And because he loved to sail, he gave up his claim to the successorship of the clan," Honora said aloud. "He went to sea."

"I suppose you could say that," Lady Lilias replied. She spoke softly so that only she and Honora could hear. "He left before Colin and I were married. And he returned once for our wedding. Colin told me then that Brec vowed never to return. Isn't it curious that when he did come, Colin died?"

"What are you trying to tell me, Lilias?" Honora asked, although she understood perfectly well what Colin's widow was hinting at.

"You have married a man who eliminates anyone who stands in the way of what he wants," Lilias said. "If I stood in his way, he would have murdered me. And what do you think will happen to you when you no longer serve his purpose . . . ?"

Honora turned her back on the portrait and on Lilias's vicious warning. Was Brec capable of such villainy? Honora wondered. Of killing his own brother? Would he murder others? His wife? She had seen murder in his face once—when he and Wallace confronted each other over the supper table. And the scene at the wedding had appeared almost as threatening.

Honora shook her head. Brec might be capable of murder. She could see him as a dark Viking wielding a battle-ax, or as a warrior striking a fatal blow in heated passion. But she simply could not envision him as a devious killer, not the ardent man who had tenderly made himself her husband the night before.

She turned to Lilias again. The hate etched in the widow's beautiful face struck Honora. She saw hunger in those lines, something monstrous and malicious that dwelled inside Lilias, an ambition that could devour them all. Lilias blinked and the monster vanished.

Honora stood frozen in disbelief. Had she truly seen that evil thing? Lilias was merely a jealous, vain, and envious woman, wasn't she? Whatever Lilias was, Honora knew instinctively that she should show no fear.

A movement in the doorway drew her attention, and she was grateful to see Ian standing there with a page who carried a brass-trimmed box. They were exactly the change she needed.

"Ian, you've brought the box I asked for, thank you," Honora greeted, a little too heartily. "While we were here in the Great Hall, I wanted to consider where to put the lantern clock my uncles gave me as a wedding gift. I was thinking about a shelf right over there near the hearth. What do you think?"

"Clock?" Lilias repeated, her lips pursed in distaste. "We have no need of such a thing here. All that noise of ticking, chains, and chimes."

Ian looked surprised, then an expression of wonderment spread across his face. "May I see it, milady. I mean, I'm sure that if Laird Brec approves, a mechanical timepiece will be a fine addition to the Great Hall. No castle in the isles has anything but a sun clock."

"Of course, Ian," Honora said. "Let's have a look at it." Carefully she took the brass-faced clock from the packing box.

Ian and the page crowded around Honora to admire the round, brass face, the shiny brass weights, and the intricately worked wrought iron hands.

Lady Lilias said nothing more and she did not join them. With a sign to Ellen, both women coolly swept out of the Great Hall.

The elderly carpenter and his assistant were summoned and with instructions from Ian they went to work immediately. When the shelf was ready, Honora and Ian set the timepiece in place. Carefully she polished the brass face and wound the clock by pulling the weighted chains. The mellow chimes rang out, echoing through the Great Hall. Satisfied that the clock was working properly, Honora turned the hands to the approximate time of day.

Ian stood back to admire the clock, his hands clasped before him and a proud tilt to his chin. " 'Tis truly grand. Something beautiful for folks to see."

"When mourning for Laird Colin is over," Honora said, flicking the last particle of dust from the clock's foot, "perhaps we can fill the Great Hall with guests again."

"In the old days, Laird Alec entertained often," Ian said, a distant look coming into his eyes as he recalled the past. "And Laird Colin too. There was always a merry time to be had at Dunrugis."

"What was it like then?" Honora asked, pleased to have the man speak with her at last and truly curious about happier times at Dunrugis.

"In those days the Great Hall was always full of lairds and ladies, pipers and harpers, dancers, drinkers, and story-tellers. The children played games in the courtyard. And the table was heavy with food and drink. And such fights would break out. Then Laird Alec sat in judgment until all was resolved. Laird Colin entertained sea captains and the families of the isles. Aye, those were great times. Dunrugis was a wondrous place to be."

"Perhaps it will be wondrous once again," Honora said.

At the supper table that evening Brec admired the elegant clock and praised Honora for placing it in the Great Hall. Lilias remained silent, bridling like a willful mare when Brec talked of the timepiece. She cast Honora a hateful frown.

Otherwise Brec continued to treat Honora much as he had before the wedding. He offered the proper kiss of greeting before the servants and performed the expected courtesies. Even when he leaned toward her and offered her the tenderest portion of venison from his plate, Honora sensed a restraint that puzzled her after the intimacies they'd shared on their wedding night.

But she took her cue from him and behaved as a lady should. She did not touch his hands as she wanted to, nor did she lean too close to him as they talked. And she never told him what Lilias had said during the tour of the castle.

But once they were alone together in that great bed with the world shut out and only the moon to watch them, Brec changed. Much to Honora's delight.

Smiling and with a hint of gentle laughter in his voice, he asked her to help him drape the banner from the under-side of the canopy so that it covered them.

"I will hold you on my shoulder, and you can tuck the banner into the folds of the canopy."

Honora agreed. "Well, I'm waiting. Aren't you going to lift me up?"

"Oh, not until you're undressed. I will not lift all those heavy skirts."

Honora turned to him with a skeptical tilt of her head. "Undressed? This doesn't sound very respectable to me, husband."

"I've no need to be respectable in my own bedchamber, wife." He grinned disarmingly, then turned her around to start work on her laces. "I'm merely honoring tradition."

In the weeks that followed, he frequently retired with her when the fire died in the hearth, but left her during the night.

Beneath the banner, the man who possessed her—sometimes passionately and sometimes playfully—wore no distant expression. He was not a stranger who treated her with courtesy, nor the laird who knew he was always being watched. He was like a true lover, tender and caring. He caressed her back and kissed her shoulders. He knew—or soon discovered—all the secrets of her body. Secrets Honora had never guessed at but that she soon took as much delight in sharing as he did in discovering.

Other times he came to her late in the night, when the castle was silent and only the breaking of the sea on the rocks could be heard. He would be carrying his sword, not wearing it. His hair would be wet and his clothes damp with droplets of mist. He would smell of the sea—not of a woman. Eagerly he would reach for Honora. Embracing her with great passion and speaking a few tender words, he exhausted her with the magical pleasure that was his only to give.

One night after Honora had spent the day making cleaning assignments to the staff, she tried to talk to him about some of the things at Dunrugis that puzzled her. She so seldom had his ear during any other part of the day.

"There is a room that I still don't have a key to," she said when he climbed into bed with her.

"I know." He pulled her down on him and gave her a kiss, not one of the public kisses.

"Your book room," Honora said, her breath coming a little more rapidly than before and her will to pursue the topic weakening. "Your room needs cleaning, dusting, and the like."

"Nay," Brec said. His voice was flat and final. "That room will remain locked. Neither you nor the staff will enter. Is that clear?"

Honora stared at her husband through the darkness, startled by his cold dictates, for he had seldom been so harsh with her, and never in the laird's bed.

"Aye, 'tis clear," she whispered. She experienced a sudden chill and reached for the counterpane.

With a smile, Brec stayed her hand. "We've forgotten to take down your hair again."

Out of nowhere—for he was as naked as Honora—he produced a silver hairbrush.

"Where did that come from?" Honora exclaimed, staring in wonder at his nakedness, at the hard smooth contours of his body. His long lean lines offered no place to conceal a hairbrush. At moments like these she had to wonder if he were more than a mere man. "How do you do that?"

"Quick hands," he said with a laugh and a shrug. He began the ritual of loosening her chestnut hair. When the locks fell about her bare shoulders, he brushed each with great care, absorbed in every stroke. First he smoothed the locks down her back, then he swept some across her shoulder until the curls curved around the aureole of her breast. He touched the strands lightly with his fingertips all the while his gaze held hers. He teased her nipple with his thumb. Honora closed her eyes and sighed, allowing the pleasure to build, no longer ashamed or embarrassed by her desires. Brec had released her from that. She put her arms around his neck to draw him to her and fell back on the pillows. He followed her, the brush forgotten, the locked room forgotten, his harshness forgiven.

Honora always awoke alone. During the day she would catch herself daydreaming about Brec's tender touch, about how his hand strayed down to her belly, about the warmth of his lips on her breasts, about the satisfaction of being filled with him, and then the lilting, cascading pleasure. She marveled at how every time he came to her, her joy grew, and she thought he found pleasure in her arms too.

Yet, with a frown she wondered why he always left her

before the dawn. Why did he place a gentle kiss on her lips, then desert her in a silent, unhurried retreat, as if he would not go, but must not linger, as if some menace had passed in the night, and he was compelled to go in search of it—leaving her cold and alone.

A jostling of her elbow and a giggle from Brenda always brought Honora back to the world from memories of the laird's bed. With a mental shake, she smiled at the little redhead and returned to the duties of the lady of Dunrugis.

While the laird spent his day about the castle, the island and the loch, making decisions, giving directions, and issuing judgments, as was the chief's responsibility, Honora dedicated herself to supervising accounts, reviewing inventories, and adjusting routines and storage procedures.

Food had to be preserved and stocked for the winter. Herbs dried. Medicines replenished. The days of summer would pass soon enough. Supplies had to be restocked and inventories consulted.

At first Ian was reluctant to let her look at his ledgers. He seemed to consider it an encroachment on his domain and a way to impugn his honesty. Honora smoothed his feathers by asking only questions to understand expenditures and assets.

From the account books she learned that the rents paid in cattle, hides, poultry, dairy products, tallow, and bird feathers—from the outer isles, also McCloud possessions— made the clan wealthy, as well as influential.

Honora leafed through the account books, noting other assets, properties owned, income sources, and expenditures. She found herself pleased, relieved, but a little confused. Brec certainly had not married her for her dowry. The McCloud was a very rich man.

14

During the month following the wedding, Honora sensed a tempering of the servants' hostility from belligerence to cool curiosity. At moments like this in the kitchen, they even seemed genuinely interested in the changes she was making.

When she appeared with her notes on the menus and supplies, the cook and her helpers gathered round and stared over her shoulder as if they could read English. She was about to talk about the new shipment of spices they had received, when the women suddenly bobbed a curtsy and receded to the far side of the room, leaving Honora and her list deserted.

She stared at their retreat in bafflement. When the cook crossed herself, Honora finally thought to look behind her. Brec loomed in the doorway, dressed in his usual black and wearing a self-satisfied smile. Dubh, with his unblinking blue eyes, sat beside him.

"Oh, I didn't expect to see you until we visited your mother this afternoon."

Brec shifted his weight from one foot to the other like an impatient boy. Honora could see that he concealed something behind his back. "A surprise arrived for you. I knew you would want to see it right away."

"What is it?" Honora asked, unable to imagine what Brec thought she valued so highly that he would make this scene in the kitchen.

Still smiling, he brought forth a letter and spoke softly. "A galley brought it this morning. I think 'tis from Rosemary."

"A letter from Rosemary!" Honora cried, her gaze latched onto the folded, wax-sealed paper in his hand.

She'd had no word from her sisters since her arrival. And how she missed them! She wrote them regularly, often putting her thoughts on paper to help ease the loneliness that descended on her in the haunted hours before dawn after Brec left her.

Sometimes just imagining Beatrix and Rosemary safe and happy in the town house among friends made life at Dunrugis easier. Every two or three days she sealed a letter and gave it to Ian, who soberly swore that each would find its way to Edinburgh. At last she had a response.

"Aye, from Rosemary." Brec waved the letter again.

With studied control Honora wiped her trembling hands on her apron, then reached for the missive.

To her irritation, Brec slipped it beneath the plaid thrown over his shoulder. "Don't frown so, sweet soul. Let's take it into the courtyard. You can read it there without servants hanging over you."

Dubh followed them into the courtyard, where Brec offered the letter again. Honora eyed him suspiciously as she reached for it. His mocking smile softened, and he released the letter to her with no more teasing.

Under the soft, cloudy sky, Honora strolled away from her husband as she examined the outside of the letter. The seal appeared intact. Brec hadn't read her letter, though it was a husband's right. She broke the seal and unfolded the paper. The sight of Rosemary's handwriting, looped across the sheets, and punctuated with ink blotches warmed her heart, and brought a smile to her lips.

15 June 1644

Dear Sister,

Beatrix and I were so glad to learn that you reached your destination without mishap. We hope this missive finds you well and happy in your new home and with your new husband. We trust the second wedding ceremony was witnessed by the people of the Isle of Myst and they shared in the celebration of your vows. Beatrix's wedding is set for next week. Her gown is almost finished. It is covered with pearls and gold, and she looks so beautiful in it. It will be a grand affair that

155

will leave the town talking at least until the next war rumor arrives. William's family will leave for their country home as soon as the festivities are complete. Theirs is not a large estate. They are converting a guest cottage for Beatrix and William. Uncle James is planning to close the town house as soon as Beatrix is wed. He is constantly in meetings with Parliament men and Englishmen. The King's army continues to be victorious. The rumor that Montrose is in the Highlands to raise Royalist support against Argyll and General Lord Leven has dithered the Convenantors. The Earl of Rothwell continues to call at the house. He speaks of you often. Beatrix and I think he misses you and would gladly allow you victory over him in bowls if you were to return. Uncle Malcolm mopes about the house forlornly because he has no one to take to the bookstore and help with selections for the library. Lanie returned a fortnight after you left and begged to serve Beatrix and me. Reverend Crawford found a place with another household. Uncle James was furious with both of them. He permitted Lanie to remain only after Beatrix and I pleaded her case. But we no longer feel comfortable with her. She deserted one of us. We do not like to think of you alone, without someone from home to share in your new life, although we are certain your husband is taking very good care of you. Uncle James is searching for a new chaplain for you. Dear Honora, please continue to send your letters to the town house in Edinburgh, but in truth, I know not where I will be. Uncle James talks of closing down the town house but the caretaker will know where to forward the letter. Give your husband and Kenneth Dunbar our warm regards.

> We love you, Sister
> Rosemary and Beatrix

With a sigh Honora folded the letter and slipped it into her pocket with her keys. Sadness engulfed her as she suddenly realized that Beatrix's wedding had already taken place and that she had not been with her sister on that most important of all days in a woman's life. And Rosemary was left to humor two ageing bachelors who were too concerned about the war to trouble themselves over her happiness.

Brec leaned against the castle wall as Honora strolled away to read her letter. He stared blindly at the clouds drifting over the loch. When he was certain Honora was unaware of him, he turned to watch her. Solemnly he took in the play of emotion across her face and tried to guess what made her smile, what made her frown, what made her shake her head in sadness.

The sea breeze teased a chestnut tendril. Absorbed in her letter, she tucked the strand behind her ear and strolled on.

Such a commonplace gesture, yet it stirred him. Brec looked out over the loch again. Their weeks together had not disappointed him. He had discovered that as a woman Honora was as passionate as he had first suspected—all that a man could want. When he closed the bed curtains around them and took her in his arms, she was responsive and willing, inventive and vibrant. And he regretted—not for the first time—that she didn't love him.

Brec glanced back at Honora to see her folding the letter and stuffing it into her pocket. She walked toward him.

"All is well with Rosemary?" he asked.

"Aye," Honora said. "Her letter is full of plans for the wedding. And news of the war. Uncle James and Uncle Malcolm are as involved as ever in the politics. And they are looking for another chaplain. Rosemary says the Royalists under Prince Rupert are victorious again and again. Is it true the king's nephew is a warlock and his big white poodle his familiar?"

Brec suppressed a laugh. "I've never had an occasion to meet the prince, so I can't say whether he's a warlock or not. Though his success hints at some favor from a higher—or lower—power. I've heard some speculation that the English forces haven't truly pulled together yet."

"What else have you heard?" Honora asked with a skeptical smile.

"News travels and 'tis my duty as clan chief to know it," he said, gesturing toward the galleys and fishing boats in the loch. "It takes no second sight to see that by winter,

Scotland will be divided between Montrose of the Gordons and Argyll of the Campbells. Montrose will be a formidable foe. There are those who still remember his success at Huntly during the Bishops War in '39. Those men will support him. And now I hear the Irish stir, determined to fight for the Royalist cause.''

When he looked down at Honora again, she was staring at him open-mouthed. ''Then war will come here?'' she asked, disbelief on her face.

''The clouds of war are on the western horizon, milady—see?'' He pointed at the darkest and heaviest of the clouds brushing the headland's hilltops and sweeping down on them.

''On the west coast, people will suffer. I suspect some of the Irish will join Montrose. You remember Alasdair mac Colkitto? He bears no good will to the Campbells for seizing his family's island home and imprisoning his father. For a man like that the war is just the excuse he needs to land on Scots soil and take revenge.''

Brec saw Honora pale at the mention of the ruthless hero of the bloody Ulster rebellion. She shivered, whether from the cold or the threat of war, he could not say. The cold breeze fluttered her lace collar. Brec reached for the corner of his plaid and cloaked her shoulders with it. As he drew her close, she snuggled against him, taking advantage of his warmth. To his surprise, his heart gave an erratic thump and his loins quickened.

He glanced at the watchman on the tower above them and at the guard below at the sea gate. But the men took no interest in the laird and his lady.

With little encouragement she leaned against him, a frown turning down the corners of her mouth and puckering her brow. Brec wondered what troubled her so. But that didn't prevent him from taking advantage of her closeness to eye the pulse in her throat and splay his hands across her ribs, brushing against her breast.

''What are you planning? I mean about the war.''

''Planning? I plan nothing,'' Brec said, suddenly finding it difficult to concentrate on talk of war. ''Events are beyond the influence of a mere laird of the isle like myself. But we'll be safe here at Dunrugis, milady. McClouds have held Dunrugis for centuries. 'Tis no reason for that to change.

"What else did Rosemary say?" he prompted. "Is it time to send for your sister?"

"What?" Honora stared up him. A rosy blush stained her cheeks, and Brec wondered whether she had forgotten her troubles and was enjoying their embrace as much as he was.

"Didn't we agree that when Rosemary needs a home, she would come to Dunrugis?" He leaned closer and whispered. "Isn't that why you chose me over the earl?"

Annoyance and embarrassment played across her face. She pushed away from him. "I made no bargain for my sister, milaird. I married you because I took pity on you. Who else would wed the devil with a black beard and ugly knees. And that beastly dog with blue eyes."

Dubh whined and thumped his tail on the grass.

Brec laughed outright and squeezed her shoulder before releasing her.

"That's more like it, sweet soul. I'll send Kenneth for Rosemary." He kissed her lightly on the cheek, but not before he heard the jingle of tambourines and voices raised in rousing song floating to them on the sea breeze.

"Look—here comes something to put a smile on your lips." He pointed to a galley that had just rounded the headland of the loch to the north.

Honora stared out over the water. "Who are they?"

"A traveling troupe of actors with some gypsies," Brec explained with a smile. "The ferry that brought your letter this morning brought word of their arrival. We see these troupes more often now that the reformers have closed the theatres. You told me once that you missed the plays. Shall I order them to perform for us tonight?"

"You can do that? And no one will . . ."

" 'Tis my island," Brec said with another laugh. "No reformer with a dour god rules here. We shall have theatre entertainment tonight."

"We'll invite the village," Honora said with a clap of her hands. " 'Twill be the perfect opportunity to fill the Great Hall again and for the people to get to know their clan chief. You will be kind—no black scowls. You'll show them your best face."

"Why?"

"Aren't you troubled when your people and servants cross themselves in fear of you?" Exasperation filled Honora's voice.

" 'Tis always been that way. I am the dark McCloud—the one to fear."

"But why should that be so?" Honora demanded. "There's no reason to fear you. You are really very warm, quiet, and generous."

"You mean, my wife does not fear me?" Brec cast her a look of mock astonishment and stifled the urge to smile. She was doing her duty as a loyal wife, and he admired her for it.

"Well, no, not really." Honora gave a little apologetic shake of her head. "You did frighten me the first night we met. I almost believed you *were* the devil. Sometimes you are so good at playing the part . . . I mean, the way you knew exactly how many cats to burn and the way you make things appear out of thin air."

Brec nodded gravely, still resisting the smile that tugged at his lips. "But if the villagers have no fear of me, how will I make them obey? How will I win their loyalty?"

"They obeyed your brother, and they didn't fear him."

Brec's good humor vanished. "I'm not Colin."

"I know."

Did she? he wondered. Did she understand what not being charming, endearing Colin meant to him? To always be the one with the black scowl, never gifted with an easy flow of words or a friendly, beguiling smile. To be the one who loved the sea and solitude instead of councils and courts. To be the second son, whose father measured him in failure at every turn, while Colin was perfect in all ways, handsome and smiling, the right words falling effortlessly from his lips, his every deed praiseworthy—always his father's golden son and heir.

She could never know or understand the pain caused by a father's anger or by the fearful acceptance of the villagers. The people had come to expect no more of Brec than his bleak looks and silences. He had grown comfortable with that. He was safe with that. No explanations were expected, no excuses to be made. He was the dark one, the sinister one. Why change that now?

If his sudden shift of mood troubled Honora, she never revealed it. She pressed closer to him as she had before, peering up into his face, her thigh firm against the inside of his. Brec wondered whether she knew what she did to him.

"But you're no devil, Brec," she said. "Why not be *you*, Brec McCloud, a caring, generous clan chief? Let your people see you as you are."

A little shock of fear trickled down Brec's spine. He was the dark son. The blood of fairies flowed in his veins. The villagers knew it. He knew it. Why reveal more? He eyed Honora suspiciously for a moment. But she awaited his answer with only concern and honesty on her heart-shaped face.

"Say yes," she whispered. "You'll be surprised how the people will respond."

"Invite the village folk if it pleases you, milady," Brec conceded, aware that at the moment he could deny her nothing. Her nearness had brought aching needs to him— the need to touch her, to kiss her, to lie with her moving beneath him. He longed to drag her off to bed right then. But he reminded himself that he was clan chief, and a certain decorum was expected.

Brec pulled Honora a little nearer. At least he was scheduled to train with the warriors shortly. Cracking a few heads would be almost satisfying right now.

Light and laughter filled the Great Hall. Honora ordered that the rush lights be replaced with bright torches for the occasion. Ghillies had been sent to the village and grooms out into the countryside to invite all to join the laird and his lady for the performance of the gypsies and traveling troupe. No one dreamed of turning down such a fine invitation from the new lady of the castle. All were curious about the new clock. In the torchlight silver brooches flashed, and women's fresh white caps bobbed among the crowd.

Ian scurried about with a harassed look on his face. As steward he was charged with feeding the troupe and seeing to the arrangements of benches, chairs, and tables for the performance. Honora wasn't fooled by his beleaguered expression; the steward was pleased to see the Great Hall full of people again. Even Lady Margaret's face had brightened with interest when Brec and Honora told her of the evening performance.

Honora observed everything from the shadows of the passage just outside the door of the Great Hall. She wanted to be certain that all was in order, but she did not wish to be seen by the crowd until Brec escorted her to their chairs on the dais.

"Psst, Honora. Is that you?" The words came from the darkness beyond her.

Honora turned, but saw only a vague movement in the shadows.

"Honora, 'tis me," the whisper came again.

A large, cool hand grasped hers and drew her deeper into the darkness before she could register any alarm.

Honora recognized the voice, yet she couldn't recall to whom it belonged. Uncertain but unafraid, she allowed herself to be drawn beyond the light of the torches.

"I'm so glad you don't wear a cap to hide your glorious hair. Honora, you are as lovely as ever."

"Alexander?" she gasped. A swirl of astonishment dropped through her. Alexander stroked her hair before she could fend off his touch. And before she could protest, he tipped her face toward his and kissed her lightly.

" 'Tis good to see you, dear Honora."

"Alexander! How did you get here?"

"I'm an actor with this troupe," the awkward young man explained with a soft laugh as though her surprise pleased him. "I left my father in London, trading horses. I hated the business, so I ran away and joined this troupe. Here I am—an actor.

"When I heard you had married the Laird of the Isle of Myst, I was shocked. That devil McCloud hasn't hurt you, has he? I was certain your uncles would force you to marry the earl. I had to know whether you were all right. Oh, 'tis so good to see you, to hold you in my arms. Honora—"

"Alexander!" Honora pushed herself free of his embrace as anxiety crept over her. She looked over her shoulder to be sure they hadn't been seen. "I'm a married woman. What if Laird Brec recognizes you?"

"He'll never know me in costume," Alexander said, his voice as young and confident as ever. "We met only once."

Dread tightened in Honora's throat. Gradually her eyes became accustomed to the darkness, and she could see that Alexander was clothed in Elizabethan costume. High color smudged his cheeks and his lips. His fair brows were darkened. He even wore a black wig.

"Lady Honora? All is ready," Ian called.

Honora turned to see the steward standing in the shaft of light from the Great Hall, anxious lines furrowing his brow. Village folk walked between them into the hall. The air hummed as the piper filled his bag and tuned up. Ian squinted at her, as if trying to see into the darkness beyond. Hastily Honora shoved Alexander farther into the shadows.

"Aye, Ian, I'll be right there."

"Will you meet me after the performance?" Alexander whispered into her ear. "I must see you, talk to you."

"Alexander, I don't know if 'tis possible. My husband—"

"Lady Honora?"

"Aye, Ian, I'm on the way."

Shaken, Honora pressed Alexander deeper into the darkness. Besides the dread that churned inside her, Alexander brought sweet memories of happy days and pleasant hours. She knew she was courting trouble, she knew it was selfish, but she wanted to talk to him too. And she knew that Brec would never understand. "Wait for me in the courtyard, outside the kitchen door," she whispered.

"I'll be there."

Honora turned to Ian. With one hand she smoothed back her hair, using the moment to clear her mind and countenance of the turmoil Alexander's sudden appearance had stirred. She took a deep breath and stepped out of the shadows.

"I'm no' sure there are enough benches for everyone," Ian fussed as Honora approached. Despite his agitation, Honora saw the pride in the set of his shoulders. "Every soul in the village and cottar on this side of the isle is here tonight."

"Doubtless they'll all find someplace to sit," Honora

said, laying a reassuring hand on his arm. "Perhaps a few will have to stand, but they'll enjoy the performance just the same. Lady Margaret, how fine you look!"

Honora managed a smile at Brec and his mother as they appeared around the corner of the passage, walking arm in arm. Brec's mother wore a dark blue gown instead of her usual black. And she beamed with pleasure, first at her son, then at the villagers as they filed into the Great Hall.

Brec grinned broadly. Honora knew his mother's attentiveness meant much to him.

A flutter of pride in her husband's dark good looks took Honora by surprise. She looked away, suddenly reminded of her duplicity. She feared Alexander's discovery more for Brec's sake than Alexander's. She had seen Brec in pain, had seen the mask slip into place when his mother called him by his brother's name. She never wanted to be the cause of that mask's coming to Brec's face. Fervently she prayed that Alexander was right, that Brec would never recognize her former lover in face paint and costume.

"Isn't this fun, dear Honora," Lady Margaret chirped. Her blue eyes were alive with interest. She greeted a villager by name; the woman curtsied in return. "Actors and jugglers. Gypsies. Guests from the village. 'Tis just like old times."

"Aye, like old times," Brec agreed as he offered his free arm to his wife.

"Thank you, kind sir." Honora placed her hand on her husband's arm. When she looked up into his face, she caught the rare glimmer of genuine pleasure in his smile.

Honora looked away and struggled again with her guilt.

Torches burned bright in the Great Hall. Nearly all the benches were filled with villagers and cottars.

With his mother on one arm and Honora on the other, Brec entered the room. Heads turned. Faces, curious and uncertain, peered at them. He waited to see someone cross himself, but there was none of that. He suspected the presence of the two women soothed the villagers' fears. At his side Honora pinched his arm.

"Smile," she demanded in a low voice with the tone of a field general.

Brec smiled and almost laughed.

164

Hesitantly at first, the people began to applaud.

Lady Margaret waved, which encouraged more approval. The applause increased. Accustomed to silent receptions when he entered a room, Brec grew uncomfortable.

"No black scowl," his wife reminded him without looking in his direction.

Still a little uncomfortable, but now amused, Brec smiled and grandly escorted the ladies to their seats on the dais. Extra torches brightened the stage area beneath the musicians' gallery at the far end. A dais of chairs and tables awaited them at the other end. From there they had a good view of the players. Brenda, Anne, Ian, Wallace, Lady Lilias, and others crowded around the dais.

The performance began with gypsy dancers and a juggler as good as any Brec had seen in the streets of Nether-Bow or at Balmoree's party. The contortionists twisted themselves into unbelievable shapes and flipped and rolled about in ways Brec thought unnatural. He glanced at his bride, glad to see her smile and laugh, then turned to see his mother clap and cheer her appreciation. She had not called him Colin all evening.

"Kind sirs, do the back flip trick again," Lady Margaret called over the heads of the crowd. The villagers roared their approval. With bows and big smiles the contortionists obliged. Brec stared at his mother in disbelief. The distance was gone from her eyes.

"Aren't they wonderful?" she asked Brec with almost childlike glee. And he agreed.

The contortionists were followed by a singer. But the crowd soon grew restless. They enjoyed good music from their own piper and harper. So the leader of the troupe, a tall man with hair like a lion's mane introduced the play, a scene from *Romeo and Juliet*.

A respectful quiet settled over the crowd as they awaited the appearance of the actors. Brec noticed Honora's hands clasped tightly in her lap and sensed a growing unease in her.

To the skirling strains of bagpipe music, actors in fancy masked ball dress whirled about the stage, glass beads and paste jewels dazzling in the torchlight. Romeo strode onto the stage, a Montague in disguise at the Capulet masked ball. The village folk clapped and cheered his arrival.

Beside Brec, Honora succumbed to a fit of choking. He turned to see whether she needed help, but she shook her head and waved his attention away.

The actors carried on.

" 'What lady is that which doth enrich the hand of
yonder knight?'' Romeo asked of a portly actor.

" 'I know not, sir,' '' the man replied.

" 'O, she doth teach the torches to burn,' '' Romeo
said, rapture glowing in his features.

" 'It seems she hangs upon the cheek of night
Like a rich jewel in an Ethiop's ear;
Beauty too rich for use, for earth too dear!
So shows a snowy dove trooping with crows
As yonder lady o'er her fellows shows.' ''

The tall actor in Romeo's role gazed directly at Honora during his speech, then looked away over the heads of the audience. Honora sat rigid and silent, trying to watch the actors with her usual aloofness. The performance continued.

" 'The measure done, I'll watch her place of stand,
And, touching hers, make blessed my rude hand.
Did my heart love till now? forswear it, sight!
For I ne'er saw true beauty till this night.' ''

A short actor stepped forward, assuming the role of Tyberias:

" 'This, by his voice, should be a Montague—
Fetch my rapier, boy:—what, dares the slave.
Come hither, cover'd with an antic face,
To fleer and scorn at our solemnity?' ''

The tall actor—the one who had stared at Honora—swept his short cape around him in a gesture that struck Brec as one he'd seen before. The voice held a familiar note too. His interest in the play renewed, Brec scrutinized the man more closely, but found it difficult to tell much about the man's face except that the jaw was long and the lips soft and animated. He knew he had seen that jaw and those loose lips somewhere without face paint. Somewhere when the sun was shining. Anger prickled the hair on Brec's neck as he recalled who the actor was. His eyes narrowed as he peered more closely at the slender young man. As impossible as it seemed, the actor on stage—Romeo—had to be Alexander Parrish.

Brec stiffened in his chair, thoughts churning through his head. Why was the boy here? He was supposed to be in London with his father. Had Honora sent for her poet lover? All those letters she'd written and given to Ian. Had some gone to Alexander, begging him to come to her?

Or had Parrish come seeking Honora on his own? Brec had recognized in Edinburgh that the boy was besotted enough with her to do something foolish.

Brec's anger grew. Whatever the reason, he would not tolerate the presence of the boy at Dunrugis. Brec knew that Honora did not love him. He could live with that if he had to, but he would allow no other to be her lover. Fury ripped through his gut and twisted his heart. He would tolerate no faithless wife.

He scraped his chair back and sprang to his feet. With one hand he flung the table aside, sent it crashing to the stone floor. Heads turned. He towered over the crowd, over Honora, menacing like a black storm.

"Cease this!" he thundered.

15

On stage the actors froze. An absolute hush fell over the hall. The villagers turned to stare at their laird. Eyes grew round and mouths gaped.

Honora sucked in her breath. Brec glowered down at her, hovered as if prepared to swoop down in attack. She turned away, unable to meet his gaze—waiting for his anger to descend on her.

He rounded on the actors and shouted, "My lady and I would hear something besides this childish story of love."

The short actor, Tyberias, bowed toward Brec. "Aye, my lord, what can we do for you? You have but to name it. *Julius Caesar*, perhaps."

"Nay. I loathe stories of traitors. I would have the song of the devil and the faithless wife." His face darkened and his elegant brows knit as one. Honora forced herself to remain straight and still in her chair, knowing that every face in the room was turned to her and her husband.

"You must know the tale I mean," Brec went on. "Where the devil, disguised as the deceitful woman's lover, lures her away from her husband and children. He sings:

" 'I'll take you where the white lilies grow
On the banks o' Loch Fyne.' "

He went on reciting the words to the old ballad, his voice hard and cold, loud enough for all to hear, but he turned to where Honora sat.

The song told of how when the woman and her lover were but a few leagues at sea, a black storm blew up and the face of the lover became that of the devil. He towered over the poor wife like the mast of the ship, his face contorted with rage. His voice mocked her.

Brec finished:

" 'I'll take you where the white lilies grow
Beneath the sea of brine,' "

The silence grew curious and heavy in the Great Hall. Honora stared at her hands, cold and white in her lap.

"Oh, Brec," Lady Margaret protested. " 'Tis a happy time we want to have tonight. Your song is so sad and full of death. Please, sir actor, do something fun and happy for us. Something from *A Midsummer Night's Dream*."

The bewildered actor looked from Lady Margaret to Brec once more.

Brec glared at the actors on the stage for a moment

168

longer. His anger radiated to Honora, seared her, hot and throbbing. He glanced then at his mother. "Aye, do something happy, as my lady mother requests."

With that he kicked his chair aside, sent it rattling off the dais as he strode from the hall.

At last Honora allowed herself to take a breath.

Lady Margaret waved to the actors. "Go on. Bring back the juggler again. I would like to see him, please."

Subdued now, the crowd murmured in agreement.

Lady Margaret leaned across the space between them and patted Honora's arm. "Have no fear. This mood of his will pass."

Honora wished that she could be as certain.

The torches in the Great Hall flickered low. Heavy smoke curled to the curved beams above.

The actors' faces grew heavy with fatigue, but they acted with enthusiasm. The laird's anger was soon forgotten, and they played to the cheers of the crowd. Only when the actors' voices began to fail did the isle folk release them. At the first chance, Honora excused herself, took a candle from Ian, and hurried from the hall.

She had heard or seen little of the performance after Brec stormed out. The urge to follow him had been strong, but to make a hasty exit after her husband would only have fired the villagers' curiosity. All she could do was wonder where Brec had gone and what he thought. Had he locked himself in his book room? Did he think she had sent for Alexander? Would he harm the actors?

Protecting the candle flame from the draught with her hand, she climbed the spiral stairs inside the castle wall to the laird's chamber. There was no sign that Brec had been there. Skirts clutched in her hand, she rounded the corner and found the door to Brec's book room ajar. A dim light flickered inside.

Surprised to find the door open even a crack—for it had always been locked before—Honora hesitated and listened. One day she had passed the door and was startled to hear voices—Brec talking with a stranger—when she could have sworn no one had come to the castle. It had been enough to send a little tingle of fear through her.

Now she was met with silence. Releasing her skirts, she gently shoved the door open and peered in with caution.

The room was empty. Fragmented moonlight glittered through the mullioned panes of the window above the copier's desk. A candle guttered on the desk. Honora sensed from the way things lay discarded about the room that Brec had been there and left in great haste.

She stepped inside.

Clutter confronted her: pottery, feathers, strange birds and animals with shiny glass eyes that peered back at her, exotic baskets unlike the wicker baskets of the isle, and leather pouches decorated with beads, claws, and shells.

A face caught her eye. Honora jumped. An empty-eyed wood-carved mask with viciously sharpened teeth glared down at her from the wall. Releasing her pent-up breath, Honora scolded herself for being so skittish.

Beneath the window sat a long-legged copier's desk stacked with parchments, maps, an hourglass, and a box of navigator's instruments. Against another wall stood a narrow, fur-covered bed without curtains, piled high with satin-fringed pillows.

The writing desk in the room was littered with quill, paper, and sealing wax. Books lined one wall.

She was so astonished by these things that she moved about the room a second time, slowly discovering an order that was unapparent at first.

She touched the smooth marble of a bust of some ancient Greek. The replica of a galley caught her eye. The vessel was painted like the real thing and fitted with a square main sail, a rudder, and tiny oars. It resembled the toy galley Brec had been holding in the portrait painted of Colin and him.

Leaning over the bookshelves, she began to read the titles: Sir Walter Raleigh's *History of the World,* Shakespeare's *Second Folio, A Glossary of Law Terms* by Henry Spelman, Sir John Hayward's *The Life and Raigne of King Edward VI.* The poetry surprised her most: Lucan's verse and Tasso's heroic poem.

Through a narrow doorway she glimpsed a small dressing room with a wash basin and shaving accessories. This was where Brec actually lived, Honora realized. This is where

170

he came when he left their bed each night. This is where he slept and dressed, shaved, and brushed his hair. With an unexplainable need to touch his brush and the razor on the table and to fold the linen towel, she started into the alcove. She put the things to order with Lanie's voice whispering in her head of secret rooms and humpbacked monsters. She shook off the thought.

Feeling like an errant child who had stolen into a forbidden place, she returned to the shelves, making note of the strange things—all souvenirs from Brec's voyages no doubt—things the island folk would not understand. And she noticed piles of documents and records concerning clan affairs. She realized that Brec's demand for privacy had some merit.

"Oh, Brec, where are you?" Honora whispered aloud. "What are you thinking? Have you gone to find Alexander? He's just a foolish boy, Brec. You're man enough to understand that."

Remembering Alexander made Honora grab her skirts again and start back down the passage toward the Great Hall. She avoided the crowd of villagers who lingered to talk with Lady Margaret. She evaded Ian and darted through the empty kitchen lit only by the banked fire.

At the door into the laundry yard, Honora stopped. Cautiously she blew out her candle before stepping into the misty moonlight. No one was there. She could hear the sea below and the pounding of her heart in her own throat. The laundry yard was deserted. She sighed in relief. Brec wasn't there lying in wait. Even Alexander was nowhere to be seen.

For a moment Honora hoped the boy had regained his senses and seen the recklessness of the meeting they had planned. No good could come of it.

"There you are." Alexander's voice broke the dark silence.

"Oh." Honora started and nearly dropped her flameless candle.

"I'm sorry, Honora," Alexander said. "I didn't mean to frighten you. It took me some time to clean away the face paint. Here, turn so the moonlight is on your face."

He took her by the shoulders and gazed into her eyes.

"Are you all right?" Alexander demanded. "That monster hasn't hurt you, has he? I'd heard rumors of his temper, but I never expected to see him turn loose on you."

"I'm all right," Honora assured him. "I don't know where Brec went. But you must leave in the morning at the earliest opportunity. Coming to Dunrugis was hardly a wise thing to do."

"I've grown tired of doing wise things," Alexander said with a cynical laugh. "Remember my father. He filled my life with wise and prudent things. I say, why grow fat and complacent on plain porridge when life offers savory puddings?"

He squeezed Honora's shoulder and gave her a sound kiss. He tasted of face paint—and spirits, as he always had. Honora had to resist the urge to wipe his kiss from her mouth.

"You must come with me," Alexander insisted. "Let me take you away from that awful dark man. You deserve so much better."

"What could I do in your troupe?" Honora asked, trying to make Alexander see how impossible his request was, yet intrigued with the idea.

"Why, play your guitar, of course, and act. Be my Juliet."

Touched by his concern, Honora looked up at him. For a moment she could see herself on a galley, sailing away from Dunrugis with Alexander at her side, her hair blowing loose in the wind. No castle keys weighing from her sash. Her guitar slung across her shoulders. Standing beside them on the forecastle the lion-maned master of ceremonies, the laughing juggler, the dancing gypsies, and the straining contortionist. All with carefree songs on their lips.

Was freedom possible? She looked up at Alexander again. His smile brightened with the possibilities.

"Come with us, Honora," he tempted. "We travel the coast. The reformers can't keep up with us. We dance. We make people laugh and hear the music of our language. The others would be glad to have you along."

Part of her leaped at the idea of being free of Dunrugis—yet, what of Brec? Could she really turn her back on him forever? And Rosemary? She needed to keep a safe home for her sister.

Honora shook her head. Alexander had chosen his path to freedom. But as wonderful and romantic as it appeared, was the path hers?

"Nay, I am well," she said with a shake of her head. "Laird Brec treats me with all the respect and honor a lady deserves. And I have vowed to be his dutiful wife. I am flattered by your concern, Alexander."

She knew she lied a wee bit, but she said it anyway. "All is well with me, Alexander. Dunrugis is my home and Laird Brec is my husband. I'm glad you and your troupe came to entertain us. I wish you happiness and prosperity in your chosen life. But I cannot go with you."

In the moonlight and with the face paint gone, Honora could see that Alexander had matured. Lines of pain and tension were drawn where once had been the smooth, carefree planes of youth.

"You won't come with us?" The smile faded from his face, and he gazed at Honora with sorrow and disappointment.

Honora shook her head. "I'm no actress. No performer. When darkness falls, I'm partial to sleeping in a feather bed with a roof over my head."

"Aye," Alexander agreed with a rueful smile. " 'Tis true we sometimes sleep on the ground beneath the stars. And sometimes we have to scurry ahead of the reformers."

" 'Tis not for me. But I would like us to part as friends."

"Friends," Alexander said with a nod. "Forever?"

"Forever," Honora agreed. She touched his cheek with her fingers and bestowed a kiss on him. The brief affectionate gesture seemed to satisfy him.

When she stepped back from him, Honora heard a footstep on the ramparts above them. She shoved Alexander back against the wall. But it was too late. If Brec was there, he had seen them together already. Yet, the instinct to protect the boy from the man was too strong.

"Shhh," she warned. She peered through the darkness to the crest of the wall above. She could see nothing, no one. She prayed silently that she had heard only the lookout on his appointed rounds.

"Honora, if you fear him so, you must come with me," Alexander persisted with a frown.

Honora wanted him to understand. "Milaird is kind in his way. Oh, 'tis so difficult to explain. You'd better go. I think it best we say farewell now. Neither Brec nor the people of Dunrugis would understand my giving you a good-bye kiss when you sail away tomorrow."

With a final clasp of hands they parted. Honora sent Alexander away first. When she was certain that he had found his way back through the kitchen to rejoin his troupe, she left the laundry yard. And though she listened very closely, she heard no more sounds from the ramparts.

Brec parted the bed curtains, pulling them back just enough to allow the moonlight to fall across Honora's face. He stared at her features, smooth and innocent. She slept peacefully on her back, with no fear of the world, like a child. Her hand curled around the edge of her pillow. A lock of her hair fell across her throat. Brec's gaze followed the chestnut curl down to the even rise and fall of her breasts.

He was calm now. The wind had comforted him, blown away the green clouds of jealousy and brought back his reason. Sailing always restored his sanity. Yet, the possessiveness lingered.

The faint glow of the moonlight disturbed Honora. She stirred, turning away from Brec's gaze. Her eyes blinked open, and she turned back to stare up at him.

"Brec?"

"Aye?"

"Where have you been?" She sat up. He was sorry to see her toss the lock of hair over her shoulder. "I looked for you everywhere after the performance."

"Why does it matter?"

"Because I wanted you to know that I didn't send for Alexander," she said. "That's what made you angry, wasn't it? You recognized him, and you thought I sent for him."

"And you met him in secret," he accused.

"Aye," she stammered. "But only to tell him that all is well with me."

"Why would he think anything else unless you had written otherwise?" Brec wondered how she could look at him with such innocence when he had seen Alexander stare across the crowd at her with adoring eyes. "I've seen your face as you go about your duties. And at the supper table each night you are quiet and somber. You have few smiles for me or anyone else. And less laughter."

Honora stared at him. Her eyes widened, turned liquid and dark. "Have I been such sad company?"

She looked so honest, so painfully bewildered by his accusations, that Brec had to turn away.

"Alexander is only a foolish boy, Brec," she went on, her voice reaching out to him. "He has just found his freedom. It has filled his head with romantic notions. Surely you would forgive him that."

"And you?" Brec put a finger under her chin forcing her to meet his gaze. "What fills your head, milady?"

"Doing my duty," Honora answered, sincerity creasing her brow. In exasperation she shook her head at him. "No, no. My head is full of Gaelic words I'll never understand and ridiculous Celtic superstitions that are impossible to observe. It's filled with stories of fairy changelings, kelpies, ghosts, and—"

Brec put a finger to her lips to silence her. When she closed her mouth and stared up at him, he grasped the back of her neck and kissed her. He was merciless, demanding she open to him immediately. To his astonishment, she kissed back. She laced her fingers through his black hair and clung to him.

"You taste of the sea," Honora gasped when he released her. "And your hair is wet. Where have you been? The guard at the sea gate told me he had not seen you all night."

"I was sailing, but I'm here now," Brec murmured as he lowered his head to kiss her throat and tongue the hollow above her collarbone where her nightgown had come untied. Against her smooth, warm skin he whispered, "You are mine, Honora. Mine. You belong to me, not some boy who writes poetry, not to a play actor. I will not have you forget that."

Roughly he pushed her back against the pillow and

175

stripped her gown from her shoulders. He planted kisses along her white neck, her throat. He savored the smooth taste of her skin. Her quickened breathing evident beneath his lips thrilled him. He worked the gown lower, trailing kisses downward until he found her bare breast. Eagerly he took the tight coral nipple into his mouth and caressed it roughly with his tongue.

He was rewarded with Honora's gasp of pleasure. She arched against him. Relishing her movement, Brec spread his hands across her ribs and impatiently sought the other nipple. Again she gasped and stirred invitingly beneath him. He ached for her in his heart and in his loins—an ache only Honora could soothe.

He grasped her around the waist, determined to master her as no boy ever could.

He ripped Honora's gown downward, pulling back the bed covers as he did. Moonlight smoothed over the flare of her hips, planed her flat belly, and contoured her swollen breasts. When he gazed into her eyes, he saw no fear. She kicked free of her gown. He tossed it aside.

Surprised by her boldness, he watched her reach for the brooch on his shoulder and felt her tug at the tie of his shirt.

"Possess me if you will," she whispered, "but with no brooches or buckles. We need only fingers and lips."

Brec stood up and began to rid himself of his clothes, tossing them aside. Then he joined her on the bed. He took no more time to inflame her, but parted her legs and knelt between them. Her eyes were dreamy, half-closed, yet curious. They dwelt on his face first, and he wondered what she saw there. Did she see him, her husband, or her lover?

Her gaze moved lower, caressing his shoulders and chest. It slid over his belly, then brushed along his thighs. Finally her dark eyes widened as if she were both fearful and captivated by the sight of what sprung from his loins.

He touched her as she watched, invading the warm, tender flesh between her thighs. At first his fingers found her dry. Relief flowed through him. No boy possessed Honora. She was his, faithful and unafraid. Victory crowed in Brec's heart.

At his touch she gasped and closed her eyes but did not

shrink from him nor push his hand away. Patiently he stroked her, certain his knowing touch would rouse her. This time her lush heat flowed. Brec caressed her again and again until she tossed her head to the side. She reached for him, opening her arms wide. Her ragged breathing and the subtle movement of her hips quickened Brec's own passion. With a steady hand on her trembling thigh, he soothed her—and fought to control himself.

Grasping Honora about the waist, he triumphantly thrust himself into her. Sweet, satin-smooth warmth melted around him. He closed his eyes and brought his knees up, forcing her to give him deeper penetration than ever before. She yielded with an anguished gasp. He was buried in her. The hot, honeyed oblivion was marred only by the fear that he had hurt her. Brec opened his eyes to find her watching him again, her eyes dark as the nighttime sea, her silken hair fanned across the pillow, and her moist lips parted. She brushed the small of his back with her fingertips. Ripples of pleasure and need built.

Restraint deserted him. He wound his fists in her hair and covered her mouth with his. He made the possession complete—exploring her mouth with his tongue, pumping himself into her, flooding her with his passion. Her moan of pleasure released him, dropped him through elation and exhilaration. He heard his own cry of conquest and gratification torn from his chest as Honora arched beneath him, sighing in her own contentment.

When he moved to her side, he felt her lips at his throat.

"Of course I'm yours," she murmured. She tucked her head beneath his chin and rested her arm on his hip. "We've been wed too many times to allow for faithlessness."

She sighed a yawn and slept, her sweet, even breath tickling the hairs on his chest.

Brec frowned and closed his eyes, but sleep refused to come. How he wanted to believe what she said was true. That she would never be false. He had seen unfaithful wives often enough even in the simple life of the isles. High society in Edinburgh and London had no monopoly on adultery.

But as clan chief he would never allow his wife to be unfaithful.

16

Honora remembered Brec covering her body with fevered kisses once more during the night and making love to her. And she remembered his parting kiss warm on her brow, then the sound of the chamber door closing softly behind him.

This was the first time that morning had paled the laird's chamber before Brec left her. Drowsily Honora envied husbands and wives who slept side by side the entire night, familiar with the tangle of each other's sleeping position, secure in each other's embrace through sweet dreams, then enticed to morning wakefulness when the other awoke. It was an ordinary luxury Brec never intended to partake of, she decided. Honora rolled over and recalled all that had happened the night before.

Perhaps Brec had been a little rough with her at first, but she basked in the knowledge that in his anger, doubt, and suspicion, he had come to her. He had not sulked off alone to brood. He had come to her and found for himself that she awaited him in the laird's bed. With a sigh she decided that she would gladly prove her faithfulness that way again if he demanded it.

Her sleepy mind cleared slowly. The memory of Brec's lovemaking blossomed petal by petal until the encounter flourished bright and vivid. Instantly she sat up. Where was that ripped nightgown? She didn't want Brenda to find it and think ill of Brec. The scene he had made before the villagers was bad enough, but she didn't want Brenda carrying tales about how the devil laird abused his lady.

After a hasty search she found the nightgown at the foot of the bed. In the mirror she discovered Brec's mark of passion on the side of her breast. Hurriedly she dressed and looked for a place to hide the gown before Brenda arrived with breakfast.

"Well, yer smiling this morn," Brenda said, a skeptical glint in her eye when she sallied into the chamber. "Did ye have a night of pleasant dreams?"

"Um hum," Honora replied, slamming the wooden chest on the nightgown. She changed the subject. "I hope Ian and Cook are seeing to breakfast for the actors."

"Nay," Brenda said. She set the breakfast tray on the fireside table. "The troupe is gone. Ian told me that Laird Brec woke them shortly after they retired for the night. He paid them well and ordered Fergus to take them back to the coast immediately."

"He was angry?" Honora asked, realizing that Brec must have sent the actors away before he came to her.

"Ian said he was cold but civil enough. Insisted that they leave before the night was out," Brenda said.

"And I suppose the villagers are full of talk?" Honora said, sorry that her plan to build a bridge between Brec and his people had failed.

" 'Tis no less than we—they all—expected of him."

With the acting troupe and gypsies gone, life at Castle Dunrugis returned to normal, to the routine that Honora had established—for a day, at least.

Working around the resistance of the staff continued to wear on Honora, but things were becoming easier. She hummed happily to herself as she went about her duties, intentionally disregarding the curious, inquiring stares from the servants. She wondered only briefly what rumors were being whispered about Brec's show of temper in the Great Hall.

Brenda moped. She wore a long face and uttered few words—because Kenneth was gone, Honora concluded. While she could sympathize with the girl's feelings, the thought that Rosemary was on her way to Dunrugis brought light into Honora's day. With Lady Margaret's help, Honora selected the chamber she'd first slept in to be Rosemary's room. How good it would be to have her sister close.

As usual Lilias had little to say to Honora or Lady Margaret and kept to herself. Honora recalled that sometimes, at night, when she lay between sleep and wakefulness, when Brec had left her, she thought she heard the hiss of the raven lady's satin skirts in the passage. Footsteps. Whispered words. What the woman might be doing about the castle in the wee hours of the morn, Honora was unable to imagine; yet, she had sensed that Lilias was biding her time. Until what, Honora had no idea.

Brec came to the laird's chamber that night, to Honora's relief. She feared that he might withdraw from her again, but he followed her through the door into the cavernous chamber, closed the door, and began to undress her. His touch had lost its playfulness, but that had no affect on his performance. He seemed more expert than ever in the intimate ways that brought Honora to pleasure. Sated and exhausted, she fell into a deep, peaceful sleep and nearly slept through the noises outside the laird's chamber door. The furtive footsteps. The whispered voices.

Honora awoke alone and oddly alert. Through the darkness she heard the mellow chimes of the clock in the Great Hall strike two o'clock. Anxiously she listened, wondering what had aroused her. Something had—some noise, some voice. Then she heard the hiss of skirts and the hush of conniving voices outside her door.

When she turned her ear to the door in an effort to hear better, she felt warmth on Brec's side of the bed. He had only just left. Was that he in the passage? She shivered and goose bumps prickled down her arms.

Cautiously she crawled from the bed and tiptoed across the cold floor. The fire had gone out and the night was moonless. Velvet darkness wrapped around her.

She wore only a nightgown that Brec had insisted on pulling over her head when their union was complete.

" 'Twill be autumn soon, with frost on the morning air," he had whispered. Honora could still hear the smile in his voice. "I will not have my bride take a chill."

He'd tugged the gown on over her head, smoothed it down her body, and across her shoulders. He tucked her in as if she were a child, flung his arm across her and fell asleep, long and naked beside her. And she had contentedly dropped into slumber with him, longing for him to remain with her till dawn, as he had done the night before.

Now alone in the darkness, she put her ear to the door but heard nothing. Slowly, with great care, she released the latch and opened the portal a narrow crack. She saw light flicker at the far end of the passage. Voices. A woman's and then a man's. Brec's? She opened the door a little wider. The woman's voice came again. Honora left the chamber and darted barefoot down the hall toward the light. The voices grew louder, and Honora recognized them—Brec and Lilias.

Honora reached the corner and peeked around. Brec's plaid was carelessly belted about his waist and thrown over his shoulder, and he wore the loose leather shoes that Highlanders favored. He carried his sword at his side and stood with his back to Honora. She had long ago forgotten to ask why he always brought his weapon to their chamber. The castle was well-guarded.

"So this was to be the night?" Brec demanded towering over his brother's widow. "Why tonight?"

"Night for what?" Lilias asked, drawing her plaid closer and shaking her head. She wore a nightgown and her hair was loose. "I don't know what you speak of."

"Why do you tread the passages of Dunrugis in the middle of the night?"

"I told you, I—I couldn't sleep," Lilias stammered, her eyes shifting from Brec to the darkness of the passage beyond him.

"Or are you on your way to find a warmer bed?"

"And what do you mean by that?" With an offended thrust of her chin, Lilias pulled her cloak of plaid even closer.

"You know what I mean," Brec growled.

"I'm a widow," Lilias replied. "You can't expect me to go on forever without a man. Colin has been dead for nearly seven months."

"But you started this little affair long before that, didn't you? Colin knew about you and Wallace."

Wallace? Honora almost repeated the name aloud. What was Brec saying? She forgot about her cold feet and stood, one foot atop the other, and strained to hear more.

"He couldn't have known," Lilias protested, too quickly. Honora heard the widow gasp as she realized that her own words had proven her guilt.

"He knew," Brec said with certainty and bitterness in his voice. "I was ready to kill you, but my good brother wouldn't hear of it."

"You're lying," Lilias said. "He didn't know. And you wouldn't dare touch me. I'm a McDonnell."

"And my brother's wife, the woman who danced in thanksgiving at my brother's wake. All the while casting me such looks. You actually thought that when Colin died, I'd marry you, didn't you?" Brec laughed, a cruel, ironic laugh. "Did you ever tell Wallace that—that you would have willingly married me if I'd have had you?"

Lilias made no reply.

"You're on your way to Wallace, aren't you?" Brec accused, his tone quieter now. "What is the plan? How am I to die?"

Before Honora's cry of shock could escape her, a hard hand clamped over her mouth and another painfully grasped her arm. Paralyzed with fear, she stared up into Wallace's incensed countenance; his eyes narrow in his beefy face. He pressed his hand over her mouth and shook her to silence. Honora regained her presence of mind enough to struggle against him—as useless as struggling against a team of horses. He dragged her around the corner of the passage, nearly wrenching her arm from its socket.

"And look who I found listening in on this conversation," Wallace shouted. "Make a move and I'll break her neck, McCloud."

Honora saw Brec's face naked with surprise. He stared at Wallace, then Honora. And she moaned, hating herself for putting her husband at a disadvantage before his enemy.

"I missed you, Lilias," Wallace said. "When you didn't come at the appointed time, I knew something was wrong. We should have been done with this by now. Their bodies growing cold in the laird's bed."

"Whom do you plan to blame for the murder?" Brec asked, to Honora's wonderment, appearing more curious than outraged.

"You made it so easy for us, McCloud," Wallace

taunted. "Parading your anger there in the Great Hall for all to witness. So all we have to do is make it look as though you, the maddened, jealous husband finally returned to your wife's bed, cut her throat, then fell on your own sword. Lilias will write the suicide note for you, milaird. And you'll be the McCloud to lie in unhallowed ground."

Brec remained still, unsurprised, but his black eyes shone cold and Honora thought she caught a glimmer of slyness there.

"Murdering me and my wife does not assure your succession as McCloud chieftain."

Wallace said nothing.

"The families of the septs must accept you," Brec went on. "Colin had lost his faith in you, Wallace, because he knew about you and Lilias. He would never give you the leadership of the clan. Not after you slept with his wife. There are those besides me who know the truth. Will you murder them too?"

"That's what you say," Wallace countered. "Tell me why the families of the clan should trust you? A man who quarreled with his father at every turn and sailed away to sea, vowing to never return, turning his back on his clan, on his obligation as second son."

"What obligation?" Brec demanded. "To spend my life waiting in the shadows in the event my brother should die before his time? Listening to my father's unending praise of him and his eternal disapproval of me? The McCloud clan was safe in Colin's hands. At least I was honest. I made my intentions clear. Were you honest, Wallace? What were your ambitions? You knew then—I heard my father tell you when you were selected as successor upon Colin's wedding—that there was little chance you'd ever lead the clan. It was but a matter of time before an heir was born to Colin and Lilias."

Silence. Lilias looked down at the floor, then turned away.

"And when there wasn't a babe, what did you do, Lilias?" Brec went on, staring at his brother's widow.

Lilias shook her head and refused to meet Brec's gaze. No haughty pride flashed in her blue eyes now.

"You looked to someone else to father a child, didn't

you? Anything to keep your place as wife to the McCloud and most importantly as lady of Dunrugis.''

Wallace's grip on Honora tightened again. She swallowed a cry of pain, instinctively aware that it was best at this moment to remain unnoticed.

"And you, Wallace," Brec thundered. "You wanted to be chief so badly that you would betray your kinsman with his wife. And consider murder. Who made the first move? Wallace? Did you flatter her? Did you touch her and make promises? Or did she come to you? I don't care. It doesn't matter. You're both traitors!"

Wallace made a noise like a snarl. He threw Honora against the wall and drew his sword.

"I'll not be called a traitor by the likes of you," Wallace shouted. "A man who deserts his clan to sail with pirates and trade in God knows what."

A wee smile of pleasure and victory formed on Brec's lips, and with deliberation he raised his broadsword. Honora knew that at last Wallace had done exactly what Brec wanted.

Rush light gleamed off the two naked blades. Honora had seen the two—cousins—train in the gun yard. Each was skillful and able. Each stood firm with his feet braced, his knees bent, the hilt of the heavy swords clasped in both hands, the knuckles gone tight and white. Their gazes locked.

Honora pressed herself against the wall, wondering how these men could wield the great two-handed *claidheamh mor* in so narrow a space. The wide, sharp blades could do terrible damage—slice flesh, break bones, lop off limbs. What if Brec was hurt? Honora's stomach turned over, and her knees went weak.

At the other end of the passage, Lilias, too, pressed herself against the wall, her face now gone as pale as her hair.

"The victor rules the clan and the Isle of Myst," Wallace declared.

"The loser is banished," Brec vowed.

17

Wallace struck the first blow. Sword rang against sword. Brec parried, the muscles of his arms and shoulders bulging to absorb the impact. Swiftly he returned the attack with powerful strokes, driving Wallace backward. To stop the advance, the master at arms brought round a lateral swipe that forced Brec into retreat. Wallace charged again, regaining the distance he'd lost.

Brec gave ground, falling back around the corner near where Honora had retreated when Wallace released her. She could hardly believe that Brec would let Wallace get the best of him so early in the fight.

Wallace hesitated. Suspicion was etched across his face. Perspiration glistened on his bare arms. The hem of his kilt swayed as he balanced on his feet, ready for the next attack.

Brec's brows were knit and his face tight with concentration. Sweat beaded on his brow. A lock of black hair dropped across his forehead.

A sick feeling lurched in the pit of Honora's stomach. Her mind chanted a fervent prayer for her husband's safety. Wallace was dressed to do battle. Brec wasn't. She wished that Kenneth were here before she realized that that was exactly why Wallace and Lilias had chosen this time to strike. Images danced through her head. Wallace menacing at the sea gate. Wallace drunk at the wedding. The glimpse of Lilias's monstrous pride in being lady of the castle as they viewed Colin's portrait. Had Brec known all along that these two plotted to murder them both? She wondered whom she could go to; who would help Brec— Brenda? Ian? Who in the guards could be trusted to follow their chief? Who would follow their master?

185

Brec launched another attack. Wallace parried. The great swords met and locked, crossed in the light above their heads. The two men strained against their weapons. At last Wallace gasped and broke away. Metal sang against metal. Sparks flew. Wallace sprang back. Brec's sword sliced through the air to clang against the floor. Wallace stood just beyond the blade. His labored breathing filled the silence.

Brec backed away. His eyes glittered black and his gaze never wavered from his kinsman.

Wallace grimaced with anxiety. He took a hand from his sword to wipe away the sweat dripping from his brow.

Brec's eyes narrowed. What did he watch for? Honora wondered. The twitch of a muscle? The feint of a glance?

Without warning, Wallace swung again. The sword arced over their heads and descended against Brec's blade. With a powerful thrust, the laird of the McClouds threw off the blow. Brec advanced on Wallace. The former clan successor staggered backward. Brec attacked again. Wallace blocked the onslaught. Blades grated against stone. Sparks flashed. Wallace stumbled backward, then recovered his balance, raising his blade in defense once more.

Tension thickened the air. Honora could hardly breathe. When she glanced down the passage, she saw that Lilias remained flattened against the wall.

Brec came even with Honora, Wallace to her right.

The master of the guard screeched a war cry and swung his weapon wildly. The blade whisked through the air. Honora felt the breath of the metal's edge. She winced away from the blade. Something tugged on her sleeve. She looked down to see her gown ripped, a thin red line slit her upper arm.

She felt nothing. But as she watched, beads of blood pearled along the red streak. Bewildered, Honora clasped her hand over the gash and looked up at the two men.

They stared at her, the stillness palpable. Slowly Brec turned on Wallace, who met his gaze reluctantly. Neither man moved.

Rage roared forth from the laird. Fury filled the air. Overhead the castle timbers shook.

Anger contorted Brec's face. His size seemed to grow with the sound of his bellow.

Wallace stepped back. Color drained from his face.

Lilias screamed, but never moved from her place near the passage wall.

Brec's sword clanged to the floor. Though Wallace was nearly as large as Brec, he was no hero. He began to step backwards, terror fixed on his face. He obviously thought his end was near. Too late, he dropped his sword and turned to run. Swifter than lightning, Brec grabbed his kinsman by the belt and swung the man around, bashing him into the stone wall.

With a thud Wallace's shoulder struck first. He bounced off and staggered, still miraculously on his feet. He thrashed his arms in a feeble effort against Brec.

Brec yanked the man around. "Not Honora. No one touches my wife!" he shouted in Wallace's face. "Cut my throat if you can, you fool, but do not harm Honora!"

Brec hurled Wallace against the wall once more. Wallace's head thumped against the stone and snapped back sickeningly. His eyes rolled in his head. His knees buckled, and he began to slide downward. Only Brec's hand on Wallace's belt kept the man on his feet.

Lilias screamed, her hands clutching protectively at her throat, but she did not reach out to aid her lover.

Honora would allow no more. She grasped Brec's arm. "Enough, Brec. No more. I'm all right."

He dragged Wallace from the wall and started to slam the man against the stones once more.

Honora pulled at his arm again.

"Brec, 'tis only a scratch. Wallace didn't mean it. Don't do this. No more, I say."

Brec turned to her, a look of fury mixed with remoteness on his dark features. He braced a slumping Wallace against the wall.

Honora stared him down, refusing to let his wrath frighten her. " 'Tis only a scratch," she repeated. To prove her words, she removed her hand from the injury. "Release your kinsman, Brec. Don't shed clan blood."

Brec paused. He studied her face almost as if he didn't recognize her. Honora forced calmness into her expression. "I'm all right. Wallace is defeated."

Grudgingly Brec released his foe's belt. The former clan

successor clung to the wall, his senses returning enough to make him cast Brec a wild-eyed look of terror. When Brec turned his back, Wallace hastily edged his way beyond Brec's reach.

Honora glimpsed others standing in the darkness beyond the reach of the rush light. Fergus, Kenneth's friend, was there. Satisfied that Wallace could not go far, Honora leaned against the wall and uttered a prayer of thanks for Brec's safety.

Brec raked his hair back from his forehead. The red haze of anger began to clear. He stared again at Honora's hand clutched over the wound in her arm. Roughly he pulled her hand free to examine the cut. He saw little blood, but his heart thumped angrily. He wished he'd killed Wallace for this injury to Honora—and for other insults as well.

Slowly he became aware of the paleness of her skin, and he saw the fear and anxiety now in her face. Gently he touched the elegant peak of her hairline to assure himself that she was genuine, that she was safe. Then he fell willingly into the clear depths of her sea-green eyes. In this nightmare of murder plots and war intrigue, she had become his only anchor. He heaved a heavy sigh from his gut. Just looking at Honora brought calmness, steadied his hands, and ordered his thoughts.

"Where is your serving woman?" he demanded. He looked down the passage where he could hear the movement of people. "Brenda? Are you there? See to your lady. Immediately."

In nightgown and shawl, Brenda scurried from the darkness.

"What are you going to do about them?" Honora asked, shrugging away from Brenda. "Did they really . . . I mean, while Colin was alive?"

"Aye," Brec said. He turned to look at Lilias. Down the passage the other way, Fergus stood with Wallace. "You are both banished. Tomorrow, both of you will leave Dunrugis forever."

"You can't banish me!" Lilias shrieked. "I won't go." Her fingertips trembled on her lips, and angry tears trickled down her cheeks. Nevertheless, she held her head high. "I won't be sent home in shame like some handfasted bride. I'm Colin McCloud's widow. I have rights."

"One of those rights is to return to your family," Brec said with rational evenness. His temper was in hand now, and the coolness of power swept over him. He had never liked Lilias, not since she had flirted with him on her wedding day. How his brother could have had any affection for this coldhearted, self-absorbed, ambitious creature was a puzzle to Brec. "There are no heirs, Lilias. No reason for you to stay. I won't have you at Dunrugis any longer."

He watched Lilias wipe the tears from her face with the back of her hand. Her lips trembled, but her eyes shone with anger. "Then I choose to be returned home, to Armadean. No hospitality is offered me here.' She shook a warning finger at Brec. "My father will be offended. This could mean a renewal of the feud."

"Don't threaten me with a feud, Lilias, unless you're ready to have your father learn what kind of wife you were," Brec said. "You sail on the morning tide. See her on her way, Fergus."

A dazed Wallace was hauled away by guards. Lilias and Ellen were escorted by Fergus. Brec turned back to Honora.

"Why didn't you stay in bed like any sensible woman would," he scolded. He looked her up and down, uneasy about the way she stared at him, pale and wide-eyed. Was she going to faint? "Woman, you wear no shoes."

That gave him the perfect reason to hold her. He picked her up, for she weighed nothing—even less than when she had first come to the isle. He carried her down the passage and into the laird's chamber, where he sat her down on the bed.

"Brenda," he bellowed, angered that the lass was nowhere about.

"I'm right here, Milaird," Brenda said at his side.

" 'Tis only a scratch," Honora protested, her voice weak.

Brec ignored her and ripped away the sleeve of the gown to see for himself. Relief washed over him when he saw that what she said was true. He never allowed himself to think of how bad the injury might have been. Brenda still hovered at his side. "What are you going to do?" he demanded.

"Clean it and bind it, if milaird will permit me."

"Be quick. Your lady needs rest," Brec declared, eager to be alone with his wife, anxious to touch Honora and be reassured that she hadn't been seriously harmed.

Brec paced to the fireplace and back to the bed.

"Please sit down, Brec," Honora said, her voice stronger now. "Your pacing disturbs me."

The edge in her voice was Brec's first warning. Uneasily he glanced at her again to read her face. She might be an innocent, but she was no fool. He would have questions to answer after this. He tried to sit but could not. Glimpses of the battle came back to him: the hatred on Wallace's face, the disdain on Lilias's, the danger Honora had been in.

"I'm going now, milaird," Brenda said gathering up the cloths and rags used to clean and bind Honora's injury. She gave Brec a curtsy, and she cast a worried look at her lady before she closed the door on her way out.

Honora's injury began to make itself known. The dull throb grew, reaching down toward her elbow, and stretching up into her shoulder, but she dismissed the pain. She waited only until the door closed behind Brenda before she began her questions.

"You knew all this time of Lilias and Wallace? And you said nothing about it to me?" she accused. Strange feelings of betrayal and anger settled over her, leaving her empty, weak, yet longing to punch the feathers from her pillow. She didn't bother to look at Brec.

When he didn't answer, she went on to speak her mind. "All I ask from you, sir, is honesty. You can surely grant me that."

"I saw no need to trouble you over this." Brec roamed from the fireplace to the window and back again, avoiding her eyes. "If you had stayed in bed like any sensible woman, you would've been safe."

"Don't treat me as if I'm to blame for what happened," Honora warned. The throb in her arm bloomed, picking up tempo, and leaving her in no mood to accept slippery answers. Her head came up. "Look at me."

Reluctantly Brec obeyed, his expression quiet, his dark eyes honest.

"Did you know they were plotting murder?"

Brec turned away again before answering. "I knew it was possible. That's why I ordered Brenda to stay with you before the wedding. And after, if you recall, I never left you alone a single night. Not until I was certain the danger had passed."

Honora gave a dispirited sigh. Of course, that's why he spent every night with her—for her protection—not because he wanted to hold her in his arms, not because he shared her pleasure. Because it was his duty to defend his wife. The painful throbbing in her shoulder spread to her head and her heart. Dry eyed, she stared at the floor.

"So you married me to thwart Wallace and Lilias." Honora's anger deserted her before the onslaught of pain.

"I married you because that's what I wanted," Brec said without turning to her. "I married you to bring a lady to Dunrugis, and to have a worthy heir. We talked of all those things in Edinburgh."

"You married me to revenge Lilia's unfaithfulness to your brother," she accused.

His gaze remained on the cold fireplace, his silence his admission.

"I understand being married for my position, for my family name and my dowry, even for my skills as hostess and household mistress. Those are accomplishments I can at least take pride in. But to be married to serve as a means of vengeance . . ."

Brec kicked at the dead coals of the fireplace. "There were many reasons why it was right for us to wed, Honora. Thwarting Lilias was only a small part of it. A very small part."

"And to think I'm bringing Rosemary into this," Honora muttered, more to herself than Brec. She wondered whether there was some way to prevent Rosemary from coming, but she knew it was too late. Kenneth was already on his way to bring her sister to Dunrugis.

"You and Rosemary are safe here," Brec said to the hearth. "I swear it. You have always been safe here, and you will continue to live here in safety and without fear."

At last he turned and started across the room toward her. "Let's go to bed now and get some rest."

She stared up at him, finally comprehending that he intended to remain with her. She shook her head. "Oh, no, milaird. I've done my wifely duty every night that you've come to me. And every night you protected me. Now the danger has passed. You have done your duty, and I have done mine. Don't ask any more of me."

"The arrival of Lady Rosemary has put a smile back on milady's face," Brenda said, watching Kenneth grimace as he lowered himself gingerly to the kitchen bench. His discomfort troubled her despite the vow she had made to harden her heart against the man who had slipped away into the forest with Lady Lilias—like a common sailor.

He groaned as he settled on the bench.

" 'Twas a hard trip then?" she asked, relenting a little and favoring him with a bit of a smile. "I'll draw that ale for ye right now."

" 'Twasn't the trip that was difficult," Kenneth replied when Brenda returned with the ale. He was rubbing his lower back. " 'Twas the baggage, the boxes of Lady Rosemary's rocks."

"Rocks?"

"Aye, they be her fancy," Kenneth said, his eyes fastened on the flagon of ale that Brenda carried. "Oh, lassie, how I've missed Dunrugis ale."

"Is that all ye missed, then?"

Kenneth grinned. "No, 'tis not all I've missed, lass, I promise ye. But 'tis all I can partake of at midday in the kitchen."

Unwillingly Brenda grinned and handed the flagon to her favorite master of arms. He immediately put it to his lips and tipped it up to take in a long draught. Brenda sat down beside him and waited for the satisfied smack of his lips.

"So, tell me about Lady Rosemary's rocks," Brenda asked, curious about the castle's newest resident. "Lady Honora has been awaiting her arrival. She set the bedchamber to rights. Sorted out the best linens. Talked of going for walks about the isle with her sister. Are they very much alike?"

"Nay," Kenneth said. "Lady Rosemary is a fair enough lass. I like the lady, but this fancy she has for rocks is madness. She is no' practical like Lady Honora. She even made us stop early one day on the shores of Loch Lomond so she could search out a rock for her hoard. But she has a good heart like her sister. Ye'll like her, I think."

That was no surprise to Brenda. She watched Kenneth take another long draught of ale and wondered what he had heard about the events that took place while he was away. She wondered if he would miss Lady Lilias.

"So, did the banishment of Wallace and Lady Lilias surprise ye?" she asked, her finger tracing the wood grain of the kitchen table before her.

"The only thing that surprised me was that Laird Brec never slayed the traitor on the spot." Kenneth frowned and studied his flagon. "The truth be that we knew they plotted from the beginning. Even on the day of the wedding, Simon amused Wallace and I diverted Lady Lilias to keep them from causing mischief. Now, donna look at me like that, lass."

"Like what?"

"Like ye want to scratch out me eyes."

Kenneth put an arm across Brenda's shoulders, but she turned away. His mention of the wedding made her jealousy suddenly flourish afresh, green and crisp. She did not trust herself to speak.

" 'Twas but a duty I did that night, lass, no more," Kenneth whispered in her ear. "I swear it. 'Twas no pleasure neither. The lady drinks like a fish. I matched her drink for drink but I regretted it later."

His breath tingled in her ear and her anger wilted a little, but still she said nothing and was sorry when Kenneth took his arm away and went on.

"Then Brec and I thought they would make their move when I left to get Lady Rosemary. I wanted to wait for them, but Laird Brec said I should go. That he was ready. That he could handle them. And he did. But I hear Lady Honora was hurt."

"Aye, 'twas only a scratch and is nearly healed already. Ye know, Lady Honora stopped the laird from striking down his cousin," Brenda said, still awed by her lady's courage.

" 'Twas kind of the lady, but it were a mistake," Kenneth said before taking another swallow of ale. "Did any of the guards choose to join Wallace? Did he make trouble when he left? I'm afraid that one might turn up again."

"A fine scene, their banishment," Brenda said, the event still clear in her mind. Her jealousy faded at the prospect of repeating the story to Kenneth. "We watched it all from the laundry yard—Lady Honora, Ian, and I. The wind carried their words straight to us."

"So tell me what happened, lassie. Donna keep me in the dark. Not now, anyway."

Eagerly Brenda leaned an elbow on the table, faced Kenneth, and began:

" 'Twas an overcast morn, the hills beyond the loch hiding in the mist. Laird Brec had the guards bring Wallace to the quay beyond the sea gate. The traitor was all wrapped up in his McCloud plaid and wore his battle gear and carried his targe. One side of his face was black and blue. But he looked bonny, a smile on his face. Always were a handsome man, Wallace."

Kenneth mumbled something and fidgeted on the bench.

"What say ye?"

Kenneth frowned at her. "Nothing, lass. Get on with yer tale."

"Well, I say Wallace is a fine-looking man. A fact is a fact."

"Umph!"

"So, Laird Brec reminds Wallace that he is banished, never to return to the Isle of Myst again—or suffer death. And Wallace only laughs and waves to the guards on the ramparts—men who answered to his command once. 'Who would go with me?' he calls. And while he waits for the answer, Fergus brings Lady Lilias to the quay. Ellen be with her. Both dressed in the McDonnell plaid. Can ye believe that? The McDonnell plaid?"

Kenneth muttered something more and shook his head.

"What was that?"

"Tell yer story," he snapped.

"So not a one of the guards agrees to go with Wallace,

them that was his own men once. Then ye can see this canny smile come over Laird Brec's face. He turns to Lady Lilias. 'Donna ye want to go with yer lover, Lilias?' the laird asks. And the lady quickly steps away from Wallace, like the man carries the plague.

'Why would I go anywhere with a banished man, one who has no place in the world?' the lady inquires, holding that chin of hers higher than her nose. Says she, 'I return to my family's holding, Armadean. I will be lady of the castle there. And my father will be angry over this insult. Ye'll see, McCloud,' she says. 'Beware of the feud.' Then she twitches that plaid at Laird Brec and marches aboard the galley and sails away.''

"And Wallace?" Kenneth asked, as if he had no concern about Lady Lilias, Brenda noted.

"He put back his shoulders and carried his head high. He was no' humble like a man who has been defeated and insulted. Like a man banished from his family's home. He sailed off in the wee fishing boat he was given with never a look behind him.''

"So, after all the talk that Brec murdered Colin, I was afraid some of the guards might follow Wallace." Kenneth shook his head in mild surprise. "Brec told me he had faith in their loyalty to the McClouds, and he was right.''

Brenda bit her lip, ill at ease with Kenneth's admission to the murder rumors. She was a little ashamed of her own suspicions, yet she found herself defending those who spoke against the laird. "You must admit that Laird Colin's death was peculiar, and came so soon after he named his brother as successor.''

"But no one has proved Laird Colin's death was anything but an accident, as Laird Brec said," Kenneth added.

"True enough," Brenda agreed. She studied the man next to her closely as she asked, "Kenneth, did ye know that Lady Lilias was sleeping with Wallace?''

"Nay," Kenneth replied without hesitation. "Not until after Laird Colin died. Then Brec told me.''

"What about Lady Margaret? She and Lady Lilias never liked each other. What did she know of Wallace and Lilias?''

Kenneth lowered his voice and leaned toward Brenda,

his shoulder rubbing against hers. She was so conscious of the warm firmness of him against her that she almost forgot to listen.

"If Lady Margaret knew, she will never admit that Colin was betrayed. Or perhaps she has forgotten by now, poor soul." Kenneth said, jostling her arm roughly now. "Where's yer flagon of ale, lass? We've a toast to make."

"What?" Puzzled, Brenda stared at Kenneth.

"Get yerself some ale."

"Aye, sir. I draw it like so. There. Now, what do we drink to?"

"Wallace and Lilias," Kenneth proclaimed, standing and holding his flagon aloft. "To their banishment and good riddance."

"Aye, good riddance," Brenda cheered. She drank to that willing enough and downed half her brimming flagon. Instantly the ale's warmth seeped into her limbs and brought a lightness to her head. She could hardly believe her good fortune. Lilias was gone, had been no more than a duty, and Kenneth was back.

"So 'tis peaceful now?" he asked when they were settled on the kitchen bench again and he had slipped an arm around her once more.

"Aye, but for the feud. Laird Brec has sent out warnings to the other isles, especially Solnarra, the isle that was part of Lady Lilias's dowry. He expects the return of the feud."

"That must account for Brec's foul mood. He's wearing a face as long as a horse's."

"May be or may be something else," Brenda said, leaning close to Kenneth's ear, taking pleasure in the pressure of his thigh against hers on the bench. "Or may be the reason for the laird's long face and foul temper is that he has no' set foot in the laird's bedchamber since the night of the duel with Wallace."

Kenneth stared back at her with raised brows. "That must be a fortnight ago now."

Brenda nodded. "They talk to each other at supper time, and he shows her every courtesy, but each night she retires alone and the laird remains in the Great Hall to drink. Sometimes he just disappears. Fergus claims to have spied him out sailing at night. I thought theirs was a love match. We all did. Do ye know?"

Kenneth shook his head and looked genuinely mystified. "I'm no' certain, lass. Truly. I donna know."

Brec sat at the supper table in the Great Hall, awaiting the appearance of Honora and her sister, Rosemary—all the while drowning his feelings of foolishness in ale.

When Colin had made Brec promise to bring a lady to Dunrugis, it had seemed such a small, but justifiable vengeance to take on Lilias. They knew Lilias would suffer the only kind of pain that she was capable of experiencing when she was forced to give up the castle keys to another. Brec admitted to himself that he had taken childish and cruel pleasure in all of it.

And Honora had looked so deliciously beautiful on their wedding day in that emerald and sapphire necklace that Lilias had never been offered. Though Lilias's envy and indignation had been gratifying, vengeance had been the last thing on Brec's mind when he exchanged vows with Honora in St. Michael's abbey. Somehow he suspected that Honora would never believe that.

The problem he and Colin had neglected to anticipate was the new lady's feelings—Honora's cold displeasure. Brec was learning the hard way that it was more difficult to foresee the reaction of a true, genuine woman than it was to frustrate a selfish, shell of a female. While his victory appeased his desire for vengeance, his loss of Honora's good faith hardly seemed worth the price.

Brec took a dry gulp from his flagon, then stared at it, perplexed. To confirm his growing suspicion, he turned it upside down; a single drop of ale splashed onto the table. The cursed thing was empty already, and he wasn't nearly as numb as he wanted to be. Briefly he considered drinking something stronger, then decided against it. Ale would be good enough company for the long, lonely evening that stretched out before him.

He had seen Honora smile for the first time in a week when Rosemary had arrived that morning. While her happiness pleased him, he knew her smile changed nothing between them. Duty was all they had now, Brec reminded himself.

Duty. He had always disliked the word. A joyless charge, and prideful. When Honora had spoken of it after the duel, the sound of the word had bitten deep, like a blade plunged near to Brec's heart. He had been a victim of duty more than once, and he had always resented it.

A nudge at his knee made him peer below the table to find Dubh there, the dog's blue eyes quiet and consoling.

"You asked too much of me, brother," he muttered, losing himself in the cur's forthright scrutiny that sometimes reminded him of Colin.

From the beginning, Brec had known that Honora didn't love him. And he had spent hours every night with her to protect her and to ensure the eventual birth of a McCloud heir. That was his duty as her husband. What he was reluctant to admit was that he had touched her with more than duty in his heart, and she had responded with such openness and warmth.

Was it duty that made her straddle him one night and wantonly offer him her breasts, the pink buds hard and tight? The curly hair of her thatch tickled his belly, and her heated moistness kissed his navel. No duty made him cup her smooth bottom in his hands and accept her offering. Had duty made her gasp with pleasure when his lips closed on those buds?

The sound of ladies' voices at the door to the hall shook Brec free of the provoking image. With pleasure he accepted his sister-in-law's kiss on the cheek. His wife merely gave him her hand. As soon as the ladies were seated, Brec forced himself to listen to what Kenneth was telling Fergus about the English Civil War.

Something about a Royalist defeat—at last. The significance of the event hauled Brec away from his glum thoughts.

"Did you say Leven and Fairfax defeated Prince Rupert at Marston Moor?" he demanded across the supper table disregarding Honora's look of irritation. He knew she wanted no talk of the war at her table, but he needed to know Kenneth's information to confirm what he had gleaned from his other sources.

"By your leave, my ladies," Kenneth apologized and turned to his laird. "Aye, Prince Rupert was defeated by Scots with the help of Cromwell and Manchester."

"Go on," Brec prompted.

"They say 'twas Cromwell's forces—the new Model Army, he calls it—that turned the tide against Prince Rupert. Only the Earl of Manchester's influence kept the Parliamentarians from overrunning the king's forces. The talk in the ranks was that Cromwell would take blood reprisals if given a free hand in pursuing the king's troops. Some speak of this being the turning point of the war. The future looks grim for King Charles."

"Do you think King Charles will give up or flee?" Rosemary asked. "His queen has gone to France to seek safety. Montrose and his army are now his only hope."

"Has the queen gone for safety or to raise money?" Brec asked. "I think the king will stay like a good ship's captain. What do your uncles say the Marquis of Montrose is doing, Rosemary?"

"They believe he has taken his Lieutenant-General commission and gone into the Highlands to gather the clans loyal to the king. But Uncle James says Argyll is confident that the Gordons and others will never support Montrose."

Brec saw Honora cast a frown at her sister. "When did you take up politics, Rosemary?"

" 'Tis all they talk of in Uncle James' house these days," Rosemary said with a girlish shrug. "Even William, Beatrix's husband, talks of little else."

"Here too," Lady Margaret agreed, leaning toward Rosemary, as if to speak in confidence. "The English and the McDonnells. War, war, war. Parliaments, kings, kirk, and reformers. We ladies are left to tend to the real business of the world. Do you like to garden, Lady Rosemary?"

"Aye, I do," Rosemary said. "I look forward to seeing your garden here at Dunrugis."

Brec leaned back in his chair and waved the women's chatter aside. "Montrose will find support among the Highlanders. "I've no doubt of it. If not for the king's cause, then against Argyll and his Campbell clan."

Kenneth nodded in agreement and reached for another piece of roast fowl.

"And will you join Montrose?" Rosemary asked. "There is much talk in Edinburgh of the strength of the Isle clans. Of experienced fighting men, they say. Men loyal to King Charles. And you have swift galleys that sail circles around English vessels. An army like that could turn the tide for the king."

"We prepare for winter here, sweet sister-in-law, not war, against Parliament and Scots or against the king," Brec replied.

"If ever there was a time when the king needed the power of the lairds of the isles, 'tis now," Kenneth said without meeting Brec's gaze. "What if Montrose comes to us?"

"Do you expect him to?" Brec asked.

"He might send one of his collaborators. Then what? 'Twas a time I remember, only a wee bit ago, when ye would've supported anyone against the Argyll cause."

"What is this, Kenneth?" Brec exclaimed. He tossed his head back and laughed. "Tonight *you* are devil's advocate?"

"Perhaps, milaird," Kenneth said. "Would ye join Montrose and the Highland and Isle clans against the Scots and the English parliament to get at Argyll? And ye with a wife whose family supports the Covenantors, Argyll and his Campbell clan."

"When Montrose comes to ask for McCloud support, I will consider his proposal," Brec promised. "Until then . . ."

Brec held up his flagon in salute. "I offer a toast to Lady Rosemary, our guest. Our kinswoman. Welcome to Dunrugis."

Lady Margaret raised her cup. "May you find happiness on the shores of the Isle of Myst, my dear."

Surprise brightened Rosemary's eyes and a blush stained her cheeks. "I'm sure I will, milady."

With Rosemary for company, Honora gladly put aside her troubled thoughts about Brec, Wallace, and Lilias. Brec had made no attempt to join her in the laird's bed since the duel. She remained unsure of how she felt about his absence.

But one night just before Rosemary's arrival Honora had

awakened suddenly with the certain knowledge that someone was in the room. The night was moonless, and beyond
the chamber she could hear the pounding of the surf against
the rocks.

"Who's there?" she called out and sat up in bed.
Through a narrow opening in the bed curtains, she could
see only a small portion of the room lit by the peat fire.

" 'Tis only me, sweet soul." Brec's shadowed form,
large and broad, darkened the opening. He parted the curtains and sat down on the edge of the bed.

She could smell ale on him and something fresh and
tangy—the sea. She touched Brec's arm and felt the cool
droplets of sea spray on her hand. In the dim light she
could see that the lines of strain in his face had grown
deeper over the past week. She had overheard him sending
out messages of warning about the McDonnells, and she
had seen the guards making preparations around the castle.

"Where have you been? Is something wrong, milaird?"

"I would see your arm," he said without making a move
to touch her.

" 'Tis all right."

"I would see for myself."

Sleepily and without much concern, Honora untied the
ribbons of her gown and slipped it from her shoulder.

"See, milaird, 'tis so well healed that Brenda took the
binding off just today," she said. "Can you see? There is
so little light."

"I need no more light." He knelt beside the bed and
reached for her shoulder. Though his fingers traced lightly
along the scar, barely touching her skin, his warmth tingled
through Honora, finally bringing her fully awake and making her conscious of what Brec's presence in the laird's
chamber meant. Goose bumps raised along her shoulder,
and her belly gave a strange hollow drop. She wondered
whether he intended to stay with her. She studied his shadowed face and wondered whether she wanted him to.

"You're chilled," he said, quickly drawing her gown
over her shoulder. He fumbled with the ribbons for a
minute before giving up in frustration. "Here, tie these."

He rose and paced the room while Honora tied her gown.

"I've had word from Kenneth," he said as he crossed

the chamber again. "He and Rosemary are well and safe. They will arrive tomorrow."

"Tomorrow?"

"Aye, tomorrow," he repeated brusquely and left, softly closing the door behind him.

The days following Rosemary's arrival passed quickly. They unpacked Rosemary's things, trunk after trunk. They ate the sweetmeats—Honora's favorite marchpanes, which Rosemary brought for her from their favorite shop in Edinburgh. And they explored the castle. Lady Margaret joined them sometimes. One afternoon she invited Rosemary to her garden.

Honora bit her lip and followed the two to the door of the garden. She hadn't had an opportunity to prepare Rosemary for the neglected flower beds.

"Oh, my," Rosemary exclaimed when she entered the wild, overgrown garden with Lady Margaret. "How lovely this is! You say you planted it yourself? What a fine design and wonderful choices in flowers. Fuchsia does so well here in the isles. I see the weeds have gotten a little ahead of you. Here . . ."

Before Honora realized what had happened, her sister and Lady Margaret knelt down and busied themselves with weeding the herbs. Rosemary pointed out where she wished to put her round white crystal rock brought along from the shores of Loch Lomond. Lady Margaret agreed and asked what other rocks Rosemary would like to put in her garden. The two wandered off, deep in conversation, their easy friendship more than Honora had dared hope for.

Supper that evening was interrupted when Ian—agitated beyond anything Honora had seen in the past—burst into the Great Hall. His thinning hair had been brushed awry in some hurried activity, and his shoulders were hunched in a posture of urgency.

"Milaird. Oh, my laird," Ian stammered as he scurried the length of the hall to the head table. He began to wring his hands. "A galley has arrived from one of the outer isles."

"Is there trouble, Ian?"

"Milaird?"

Brec rose from his chair, his voice harsh with impatience. "Out with it, man."

"The McDonnells raided the McClennons of Solnarra, milaird." Ian looked over his shoulder as if expecting sword-slinging McDonnell warriors to charge into the hall that very moment. "The McClennon galley brings the injured. Some men. Women and children."

"Oh, no," Lady Margaret gasped. She pressed a hand against her heart. " 'Tis the feud again. Sooner than I expected."

Honora started out of her chair. She loathed feuding. The practice was nearly dead in the east, Lothian and Fife, where she had been born and raised. Boundary disputes and clan conflicts were more often settled in English-like courts. Whether she approved of feuding or not, she knew what to do. "Send for Oleen. And Father Andrew," she ordered.

Kenneth nodded. "Fergus, put the guard on alert."

"How many aboard?" Brec demanded.

"A dozen or more," Ian said. "Most of them injured." Lady Margaret groaned.

"Is the McClennon with them?" Brec asked.

"Nay," Ian said. "He remained to defend the isle but sent his wife and some bairns."

"Clear away the tables and bring the children in here," Honora directed. "Put more peat on that fire. I'll have no sick children sleeping in a cold room in my castle."

Brec spun around, an expression of surprise and approval on his face. Honora glimpsed it.

"What is it, milaird? Is there something else you would have me do?"

"No, lady, proceed." He bowed to her. In a gesture quick, genuine, and unpretentious, he took her hand and kissed it. Then he was out the door after Kenneth.

"Aye, milady." Ian motioned to the pages to do as they had been ordered.

"What can I do?" Rosemary asked. She leaned forward in her chair and patted Lady Margaret's hand reassuringly.

"Have Brenda gather my remedies and bring them to me," Honora ordered. "Tell Cook we need more milk and hot porridge for the children. Lady Margaret, if you would, please, we will need all the linens.''

"Aye, of course." Lady Margaret rose from her place to follow Rosemary out the door.

The Great Hall quickly filled with crying children and frightened mothers. Some screamed in their distress, upsetting their children and the other women about them. Others stared out in silence at a world that had betrayed them—stolen away their quiet daily life and brought them pain and sorrow, grief and loss.

Father Andrew ministered to the dying—a boy near manhood and a cottar and a fisherman. Oleen bound their wounds. Because Honora had a weak stomach, she couldn't bear to look at those men's injuries. But Oleen needed help so badly that Honora forced down her nausea and did what she could to stanch the bleeding and relieve the pain.

Oleen tended the men struck down in battle and the women who were wounded as they defended their homes and children. Rosemary sat with a bruised and battered dry-eyed lass that Honora suspected had been raped. Lady Margaret and Anne made sleeping pallets and directed the kitchen servants in preparing food. When Honora saw the faraway look grow once more in Lady Margaret's eyes, she ordered Anne to see the lady to bed.

Honora worked all night. Rosemary worked beside her until she fell asleep in a chair. Dawn brightened the mist in the east when Brec reappeared. He looked haggard.

An orphaned child that Honora held in her arms had slipped into a peaceful sleep. The child's aunt took him from Honora.

Brec led Honora to the bedchamber, where he insisted that she rest. She asked about the raid, but he refused to talk of it. When she saw the lines of weariness about his eyes, she knew he needed rest too.

"I'll sleep only if you'll rest with me," Honora bargained.

Reluctantly he agreed and fully dressed, he slept beside her for a few hours.

18

The morn dawned cool and gray, heavy with anticipation. Honora stood with the other women—Rosemary, Brenda, Lady Margaret, and Anne—in the garden where Brec had asked them to meet.

With Rosemary's help Lady Margaret's garden had begun to take shape once more. Some shrubs remained wild and overgrown while others needed deadwood cut away, but the flower beds had been plucked free of weeds, and the rose buds burst forth with vitality.

Honora noticed little of this; her mind was on the wounded. When she'd checked on them, she found no more had been lost during the night. Satisfied with that, she turned to speculating on the reason for this gathering Brec had called, and she knew she wouldn't like what he was going to say.

Distractedly she pinched a faded blossom from a fuchsia. When she heard Brec enter the garden, she turned to see a warrior prepared for battle. He wore the kilted-plaid, a black linen shirt, and a leather doublet. His *claidheamh mor* swung at his side from a belt. A dirk was tucked into his knee-high leg coverings. Grim-faced Kenneth stood behind him, bearing their brass-trimmed leather targes.

Honora shivered, suddenly chilled by a mysterious draft. Behind her, Lady Margaret began to whimper. Rosemary put her arms around the woman to comfort her.

"Is this really necessary?" Honora asked. "Do you have to return the raid? Couldn't you leave the McDonnells waiting for a raid that would never happen?"

A wry smile twisted his lips. " 'Tis unheard of to not return a raid. We are bound to help those who remained on Solnarra. Besides, the McDonnells would but raid again, and do more damage to make sure they were not *neglected*."

Honora shook her head. She eyed the breadth of him and finally surrendered to the need to touch him, to straighten his shirt collar, and to smooth the fabric across his shoulders.

Brec's stance stiffened with her touch. But she dismissed his wariness and went on to satisfy herself with the placement of the brooch in his plaid and the feel of his solid body beneath the fabric. How long had it been since she had stood this close to him, in the shelter of his body? With sudden regret she realized how much she had missed his touch, the warmth of his lips on her shoulder, his hand on her thigh.

"Doesn't my apparel suit, milady?"

" 'Twill do," Honora said, brushing invisible lint from his plaid, reluctant to desert her nearness to him. "If only we could do something about those knobby knees."

Brec smiled, surprise and pleasure lighting his dark eyes. She smiled back at him and let a cool sea breeze sweep away the gloom and ache of the past few weeks. Neither of them spoke. Honora wanted this moment to last as long as possible.

Lady Margaret heaved a horrific sob and broke away from Rosemary. "Oh, my son!" Imploring hands outstretched, she tottered toward Brec.

"Don't go," she pleaded. She clutched his arm as if trying to drag him back from a terrible fate. "Don't go, Colin. Last time you went away, I never told you how much I loved you. This time, you must know. You have made me proud, Colin. No mother ever had a better son. If I never told you before, I tell you now. I love you. Your mother loves you, Colin. You know that, don't you?"

Honora saw Brec's impassive mask drop over his face. She glanced at Rosemary, who stared at the woman in helpless horror.

"Lady Margaret—" Honora reached for her mother-in-law.

" 'Tis all right, Honora." Brec motioned her to stay where she was, then took his mother's hands and peered into the weeping woman's face.

"Aye, Mother, we have not spoken of these things before. But I know you love me. And I love you."

He put his arms around his mother and held her for a long, loving moment. Honora watched peace smooth Lady Margaret's rumpled face and tears of relief glisten in her eyes.

"God be with you, my son." The lady released Brec.

With a barely perceptible nod, Brec turned and strode from the garden.

"Now he knows," Lady Margaret said, satisfaction and happiness glowing in her smile.

Honora bolted past Lady Margaret, determined not to allow her husband to sail into battle with this sorrowful farewell. As soon as the door to the garden closed behind her, she called after him. "Brec?"

At the top of the spiral stairway, Kenneth stopped and waved her on. Honora grabbed up her skirts and followed.

The three of them, one after another, pounded down and around the stone stairs. Honora called Brec's name again, but he ignored her. They reached the long ground floor passage that led to the sea gate: Brec first, then Kenneth, and then Honora, striding along as quickly as possible.

"Brec?" Honora called again.

"Milaird," Kenneth shouted. "Lady Honora wants to talk to ye."

Brec marched on without answering, his long-legged step outdistancing the two of them as they neared the sea gate door.

Desperate, Honora was about to break into a run. Ahead of her, Kenneth threw himself between Brec and the door.

"Speak to your lady," the master at arms commanded.

Brec hesitated, shifting from one foot to the other like a trapped animal. Finally he turned on Honora. The mask had slipped and split. Through that thin, cracked facade Honora saw anger and pain. She glimpsed the sailor who longed to sail away and never return. Instinctively she knew it was not she whom he wanted to escape, nor even his mother, nor the specter of his brother. It was the pain of duty unrewarded—of love unaccepted.

Honora slowed her step. The image of the black-haired boy sitting in the shadow of his blond brother blinked through her mind. She recalled Brenda's tale of a body readied for burial by Brec. A mother refused her right to prepare her son for the grave. Honora could only guess what was between the three—mother, son, and brother. She prayed that she'd guessed enough to tell Brec what he needed to hear.

"Don't be angry with your mother," she pleaded.

"Stay out of this, Honora," he growled. "You don't know anything about it."

"I know that your mother didn't mean what she said to hurt you. The grief still troubles her."

"Aye, grief over Colin."

"You did a beautiful thing," Honora said. "She needed to say farewell to Colin. And you helped her do that."

Brec turned away, facing the other branch of the passage. His fists were planted impatiently on his hips, his head bowed.

Honora wanted to know what he was thinking, what it was that hurt him so. But she knew he would not tell. All she could do was make certain that he did not sail away into danger—even to his death—thinking that Colin was the only one missed.

"I want you to take something with you," Honora said. "Something of mine. You know, like a token, a favor."

"I don't need anything from you," Brec snapped and reached for the door latch. Kenneth pressed himself firmly against the door, between his laird and the exit.

Surprised by this sudden alliance from a man who she knew had once disapproved of her, Honora cast Kenneth a grateful glance before she went on. "A token, like the ladies of old gave their knights. I'm your wife. You can't refuse me."

Over his shoulder Brec cast her a quizzical look.

"Give me your bonnet."

"What? Why do you want my bonnet?"

"Give it to me," Honora demanded. "You'll not leave Dunrugis before I bestow a token on you."

He pulled the blue cloth hat from his belt and handed it to her. "Make haste, woman. I want to sail with the tide."

"I won't be long," Honora vowed. She turned to dash down the passage.

In the laird's chamber she tore through things in one chest then another. Unsuccessful, she turned to a third. Where was Brenda when she needed her? Honora wondered as she tossed things aside.

Then she remembered where to find the token—wrapped in a cloth with her favorite pearls and stuffed into the trunk with her walking shoes. Victorious, she threw the packet on the bed, pulled from it the token—a keepsake that belonged to them only. A charm he would understand. She raced out of the room.

Brec paced impatiently at the door, still blocked by Kenneth when she returned. Her husband glared at her. "Well?"

"This is a rare charm given to me by a brave sea captain who has sailed to strange and exotic places," Honora began.

The hardness about Brec's mouth softened. His curiosity was obviously piqued. He stepped toward her, his gaze fastened on the thing she held in her hand.

Encouraged, Honora held up the bonnet and let Brec watch her pin the white, blue, and green feathers to the headband.

"This charm is said to have the power to ward off the advances of ambitious earls," she continued. "And I have little doubt that it would also ward off the spears and arrows of the Clan McDonnell."

"So it would," Brec agreed, his voice low, as if begrudging the words. At last his dark-eyed, searching gaze met Honora's.

"Return safely and soon," she whispered. The lump in her throat robbed her of her voice. She stared up into his eyes—shiny black eyes, keen, and warming now. She tried to swallow the lump again, but it refused to budge.

"You will be missed." Somehow she knew those weren't the right words. She blinked and tried again. "I will miss you."

He bowed before her, head low, and didn't move. Honora stood there, wondering what he wanted her to do. She knew she wanted him to kiss her.

His head came up a wee bit, and he cast her a questioning glance. "My bonnet? Will you bestow my bonnet on me, milady?"

"Oh, aye," Honora gasped. What a dunce she was. She set the bonnet upon his dark hair just so the point met the center of his brow. Shyly she touched the lock of dark hair that fell to one side of the cap's point before she gave the bonnet a firm pat. When he stood up straight and grinned, he made a bonny sight. She grinned back at him, her heart suddenly lighter.

Kenneth cleared his throat. "Fergus is calling. He says the tide is turning."

"Aye, I'm on my way," Brec said without looking away from her. To her disappointment, he bent to kiss her—on the cheek—and was gone.

Islemen, fired by the insult and prospect of feuding, hauled on the oars, sending the *Dal Riata* skimming along before the wind. The single square sail filled taut and full. They made good time to the isle of Solnarra. In the bow forecastle Brec watched the horizon for McDonnell's galleys and others. Kenneth stood at his side, also watching. They said little.

In the clean, fresh sea air, things drifted unbidden into Brec's head. His mother's words—meant for Colin—raked across his raw emotions. The first sting of those words was gone. Honora, with her hand on his brow, had soothed the pain.

After she bestowed the token on him, he walked down the gangplank and boarded his galley with a new feeling growing inside him. The familiar eagerness to be at sea still flowed strong, but something hauled at the underside of that familiar eagerness. Even as he gave orders to set sail and climbed into the forecastle where he always stood, the feeling could not be ignored. It tugged like a stubborn snag in a river waterway. The snag was Honora.

"I will miss you," she whispered. 'Twas her duty to say so, Brec told himself. She knew her duty as a loyal wife. But he looked down into her face to find the sea in her eyes. He recalled how she had nibbled at her bottom lip as she hurried to pin the parrot feather to his bonnet. Her hands trembled. Did she really care whether he returned?

Was he more to her than a husband she had vowed to serve? The man she married because he offered to give her sister a home?

The image of her pinning the feathers to his bonnet was so powerful—her tiny hands, their pink oval fingernails fumbling with the fabric and the clasp—that he had to brush his fingers along the side of his bonnet. To touch the token was almost like touching her hand. He regretted that he hadn't really kissed her when he left, hadn't pressed his lips against hers and taken the taste of her away with him. A movement at the corner of his eye made him turn to his master of arms and catch the knowing glance of amusement that Kenneth gave him.

"We'll catch the McDonnells at their game and be home soon," Brec prophesied. He let his hand drop to his side.

"Aye," Kenneth agreed, still smiling. "No long sea voyage today."

At midday the lookout spied the smoke rising from Solnarra. As they sailed closer, the lookout spotted another vessel.

"Three masts," the boy called down from the crow's-nest.

"Simon LaFarge?" Kenneth asked. "Would be no McDonnell galley. They'll be gone by now."

"Flag?" Brec called up.

"None, sir," the boy answered. "Aye, now they run up the French flag."

"Simon," Brec confirmed.

Kenneth agreed and gave orders to close in on the ship.

Moments later the *Dal Riata* slipped along the lee side of the pirate ship and slewed around, bow to gunwale. In a blink of the eye Simon threw a rigging rope over the side, and the McCloud clan chief swung aboard the *Sea Gull*. Simon laughed.

They greeted each other with a hearty embrace.

"We saw the smoke on the horizon and decided to drop in to see what was happening," Simon explained after they exchanged greetings. "When the raiders saw us, they hauled anchor and sailed. I don't think they cared to meet up with fighting men. Hey, look at ye. A feather in yer cap like a cursed pirate." Simon laughed at his own joke.

"Did you send men ashore?" Brec asked, peering at smoke rising from the smoldering thatch-roof and stone-walled cottages.

"Oh, no," Simon said as his laugh died. "I never waste good men on the likes of that. Nothing there to loot. The raiders took it. But there still be men on the isle. In hiding."

"Good," Brec said. "We brought them arms, food, and reinforcements."

"So the feud is alive?"

"I sent Lilias back to the McDonnells," Brec explained. "She was unhappy. What are you doing in these waters? I thought you were off to harry the English in the channel."

"Too many ships about," Simon said. "And they all carry cannon bigger than mine. This bloody English war has taken all the fun out of pirating. And I thought ye should know, Alasdair mac Colkitto set sail from Passage on the River Barrow aboard the *Harp* in June."

"Aye, what else have you heard of that man?" Brec asked well aware that Alasdair mac Colkitto was a dangerous man whether he fought with you or against you.

Every Isleman knew that Colkitto and his son had pledged their vengeance against the Campbells the day Argyll's clan had destroyed Colkitto's household on Cononsay isle five years ago

Since then, the legendary Scot-Irish warrior had fought hundreds of Irish skirmished and pitched battles, many against the Scots Convenanting army in Ulster. Dark tales were whispered that on occasion he'd murdered his own Scot Royalist allies as well. He even enjoyed something of a reputation as a pirate.

"We heard that he overtook a convoy in the Irish Sea, two supply ships and a passenger vessel. He made the Protestant passengers walk the plank. Early last month he sailed into the Sound of Mull and landed his half-Irish forces on Ardnamurchan ground." Simon stopped. The jolly glint faded from his eyes and his smile disappeared.

"What is it, Simon?" Struck by his friend's rare look of fear, Brec turned to look behind him. "Have you seen a ghost?"

"Might as well have," Simon said. "I tell ye Brec McCloud, the judgment of the Lord is about to descend upon Alasdair and the king's cause. We sailed just off the isle of Coll that day ourselves—only leagues away from Colkitto's landing site. The sky was clear and the sea calm.''

"Aye, so?" Brec didn't understand the furtive looks the sailors had begun to exchange.

" 'Twas peculiar at the time of Alasdair's landing. There came the boom of a mighty explosion,'' Simon said in a low voice, as if to be overheard would call up the devil himself. Members of the pirate crew who were close about became quiet and drifted toward their captain. "Aye, a blast like a dozen enormous, brazen cannon fired all at once.''

"Shook the main mast, it did,'' one grizzled sailor piped.

"Aye,'' one with a missing front tooth agreed. "There is more. I heard from a sailor down south that the loud tucking of drums was heard in Mar and that unearthly trumpets, bagpipes, and bells were played at Peterhead.''

"I tell ye, Brec,'' Simon said, settling a hand on Brec's shoulder, "beware of the alliances ye make. This thing with Alasdair mac Colkitto will come to no good.''

"What happened after the landing?" Brec asked.

"Well, they made quick work of the Campbell castles of Lochaline and Mingarry. I think they'll be calling on ye and the others, too, for men and arms. McDonnells. Clan Ranald. The McNeils. But none can call forth as many fighting men as ye McClouds and the McDonnells. He'll be doing his all to get yer backing for himself and the king.''

"I know what you're saying,'' Brec said. He still watched the isle of Solnarra before him. The fortified house on the isle had been gutted and burned. The livestock were gone. He had homeless families and injured people to mind. And a dutiful wife at home who missed him.

Simon stepped closer to Brec's shoulder and lowered his voice. "The *Sea Gull* needs to lay up for repairs for a while ye know, before that run we promised to make for ye. There's a good loch on the west side we had in mind.''

"Aye. You'll be safe there,'' Brec said. "No McCloud will tell of your whereabouts. Besides, I might have some need of your help.''

* * *

Two days later the *Dal Riata* sailed into Dunrugis Loch with Brec in the bow forecastle. He found himself searching Dunrugis's ramparts for a small figure. He was mightily pleased to see Honora appear with Brenda at her side. Honora gave a proper, ladylike wave, but the red-haired lass swung her arm wide and jumped up and down with unladylike eagerness. Brec cast Kenneth a look of amusement.

"Now I know why you've no interest in long voyages any more," Brec said to his master of arms. Kenneth's red blush clashed with his orange hair.

The women scurried out of sight, only to reappear in the lower courtyard. Brenda threw herself at Kenneth. He swept her up in his embrace, her ankles and petticoats visible to all, and he kissed her. The galley crew cheered, and Honora laughed.

As she stood before Brec at the sea gate, she cast a quick, shy glance at him and the people around them. Brec smiled.

"Is all well, milady?" he asked.

"Aye, milaird," she said, taking his arm and walking beside him. "Everyone is healing and eager to return home. What did you find on Solnarra?"

"Old man McClennon was hearty enough and ready to do battle again," Brec said as he steadied her up the steps into the courtyard. " 'Twas a small raiding party—one galley and a dozen men or so. The McClennon said he thought the leader was Donald McDonnell, the eldest son. We helped clear the rubble and gather up what few animals were spared. Left them provisions, some arms, some fighting men. I don't think the McDonnells will bother them again soon."

"Is that important?" Honora asked. "The leader of the raid?"

"Aye, in this case it is," Brec said. "Lilias has several brothers. Donald is her favorite and has the hottest temper. 'Tis possible the McDonnell knows nothing of the raid."

"Brenda says Solnarra was considered part of Lilias's dowry."

"Solnarra has always belonged to the McClouds," Brec corrected her. When he saw her blink in surprise and embarrassment, he realized he had spoken harshly. He softened his voice. "The McDonnells have no right to Solnarra. And they certainly have no right to kill and steal from the McClennons. And if I get my hands on Donald, I'll make sure he knows that."

"Of course," Honora said.

They stopped before the door into the castle. Brec saw that the guards and the crew of the galley were watching their laird and lady. "When I left, you gave me a token, fair lady. Have you no kiss for your laird upon his safe return?"

She smiled, nodded, and lifted her face toward his, her dark lashes fluttering against blushing cheeks. Brec longed for something more passionate, but he took her hands in his and leaned over her to kiss as they had so often before the wedding. When he drew away, she smiled shyly, pleasure on her lips and in the pressure of her hand in his. Brec's heart warmed, and desire seeped through him. He resolved that he wouldn't sleep alone tonight. He followed Honora into the castle, thinking that perhaps duty needn't always be a joyless thing.

In the weeks that followed the raid an uneasy peace prevailed between the McDonnells and the McClouds and between the laird and his lady.

The McClennon families were returned to Solnarra. But within a week, word reached Dunrugis of a fishermen's skirmish at sea between McDonnells and McClouds. A net had been slashed, then insults and fish hurled across the water at each other's galleys.

With the departure of the last of the McClennon guests, Honora soon had Dunrugis put back into order and the routine reestablished. Brec came to the laird's chamber from time to time but never remained for the entire night. Honora gave up trying to understand him and accepted him willingly when he chose to come to her. Her solace was Rosemary's company.

Honora stared longingly out the chamber window at the clear morning washed clean by the squall that had blown over during the night.

"This would be a good day to collect rocks, don't you think?" she suggested to her sister, who sat at the breakfast table in the laird's chamber as she had nearly every morning since her arrival.

"Aye, but you know, I'd like to see the kelpie that Laird Brec and Master Kenneth told us about," Rosemary said. "Remember?"

"That's right," Honora agreed. "I'd forgotten about that silly story. I've never seen the kelpie either. Ian tells me there is one. He said 'tis the stable master's pride."

"So 'tis time for us to explore the island some," Rosemary said. She drained her cup of milk. "I think the shore will offer some beautiful rocks for my collection and for Lady Margaret's garden too."

"There be yer Kelpie," Master Angus said and chuckled—a sinister chuckle that Honora disliked. She had met Master Angus before, when she came to check on her mare, Brownie. She had sensed a resentment in him, although he had been polite enough then when she was in Brec's company. And this day he seemed mannerly enough.

Warily she stared at the pony that Rosemary was watching.

From the box stall the shaggy black pony glared back, a hostile gleam in his black eyes and a sullen twist to his pointed ears. He munched on his hay with stubborn jawing. His tail switched in vexation.

"Kelpie doesna like to have his meal disturbed, nor his nap for that matter," Master Angus said. "Truth be, Kelpie doesna like much. But he's a sure-footed creature with a sturdy back. He's no' afeared of the water. But he has his uses whether he likes it or no'. He'd make a perfect mount for ye, Lady Rosemary."

Rosemary laughed. "He's delightful."

Honora glanced doubtfully at the sour island pony. "I don't think—"

"I like him," Rosemary said. "May I ride him?"

"Of course, milady."

Before long, Honora was mounted on Brownie, with Rosemary on Kelpie trotting along at their side. The black pony's stubby-legged gait bumped along double-time beside Honora's long-legged mare.

"Is he a rough ride?" Honora asked, looking down at

her sister as they jogged along the path toward the headland above Castle Dunrugis. Dubh loped along ahead of them.

" 'Tis not as rough as it looks," Rosemary managed to say, her voice quavering with the pony's gait.

Honora sighed. Her sister would never complain.

She looked back at the groom, who followed them with a basket of food for a midday meal and a basket for the rocks. He was but a boy, Brenda's brother, Walter. Honora could tell from the smirk on the lad's face that the whole isle would know by nightfall of the sisters' ride on the kelpie. No doubt Laird Brec would find the whole kelpie story amusing too.

Walter directed them north of the castle through a ferny forest along a narrow footpath. When they reached open ground, shaggy-faced, long-horned cattle on the hillside turned to stare at them.

"On the other side of the hill is the bog where the peat is cut," Walter said. "The valley beyond the bog is good grazing."

Soon the countryside leveled out. The wind became stronger and the black rocky shingle beach came into view. Across the green turf to the west, Honora saw the blue water stretch itself out toward the faraway horizon where sea met sky. Ahead of them to the north lay the green headland above Dunrugis where the waves dashed themselves against steep golden cliffs.

Honora shook her head, loosening her hair and taking pleasure in the refreshing tingle of the sea breeze against her skin. She rejoiced in this freedom from the castle, and she looked around for Rosemary, grateful to her little sister for bringing her out to the sea and fresh air. Rosemary seemed to be enjoying herself too.

"Whose cottage is that?" Honora asked, pointing out the lonely rock beehive-shaped hut that she saw on the hillside beyond her sister.

" 'Tis the witch's cottage," Walter replied, looking away quickly, as if to look at the hut endangered him. "Mistress Oleen lives there. 'Tis an ancient place, built by druids and the old folks say that Mistress Oleen traffics in their spirits."

"Don't listen to them," Honora said. "Oleen is a good healer."

"Aye, milady," Walter said, without conviction.

"This looks like a good stretch of beach to search," Rosemary said from atop Kelpie. She pointed to the rocky shore.

" 'Tis what ye asked for, milady, but 'tis nothing there but black rocks and kelp," Walter protested.

"We'll bring back something fine, Walter," Rosemary said. "You'll see."

Before she could say more, Kelpie tossed his head. The pony lifted his nostrils to the air and sniffed the sea breeze.

"Oh," Walter groaned. "Did Master Angus no' tell ye that Kelpie has a passion for fresh seaweed?"

"A passion for seaweed?" Honora repeated, about to laugh at the absurdity of the remark.

Walter's warning came too late. Head up, nostrils to the wind, the pony caught a scent of what he wanted and took off in a short-legged, but amazingly swift gallop.

"Rosemary," Honora shouted. "Haul back on the reins. Oh, that infernal animal has the bit in his teeth."

Terrified that the uncontrolled pony would hurt himself and Rosemary, Honora dug her heels into Brownie's side and pursued them until Brownie veered aside where the turf ended. Ahead, Honora could see that the shingle beach had slowed Kelpie's headlong pace.

Rosemary looked back and waved. "I'm all right, Sister. Don't worry. He will probably stop when he finds the kelp."

Relieved, Honora halted Brownie and relaxed in the saddle. Swiftly she dismounted, threw the reins to Walter, and took a basket. She trudged on down the beach after her sister—and that mad pony feasting on seaweed.

"Look," Rosemary called as she dismounted. "Here's an oar washed ashore. Should we take it back with us? Do you think one of the fishermen lost it?"

"Perhaps," Honora said as she reached her sister's side. They stared at the oar grounded on the rocky beach. A wave washed over it, then sucked away. "Or 'tis from some poor boat lost at sea. Leave it here. I'll pick it up when we come back."

They went on, avoiding a dead fish that Dubh had to linger over sniffing with relish. They skirted the black kelp, shiny and ruffled, freshly washed up on shore. Kelpie stopped to steal another mouthful.

Rosemary found several rocks she fancied. She popped them into her basket and went on chattering about Lady Margaret's rose garden. Honora wandered ahead of her sister, past an outcropping piled high with round black boulders and bleached white driftwood.

"Lady Margaret is going to ask the gardener to order more rosebushes for the walled garden," Rosemary said. "Isn't that old Quaker an interesting fellow. And a good gardener. I think . . ."

Honora walked on, soothed by Rosemary's chatter and the rhythm of the waves. Unconcerned, she idly let the water lap over her boots, then drag the sand from beneath her foot.

"Sister? Come look at this."

Honora caught a new tone in her sister's voice. When she turned around, she could just see the top of Rosemary's head above the boulders. Honora nearly twisted her ankle in her haste to get across the rocky beach. Something in Rosemary's voice told her to hurry. "Aye. What is it?"

She saw only Rosemary's back when she first rounded the outcropping. Her sister was bent over something lying on the rocks, and her basket had been flung aside and forgotten.

" 'Tis a man," Rosemary said over her shoulder. "Look. He still breathes."

Honora knelt beside the body and put her hand to his throat as Oleen had taught her to do. The pulse there was weak and uneven.

"Aye, he lives," Honora whispered, as if speaking aloud would awaken him.

"His clothes are soaked and his skin is so white," Rosemary said. She took his hand between hers and chafed it roughly. "I think he was in the sea a long time. Maybe washed overboard in the squall last night. Who is he? Do you know him?"

The lad moaned and tried to move. His eyes opened for a moment, dark blue eyes that rested on Rosemary.

"You must be the mermaid who pulled me from the sea," he murmured. "You have my gratitude, sweet lady." He managed a sweet sleepy smile, then, with a sigh, fell unconscious again.

"Me?" Rosemary stammered. She turned to Honora. "Did you hear? He thinks me a mermaid!"

Honora nodded. She would not tell her softhearted sister that the man was ill and out of his head—perhaps even dying.

Rosemary turned back to him, touching his cheek and stroking his golden beard. "We must help him."

"I don't know," Honora said, peering down at the young man. The plaid he wore—Honora couldn't recall that she had seen any like it before. No blues, greens, yellows, and whites like the Isle of Myst weavers favored. This plaid was gray and green, with red threads. And the brooch that pinned the garment into place bore the great sea eagle that reminded her of the McDonnells' flag.

She had seen no blond man like this on the isle either. He had a pale beard, fair unweathered skin, and almost white eyelashes, yet there was something familiar . . . Then she recalled where she had seen this fairness before—Lilias. And the widow had wrapped herself defiantly in the McDonnell plaid when she sailed away. Hadn't it looked like this—the gray and green? What had Brec said? That Lilias had several brothers?

Her first reaction was to pray that she was wrong. This was no McDonnell. At Dunrugis feelings still ran high over the raid. No member of that clan would be welcome in the castle or the village either. Nor could they leave him here on the beach. Honora did not consider herself any kind of healer, but she doubted that this man would survive without care and nursing. She groaned when the blow of all the mounting problems struck.

"What is it, sister?" Rosemary asked. "Is he dead?"

"Nay," Honora said. "I think he is a McDonnell. I think this must be one of Lilias's brothers."

"This beautiful man?" Rosemary shook her head. Honora had told her all about Lilias. "He is so innocent looking. Not like an evil McDonnell."

"Well, what did you think a McDonnell would look like?

A hoary monster?'' Honora replied, her words short and sharp. "No more than that misbegotten pony looks likes a sea dragon.''

"Oh,'' Rosemary sighed. "What will we do? If we tell anyone about him, they will throw him into the dungeon, let him starve to death.''

"I know. But he's in danger now of dying of the chill,'' Honora said. She looked back down the beach. Deserted— except for Kelpie. Walter had remained with the other horses back on the green turf. She looked out to the sea, no boats there. She prayed that no one had seen them. "Maybe we can get him to Oleen's hut.''

"Will Oleen hate him too? Can we trust her?''

"Oleen will help,'' Honora said. "She's pledged to heal. But we must send Walter away. Then maybe we can get Kelpie over here and lift the man onto his back.''

Honora again looked down at the unconscious youth. He appeared so harmless. How could they hide him, care for him without someone learning they had hidden a McDonnell? Neither she nor Rosemary was any good at deception.

"I'll help,'' Rosemary said. "I can help lift him. We can do it. You'll see. We can save him.''

"Aye, what shall I tell Walter to get rid of him?'' Honora asked. "The oar. We'll send him back to the quay with the oar.''

19

At first the only change Brec noticed was the disappearance of Honora's smiles.

She had been smiling and busy since her sister had come, since he had returned from Solnarra wearing Honora's token. Depending on the time of day, she was to be found in his mother's garden, or in the accounts room where she conferred with Ian, or in the Great Hall where she played the guitar and Rosemary sang.

Then suddenly her smiles became fleeting, uncertain. She rushed in late for meals. When she was on time, she fidgeted in her chair, flustered and distracted. Tension quivered at the corners of her mouth.

Even Rosemary seemed different. She carried a faraway look in her eye and a dreamy smile on her lips.

Brec heard a strange story from Kenneth—who had heard it from one of the grooms—that Lady Honora had taken Stable Master Angus to task over mounting her sister on Kelpie.

"The stable master neglected to warn the ladies of Kelpie's fancy for seaweed," Kenneth told Brec.

Kenneth's smile made Brec curious about the rest of the story. He looked up from the dispatch from the mainland that he was reading. "And what happened?"

"Lady Honora gave Angus to understand that he had erred most grievously. Walter said her wrath was so great that when the poor man begged her not to tell you, she informed him that he had nothing to fear from his laird, that she was the one who was angry. When the lady did finish with the stable master, Walter said Angus was practically on his knees and weeping for forgiveness."

Brec turned back to his dispatch and smiled to himself. He had never been fond of Master Angus, but he could almost sympathize with the man who received the brunt of Honora's anger. Still, he saw no reason to make amends for his wife's uncharacteristic fury. Angus should have at the least warned the women, if not found another mount for Lady Rosemary.

He took closer notice of the changes in Honora when his clothes did not reappear promptly after laundering. And Honora lost interest in her guitar. She and Rosemary spent all their time on the beach, searching for rocks, or at Oleen's beehive hut.

At first he considered these oversights natural enough. The weather was perfect for spending long hours in the fresh air. Honora and her sister enjoyed each other's company. And Honora had been so strong and resourceful during the Solnarra crisis that he thought she deserved any diversion that amused her.

But as the weather grew colder and the sky darker, Brec began to suspect that something else distracted his lady.

And he didn't like what he was thinking. She never denied him when he came to her, yet her passion remained subdued. Each time, afterward, as he held her in his arms he sensed something unsaid between them, the hovering of important words unspoken. He wanted to ask her what was kept in her heart that he should know, but she fell asleep, her breathing deep and worry puckered on her brow. Brec put his lips against the pulse in her temple. He closed his eyes, inhaling her sweet, rosy scent and spreading his hand along her narrow, delicate back.

Perhaps he didn't want to know.

" 'Tis true," vowed the blond youth sitting in a box bed in Oleen's beehive hut. "At first I thought I was dreaming. But when I opened my eyes the second time, there was the mermaid with red-gold curls who had carried me to shore and saved my life."

Brenda watched Robert McDonnell take Rosemary's hand in his and smile lovingly at the lady. Rosemary sat on the edge of the bed with eyes only for the fair, young man, one who looked uncomfortably like Lady Lilias.

Rosemary took up the story. "And I told him, 'Sir, you see, I am but a lass with a clubfoot.' " She blushed, and Brenda could see that the lass had received little flattery in her life.

"I still swear that your foot is but a mere vestige, proof of your former life in the sea," Robert finished, reaching for Rosemary's other hand to entwine with his.

Heaven knew Brenda had no desire to like the young McDonnell, but she did. He was obviously as enamored with Rosemary as the girl was with him. Now Brenda knew what had preoccupied Lady Honora for almost two weeks, what had kept her and her sister from the castle until the early hours of the evening. When Lady Honora finally confessed, pledging Brenda to secrecy, Brenda never dreamed she was promising to help hide a McDonnell. What would

Laird Brec think? What would Kenneth say? Brenda shuddered and cast aside the unpleasant questions.

Forgotten by the lovers, she wandered away and seated herself at the table where Oleen and Lady Honora plotted a voyage set for the next day.

"I know you disagree with me, Oleen, but I think returning Robert to Armadean is the only way," Lady Honora was saying, her voice edged with irritation. Brenda had noticed that this deception had made her lady short-tempered.

Brenda's heart started to thump faster, like it did every time she thought about the voyage to Armadean, home of the McDonnells. She'd never sailed beyond the shores of the Isle of Myst and now Lady Honora wanted her to sail them to Armadean.

"But look at Rosemary and Robert, milady, so perfect a pair," Oleen whispered, leaning across the table. "They were meant to be together. Robert is a gentle man, unlike his father or his brothers and sister. He's no warrior. He has strong ties to the church, even considered the priesthood. Perhaps 'twould be best to make the McDonnells come here."

"After what happened at Solnarra, do you think they would come in peace?" Lady Honora glanced over her shoulder at the lovers. "Do you think they would be received in peace? If only he had become a priest. Then we wouldn't be worried about his breaking Rosemary's heart."

"I fear it may be too late for that already," Oleen observed.

"Robert McDonnell must be returned to his family before Brec or anyone knows he's been here," Lady Honora insisted. "As much as I know the parting will hurt Rosemary, as much as I want happiness for her, this deception cannot go on. Robert endangers all of us, as well as himself. If there is to be anything more between Robert and Rosemary, the young man will have to make his wishes known to his family."

"I'll find a boat for you," Oleen agreed with a reluctant nod. "But I'm concerned about this manner of getting the boy back to his kin. You don't know that much about sailing, milady. And Brenda, I know you've grown up sailing, but only around the isle. Can you do this? Remember, young Robert is still too weak to be of much help."

"I think I can," Brenda said, hardly believing she was agreeing to this scheme. "If the weather be good."

"Brenda will do well," Lady Honora said. "We'll need clothes too. We don't want to draw attention to ourselves. We should look like fisher wives."

"I can get gowns for us," Brenda volunteered.

"And Lady Rosemary. Are we going to take her along?" Oleen asked.

"I don't think she will remain behind."

"Maybe *not,*" Oleen agreed, looking back at the lovers again. Suddenly the wise woman sat up straight and spread her hands across the table. She stared into the distance, as if listening to something. Brenda had seen that entranced look before, when the healer was about to "see" something.

"What is it?" Lady Honora asked. She exchanged a look of alarm with Brenda.

"Riders are coming," Oleen replied.

"Riders? Who would ride up here?" Brenda asked, answering her own question. "The villagers and cottars always walk. That could only mean someone from the castle is coming."

"Robert, hide, at once," Lady Honora ordered.

Without question Robert disappeared into the shadows of the box bed. Rosemary helped him, then stood up, smoothed the bed linen, and partly closed the bed's shutter doors, before turning toward the hut's doorway.

The tattoo of cantering horses grew plain. In expectant silence the four women stared at one another as the riders neared.

"Can you tell how many?" Lady Honora asked.

"Two, I believe," Oleen replied. " 'Twill be all right. Remember, Brec does only what a good clan chief would do."

If one of the riders was Laird Brec, Brenda thought, the other could only be Kenneth. She didn't fear the laird's wrath as much as she dreaded Kenneth's disappointment in her.

The horses halted outside the door already open to provide a view of the sea and a breath of sea air. A deep voice addressed the occupants. "Mistress Oleen? May I enter?"

Oleen met Lady Honora's gaze before she answered. "Enter and welcome, Laird Brec. Your lady is here with me."

Laird Brec ducked through the low doorway, his large shadow filling the smoky darkness of the hut. He stood for a moment, blinking.

"So you are here," he said when he spied Lady Honora standing by the table.

"Of course," she said, her face calm and her hands quietly clasped before her. "This is where I said I would be, milaird. Oleen was just describing to Rosemary and Brenda and me a better way to dry basil and thyme."

"Aye." Brenda and Rosemary agreed with a furious nodding of heads.

" 'Tis a while since you've called on me, milaird," Oleen said. "I'm pleased to see you again. Won't you join us in sharing a cup of fresh milk."

"Aye, 'tis been a long time, hasn't it?" Laird Brec walked farther into the room without looking at the women who stood around the table. "Colin and I spent a lot of time here once long ago, when we were boys."

Brenda saw the look of surprise on Lady Honora's face.

"Truly? You and Colin, together?" the lady asked. "I always thought of the two of you as going your separate ways."

"Oh, no," Oleen imposed. "Colin and Brec were near inseparable. 'Twas their father, Laird Alec, who never liked you two to spend much time here. He feared I'd fill your heads with druid nonsense."

"Aye," Laird Brec agreed. "My father seldom approved of anything I did."

In the silence that followed, Brenda, Honora, and Rosemary watched him prowl about the hut, examining the bunches of drying herbs and the stacks of wicker baskets along the wall. When he neared the box bed, Rosemary paled and stared helplessly across the room at Lady Honora, who remained silent and composed.

"Oleen has told us a lot about the islands," Rosemary said, beginning to stammer as if she felt a need to fill the silence. "Things that the villagers don't think to tell us, about how to read the clouds and sniff the wind. How to protect the milk cows with a collar of rowan or honeysuckle."

Laird Brec turned to the box bed. Brenda glanced at the other women. Their simultaneous intake of breath was almost audible. He lingered by the bed, brushing one of the shutters back and peering briefly into the shadows.

Brenda was certain that their silent prayers for Robert's successful concealment must be loud enough to be heard by the laird. He loitered by the bed. Finally Brenda could bear the suspense no longer. She lurched across the room and grabbed the cup of milk that Oleen had poured.

"Your refreshment, milaird." She thrust the cup at Laird Brec.

"Would you have some oat cakes as well?" Oleen asked, offering a plate of the fresh-baked fare.

"Nay, no milk or cakes." Laird Brec turned from the bed, waving Brenda and the food away, and gave Rosemary a doubtful look. "To read the clouds and protect the milk cows from evil? Are those things you need to know, milady?"

"Aye. To be sure. And other things such as cures and omens," Rosemary babbled, casting a quick, uncertain glance in her sister's direction. "Where to find wild carrots for St. Michael's Day. And Oleen tells the most peculiar stories about the Sight. About people seeing their own ghosts sometimes before they die. Like Oleen and your brother coming upon his ghost walking the halls of Dunrugis before . . ."

Rosemary clamped her mouth shut the moment Lady Honora cast her a disapproving frown. Brenda stood rooted to the spot near the laird, still bearing the cup of milk in her trembling hand.

Laird Brec turned slowly, with measure, toward Oleen. Brenda stared at the floor and cringed, awaiting the blast of his temper. Everyone knew the laird was sometimes touchy about his brother's death. After a moment, when no explosion came, Brenda stole a curious look up at him. His brows formed one dark line, and his voice issued low, almost a growl.

"I do not care to have the story of my brother's sighting of his ghost prattled about like some common tale."

" 'Twas the most recent instance I could think of when we were talking of the Sight," Oleen explained calmly. She met his piercing, black-eyed glare without wincing. "Lady Rosemary is family. And there's no evil in talking of your brother's death, Brec."

Oleen and Laird Brec regarded each other for a long, heavy moment. In the silence, a smoldering brick of peat collapsed on the stone hearth in the middle of the room. The musty, sweet smoke coiled lazily upward to the open hole at the center of the beehive hut.

"I must go," Laird Brec said at last, and with no more words of farewell, he turned abruptly and walked from the hut.

Brenda heaved a sigh of relief. Lady Honora hurried after him. She wondered whether the lady really understood the risk she took in deceiving the laird. Not everyone was protected by the Sight like Oleen.

Outside, the sea beat against the yellow cliffs of the westernmost headland of the loch. The spray plumed white against the blue sky. Above, two gulls floated on the updraft along the bluffs.

The mist sprinkled on Honora's cheeks as she followed Brec to his horse, uncertain of what she wanted to say. "Brec?"

He stopped, turning on her with a hopeful light in his eye. "Will you return with me?"

"Nay," Honora said, surprised and pleased to see that his anger with Oleen had already evaporated. "I wish to have Oleen complete her lesson. I just wanted to say that . . . that I'm glad you came to see us here."

"Aye?" Brec said. He looked out over the sea.

Honora watched the wind ruffle his dark hair. Trouble furrowed his brow. A muscle in his jaw tightened. She wondered whether he suspected something.

When he turned back to her, she caught a quick flick of his hand, and he flourished before her a small bouquet of wildflowers—blue, yellow, and pink with forget-me-nots, buttercups, and wood anemones.

"Oh," Honora gasped. Startled, then touched, she smiled

up at him and let her hand linger on his as she took the flowers. "Thank you, milaird."

"Honora? I know you've kept secrets from your uncles and from me—" he said, releasing the flowers slowly.

"Only to protect Alexander," Honora reminded him. Her back stiffened.

"You have no Alexander to protect now," he said. "Tell me the truth."

Honora looked up at him to find him studying her, searching her face.

"Have I your word that nothing is amiss? That there is nothing that I should know about? That you would keep no secrets from me?"

"I would keep no secrets from you," Honora lied. The words slipped out more easily than she wanted them to. But she could not endanger Robert, not for Rosemary's sake, nor for the sake of peace. She stared up at Brec, astonished at her duplicity. Guilt tugged at her heart. She held her breath, waiting for lightning to strike her down. When none did, she had to go on. "I know my duty, milaird. I vow I will always do my best for you and the clan and the Isle of Myst."

Pain flickered in his expression for an instant. "I know you do," Brec said with a brusque nod, then turned away. "Kenneth, bring the horses. I've a cottar to see on the other side of the isle before the day is out. 'Til supper, milady."

As Honora watched Brec ride away with Kenneth, she pleaded—bargained—with God—*Help us get Robert home safely, and I'll never tell another lie, Lord, I promise. And I'll give up marchpanes. I'll give up anything you ask.*

Supper was interrupted by the arrival of a galley Brec insisted on inspecting. He left immediately. Honora slept alone, but she didn't sleep much. Her penance for lying to Brec, she supposed.

The next morning dawned clear and peaceful—just as Oleen had forecast. As planned, she, Brenda, and Rosemary slipped away from Dunrugis early on the excuse of visiting Oleen again.

Robert had agreed with their plan the day before. They would send Walter off with an herb remedy for some inland cottar. Dressed as fisher folk, they would sail from the headland and out of sight of Dunrugis to within a few leagues of the McDonnell castle.

They would land Robert where he could reach a cottage. Afterward Honora, Brenda, and Rosemary would sail back to the Isle of Myst. Robert would be within an easy walk of home. Oleen would tell anyone who asked that Lady Honora, Lady Rosemary, and Brenda had spent the day with her, as the ladies frequently did. The women would be home in time for supper.

No one ever need know that a loathsome McDonnell had been nursed back to health on the Isle of Myst.

With Brenda's and Honora's help Robert stumbled along the narrow switchback path down the cliff to the beach. Rosemary followed, carrying a bundle of food and a jug of water for provisions. Oleen served as lookout.

"Aye, 'tis the kind of boat the isle folk use," Robert said when he saw the craft Oleen had borrowed for them. Stiffly he climbed aboard and tugged on the rigging. Honora was reassured to see him pat the furled sail as if the boat were a familiar friend.

"These little craft almost sail themselves," he added. Then he stretched a trembling hand toward Rosemary to help her aboard.

Brenda agreed. "We'll land on Armadean before ye know it."

Honora looked from the weak, pale youth who she was certain was not quite well, to her sister, who knew nothing about sailing, and to Brenda. "I hope so," she said as she climbed aboard.

When they hit the open sea, the sails snapped then filled, billowed tight, pulling the boat along, humming over the blue water. Brenda seemed satisfied.

So Honora settled herself, trying to become accustomed to the galloping rhythm that grew as the speed picked up. The feel of skimming over water in such a small boat was new to Honora. She forced herself to turn away from Myst as it receded behind them. She looked toward the northeast. She could not worry about Brec now, about what he would think or how angry he would be. They were on their way.

Robert sat at the tiller to hold the heading. The sun and wind brought color to his cheeks. But Honora noted that when he looked at Rosemary, sadness filled his eyes.

She turned away from the lovers to watch the jib. It held, full and taut. The sun warmed her, but the shadow of the lovers' sadness settled on her shoulders. She wished she knew another way. Why did Rosemary's one chance at happiness have to be with someone whose clan was at war with the McClouds? Why did they have to go through this deception, risking Brec's anger and their own safety to keep a man alive?

They sailed east for some time, the little craft surging along, carried forward over the waves in rocking motion. They shared the meal Brenda had packed for them and watched the horizon.

All went well for some time. Finally Robert looked so exhausted that Honora suggested that he rest. Brenda took the tiller. And when Honora felt the coolness of a shadow on her cheek, she looked up to see that the sky had washed gray with clouds. She turned to Robert, dismayed to see that he had fallen into a heavy sleep, his head pillowed in Rosemary's lap. Brenda watched the sky too, and pointed to the horizon. Land was in sight, but so was the enemy castle.

"Armadean," the serving girl shouted over the wind.

"Will anyone be watching, a lookout?" Honora asked.

"They'll no' be concerned about a wee boat like this," Brenda assured her.

Honora watched Robert for a moment. She didn't like his coloring. He had grown paler. His shoulders slumped. His strength had slipped away. Anxiously Rosemary looked at Honora.

"Do what you can for him," Honora ordered.

The sails flapped. The hum faded. Honora stared up at the mainsail and watched it go slack. The mainsail boom wobbled to and fro. The boat slowed.

"What do we do now?" Honora asked.

"Patience," Brenda counseled, remaining at the tiller. Honora didn't miss the worried look on the lass's face. "The wind is just waiting to switch."

The three women sat in silence, each looking out across

the water and waiting for the wind to return, searching for the sheet of ripples that would tell them that a breeze approached.

More clouds scattered across the sky. The boat bobbed aimlessly on the waves. Rosemary took the quiet time to hand out some food and pass the water jug around.

Honora grew impatient, an hour lost already. If this voyage was not completed as they planned, they would not get back to Dunrugis until after dark, after supper. What kind of a story would she tell Brec then? she wondered. They had just decided to go sailing dressed as fisherwomen? He'd never believe that.

"Let's row," Honora ordered, reaching for the oars. "Brenda, you take one side I'll take the other."

"Nay," Brenda said with a shake of her head. "The wind will come. Ye'll see."

She was right. After a few more minutes it did come, ruffling across the smooth water and catching the sails. The mainsail whipped across the boat to the other side. Honora ducked and turned to Brenda. " 'Tis back."

"Tack," the lass shouted and shoved on the tiller. "Let the jib out on the other side."

"Tack?" Honora repeated. She didn't know what that meant, but she ripped at the rigging ropes to free the front sail. She tore three times at her sloppy knot before it loosened. Freed, the jib swung around enough to fill with the wind.

Canvas snapped. The boat surged forward. Little by little the hum built again until the rocking speed resumed. Honora sagged to the bottom of the boat in relief.

"Lady Honora," Robert called.

Honora turned to him, surprised to realize that he'd awakened to watch their frantic efforts.

"You can sign on with my crew anytime."

Honora gave him a weak smile of thanks and turned to look ahead. She prayed that soon this voyage would end.

They sailed for an inlet that Robert pointed out just above Armadean castle, but as they neared the shore, the wind died again. In frustration Honora stared at the sagging sails.

"Look," Rosemary said, pointing off the port stern. She sat next to Robert, who had fallen asleep again.

When Honora turned to see where her sister pointed, a billowing wall of fog rolled down on them. No one would see them, but they would be unable to see as well. And how would Brenda sail them home after they had landed Robert?

Urgently Rosemary shook Robert. "Sweetheart, what do we do now? Robert? Please, Robert?"

He stirred. "What is it? Rosemary . . ."

"Robert? The fog—what do we do about the fog?"

Slowly he sat up and looked about them just as the mist rolled over them and the boat.

"Fog? What to do? Listen. Sounds carry. You'll be able to hear the big vessels. The singing and the drum. Row away from them." He struggled to reach one of the oars but fell back, too weak to move that far.

Honora motioned to Rosemary to cover him with a blanket. The fog descended on them and chilled the air. The young McDonnell had no strength left to help. What would they do when they reached shore?

Honora groaned. "This seemed so simple when we planned it."

"I know," Rosemary said. "To take Robert home is the right thing to do. But we can't just put him out of the boat and leave. We have to be certain that he finds someone to help him."

"Can you take the tiller, Rosemary? Brenda, we'll row." Honora reached for one of the oars.

Rosemary took the tiller. Brenda took the other oar and the women began to row. Honora pushed forward. Brenda pulled back. The boat swung in a circle.

"This way," Honora said, pointing ahead of them. "Can't you hear the waves against the rocks?"

"Nay, shore is this way," Brenda argued. "The boat swung around when the mist rolled in. I hear the waves over there."

"I hear the waves too," Honora said. "And I'm sure the sound comes from over there."

They listened again. Honora turned in the direction where she was certain she had last seen shore. She turned to another direction and the sound seemed the same. "Rosemary, which direction is shore?"

Rosemary, more gray now than green, returned her gaze. "I don't know, sister. I'm so dizzy I can hardly sit up."

Through the mist the music of a song drifted to them, the rhythmic sound of weary oarsmen returning from sea. Oars rushed through the water.

"Are they near?" Brenda whispered.

"I'm not certain," Honora said, looking behind her, then ahead. "Must be McDonnells."

The singing grew louder and more wistful.

"What if they run over us?" Honora gasped.

"Maybe we should call to them. Tell them we are here and that we have Robert," Rosemary said. "They must be frantic about him. Surely they wouldn't harm us for returning one of their own."

Honora stared in horror at her little sister. For the first time she had to consider what would happen to them if the McDonnells captured them. For some reason she had never thought of that; she had thought only of keeping their secret from Brec.

"They might use us as hostages," Honora said, thinking of Lilias. Colin's widow would be no ally. "Nay, we can't fall into McDonnell hands. Row this way."

But the oarsmen's singing grew louder. She stopped rowing and tried to listen to the voices, to detect from which direction the singing came. But every direction she turned in, the voices seemed to be almost upon them.

Suddenly a deep voice called out in Gaelic. In near panic, Honora looked up to see a towering forecastle emerge from the fog. A relentless row of long, dripping oars lifted and descended upon them.

20

"Get out of my sight!" Brec roared. He lunged down the abbey steps where he had come in search of Honora and clenched his hands into fists to keep himself from throttling the lad who cringed at Kenneth's side.

Walter, white-faced and trembling, twisted his bonnet in his hands. To his credit, the boy didn't flee, but his voice squeaked. "Please forgive me, milaird. I'll do whatever I can. I want to be in the first search party. I canna forgive myself for losing yer ladies—and my sister."

"You were slack in your duty, lad," Brec said, lowering his voice with great effort. A moment more and he was going to grab the boy by the throat. "I said, out of my sight."

Walter winced and scuttled sideways down the path from the abbey, toward the safety of the forest, casting looks over his shoulder as if he feared pursuit.

Oleen and Kenneth remained silent, side by side in the twilight. Oleen serenely tucked her hands into the sleeves of her oversized coat. Kenneth restlessly braced his legs and clasped his hands behind him. Dubh sat motionless at Brec's feet.

"And what have you to do with this?" Brec demanded. He glowered at Oleen. Only his grudging respect for his old teacher, wise in the ways of the spirits and learned in the art of medicine, kept him from shouting at her as he had at Walter. He had no desire to believe she had any part in Honora's betrayal; but if she did, the witch would not be spared. "I've known for some time that Lady Honora didn't visit you each day for lessons in herbs. What kind of fool do you take me to be?"

"We never thought you a fool, milaird," Oleen replied.

"I of all people know of your shrewdness. We women only feared more bloodletting where none was necessary."

Brec's eyes narrowed as he peered at her, searching for any hint of deception. "Speak the truth, woman."

Oleen told him all—of how Lady Honora and Lady Rosemary had appeared at her door one day with the young, half-drowned McDonnell draped over the black pony's back.

As she spoke, Brec paced from the abbey steps to the kirkyard gate and back.

Oleen told of Robert's slow recovery and the rapid blossoming of romance between him and Rosemary. Of secrets kept and lies told. Of Honora's fears for the young man and her sister and of her daring plan to return the youngest McDonnell son to his clan with Brenda's help.

"You let Honora sail off to Armadean alone?" Brec thundered. Startled doves fluttered from their nesting place beneath the abbey eaves. Dubh slunk to the far side of the steps.

Oleen remained unperturbed. "Her will is nearly as strong as yours, milaird. Once her mind is set—"

"Aye, aye, I know that." Brec waved at Oleen to be silent and rubbed his hand across his brow to hide his face from her for a moment—for one instant of exultant relief and tortured joy.

Honora had not left him for another man, *but* she had lied—he had known it as soon as she and Rosemary had not appeared for supper. He had ordered an immediate search of the castle and village, but he had known she would not be found on the island. She'd deceived him—to protect a McDonnell, one of Lilias's kind. She had sailed off without a care for him or for the clan or for her place as his wife, the lady of Dunrugis.

Knowing that there was no other lover gave him little satisfaction. He had given her every opportunity to reveal her secret and she'd denied there was one. And now she had probably fallen into the hands of the McDonnells—or worse.

Brec swore a seaman's oath. He pounded his fist against the abbey's stone wall until his knuckles purpled with bruises.

Oleen frowned, but went on undaunted. "If the weather had held, I'm certain Lady Honora and Lady Rosemary would have gotten back all right. But the signs betrayed us. When I saw the fog roll in, I knew there would be trouble. Have faith, Brec, Robert should be able to advise Brenda and Lady Honora. Surely the boy will speak to his father on their behalf. Roderick McDonnell would not dare harm McCloud ladies."

"Perhaps not, but he can hold them for ransom," Brec muttered. "And Lilias will give them no gracious reception."

"Brec," Kenneth said, stepping forward, his face pale and his mouth small with fear. "We should set sail immediately. A show of force will prove to the McDonnells that we will no' tolerate any harm coming to Bren—the ladies."

"Aye, we sail in an hour," Brec ordered, somewhat mollified by this suggested course of action. "No matter what we do, Roderick McDonnell won't be easy to deal with. And there are others out there besides Lilias's father. Alasdair mac Colkitto sails among the isles, recruiting Royalist allies. And that Scot-Irish renegade has no liking for Campbells or Lowlanders."

"In an hour," Kenneth repeated and hurried down the path toward the castle. Oleen lingered.

"I have no more to say to you," Brec bit off, turning his back on the wise woman.

"Well, I would tell you that your wife has a good heart and great courage," Oleen said. "And to mind your black temper, Brec. Don't be too quick to condemn her for doing what she thought was best for everyone."

"I condemn no one, *yet.*"

"I'm glad to hear it," Oleen said. She turned and strolled down the path after Kenneth.

Certain that he was alone at last, Brec opened the iron work gate and entered the kirkyard with the reverent, unhurried tread of one marching down a kirk aisle. He wound his way between the ancient lichen-speckled stones to the far corner and stopped at a new grave. He touched lightly the new white rock, tracing the plaited vines carved into stone. He looked away, out over the trees, through the twilight, and down on the gray waters of the loch where he could see Kenneth and the oarsmen readying the *Dal Riata*.

"Was it this painful for you, Colin?" Brec asked, with visions of his brother and Lilias in his head. With his face turned to catch the sea breeze that swayed the treetops, but with his hand still resting on the stone, his only connection with the dead.

"When you knew for certain that Lilias had betrayed you did it feel like this? The heavy ache in the chest, the hot twist in the gut. Everything was always so perfect for you, Colin. When you found that the union of bodies was only that—two separate souls embracing—a fleeting pleasure, an illusion of oneness, like a trick of magic. Now you have it, now you don't."

Dubh followed Brec to the grave side and sat peacefully beside the stone and at Brec's feet. Distracted by the movement, Brec looked down to stare into the dog's blue eyes.

"I did as I promised you, brother, I brought a lady to Dunrugis. There was no mistake in that. And I don't regret the price. Even the servants have accepted her. But then I let myself believe that the half-measure of happiness that I found with her might grow into something. I let myself believe that in a moment of union we shared something, at least the desire to please each other, if not more. But I was a fool, Colin."

Brec gave a bitter laugh that made Dubh perk his ears.

"If father had been here he would have been the first to see it, the first to laugh. 'Fool,' he would shout at me. Wave a belittling hand in my direction. Even when I was old enough to take command of my own galley he could always make me feel like a boy too young to be out of the nursery."

Brec shook his head at the dog. "I never had your success, Colin. Why should I ever think I would find loyalty, love, and happiness in marriage where even you failed?"

The cold of the castle chamber crept through the wool plaid to Honora's shoulders, settling on her arms and numbing her fingers until no matter how tightly she pulled the blanket about her, she shivered. But she made no complaint. She never thought she would prefer a below-ground room in the McDonnells' castle over other accommodations. But the icy chamber proved infinitely better than the stinking hold of the Scot-Irish pirate ship.

She had recognized the monstrous red-haired captain of the galley as Colkitto before he introduced himself. The man was reputed to give no quarter to Lowlanders and those of the reformed religion. Her knees had gone weak and she had nearly lost her voice as she stood before him and boldly demanded safe return of herself, Rosemary, and Brenda. Robert had roused himself enough to insist that Colkitto at least put all four of them ashore at Armadean. Of course, that had put them right into McDonnell hands.

Beside her on the bench slept Brenda in a deep and trusting slumber, her head resting heavily against Honora's shoulder. Honora had slept little. She watched dawn's watery light pour through a window slit high in the wall of Armadean castle.

They would have been missed at Dunrugis by now. She wondered what Brec had said when her chair at the supper table had remained empty. Had he flown into a rage? Had he searched for her in the laird's bedchamber? Or was he relieved, glad to be free of his duty beneath the fairy banner? In the end, would Oleen tell him the truth about their visits? Would he think her and Rosemary traitors for aiding a McDonnell? And where was Rosemary now?

Against Honora's shoulder, Brenda stirred and sighed in her sleep but did not wake. How could the lass sleep? she wondered, then reminded herself that Brenda had no guilty conscience.

And just where were Robert and Rosemary? Honora asked herself. Perhaps she should never have allowed Rosemary to be separated from her.

Upon their coming ashore from the pirate ship, old Laird McDonnell had nearly collapsed in blubbering tears over his youngest son.

"Robert, Robert, we thought ye lost in the storm and feared ye'd drowned," the rough old man had cried, snatching his son up in a bearlike embrace.

Robert, weak and somewhat dazed, had endured the embrace and steadfastly refused to be separated from Rosemary. So when Rosemary began to interrupt on Honora's behalf, Honora had silenced her sister with a warning shake of her head.

Lilias, dressed in black with the Armadean keys worn around her neck on a gaudy gold chain, hovered at her father's side. She had changed little in her weeks away from Dunrugis, remaining as haughty and cold as Honora remembered her. Face to face the raven lady's ice-blue gaze flamed with hatred the moment she recognized Honora. Outwardly Honora managed to remain calm, but she cringed inside. She would receive no favors from this woman.

But Lilias didn't know Rosemary and apparently saw no reason why her ailing brother's fancy for a common lass shouldn't be indulged. Lilias and her serving women had whisked the young McDonnell and Rosemary away.

Though Honora was reluctant to be separated from her sister, she made no protest. She hoped that under Robert's protection Rosemary would be spared Lilias's vengeful wrath.

A grim-faced master of the guard locked Honora and Brenda away in a tiny, below-ground chamber—not a true dungeon, entered only through a trapdoor. But it was without a hearth and horribly cold. Honora had beat on the door and decried their treatment to the guard. If he'd understood her Gaelic, he made no sign.

The hours of the night had been long and dark for Honora. She listened to morning sounds—servants lighting fires, carrying water, and preparing food. But the passage outside their cell remained silent. Beyond the castle she heard the song of birds and the distant roar of the sea.

Armadean was not the grand castle that Dunrugis was, Honora had discovered. Dunrugis towered on rock with its skirts trailing gracefully in the water, while Armadean perched on a hillside above the sea, forest bound. What little of Armadean she'd seen revealed damp barren walls in need of repair, dark rooms with little furniture, and uneven floors of worn stones. No wonder Lilias had coveted the position as lady of Castle Dunrugis.

What happened now, Honora wondered. Had they saved Robert from a fate of starvation in Dunrugis' dungeon, only to meet it themselves in the bowels of Armadean?

Without warning, keys rattled in the lock. Honora and Brenda sat up. Honora's stiff muscles ached, but she stood, smoothing her windblown hair and her wrinkled tartan skirt.

The door was thrown open by the guard. In the doorway stood Lilias and the McDonnell.

"Which one did you say is Brec McCloud's wife?" the McDonnell asked. He was a man of average height, but with a distinctive face—a big nose, full lips, broad brow, and a wild brown beard streaked with silver and something that Honora took for dried gravy. He pointed at Honora, disbelief on his face. "She looks like another fisherwoman to me."

Honora realized that in her common dress and cap she bore no resemblance to a clan chief's lady. But she summoned her courage and decided to face down Lilias and her father as best she could. She had done it with the Scot-Irish pirate who had fished them from the sea. She could do it with a McDonnell.

"I am Lady Honora Maitland, daughter of the late Duke of Rosslyn and now Lady McCloud of the Isle of Myst," Honora announced in her best Gaelic. She didn't trust Lilias to translate for her.

The McDonnell stared at her, the derision on his lips dissolving into curiosity.

Encouraged by this expression of interest, Honora went on. "We found your son Robert near-drowned on the beach. We nursed him back to health and have returned him to you. For such a service, we—all three of us—ask to be returned to Dunrugis."

After another moment of silence, the McDonnell turned to Lilias and spoke in English. "Colkitto said she was a good talker with a lot of bluff."

The slight infuriated Honora, but she disclosed no anger.

"Don't be fooled by her, Father," Lilias warned, her gaze fixed on Honora's face. "McCloud sent her here to spy on us even as they prepare to return the raid on Solnarra."

"Then why is the *Dal Riata* out there in the loch with the French pirate ship *Sea Gull?* Nay, I think the new McCloud is eager to have his lady back."

"Oh, thank God, Laird Brec is here," Brenda whispered in Honora's ear, squeezing her arm. "I hope Kenneth is with him . . . but maybe no'."

Honora's heart gave a little leap. Brec was here already to take her home. Then, like Brenda, she thought again. She could well imagine his roar when informed he had to deal with a McDonnell for the return of his wife and her sister. She knew the McDonnell would demand something for their return.

Without realizing what she was doing, she took Brenda's hand and drew the girl closer. "Where's my sister? Where's Rosemary?"

McDonnell glanced at Lilias. "There was another?"

"Other? There was only the crippled girl who spent the night with Robert."

"Nay," Honora groaned. "They didn't . . . You didn't allow . . . I demand to see Rosemary—now." Unspoken fears chilled her, making her bolder and more insistent. "Where is Rosemary?"

"Rosemary must be the spy," Lilias said in her father's ear loud enough for Honora to hear.

The McDonnell shook his head. "Nonsense, daughter. McCloud would never send a spy to Armadean in such an obvious fashion. And I think if McCloud had known that Robert was on the Isle of Myst, he would've held him hostage instead of sending the boy to us in the company of his wife. Nay, we have the advantage here."

A sweet tinkle of laughter drifted into the room from the passage. Honora turned eagerly at the door in time to see Robert appear, followed by Rosemary. With a laughing smile, Honora's sister hobbled lightly past the McDonnell and Lilias and threw herself into Honora's arms.

"I'm here, Sister. No harm done. Robert has asked me to marry him."

Honora staggered under the impact of her sister's body and her words as well. Over Rosemary's head Honora noted the flush in Robert's pale complexion. He wore a lover's euphoric smile. And he had seemed so weak only the day before, she thought ruefully.

"I'm so happy," Rosemary said, gazing up at her sister.

A blissful smile touched Rosemary's lips, and she glowed with the happiness she had just declared.

Robert stepped closer to put his arm around Rosemary. "Lady Honora, I want to ask for Rosemary's hand in marriage. Today. I'm afraid that if I let her out of my sight, she'll turn into a mermaid, slip into the sea, and be gone from my life."

"Marriage?" Honora turned to Rosemary. "Today? Is that what you want, Rosemary?"

"Aye." Rosemary gazed into Robert's face. "This day, if he wishes it. 'Tis what I want, Sister. I belong with Robert."

The lovers drowned in each other's gazes. Only a dullard would be unable to see that they truly loved each other.

"Another marriage with the McClouds?" the McDonnell exclaimed. "One has been more than enough trouble."

Lilias snorted a derisive laugh. "Robert, you must know there is no power in marrying this McCloud kinswoman."

"I don't care," Robert said, watching Rosemary's face. "I don't have to marry for duty or power. I marry to spend my life with Rosemary."

Deep inside, a sharp pang of bittersweet envy pierced Honora. The stab came so swiftly, with such unexpected sting that she had to place her hand over her heart to smother her gasp of pain. Rosemary, her lame sister, who she feared would never marry or have children or love and happiness—Rosemary had this chance to have everything.

Honora studied the floor, pressing her hand to her heart, struggling to catch her breath. Once long ago she had hoped for all those things for herself. And when she married Brec she wanted to believe that somehow, sometime they might come to love each other. She wondered what hope she had now for ever gaining Brec's love. The possibility seemed farther away than ever. But that was no reason for Rosemary's future to be snatched from her. With effort Honora quelled her own pain and set her mind to securing Rosemary's happiness.

"This is your sister?" the McDonnell demanded. He looked Rosemary up and down before turning to his son. "We thought her a common wench. Robert, ye wish to marry a McCloud?"

"A Maitland," Honora corrected. "Daughter of Thomas Maitland, the late Duke of Rosslyn. Sister-in-law of the McCloud. Your daughter married a McCloud. What objection could you have to your son's match with my sister?"

Before the McDonnell could respond, weapons clanged in the passage. Boot leather slapped against stone. Out of the noise blustered the huge man with red hair and a bright bushy beard—the one who'd dragged them from the sea.

"I have news, McDonnell."

"There you are, Colkitto," McDonnell greeted. "Did McCloud answer our invitation to a meeting?"

"Aye, McCloud agrees to a meeting, but only aboard a neutral ship—the pirate's *Sea Gull*."

" 'Twill do," McDonnell said, giving a look of satisfaction to the huge Scot-Irish pirate. "You and me will get what we want as a trade for these ladies."

Brec settled back in his chair, feeling oddly at home in the confines of the *Sea Gull*'s low-ceilinged captain's quarters. A peat fire glowed in the brazier. Simon's pipe smoke curled about their heads. The Frenchman had not been pleased about joining this expedition, but Brec had reminded Simon of what he owed the McClouds.

Four big men—Simon LaFarge, Roderick McDonnell, Alasdair mac Colkitto, and himself—sat crowded around the table, knee to knee, a flagon of ale set before each.

"Are ye saying ye refuse to join us, McCloud? Remember, we have yer lady," McDonnell sputtered, thumping his empty flagon down on the table.

Brec made no reply, satisfied to let the McDonnell stammer.

"I heard that ominous signs marked your landing at Ardnamurchan," Brec remarked to Colkitto while the McDonnell pondered refusal.

" 'Tis no ill omen," Colkitto said with a laugh. "Were a warning to the bloody Campbell clan. We're here to defeat the usurper and to win the king's cause."

McDonnell joined in Colkitto's laughter. Neither Brec nor Simon smiled. The group fell into an uncomfortable silence.

The legendary Alasdair mac Colkitto leaned forward. In

his youth the Scot-Irish pirate was said to have held a cow by the horns with one hand while using his other to sever its head with a single ax blow. He was an imposing man— arrogant, ruthless—with more courage than brains, Brec suspected. A dangerous combination.

"Ye'll have more ale, Colkitto?" Simon offered as he filled the three other flagons on the table.

Brec refused the offer. He had no real interest in the food or drink and had accepted the first flagon only to avoid offending the others. He wanted to see Honora. He wanted to see for himself that his wife was well, that McDonnell and Alasdair mac Colkitto hadn't abused her. Then he would throttle her himself. He could not imagine what had induced her to attempt such a foolish voyage, to lie to him and to the clan.

"Are ye hungry, McCloud?" McDonnell cast Brec a sly look. "I can send for some fine Solnarra beef."

"I'm not here to discuss Solnarra," Brec replied. His anger and impatience was rising, but he controlled it. "The issue is the return of my wife, her sister, and serving woman."

"Perhaps we should discuss the isle," McDonnell said, wiping a trickle of ale from his chin whiskers, then drying his hand on the front of his saffron shirt. He leaned across the table toward Brec as if to confide something important. "Ye put me in a devil of a spot when ye sent Lilias home, McCloud. The lass is no' accustomed to being told where to go and what to do. Took the dismissal as a real insult. And her brother Donald did too. Ye know how hot-blooded he is. 'Twas off on that raid before I could stop him. Of course, there is the question of the dowry, Solnarra and all."

"Lilias was given her proper dowager settlement."

"Aye," McDonnell said, "but it doesna mend her grieving heart. Her man is gone. Why didna ye marry her, McCloud? Would've made life simpler for all of us."

Alasdair grunted his agreement.

"Lilias is a strong woman, a McDonnell," Brec said. He had no intention of enlightening the father about his daughter's sins unless that became necessary. "I think her heart will recover."

"Aye, but the rest of us will suffer in the meantime,"
the McDonnell lamented. "And while I had the chance I
looked over yer wife. Truth of it be, I might've considered
a Lowland lass myself if I'd met one like her. Sailed herself
right up to Alasdair's ship and demanded protection for
herself, her women, and Robert." McDonnell elbowed the
Scot-Irish pirate beside him. "Brazen courage for a
woman."

Colkitto grunted agreement without taking his lips from
his flagon. Brec wondered why Alasdair was so quiet.

"Too bad she's from a Covenantor family and all. Took
old Alasdair by surprise. He was ready to throw them all
overboard until he recognized Robert. Then he wanted to
use the ladies as hostages to win your five hundred fighting
men. See, I told him how I thought ye might refuse to take
up the cause of the king. But when I realized yer lady and
her sister brought my Robert back, well, we couldna repay
a kindness like that by using her as hostage, now could
we?"

"I want to see my wife," Brec demanded in an even
voice. He never blinked, never displayed his anger, his
fear. He had known McDonnell would do something like
this—hold Honora for an exchange—fighting men, rights to
an island, even money.

McDonnell shrugged. "Donna refuse before ye hear our
plan to save the king's cause. Alasdair, tell him."

"I'll hear your plan after I see my wife." Brec met the
McDonnell's gaze across the table. "No more talk until
then."

The McDonnell blinked first. "Signal Donald to bring the
women aboard."

Simon went to the cabin door and passed along the order.

"While we wait, Alasdair, show McCloud here yer
sword," McDonnell suggested over his flagon.

Alasdair rose, ducking to keep his head from striking a
ceiling beam. Steel raked against the scabbard and he flourished a huge *claidheamh mor*.

To belie his wariness Brec leaned back in his chair and
watched the great red-haired man display a sword of
unusual design. He noticed that Simon who remained in
the doorway turned pale at the sight of the weapon.

Brec knew the game of intimidation when he saw it—
he had used it often enough himself. He would not give
McDonnell or Colkitto the satisfaction of turning a hair in
concern. And he was fairly certain that the two wanted him
alive rather than dead. Dead, he was useless.

The polished steel of Alasdair's sword flashed in the dim
cabin light, catching Brec's interest. Alasdair pointed to the
steel rod that paralleled the blade. Upon the rod floated a
steel apple, or weight.

" 'Tis an improvement I had added to give the Covenantors a quick and merciful death. Seems the least we can do
for the ignorant brutes. Me own design," he bragged, his
square white teeth gleaming in the lamplight.

His attention captured at last, Brec rose from his chair
to inspect the weapon more closely. With growing admiration he noted how the metal globe slid down the rod, adding
extra weight to the sword tip when swung downward. He
turned the sword slowly so all in the cabin could see each
side of the lethal blade and weight.

"Ye want a demonstration?" Alasdair asked, eyeing the
table they sat at.

"Not in me quarters," Simon protested from the cabin
doorway. "Let's go above. 'Twill make for great tale telling
and 'twill be an honor to show me guests where Alasdair
mac Colkitto buried his sword shaft on the *Sea Gull*."

The men roared with laughter at the joke, at the innu-
endo, and in release of the tension.

Alasdair led the way to the deck, leaping the steps two
at a time. When all had gathered on the deck, he raised the
weapon over his head, then swung it down into a bench
just abandoned by two of Simon's crew. The oak wood
split, shivered with the thud. The bench groaned, then
collapsed, the wood screeching protest. The men on the
deck—pirates, McDonnell and McCloud men—backed
away, putting more steps between themselves, the sword,
and Alasdair mac Colkitto.

McDonnell threw his head back and roared with delight.
Alasdair grinned. He brandished the sword proudly before
him.

Brec stared in awe at the menacing, gleaming steel.
" 'Tis an uncommon weapon."

"Aye, uncommonly effective," Alasdair admitted. "I've never needed more than one blow to behead a foe. Try it?"

"I have no more benches to spare," Simon objected. "Ye may have to start on the sailors."

The *Sea Gull*'s crew grimaced nervously and retreated to the ship's rail.

Alasdair laid the hilt of the weapon in Brec's hand.

Brec had trained in the use of weapons since he was a boy. With his quick reactions and his size he was a more than competent swordsman. He had always bested Colin in swordplay and sailing. But he had never had the fascination with weapons that others did. He was a man of the sea. He admired the well-cut sail and the fine line of a hull. But this sword intrigued him. He respected its macabre beauty and deadly efficiency.

"Does the weight pull it from your grip as it strikes?"

"It can," Alasdair admitted. He stepped around to Brec's side. "I train for that. Make your grip like this."

The Scot-Irish pirate demonstrated the grip.

"Would ye no' like to join our little band, McCloud?" McDonnell coaxed, obviously encouraged by the McCloud's interest in Colkitto's sword. "We have a great warrior with a unique weapon to join us. Ye be our transport with yer fine ships. With yer fighting men, ye'd keep the English from our backs."

Brec weighed the weapon in his hand. Despite its ungainly appearance, the sword balanced well. The old restlessness stirred in his heart, like the tug of a long-planned voyage. The excitement of laying the plans, studying maps, plotting the course. The work of gathering the men, training them, oiling the weapons, and readying the rigging. To defy the fates. To spurn the odds. To believe that one will be the victor despite the obstacles. The siren of battle called to Brec's Celtic soul as clearly and seductively as a march droned by bagpipes.

Cold concentration hardened Brec's face. He lifted the weapon, and when the blade arced down, the oak bench flipped and split again. Splinters flew. The steel weight spun to the end of the rod. With a thud the sword tip buried itself into the *Sea Gull*'s deck and quivered.

Silence reigned.

No foe would survive a direct strike from this weapon. Brec pulled the blade from the deck to admire it once more. Colkitto roared with obvious delight in Brec's demonstration. He slapped Brec on the back. "Ye must join us, McCloud. Help us send those Covenantors to their misbegotten heaven."

A commotion near the railing wrestled Brec's attention from the weapon. He looked up in time to see Simon help Honora climb over the railing. Rosemary was already aboard in the company of a fair young man Brec recognized as Lilias's brother. Lilias followed Honora.

But Brec had eyes only for his wife. To his relief, she appeared unharmed and composed. Even her plain gown and the cap on her head could not hide her quality. Her face was pale and a hint of purple smudged beneath her eyes as though she hadn't slept—neither had he. Soberly she stared at him and the weapon he held.

Abruptly Brec lowered the sword. For her he had given his word to not go into this battle.

"Here's yer lady, McCloud," the McDonnell said. "She's no' much worse than when Colkitto put her ashore. Listen to our plan. Ye'll want to join us when ye hear how we will win this war for the king."

At the sight of her husband wielding a strange, vicious-looking sword, Honora lost what little courage she had left. She watched in frozen fear as he lifted the blade and admired the monstrous weapon a moment more.

At her side Brenda muttered a prayer and crossed herself.

Then to Honora's relief, Brec returned the weapon to the pirate. As he did, he glared at her, his anger and resentment clear. She clutched Brenda's arm for strength and Brenda clutched hers.

"I will speak with my wife before I hear any more about plans," Brec said, turning to Honora. In a gesture that surprised her, he held out his hand. Invitation or summons? Honora hesitated.

In the darkness of the night she had feared that he wouldn't come for her, that he would consider her a traitor. Yet here he was reaching for her—but did he reach because he cared or because a McCloud could not desert his wife? Because the clan could not lose face before an enemy?

Honora caught a leer from the Alasdair. She collected herself with as much poise as she could muster and walked across the deck to Brec. He took her hand in a bone-crushing grip. With surprise and determination, Honora choked back a yelp of pain. She would allow neither her husband nor his enemies to witness her weakness. Brec held her gaze, his brows lowered a hard, black line.

"You lied to me," he said, so quietly, so deadly.

"Aye, milaird," she replied just as quietly. Before she could say more, he drew her to his side, his grip easing only when she stood with her arm pressed against his.

"Are you all right? Have you been mistreated? Is Rosemary all right?" He looked to her sister.

Still in pain, Honora nodded her head yes first, then no, and then yes.

"I'm satisfied, Alasdair," Brec declared. "Now explain the price of my wife's and her sister's return."

"And Brenda," Honora prompted in a whisper. "Don't forget Brenda."

"And Brenda," Brec amended, his brows quirked in irritation. Aside he muttered, "How can I forget, between you and Kenneth?"

Honora looked over Brec's shoulder to see Kenneth standing near the ship's rail, arms folded stubbornly across his chest and his glare fixed on her serving woman.

"Here's the plan," Alasdair began. "We march inland by the end of the month to join with Montrose. With his Highland forces and our seasoned Irish and Islemen, we will drive Campbell's forces from Scotland and south to London, where they belong."

"Do you know where Montrose is?" Brec asked. Honora sensed immediately that Brec did know. "Does he expect you?"

"He's in the Highlands gathering forces," Alasdair said. He and McDonnell exchanged awkward looks. "We don't know exactly where. McDonnell says you might know. That you have spies."

"Spies?" Brec repeated with a wry chuckle. "I may have some information that could help you."

"Where is Montrose? Tell me, man," Alasdair ordered. He started toward Brec. "I can send word to the Montrose today that the Islemen come with ready forces."

Brec studied Colkitto, then McDonnell. "Is that the price of the return of my wife then? How to reach Montrose?"

McDonnell blinked at McCloud. After exchanging glances with Colkitto once more, the clan chief spoke up. "We want more than the knowledge of where Montrose is. We want your fighting men."

Brec shook his head. "I've told you, I'll not take up arms against either side. That's final. But I am willing to share the information I have gained through my shipping, ah, sources."

Again Colkitto and McDonnell muttered between themselves.

"McDonnell, you test my patience," Brec warned. "I came here for my wife, who in a moment of charity—granted, foolhardy charity, but charity nonetheless—saved your son and brought him home alive. Where is this McDonnell who owes my wife his life?"

From Rosemary's side Robert stepped forward, his face sober with earnestness, his hand clasping hers. "I'm Robert McDonnell, Laird McCloud. Your wife and her sister saved my life. And I wish to ask for Rosemary's hand in marriage."

Rosemary stepped forward. "Aye, we wish to be married."

"None of this foolishness now," old McDonnell warned. "Donna listen to the boy, McCloud. He is ill."

Brec glanced at Honora. "Did you know of this?"

"They told me only this morning," Honora murmured so that others couldn't hear, and praying that Brec's fondness for Rosemary would make him sympathetic to their cause. "They were together last night, and now they refuse to be parted. What can we do? I don't want to deny Rosemary happiness, but I cannot leave my little sister here among the McDonnells. Alone with Lilias. Can you help us, milaird? Help Rosemary."

Robert spoke again. "Milaird, if 'tis the dowry that concerns you, I will gladly forgo that. Rosemary saved my life. I will ask for no more from her."

"Donna be hasty, boy," old McDonnell advised, a more

serious expression coming over his features. "A wife has a right and a duty to bring something to a marriage."

Rosemary cast Honora a woeful look.

"Aye, I didn't come here to settle a marriage contract," Colkitto interrupted. "Where is Montrose, McCloud?"

"You'll get nothing from me until this matter of my wife, her sister, and Robert is concluded," Brec retorted.

Gratefully Honora squeezed Brec's arm. "Ask what he would accept for a dowry," she whispered. "I can offer land."

"So what would you accept, McDonnell?" Brec demanded, a narrow-eyed look of defiance on his face. "How about Solnarra?"

"Solnarra is my island," Lilias objected, making her way from the rail to her father's side. "You can't consider giving it away."

" 'Tis always been a McCloud holding, Lilias," Brec declared.

"Oh," the McDonnell groaned. "I've no stomach for quarreling over that damnable isle now."

"Grant them the cursed island," Colkitto said, pacing the deck. " 'Tis no time for feuding. We've a war to fight."

"Nay, Solnarra is my isle." Lilias turned to face Brec and Honora with her arms folded across her breasts. "I won't give it up, not even for my brother."

"You already rule Armadean," the McDonnell reminded his daughter. "What more do ye want, lass? And we need the McCloud's information."

"And I'm sure you would be pleased to rebuild the fortified house on the isle for the bridal couple," Brec suggested. "As you may recall, 'twas recently destroyed in a raid."

"Aye, father," Robert agreed as he smiled down at Rosemary and put his hand over hers tucked under his arm. "My bride must have a proper home."

"Oh, aye," McDonnell said, a look of exasperation crossing his face. "Aye, 'twill be rebuilt."

"Father, you can't do this," Lilias protested, her voice becoming high pitched, and she clutched at her Father's arm.

"Silence, daughter," the McDonnell ordered, shrugging

her off. "Think of it as a wedding gift to your brother. You can add that tower you want to Armadean Castle if ye don't trouble me over this island."

Lilias hesitated, her hand dropping away from her father and her expression lit with avarice. "Truly? A new tower with a wood-paneled drawing room—and a virginal. I'd like to have a virginal."

"Aye, aye," the McDonnell agreed with another sigh and a helpless wave of his hands.

"And you will replace the McClennon livestock that were stolen," Brec suggested. "And you will make it clear to Donald that he will lead no more raids."

McDonnell drew in a long breath and his back stiffened. "Ye ask for a lot, McCloud."

" 'Tis for your son and new daughter," Brec prompted.

" 'Twill be done," McDonnell grumbled.

Honora could hardly believe what she was hearing. The McDonnell and the McCloud had agreed to something. Rosemary was to wed her true love and live on the isle of Solnarra. Peace would reign again between the McClouds and the McDonnells. Honora squeezed Brec's hand and smiled up into his frowning face. Her husband had performed magic once more.

21

McDonnell slapped Brec on the back and proposed the wedding be held at Armadean. Brec frowned. "More than one assassination has taken place at a wedding celebration."

"Ye insult my hospitality, McCloud."

"I accept your son into my family, McDonnell, after you threatened to hold my wife hostage. That is no insult. I will see the couple wed on this deck."

"Then we'll bring the celebration to the ship," McDonnell declared. "Lilias?"

The raven lady regarded her father with a stubborn frown.

Despite his daughter's refusal to act as hostess, the McDonnell ordered that refreshments and the harper be ferried out to the *Sea Gull* without delay.

Simon gave up his quarters to the bride-to-be and her attendants. Before he left them alone, he found a fine, Spanish lace shawl in his locker for the bride.

The women had only as long as it took to bring the priest aboard to prepare for the ceremony. Honora smoothed Rosemary's hair and arranged the Spanish shawl. Brenda fussed with the lame girl's kerchief collar. Tearfully the sisters embraced.

"This is truly what you want?" Honora asked again, wondering whether her little sister understood all the difficulties she would face. Suddenly she thought her Rosemary looked helpless and innocent—too innocent to be married and left on her own on a small isle. "This marriage is happening so fast. If you have doubts, now is the time to say so."

"I know 'tis an uncommon betrothal and wedding, but it is right," said Rosemary, smiling through her tears. "Tell Beatrix that Robert and I are as perfect for each other as she and William. We'll live on Solnarra like a prince and his mermaid."

All was like a strange, feverish dream to Honora. Her sister Rosemary wed on a pirate ship—to a McDonnell!

Brenda had no cake to break over Rosemary's head, and no grand table of food was laid out. But the music was loud and merry. The bride danced with her groom, and nearly every pirate claimed his kiss. Rosemary's cheeks glowed with happiness, and pride flushed Robert's face.

Brenda and Kenneth danced merrily. After some ale and some bread and cheese, Honora began to enjoy the celebration. She especially took pleasure in seeing Colkitto grab Lilias about the waist and whirl her around the deck. The widow had no escape.

When Honora caught sight of Brec, he was leaning against the ship's railing, his arms folded across his chest. He watched only the dancing, the look of anger never far from the slant of his brow.

But Honora had to dance at her sister's wedding, first with Robert, then Simon, Kenneth, the McDonnell, even some of Simon's crew: Red Dog, Little Ned, and a strange shiny-headed fellow named Bald Bill. She drew back when Colkitto invited her to dance. His reputation for murder frightened Honora. Thankfully, Brec appeared to lead her away. Alasdair only laughed.

The dancing went late into the night.

Simon gave up his cabin to the newlyweds. The other merrymakers slept on the deck. Aboard the *Dal Riata*, Brec pointed out a small enclosure below the forecastle, where Honora found a warm plaid and a pallet on which she and Brenda slept.

The next morning the *Dal Riata, Sea Gull,* and the McDonnell *Sea Eagle* prepared to sail to Solnarra. As supplies for the isle were loaded on the McDonnell galley, the Scot-Irish pirate and McDonnell rowed a small boat out to the McCloud ship and hailed Brec.

"Where is Montrose?" Colkitto demanded. "You said you would tell me, McCloud."

"He is in hiding," Brec called over the gunwale. "Send word to his cousin, Black Pate Inchbrakie, near Tulliebelton. He will forward any message to the Marquis of Montrose."

"Join us," McDonnell urged. "We could use your five hundred men at arms, and I see battle fever in your eye, McCloud."

"Nay," Brec said with a shake of his head. His gaze fell immediately upon Honora. "I have sworn to take up no arms against the Covenantors. I will not break my word."

"Ye are sworn?" McDonnell asked. The man's lower jaw went slack with astonishment. "Why? Who? Donna tell me the lady's family? 'Tis a high price for a woman, McCloud."

Honora thought so too, if it were true, and she wanted to ask Brec about it.

But he merely shook his head at all of them and signaled to the master of the *Dal Riata*, who shouted orders to the oarsmen, and they sailed for Solnarra.

*   *   *

Throughout the voyage and once on the isle, Honora's head was so full of plans and the details of setting up Rosemary's household that she forgot about McDonnell's words.

"Maybe you should stay here with Rosemary while I return to the Isle of Myst," Brec suggested the third day they were there. He came up behind Honora and spoke as she was supervising the meal preparation. She gave little thought to his words at first.

"I thought about that, but I believe Rosemary will be all right after all," she said, without looking at him, her mind set on getting the meal served to the men and women who had agreed to serve Rosemary and Robert.

"Brec, you know, I think the McClennons like Robert, even though he's a McDonnell. They know he wasn't responsible for the raid and that he's a devout man of peace. Rosemary speaks enough of the language to get along. 'Tis kind of you to suggest it, but my place is with you at Dunrugis."

When he made no answer, Honora turned to see him frown at her once more, a hard turn of the mouth full of reproach. She had been so caught up in Rosemary's happiness that his expression startled her. With a pang of remorse she remembered that they had things to settle between them yet.

"Why do you ask? Do you wish me to stay here?"

"Whatever you wish," he said with an indifferent shrug. Before turning away, he added, "We leave tomorrow morning."

As helpful as he was to Robert and the men in getting supplies unloaded from the galleys and stored on Solnarra, Brec had nothing more to say to Honora for the rest of their stay.

The next morning Honora and Brenda boarded the *Dal Riata* and stood at the stern rail, watching Solnarra grow small on the horizon. Without the confusion of directing servants and setting things to rights in the partly built house, the McDonnell's curious words came back to her. Had Brec forsworn taking up arms for the king? That sounded like something her uncles would demand, were they unable to recruit him for their cause. Would Brec have given such a promise to wed her? Surely he had not wanted her that badly. Such an oath would be an unthinkable sacrifice of independence for a clan chief.

Solnarra forgotten, Honora whirled around to see Brec standing in his customary place on the bow forecastle, looking out over the sea. Would he tell her why he made such a promise if she asked? It was time for them to talk of the matters between them, she decided, as she made her way between the rows of oarsmen to her husband.

" 'Tis true, what McDonnell said?" she asked breathlessly, without preamble when she reached the rail next to Brec. She realized that her hands were trembling, so she clutched her plaid and peered into his face. "Did you agree to not take up arms for the king because of me? Did my uncles demand that?"

"Aye," he said simply, never taking his gaze from the horizon. "I thought having you worth it at the time. I didn't believe you capable of lying to me and disgracing the clan."

Unprepared for this quiet attack, Honora caught her breath and tried to think how to explain her deception to him. She had expected an explosion of rage, not this deadly calm. Bewildered, she searched for the words to make him understand how important it had seemed at the time to protect the young McDonnell from the McClouds. "Robert was so innocent and Rosemary fell in love with him. I didn't want to see anyone hurt."

"Romantic nonsense," Brec said. "You lied to me. You betrayed my trust. A clan chief must have a faithful wife. A loyal wife." Brec's hands gripped the rail until they whitened, but his stoic gaze remained on the sea.

"I have not been unfaithful, Brec. There has never been any man but you. You know that," Honora insisted, her heart aching to make him understand and a sense of panic descending on her.

Heads of the oarsmen came up, staring at her, and she realized she had spoken too loud. She lowered her head and moved closer to Brec. She'd rather have him explode at her in white-hot anger than turn this coolness on her. She could deal with open anger. This cold remoteness took him away from her, to an icy isolation beyond her reach.

A sudden large swell threw her off balance, and she grabbed for the rail. Brec caught her arm to steady her and their gazes met. The moment she regained her balance, he released her. But not before Honora glimpsed the doubt in his dark eyes.

"Why, Brec? Why do you insist on mistrusting me?"

"Why?" he echoed bitterly. "There was the first meeting with Alexander that you lied to your uncles about. Then Alexander came to the island. Will I ever know the truth of that? But I wanted to forget it, so I did. Weeks went by, but I knew something was wrong. When I held you in my arms, I knew you weren't telling me something. I even asked you about it. But you lied to save a McDonnell. You lied to me, your husband and your clan chief. That's the truth, isn't it?"

He turned to her and held her gaze, his dark brows low, like a line of angry squall clouds over the sea.

Honora hesitated. She saw the trap in his question, like a pun or a riddle that made the respondent the victim, the fool. In that moment she hated him for making her say what she didn't want to admit. But she said it and spared no words.

"Aye, I lied about Robert, and I'm not sorry. Rosemary is loved and wed. At what price? The clan's pride? Your trust? Our carefully negotiated marriage? A marriage you wanted only in order to thwart Lilias? I'm not sorry for what I did. At least my little sister and Robert will have love and happiness."

The unspoken words hung heavy between them. Rosemary and Robert would have happiness, even if she and Brec never would.

For a moment Brec stared at her. A rainbow of emotions—surprise, pain, and sorrow—played across his dark face. Abruptly he turned away, but not before the extraordinary glimpse of him touched Honora. Her breath caught in her throat. Astonished, almost disbelieving, she reached for his arm, but he shrugged her off and refused to look at her again. When she was able to see his profile once more, the subtle mask was in place. Had she really seen all those tender sentiments in the black glimmer of his eyes, in the eloquent arch of his brows, in the lines around his mouth?

At that moment the lookout called down that he had spotted a ship at anchor in Loch Dunrugis.

They both turned to look ahead as the *Dal Riata* rounded the headland and the castle and cove came into view. Honora leaned forward against the rail, surprised at her own eagerness to catch the first sight of home, of Dunrugis. In the late afternoon sunlight the castle rose proud and golden from the blue water of the loch. Before it, a double-masted ship lay at anchor. From the main mast flew the insignia of the Earl of Rothwell.

Honora blinked and peered at the flag again. Why was the Laird Ramsay here? She eyed Brec uneasily. "I suppose you are going to accuse me of sending for the earl now?"

"Nay," Brec replied quietly. "No doubt your uncles sent him to make sure that I'm keeping my word." He glanced at her before going on. "So this is your chance, Honora. If you are unhappy, you have my consent to pack your boxes and sail home with the earl."

Before Honora could say any more—before she could recover from the suffocating drop in the pit of her stomach—Brec turned away and began to issue orders for their landing.

"Laird Brec, your charming mother offered me a most gracious welcome when I explained that I had come with a new chaplain for Lady Honora." Rothwell cast a polite smile in Lady Margaret's direction. "Alas, I'm sorry to say that the poor man is still so seasick that he can't be here to sup with us tonight."

"Did you know Brec, that Laird Ramsay met Colin once?" Lady Margaret asked.

"Aye," Brec muttered, more occupied with his own surprise over the seating arrangements. Honora had seated Rothwell next to his mother, not herself. "I believe he mentioned the meeting once."

"Colin and I met in Glasgow years ago," the earl explained. He swept a gesture toward the Great Hall. "Of course, I knew the McClouds by reputation, but I had no idea that Castle Dunrugis was so grand."

"Then you know that the McCloud family has a long, proud history," Lady Margaret chattered on. "And the clan has been blessed with strong, wise, and brave men to lead us—men like my husband Alec, and my son Colin, and now Brec.''

Unexpectedly Brec's mother took his hand and squeezed it. She looked up at him, her eyes clear, her smile brightened. She had not mistaken him for Colin now, nor had she since that morning in the garden when he had prepared to sail for Solnarra.

Laird Ramsay asked another question, and Lady Margaret turned to him to answer.

Brec glanced at Honora, who sat silently on his other side. Her first greeting to the earl had been no more cordial than required of a hostess, and she had spoken to the man only when necessary during the meal. There was nothing unusual in that, Brec told himself. She had never really liked Ramsay.

He watched her toy with her food and he longed to bridge the silence between them. He desperately needed to hear a note in her voice, to catch some glimmer in her eye to give him a clue to her thoughts.

A damp chestnut tendril dropped across her temple as she pushed food across her plate with her fork. She had taken the time to bathe and wash her hair before supper. The clean, fresh scent of her reached Brec, bringing him the vision of her sitting before the fire drying her hair—a sight he had never seen and suddenly longed to see.

He had never had the courage to take full advantage of his husbandly rights. He'd never lived with his wife in the everyday way—never taken pleasure in the sight of her drawing her stocking over her toes, around her ankle, and up her thigh, or in watching her preen before the mirror as she fit earrings in her ear lobes—all the ordinary and mysterious things women seem to occupy themselves with in their bedchamber.

He'd missed all that because he lived his life in the shadow of another. And as unreasonable and illogical as he knew it to be, he knew he could never bear to hear Honora murmur another's name in a moment of grief or anger—in the innocence of her dreams. For all his vows of possession there would always linger in his heart the painful doubt that if she didn't love him, she must love another.

He had not been a good husband to her and began to

wonder if he could ever be. She had been right when they had argued on shipboard; he could give her little happiness. Perhaps it would be best to let her go, if she wished to leave.

Lady Margaret left the table for a moment and Ramsay turned to Brec.

"You know, Laird Brec, I doubt Rosemary's marriage to a McDonnell will please her uncle, the duke," the earl said, intruding on Brec's musing. "That clan is a rough lot."

"The McDonnells have made no secret of their support for the king's cause," Brec agreed.

"And you will not join the Covenantors' cause?"

"Nay, I gave my word to the Duke of Rosslyn," Brec reminded the earl. "I will join neither side."

"Now you have a new McDonnell brother-in-law," Laird David said. "And you refuse to join them in the king's cause? That's hard to believe."

"Why?" Brec asked. "McDonnells and McClouds have seldom been aligned on any issue."

"But I heard in Glasgow that there is so much more to your interests than meets the eye," Laird David said with a sly smile.

"Are you accusing me of something?" Brec demanded coolly.

"Only of doing what is best for Brec McCloud," the earl continued with an ingratiating smile. "Your interests in the New World are successful, are they not, and take up much of your time? Does Honora know of your shipping enterprise? Of course not. But I imagine the East India Company would like to know more. How many flags do your ships fly, McCloud?"

"No more than is required," Brec replied. "And don't threaten me, Ramsay. There are no stolen goods involved in my shipping ventures to the New World. This is the most honest work Simon LaFarge has ever done."

"I make no threat, McCloud," Ramsay simpered. "I merely express interest in such an investment."

Brec said nothing. He had no intention of inviting the earl to join his enterprise.

"Think about it," Ramsay offered. "If I may, I'd like

to speak alone with Honora. I have a message from her uncles.''

Nor did Brec care to have this weasel of a man speaking alone with Honora, but if Ramsay had word for her from her uncles, Brec would not interfere. He rose. ''I'm sure Honora would be glad to hear from her uncles.''

With some concern Honora watched Brec stride from the Great Hall. His anger was still plain in the set of his shoulders, but she did not know what to say to him, how to make him see that she had done what she did out of love for Rosemary and concern for the clan.

And she had no desire to be left alone with the earl. She looked at her guest and momentarily thought of offering to go to one of the smaller receiving rooms but decided to stay in the company of the servants, who were clearing the table.

''I thought we'd never get a few moments alone,'' David said. ''Your uncles want to know whether you are well and happy.''

''Of course I am,'' Honora said. She wasn't about to admit the truth about her differences with Brec to David Ramsay and her uncles.

''They told me to bring you and Rosemary home if there is any question of your happiness or safety,'' the earl added. ''They are concerned about these rumors of Colkitto in this part of Scotland.''

''I met him at Armadean,'' Honora said. ''In fact, he was a guest at Rosemary's wedding. I think he is too busy with his war against the Campbells to threaten the Isle of Myst.''

''But think about returning with me, Honora,'' the earl said leaning toward her. ''You don't belong in a heathen place like this. Have you thought of returning to Edinburgh or even going to London, where you can have the fine things you deserve?''

''Milaird, I'm a married woman,'' Honora protested. ''My place is with my husband.''

''But this is a time of war. When this war ends, some people will be influential and wealthy,'' the earl said. ''Others will lose everything, including their family fortune and title.''

Honora rose slowly. She didn't like what he was hinting at. It was all she could do to resist running away from the man. "After the excitement of my sister's wedding and getting her settled on Solnarra, I'm very tired, milaird. I believe Ian has settled you in your room. You'll forgive me if I retire early."

"Of course, my dear," he said. He seized her hand and kissed it, lingering over her fingers longer than was polite. His touch repulsed Honora. She drew her hand away, almost too quickly to be polite and hurried from the hall.

Brenda fussed about the laird's bedchamber, putting things in order. Her chatter which Honora heard, but did not listen to, was comforting.

Honora crawled to the middle of the laird's great bed, sat down, and tucked her silk nightgown about her feet. Brec's suggestion that she consider leaving with the earl hung over her like a cloud. She didn't want to go anywhere with Laird Ramsay. She wanted her husband to come to her bed and sleep there through the night. Was that so much to ask?

"The story is spreading of Lady Rosemary's wedding on a pirate ship. Now that's something to tell my grandchildren about. And Lady Rosemary was a beautiful bride, was she not? The villagers think you and Laird Brec are heroic for making the match with the McDonnells. What are you going to tell Beatrix?"

"That Rosemary married her true love," Honora said, but her thoughts were no longer on her sister's wedding. Instead, she was haunted by Brec's words to Alasdair. *I am sworn to not take up arms against the Covenantors. I will not break my word.*

"Do you wish anything else?" Brenda asked when she was finished. "Ye best get into bed, milady. 'Tis growing cold, and I donna think Laird Brec is coming tonight."

The serving girl was right; Brec wasn't coming to her tonight. Obediently Honora let Brenda tuck her in, snuff the candles, and bid her goodnight.

The expression on Brec's face played vividly through Honora's memory once more as she was drifting off to sleep. The pain, surprise, and sorrow haunted her. What had she said to him to bring such emotions out? *At least my little sister and her husband will have love and happiness.*

A cold wave of revelation washed over Honora. She sat up in the darkness, her mind racing to review words, reread expressions—a lift of a brow, a frown, a refusal to meet her gaze. Could Brec want love and happiness too? *For them?* He had given up the right to fight in this war to have her. He admitted that. To have her to thwart Lilias when any woman would have done as well. That was plain enough now. But Brec had wanted her.

The astonishing obviousness of the possibility shook Honora. But why did he stay away from her bed? Their nights together were the one beautiful thing in their marriage. The one thing that made sleeping in the great, cold cavern of the laird's chamber tolerable. She was convinced there was no other woman. It was only the compelling affairs in that book room that kept him so preoccupied—whatever those were.

The peat fire flickered out and the cold crept along the floor, then up across the bed as Honora pondered the possibilities.

Perhaps there was a way to learn why Brec had married her.

The candle flame flickered as Brec leaned over the dispatch to concentrate on the correspondent's handwriting. The English were so occupied with their war that his shipping business was doing extremely well. A draft from the passage made the candle flicker. Dubh lifted his head. Brec looked up at the door. Had he forgotten to turn the key in the lock?

Without a knock or a greeting, the door swung wide. Honora stood there, barefoot, with only a nightgown covering her. She held a rush light in one hand and dragged her pillow in the other. Her hair fell loose about her shoulders and glowed garnet red in the light. Fragile determination paled her face.

An odd sensation fluttered in Brec's chest as he scraped back his chair to rise from the desk. "Is something wrong?"

"Aye," she said. The word seemed to give her courage.

"I hate that great cold cavern of a bedchamber. And those yellow spots on the blue fairy banner hanging from the bed frighten me . . . like eyes staring down at me."

"Those spots never bothered you before," Brec said, nervously trying to make light of her fear.

Her gaze strayed to his fur-covered bed. "So I've come to sleep where 'tis warm. With my husband. 'Tis my right, sir."

Before Brec could think of anything to say, Honora marched into the room, around his desk, to his bed. She blew out her rush light and set it on his desk. Then she threw her pillow down on the bed and crawled to the far side, offering Brec a tantalizing glimpse of her swaying derrière enticingly draped in silk. He caught the sight of bare ankle as she slipped her legs between the furs and blankets. With a sigh she lay down on her side with her back to him.

Brec remained behind his desk, his mouth gone suddenly dry. He watched her, admiring the way the fur dipped into a valley at her tiny waist, then rounded again to cover her hips. What did he do now?

Without warning, Honora sat up and looked at him. She brushed a lock of hair from her face and leaned back on her hands, her breasts thrust forward, the dusky, nubbed peaks evident through the silken gown. Brec could hardly take his gaze from the inviting view.

"Are you going to keep that light burning long?" she asked.

He forced himself to look away at the papers on his desk. He couldn't even remember what he had been reading. "Uh, I don't know."

"Well, 'tis of no importance," she said, slipping beneath the bedcovers. "I'll just pull the blanket over my head."

Brec stared at her a moment longer. His pulse was thrumming in his temples so loudly that he could hardly think. He tried to remember all the reasons she wasn't supposed to be in this room. Not a one of them seemed important now. No messenger was expected this night, but he could never be certain who would turn up at the secret castle entrance.

His wife had just walked into his room and crawled into his bed and he wasn't about to send her away.

Pulling at the brooch on his tartan sash, Brec blew out the candle and threw off his clothes as he crossed the room. When he crawled into bed and reached for Honora, he found that she had already turned to him. Slowly she opened her arms and drew him into her embrace.

Honora had hardly breathed in those moments before Brec blew out the candle. She had waited for an explosion of temper, for him to order her to leave. She had almost expected him to stomp to the bed, throw back the covers, and drag her to the door. But when he blew out the candle, she knew she was safe. At least for one night.

As he stretched out beside her, she wrapped her arms around his neck and found his lips in the dark. More than a week had passed since they had come together as man and wife, and Honora realized as she accepted Brec's kiss that she needed his touch. His deep kiss left her weak and breathless. Relentlessly he covered her face with hundreds of little kisses as he tugged at the neckline of her gown.

When he was like this, he had little patience for clothes. Hastily Honora wiggled out of the gown to avoid any more rips that would have to be explained to Brenda.

With a sigh of satisfaction Brec spread his hands across her bare ribs before he grasped her by the waist and pushed her back on the bed, straddled her, and nourished her need for him with kisses—down her throat, around her breasts, down the center of her belly to the patch of curls between her legs.

Honora longed for him to take her breasts into his mouth as he had done so often and so well, but she forgot about that when his hot breath tickled her inner thigh. Honora felt her own desire turn liquid. In embarrassment and alarm, she reached for Brec, but he took her hands firmly in his and went on, his tongue never failing to find the most sensitive part of her.

When she finally surrendered to his strength and skill, pleasure warmed through her, building bliss and creating the craving for more. The bliss toppled when he rose over her. She whimpered in her need. Heedless, Brec parted her thighs and knelt between them. His erection stood proud and ready. Leaning forward, he scooped Honora's hips up in his hands, guided her along his thighs and onto him. Smooth and quick. Honora gasped with the first satisfaction of completeness. At Brec's prompting she clasped her legs around him. With his hands on her waist, he encouraged her movements, rocking at first, inviting her to find her own rhythm.

Adrift in the delight, Honora opened her eyes and touched his face. He stared into her eyes, his lids hooded, his face soft and serene with pleasure.

"Take what you want from me," he whispered, carefully stroking the tenderest flesh open to him. "Now, sweet soul."

Honora arched her back and reached the heights deep inside, tingling with ecstasy, soaring to fulfillment.

When she lay sated and quiet at last, she knew Brec had yet to be given his release. He filled her still. She rested while Brec leaned forward to stroke damp curls from her face.

"More?" he asked.

Honora didn't think she could bear more, but she wished to satisfy her husband. "Aye, but you'll have to show me how."

Brec bent over her, slipped his broad hand behind her head and splayed the other across her back. With a quick roll he pulled them over so that Honora rested on top of him, still filled. With his fingers laced through her hair he drew Honora to him for another kiss.

"I need you," he whispered.

"I'm not sure . . ."

"Just follow your instincts."

"My instincts? You mean to do this?" She swept her hair forward. With great care and calculation she brushed her tresses down his body, sweeping her hair across his chest, kissing his paps and his ribs as she went.

Brec groaned. With his hands on her hips, he encouraged her to renew the rhythm of their mating dance. She moved above him as nature told her until they both knew the bliss of union. Weak and swaying with exhaustion and pleasure, Honora allowed Brec to pull her against him. Tangled together, they slept.

* * *

Sudden light teased Honora's eyelids. She awoke enough to realize that a candle had been lit. Languidly she stretched and turned toward Brec's desk, thinking he had decided to finish his work. Instead she saw a strange figure bent over his desk. The hulk of a man was flipping through the piles of papers. When Honora moved, he turned to her, surprise on his face.

Honora's sleep-befuddled mind fumbled with memories. She tried to remember where she had seen his shiny bald head—no brows and no beard. Tattoos adorned his bare arms, and golden earrings dangled from his enormous ear lobes. The hoop's flash reminded Honora of Simon.

When the intruder saw her, he left the desk, prowling across the room to stand over her bed. Honora retreated, pressing up against the stone wall and drawing the furs up to her neck.

The freakish man peered at Honora as if he were as startled to find her there as she was to see him. He leaned closer, his bulk blocking the light of the candle, his expression curious. Honora could see his chest beneath his jerkin was just as hairless as his head. His gaze rested on her hair. For a moment Honora thought he was going to touch her.

He bent closer; Honora caught his scent—tobacco and ship bilge. Dubh sneezed. The man smiled down at Dubh and gave the dog a pat. Dubh wagged his tail. Obviously man and beast had met before.

"Remember me, milady," the man drawled. "Bald Bill. We danced at yer sister's wedding. So, the McCloud keeps ye here does he, close at hand. Canna say as I blame 'em."

"Stay away from her," Brec ordered. He appeared from the dressing alcove, wearing his black leather breeks and doublet.

Bald Bill turned on Brec, a greedy grin spreading across his ugly face.

"Get out, Honora," Brec ordered, his face harsh with annoyance. "Go back to the laird's chamber. Stay where 'tis safe. I don't want you here."

Before Honora could open her mouth to object, Brec shoved the man aside, wrapped a bed linen around her and pulled her from his bed. "Keep this around you and get out."

"What's happening?" Honora protested. "I just woke up to find him here. What are you doing?"

" 'Tis too dangerous for you to be here. Go back to the laird's chamber. Go."

Brec led her to the door, lit the rush light for her, and pushed her out of the room. A resounding thud echoed in the passage when he slammed the door behind her.

For a moment Honora stood there, too shocked and too sleepy to react. Then the more she recalled, the angrier she became. She turned on the door and pounded with her fist. "Let me in. You can't do this to me, Brec. I'm your wife."

Silence.

She pounded on the door again and uttered an oath she had once heard Brec use.

Her only answer was more silence, the silence of an empty room. Honora hesitated another moment, reluctant to believe what had just happened. She thought she had won her husband. But just like that, she had been shut out of his life.

Alone—Dubh hadn't even come with her. Exiled, Honora padded her way along the passage to the laird's chamber. The room was like a cold prison.

She sat down on the icy, empty laird's bed. Where had Bald Bill come from? Was there a secret door somewhere in that book room? That was the only explanation. A secret entrance explained why he would admit no one to the room to clean for fear of discovery; why he kept the room always locked; why on the night of the troupe's performance when she had gone to find him he was nowhere to be found, and no one in the castle had seen him. He'd gone sailing, just as he said; he'd left by the secret door.

Yet, he refused to share that secret with her, his wife, the lady of Dunrugis. He'd shut the door in her face, closed her out of his life.

She pulled back the counterpane and crawled under it. Between the linen sheets she lay cold, bereft, and shivering. When Brec had blown out that candle and come to her, she was ecstatic. She'd opened her arms to him believing that there was hope for their happiness together.

That he wanted love from her as she did from him. She had given and accepted with all her heart.

She'd let the power of their union drive out the memory of Brec's invitation to leave with the earl. Surely he'd spoken those words in anger.

But then there had been the strange man, Bald Bill. Brec had dragged her from his bed, shoved her toward the door, and slammed it in her face. Shut her out. Refused to answer her. He'd locked the door between them once more. What did he want from her?

Hurt and confused, Honora let the tears come then—hot, stinging, angry, and bitter—soaking Brec's pillow. When dawn glimmered in the east at last, Honora fell into a lonely, exhausted slumber.

22

"My ship is nearly provisioned," the earl said. He leaned eagerly toward Honora, and she could hear the hope in his voice.

Gray clouds cluttered the blue sky above as they stood on the wall of the castle courtyard and viewed the earl's double-masted frigate at anchor in Loch Dunrugis.

"And the captain's quarters are quite comfortable," he went on. "There is no need to trouble yourself about appearances. Your uncles and I will see to that. Annulments are more easily come by than you might think. Your uncles would not want you to suffer in an unfortunate marriage."

Honora remained silent. Numbness had settled over her when she heard that Brec had sailed off early this morning. He had left her alone to entertain the earl, as if he had no concern about her leaving with her former suitor. According to the message he left, he had to tend to some crisis on the other part of the isle and would not return until evening.

Was this how her married life was to be? A few moments of warmth in his bed—primarily to beget children—and the rest of her days filled with empty rooms and closed doors? Distrust and accusations?

She shook her head against the thought.

"Don't answer now," the earl exclaimed, lightly touching her arm, his anxiety that she would refuse to go with him almost tangible. "Think about returning to Edinburgh. We'll talk later."

Honora stood at the wall long after the earl had left her, her bleak thoughts drifting like the dark clouds above. She saw Laird Ramsay appear at the sea gate below to give instructions to sailors who were ferrying food and water out to the ship and speak to a big man in a shapeless black suit, the kind the reformers preferred. This must be her new chaplain, she thought. And she wondered why the man hadn't presented himself to her before now. He and the earl crossed the gun yard and disappeared into the castle.

Old habits nattered at her, and she wondered how Ian was managing with the castle larder. Generous hospitality was expected from Dunrugis and was always given. Still, she wanted to be certain that things were handled in a reasonable manner. With a sigh she went to the kitchen, threading her way between busy servants to find the larder Ian issued provisions from. She found a door unlocked and wandered between barrels of pickled herring, oatmeal, and clay pots of honey. Behind a stack of wooden crates she found Ian's inventory. As she looked it over, trying to make sense of his marks, she heard men's voices in the hallway. One was the earl's. The other was familiar, but she couldn't quite place it.

"I told you not to come into the castle," the earl hissed.

Alerted and curious, Honora listened more carefully.

"Nobody has recognized me, dressed like this," the unidentified voice said. "And no one here wants to look a preacher of the reformed church in the eye. McCloud is expected back by sundown. Can you have her on the ship by then?"

"I'll have her there, one way or the other," the earl said,

his voice edged with cruel determination. With a strange certainty, Honora knew they were referring to her.

"But we don't want to make the servants suspicious," the preacher warned. "I plan to take him in his room, when he is alone. When I declare myself clan chief, I want Brec McCloud's body cold and his lady gone from the castle."

Honora clapped a hand over her mouth to stifle an audible gasp. The voice was Wallace's.

"You're certain the people of the Isle of Myst will rise up for the king?" the earl said.

"Give me your men and leave this to me," Wallace replied. "That was our agreement when we decided to join together in Glasgow. You get the lady, I take care of McCloud. When the islanders know Brec McCloud is dead, they will accept me. I'm a McCloud cousin. Until he returned, I was his brother's successor. They will follow me. Kenneth might be a problem, but he can be eliminated easily enough."

"That is your concern. All I want is the lady and Isle of Myst forces for the king," the earl said. "Now keep out of sight until the time is right. If anyone recognizes . . ."

The voices faded away.

"But the Earl of Rothwell is for the Covenantors," Honora whispered to herself. "He had turned against Montrose and the king. He told my uncles so. I heard him myself."

The clock in the Great Hall struck noon as Honora sorted through the facts—throwing things out, putting things together. Had the earl returned to the fold of his old friend, Montrose, after she left Edinburgh? In spite of the earl's assurances her uncles had been uncertain of him and thought her marriage to Laird Ramsay would seal allegiances. That aspect of the arrangement had made her even more defiant about her uncles' matchmaking.

She ducked behind the barrel again when she heard footsteps turn into the larder and walk right to her hiding place. She blinked at the knobby knees that stopped before her.

"Lady Honora?" Ian exclaimed.

"Oh, Ian." Honora struggled to her feet. "Do you know where Laird Brec went? Is Kenneth with him?"

"Milady, what's wrong?" Ian stammered, staring at Honora as though she had lost her mind. "We can light signal fires if we must alert the McCloud and the fighting men."

"Nay, nay, that would reveal that we know what he's planned." Honora waved that option away. "We must warn Brec without our guests knowing."

As Honora told him what she had overheard, a dumbstruck expression froze on the steward's face.

"Where is Lady Margaret?" Honora asked.

"In her rooms."

"We must get her to safety and the others as well," Honora said. "I'll have Brenda take her to visit Colin's grave and attend chapel. Can you make excuses to clear out the kitchen?"

Ian nodded. "But there is another in the castle. Mistress Oleen is here. One of the cook's helpers has a fever, and mistress brought a remedy for her."

"We've got to get Oleen and her patient out of here too," Honora agreed. "But we don't want the earl or Wallace to think anything is amiss. Don't tell Fergus or the guards any of this yet. I fear Wallace would use the earl's men to overcome them."

"Ye can count on me, milady," Ian vowed.

At the door to Brec's room Honora tried the latch again. Still locked. She wanted to search for the secret door. She wanted to leave a message for Brec in case he entered that way. Frustrated, she rattled the door once more, praying that Brec would suspect somehow that he was walking into a trap.

In the laird's bedchamber, she pulled the fairy banner from the canopy, where she and Brec had tucked it weeks ago. For a moment she savored the silken texture between her fingers then rubbed the banner against her cheek. Memories of another touch filled her.

"Milady?" Oleen burst into the chamber.

"Oleen? Didn't Ian tell you to leave?"

" 'Tis not the time to leave," Oleen rasped in her deep, husky voice. "You have the banner? We must warn Brec."

"You know of the earl's plot? Ian told you?"

"Ian? Nay," Oleen said. "I happened to address that ridiculous chaplain in the kitchen. Ducked his head and pitched his voice high. Wallace is more of a fool than I thought if he thinks he can disguise himself from me. The banner must fly over Dunrugis to warn Brec upon his return."

"But will that be too late? Will he believe the warning?"

"Brec will understand. I will have Ian see to raising the banner. And you, milady, must keep the Earl of Rothwell occupied this afternoon. But whatever you do, don't board his ship. If you do, you'll never see Brec again."

Honora surrendered the banner to Oleen and thoughtfully closed the door behind her. Never see Brec again? Only an hour ago she had thought that that was what she wanted. Now she knew differently.

She loved Brec. It seemed so clear, when faced with the prospect of never seeing him again. She loved him, but not with a love that filled stanzas of poetry. She loved him for accepting Rosemary as no burden, for accepting his mother's words of love for a dead son, for his magic, tender touch in the darkness.

She leaned against the door and closed her eyes against her tears. She didn't delude herself that saying, "I love you" would change Brec's feelings about her now. She had lied to him. Nothing could change that. Nevertheless, she loved him and she wished with all her soul that she had told him so. That she had given him her heart, as well as her body and her loyalty.

But what was more important now was to keep Brec from walking into Wallace and Ramsay's murderous ambush.

"I'm still packing, milaird," Honora insisted. With a false smile she tried to squeeze the chamber door shut on the earl. Angrily he shoved his way into the room.

He stopped in the middle of the chamber and stared at the trunks in the room. He kicked at a leather valise and demanded, "What is all this?"

"My luggage. This is rather improper, sir," Honora protested with a frown. "I seldom receive gentlemen in my bedchamber."

"Your cabin is prepared for you," the earl said. "We sail very early in the morning, so you must be on board by sundown."

"That's several hours away. I'll be packed by then."

"How much more? My men have hauled three trunks out to the ship already," the earl complained. "Two of them were as heavy as a load of rocks."

Forgive me, Rosemary, Honora prayed silently. She smiled coyly at the earl. "I will have several more. A lady's costumes require careful packing and more trunk space than a gentleman's. I'm sure you understand, sir."

As if on cue, Oleen swept into the room and began to painstakingly lay a gown into a trunk and arrange the yards of fabric. The earl eyed Honora suspiciously. She smiled back and wished Brec could see her now. He'd realize that she wasn't as good at lying as he thought.

"I'll send word as soon as I have another trunk packed," Honora offered, holding open the door.

Laird Ramsay made a disgruntled noise, then retreated to the doorway, where he stopped to look around again. "The wind is rising. We can afford no delay."

"Of course," Honora agreed. "No delay."

She closed the door on him, listening to his footsteps fade in the passage.

Oleen straightened from her work in the trunk. The women exchanged a look of understanding.

"Lady Margaret?" Honora asked.

"Gone with Brenda," Oleen replied. "Fergus is still about, but most of his men have disappeared."

"Do you think they know Wallace is here?"

Oleen shook her head. "I don't think so, but Fergus lifted his eyes to the banner flying from the tower when I spoke to him. He said nothing about it, only the look. Ian has made excuses to get the kitchen women out of the castle and to the village. Only a few ghilles remain."

"Good," Honora said, satisfied that they had done all they could. "You have the Sight, Oleen. What do you see for us? Have you seen any visions? Have you seen Brec's ghost?"

"The Sight is a willful thing," Oleen explained, facing Honora. "I have seen no ghosts. But I do know that the McClouds will rule the Isle of Myst for centuries to come."

"Tell me. You must know. Brec is no murderer. Wallace killed Colin didn't he? Why did Brec never accuse him before the people?"

"Brec never protected Wallace," Oleen said with a shake of her head.

Surprised, Honora stared at the wise woman. "Then Colin's death was an accident?"

"Nay, 'twas no accident. Colin was dying of a brain fever."

Oleen's revelation was so unexpected that Honora could only repeat the words. "Brain fever?"

"Aye. We knew there wasn't much time. Colin sent for his brother. Brec came as soon as he could."

"His mother? Lady Margaret, how much did she know?"

"She knew the truth about the illness, but Colin hid the suffering from her. By the time Brec arrived, the bouts of pain were becoming almost unbearable. My potions were losing their effect. Colin named Brec his successor as soon as he arrived. 'Twas a bad time for Brec. He adored his brother as much as, or more than, the rest of us. Often it was Colin who came between Brec and his father, who kept them from going at each other's throats."

"He has never told me any of this," Honora said, mystified and a little hurt. "He never said how he felt about Colin other than to insist on mourning. Why didn't he tell me himself?"

"He will," Oleen said. "His brother's death has been hard on him. Before Colin died he made Brec pledge to do two things: to keep the clan McCloud together and to bring a true lady to Castle Dunrugis, a woman of courage and virtue."

"Oh," Honora whispered. "And I have failed him."

"Oh, no," Oleen said with a laugh. "I think he is very pleased, and he will be especially pleased to learn that you conceived last night."

"What? But last night I . . ." Honora stopped and blushed.

Oleen smiled broadly and nodded. "A daughter."

Honora's knees went weak. She sought the edge of the bed and sat down. "Truly? A daughter?"

"Truly. In nine months you will deliver a beautiful black-haired girl with sea-green eyes. That will please Brec. Does it please you?"

"Aye, I'm very pleased," Honora said with a delighted

laugh. She covered her belly with her hand. A child lived there already. Then she remembered why trunks filled the chamber. "If only we could be sure that Brec will see the banner and be warned."

From the forward forecastle Brec peered at the blue fairy banner flapping above Dunrugis against the pinkened clouds of twilight. Honora's disparaging words about the yellow eyes of the flag rang through his memory. His gut twisted.

Behind him the *Dal Riata*'s master relayed the McCloud's orders. The oarsmen shipped oars but remained ready. The gallery drifted silently at the mouth of the loch.

"What do ye think it means?" Kenneth asked, turning to Brec. "That banner hasna been raised for three generations."

"Honora knows the story of the banner. I don't think she would have it raised on a whim. Look at the activity around Ramsay's ship."

The frigate, anchored in the shadow of shore near the castle, was alight with lanterns and aswarm with sailors. Over the wind Brec and Kenneth could hear the shouts of the men aboard the ship and the whine of the windlass.

"We havena been spotted yet," Kenneth observed. "They appear to be prepared to sail."

Brec's heart hammered a protest. Was Honora preparing to leave with the earl? he wondered, recalling how in the heat of his anger on the very deck where he stood he'd foolishly bid her to leave if she wished. He'd regretted those words a thousand times that day.

But she had come to him in the night, he tried to reassure himself. She'd stood in the doorway, draped in white silk and with her hair aglow like dark fire—a passionate angel materialized in answer to an unspoken prayer. And he loathed himself for his cowardice. For locking her out. For leaving her alone with the earl all day because Simon needed him and because he feared the choice she might make. If she chose the earl, she was gone from his life forever. If she chose to stay, he would have to admit how much she meant to him. He wasn't certain he had the courage to give her that much of himself.

But Brec had found no answer to the question. Why did

the fairy banner fly above Castle Dunrugis? Simon had needed his help with the repair in the hull, but what if Honora had needed him too? Was that why the banner was flying? Or was it a gesture of derision? Brec shook his head. He didn't believe that.

No doubt he had made Honora angry when he shut the door on her, but ridicule wasn't part of Honora's nature. That wasn't the way of a woman who established her dominion with the addition of an elegant clock in the Great Hall. Of a woman who had pinned a feather token on her husband's bonnet before he went into battle. Honora never took symbols lightly. The banner had to be a warning.

"I'm going ashore from here," Brec said aloud to Kenneth. "Send one of our best swimmers out to cut the frigate's anchor ropes. Seize them when they have discovered they're adrift and are trying to gain control."

Kenneth nodded.

"After you anchor, present yourself at the sea gate with fighting men. Find out what you can from Fergus if he is there. Be prepared to be attacked. 'Tis possible that our guest has readied a surprise welcome for us."

"Where are you going?"

"Ashore to find out what I can," Brec said. "Where Mother is. Where Honora is. Don't press too hard if you encounter resistance, not until you've heard from me. Let's know what we're up against before we risk many lives."

The earl threw a cloak over Honora's shoulders. "The boat awaits to take us out to the ship."

He grabbed her elbow roughly and hurried her down the stairs, their footsteps clattering on stone. The castle echoed empty. Honora was satisfied that everyone was gone.

"There is no time for packing more trunks. You will have to do with what's aboard the ship."

Honora struggled to keep up with the little man, his feet flying down the stairs as if he were pursued by the devil himself. At that thought Honora twisted to peer back at the darkened top of the stairs. For a moment she thought she sensed a presence and saw something move.

Black on black. Shadow against shadow.

"Honora?" The earl yanked on her arm so hard that she

stumbled against him. "Why are you so slow? Am I to believe that you really want to remain with this warlock you call a husband?"

"Well . . ." Honora fumbled for some excuse. The clock in the Great Hall chimed eight times. "I was just thinking of the clock. 'Tis my uncles' clock really. I must take it with me."

The earl hesitated, a look of irritation sharpening his features. "Get it."

He dragged her down the few remaining steps. With a hand pressing on the small of her back, he guided her to the doorway of the Great Hall.

"I must have the proper packing box for it," Honora insisted. " 'Tis a very delicate thing, this clock. It must be packed just so."

The earl hesitated again, and Honora was afraid he was going to refuse this time.

"All right," he growled. "Do it quickly. Where is your steward? What's his name?"

"Ian?" Honora whirled around to find the thin old man there in the doorway, his face lined with apprehension. He looked as if he had aged eight years in the last eight hours. Honora knew his feeling well. "Oh, there you are. Would you bring me the box for the clock?"

"Aye, milady." Ian shuffled off with gratifying sloth.

"The old man will take all night," the earl snapped.

"Ian is very thorough. He'll be back with the box before you know it." Honora turned away to hide her smile over this small victory—one more delay. She hoped Ian would never return. Beyond the earl, near the passage stairway, she caught sight of a movement again. Torches cast long shadows, restless and sinister. It was difficult to be certain about anything. Honora blinked and looked again.

Amid the shapeless darkness Brec's face emerged: pale, bonnetless, seemingly disembodied.

Honora's mouth went dry.

She whirled around, back into the light of the hall. She gulped a deep breath. Her hand fluttered to her throat in an attempt to shove her heart back into its proper place. Tension and fatigue had muddled her senses, she tried to tell herself.

But the pull was irresistible. Honora peeked over her shoulder again. Barren shadows, empty and stark. He—it was gone. Brec's ghost? Dear God, she prayed, not Brec's ghost.

"Haven't you gotten her out of here yet?" demanded the man with the broad-brimmed hat who appeared at the other end of the passage.

Honora started. The man marched down on her.

He jerked off the hat and threw it aside. Torchlight fell on Wallace's round, beefy face. He stalked into the hall and glared at Honora briefly. "Is she causing a problem?"

"She wants to take the clock," the earl explained.

" 'Tis too late now," Wallace said, casting the earl a belittling look. "The *Dal Riata* has just anchored."

Hope and fear pounded in Honora's heart.

The earl cursed. "Any sighting of the McCloud?"

"Not yet," Wallace said, reaching for Honora. "Actually, this may work best. One way to be sure we lure him into our trap is to let him see his wife in our hands."

Honora swiftly stepped beyond Wallace's reach. "Nay, I will not help you assassinate Brec."

"I told you she wouldn't help us," the earl said.

"She doesn't have to be willing," Wallace said. He lunged after Honora this time. He caught her wrists in a grinding grip. She yelped in agony. Frantically she pulled away, but he drew her to him relentlessly until all she could do was fight his grip and kick his shins.

"Cease this!" he ordered. With the back of his hand Wallace slapped her face, snapping her head back. The smack echoed through the Great Hall.

Torches flared and maddened shadows danced.

Honora gasped in pain and surprise. Tears sprung to her eyes. She had never been struck by a man before. In truth, until now she had never considered how much danger she might be in. Speechless, she stared at Wallace's ugly countenance, into the face of a banished man, a man with no home or family, a man who had nothing to lose and everything to gain if he made good this plan to kill Brec and perhaps herself.

"That's enough, sir," the earl shouted. He grabbed for Wallace's arms, but the warrior shrugged the little earl off.

"I'm going to handle this now," Wallace said. He dragged Honora out the door of the Great Hall and down the passage toward the door to the sea gate.

She tried to plant her feet, but the man dragged her along, her slippers sliding across the stone floor. Her cheek still stung. But she didn't care how much danger she was in. She wasn't going to be used as bait in a trap for Brec. She looked over her shoulder to appeal to the earl. Surely he would not allow her to be treated like this.

But the earl was gone—vanished into the darkness.

Charging ahead, Wallace hauled Honora around a corner in the passage. She took the opportunity to glance back again, hardly believing the proof before her. The earl had indeed disappeared.

When they reached the door to the sea gate, Wallace looked around for the first time to find his ally missing.

"Where'd that fool Ramsay go?" he demanded.

As mystified as he, Honora shook her head and prayed that Ian had somehow overpowered the earl.

Distant screams and shouts reached their ears. Wallace threw open the door to the gun yard. Orange light licked across his face and glared off his jowls.

"The frigate has been set afire!" he exclaimed. "Connor, where are you? Where is that cursed guard?"

No one answered.

The light of the burning vessel glared off the waters of the loch and silhouetted small boats full of fighting men. War cries carried across the water. Metal clanged against metal. Splintering wood whined as one of the frigate's masts crashed into the sea. An explosion shook the ship. The loch lit up as if lightning had struck.

Wallace cursed again and dragged Honora out into the gun yard to the top of the steps leading to the sea gate.

The iron grill rattled against the lock, and Honora heard her name on many tongues.

"Lady Honora. Lady, have courage."

She looked down the curving, stone-lined passage to see Kenneth's bearded face peering through the grillwork, his fists rattling the bars. In vain Honora looked beyond him for Brec. Faces from the village filled the darkness beyond the master of arms. And those people—men and

281

women—raised their weapons and their voices in disapproval at Wallace. The gate was securely locked. Honora wore the castle keys.

"Surrender and open up," Kenneth demanded. "Your men are overcome and the ship burned."

"I want to talk to Laird Brec," Wallace shouted in reply. He glanced uneasily about him and drew Honora closer. She struggled, but he was far too strong for her. He clutched her against his chest, her delicate wrists gripped in one of his large hands. "Bring the McCloud to me, else his lady . . ."

Honora winced at the flash of his dagger. From the corner of her eye she saw the blade near her jaw. She closed her eyes against the thought of death. All she could think of was her unborn babe and her unspoken love.

Without warning, Wallace jerked Honora backward. He lurched and arched his back lifting her from the ground, while his feet remained solid and braced against his unseen foe. Honora kicked him.

"Release the lady," Brec's deep voice demanded.

Honora fell still, hardly believing her ears. Brec? Here? No ghost?

"Nay, McCloud," Wallace panted. "She dies and you die. The clan is mine and the king's."

Confused, she ventured to look again, only to see that the trembling dagger hovered closer, only a fraction of an inch from her jaw, where a pulse beat wildly in her throat. She strained away, but the point grazed her skin. Filled with dread, Honora closed her eyes against the coming pain.

Wallace clutched Honora tighter as he struggled against Brec's hold from behind. She opened her eyes only to see the knife wavering closer to her throat—nothing between her and a bloody death. No way to break Wallace's hold.

Then she saw Brec's hand—and stared in horrified disbelief as his fingers curled around the well-honed edge, covering the glittering knife, protecting her from the lethal blade. Blood welded between his fingers, trickled down his knuckles, and dripped from his thumb. Honora nearly cried out for his pain.

Wallace grunted, his single-handed grip on Honora never slackening. Now she fought with renewed effort. With strength she never knew she possessed, Honora pulled against Wallace's hold until she felt it slip, then she lunged against it, and broke free. Her release came so suddenly that she stumbled forward, tumbling head over heels down the sea gate passage. She didn't stop to think of her skinned knees and scraped hands. She didn't even look over her shoulder. She wore the key to admit Kenneth and help. She never allowed herself to think of the iron blade that had bitten into Brec's hand and that could end his life as easily as hers. She thought only of the key. Scrambling to her feet, she grabbed the brass key ring. Grasping it between her shaking fingers, Honora watched as she miraculously drove the key home into the lock.

The gate flung open, pinning Honora against the wall. The loyal islanders, with Kenneth in the lead, flooded through the sea gate and thronged up the passage to rescue their laird.

Brenda and Lady Margaret pulled Honora from behind the gate and huddled around her to protect her from the crowd. They embraced, all three women in tears.

"How did you know?" Honora managed to ask between sobs.

"We saw the fairy banner," Brenda replied, as if the answer was obvious. "We knew 'twas time to do battle for our clan and our chief. Fergus reminded us that 'tis our duty for all the times the McCloud has done battle for us."

The women watched the islanders swarm into the court-yard and overwhelm Wallace, seizing his dagger, forcing him to his knees, and shielding their chief from the traitor. Brec stepped back, towering dark and triumphant above the crowd.

"You care for your husband now," Oleen ordered, thrusting the white linen binding cloth into Honora's fumbling fingers. "I have finished the stitching, and there are others to see to."

The little woman bustled away into the swarm of villagers gathered in the Great Hall. Honora and Brec were left to themselves.

Wallace and the earl—whom Ian had captured by dropping the clock box over his head—had been safely locked in the dungeon.

At Lady Margaret's direction flagons of ale were being served, and the fire in the hearth had been built up into a roaring, cheery blaze. Kenneth hugged Brenda to his side and stood in the center of the hall, where he was toasted as a hero. The people's mood was exultant, and no fearful glances were cast in the direction of their laird or his lady.

The sight of Oleen's neat stitching of Brec's flesh stirred the queasiness already churning in Honora's belly. She had but to close her eyes to see once again Brec's hand close over the gleaming knife blade to protect her from injury, even death.

" 'Tis not deep, is it?'' she asked, her voice weak and wavering. She glanced at his face for the first time since the night before—since he had locked her out. She was surprised to find him studying her in return, his dark eyes keen, his mouth grim.

" 'Tis not deep. Sit.'' With his good hand, he pulled her down beside him.

Gratefully she dropped onto the bench and began to work with the binding. "We must be certain the wound doesn't bleed more,'' she fretted, uncertain whether she worked quickly for his benefit or for hers. She had never had a strong stomach. And her strength and courage were ebbing quickly now. If she were to be reminded once more of how close they had both come to their end, she would not be able to go on.

"Your cheek is bruised,'' he observed softly, without anger.

"I'm all right,'' she replied, with fierce concentration on the binding of his hand. "And Oleen says you will be all right also.''

"Aye.'' He touched her cheek with his good hand. "I shouldn't have left you alone with the earl. I should have known that he was lying, that he had some plan. I should have known that Wallace would return somehow.''

"You shouldn't have locked me out of your room,'' Honora replied, her head coming up to look him directly in the eye. "That's what you shouldn't have done. I'm your wife. I deserve better."

"I know," he agreed without hesitation. "But—you must have guessed—there is a secret entrance to the castle through the book room. Messengers arrive from time to time. Men I don't want anywhere near my wife."

"Like Bald Bill?"

"Aye, like Bald Bill. Simon sent him."

"Why?" Honora eyed her husband expectantly.

Brec hesitated, then gave a shrug of resignation. "Simon runs cargo for me to the New World. Because of the East India Company's monopoly the venture requires information and some discretion. Like knowing what flag to raise over your ship and when." He smiled self-deprecatingly. " 'Tis an intriguing game, milady. Difficult for me to give up. And if anyone ever asks about it, you know nothing. Do you understand? If I'm ever called to account for this, I will not have my wife implicated."

"Aye, I understand," Honora said, appraising Brec with renewed wonder. "But why didn't you tell me about Wallace and Lilias and Colin? You've never told me anything about Colin, how you felt about him. What truly happened. Brec, why don't you trust me?"

"I don't know." Brec shook his head and stared down at his wounded hand, which she cradled tenderly in her lap.

"But you *do* know," Honora insisted. "You cannot slip away from me into the darkness or distract me with magic tricks. No seduction this time, husband. I will say it if you won't. You don't trust me, Brec McCloud, because you think I'm going to be like Lilias, faithless and demanding. Or like your mother, too gentle to accept reality. And look at her now. She is strong again. You underestimated her. You underestimated me."

Brec watched her from the corner of his eye, a questioning tilt to his brow. "So I have."

"Indeed you have." Satisfied that her point was taken, Honora began to work on the binding of his hand again, her hands steadier now. "I want to know about Colin. Oleen said he was ill."

Brec remained silent. Without looking up, Honora said,

"I would have it all now, husband. I've been near-murdered tonight by Colin's disgruntled successor. 'Tis my due to know it all."

"Aye, milady." With a sigh that seemed to come from deep within—a sigh filled with regret, guilt, and relief—Brec began to speak. "Last fall Colin sent word that he needed my help. I had promised it to him when he and Lilias were wed. You can imagine how shocked I was to return and find him dying. Not that he looked unwell, but Oleen assured me there was no doubt. At times he was in terrible pain from headaches. He kept the pain from mother. He told Lilias, which was a mistake. She had no strength to give him. No love, no courage. When he suffered, she only turned away."

Brec hesitated, squeezing her hand painfully, a faraway look coming into his eyes. Honora realized that he was reliving the sorrow again, and she returned the pressure so he would know he was not alone.

"Then Colin told me that he suspected Wallace and Lilias of adultery. I wanted to banish them, then."

Brec took a deep breath. "Nay, the truth is I wanted to do away with them, but Colin would have none of that. He was a good man and fair, not a schemer or a usurper. He insisted on naming me successor. I was his brother—the true, direct line, he said. The septs would accept me without question. I agreed only because nothing else seemed to comfort him. One night, after I had agreed to all the things he wanted, I guess when the agony and despair became too much, he put a pistol beneath his chin and he shot himself."

Honora bit her lip to keep the tears at bay. They shared a long, pain-filled moment in silence before Brec went on.

"Father McGregor took a literal view of my brother's death. I could not allow that. Colin was my brother, my friend. He made what little peace there ever was between my father and me. Colin had been dying, suffering. The end would have been the same, regardless. He was a good clan chief, loved by his people and his family. He deserved to lie with honor among the proud McClouds who have gone before him. I could not allow him to be buried apart with sinners and criminals."

Brec gave Honora a strange, twisted smile. "So I invited Father McGregor to leave the Isle of Myst. It did nothing for my reputation, I know, to escort a priest from the isle, but I didn't care. And I had heard that Father Andrew was a compassionate man of God. So I sent for him. Now Colin lies in peace with his clan."

Brec stopped to look about at the gay crowd that filled the hall with laughter and good cheer.

"No one knows the truth of Colin's death, Honora. No one but you and I, Kenneth, Oleen, and Father Andrew. We must not speak of it again. I think Mother should never know."

"We will tell her only as much as she wants to hear, and only when she is strong enough to ask," Honora said. Carefully she resumed binding Brec's hand, full of love and tenderness for this man who had gone to such lengths, made such sacrifices for others, suffered for it, and kept the pain to himself.

Honora gently smoothed the binding on his hand with her fingertips. "I love you, Brec" she whispered, without looking at him, almost afraid to utter the words that he had never spoken to her and that she longed to hear.

"What? What did you say?" Brec demanded in clipped words that startled Honora. Roughly he grabbed her hand.

Honora swallowed the lump in her throat. He must have heard her. What did she say now?

"No, wait. Don't say anything yet." He waved to Ian. "Bring the best cognac from the cellar. Hurry, man. Lady Honora needs warming."

Perplexed, Honora watched Ian scurry away. She was afraid to look up at Brec. Instead she held his hand in her lap between her own and was surprised to see her own tears drop onto the bandage. Hastily she brushed them from the fabric.

Without a word Brec brushed them from her cheek with the back of his good hand.

"I wasn't going to go with him—Laird Ramsay—you know. I thought about it. I was hurt when you shut the door in my face."

"I didn't really want you to go. I shouldn't have said the

things I did." Brec took a goblet of cognac from a breath-less Ian. "Drink this."

Thankful for the interruption, Honora sipped from the pewter goblet. The brandy burned her throat, and its warmth trickled into her limbs. She relaxed, aware for the first time that she had been trembling. She could feel Brec scrutinizing her every movement. She heard him take a deep breath.

"A moment ago you spoke of love?" he said evenly, as he took the goblet from her.

She thought of denying her words, lest he laugh at her, think her feminine, frivolous, and overwrought. Lest he dismiss her declaration as unimportant and silly. She glanced up at him. He met her gaze and held it. There was no amusement in his expression, no condescension, no disdain. His eyes were dark and soft and inquiring. With a quick gasp for courage, she spoke again. "I said, I love you."

His expression remained intent and unchanged. She hur-ried on. "I think I've loved you for quite a long time, but I was too fixed on my duties to listen to my heart. And when I realized that Wallace was here to kill you, I regret-ted that—that I'd never spoken those words to you."

There. She had said it. She ducked her head, staring down at his injured hand, waiting. She listened to Brec's silence and wondered what he was thinking—how would he respond?

A roar of laughter erupted from a group of villagers gath-ered around the McCloud bard. Lady Margaret stood in the midst of them in lively conversation with one of the village women. The harper tuned his harp and began to sing a sweet air.

Brec released a long, slow breath and studied the top of Honora's head. He could take no chance on this. He didn't care who was watching them, or who heard. He had to be certain that he heard her correctly; that she spoke the truth. She had lied to him once out of a sense of loyalty to her sister. He was willing to forgive her that. But he had to be certain now that she spoke the truth from her heart. Slowly he lifted Honora's face to his and steeled himself against the tears that streaked her face.

288

"Say it again, Honora," he asked, trying to keep the anxiety from his voice. "I must have the truth. No flattery, no deceptions, no dutiful declaration from a good wife. If you truly meant those words, say them again."

Her stormy sea-green eyes cleared as if some sudden understanding had come to her. Her face brightened. Her lips trembled.

"Say it again," he demanded, more roughly than he intended.

"Aye, I'll say it again." She gave a vigorous nod. But she hesitated as a sob erupted. Tears rolled down her cheeks.

Brec squeezed her fingers tighter. Her delay was unbearable. These words were so important, and she had spoken so softly before, so uncertainly.

"Brec," she began in a small but steady voice, holding his anxious gaze with her determined one. "I love *you*. Not Alexander. Not David. No one else. Only *you*, Brec. I love *you*."

Tears stung Brec's eyes as no salt spray ever had. He bowed his head over their entwined hands.

"I think you love me too." Honora spoke breathlessly. "Even if you can't say the words. You have proved it over and over. You even gave up the right to fight in this war for me. Why else would you give that up? Brec, you *must* love me."

"I do, sweet soul," Brec whispered. "I love you. I have loved you from the first, from the moment you scolded me for introducing myself as Ol' Nick. You weren't frightened or awed, just annoyed with me for pretending to be what I was not."

"But I was frightened," Honora said with a smile. "And I thought perhaps you really were the devil, come to punish me for defying my uncles once more."

They laughed together. Honora sobered first and searched his face as if she still had doubts and questions.

"What is it, Honora?" he asked, anxious that all be set straight now.

"If you love me, then sleep with me tonight, stay with me until dawn. Don't slip away as if we don't belong together. As if you fear lying too close to me."

"Is that all you ask?" Brec inquired, admiring the tremulous smile on her face, unable to believe that she requested so little.

"Aye. Sleep with me the night through, husband."

"If 'tis what you desire, sweet soul, you shall have it. I will forever lie with you until sunrise."

"You will, truly?" Honora's smile broadened, her look of doubt disappearing like shadows before the noon sun. "Does Oleen always foresee the truth?"

Brec stopped, confused by this sudden, unexpected turn in their conversation. "I've never known the good healer to be wrong. Why?"

"Because Oleen told me that I—that we conceived a daughter last night."

"A daughter?" Stunned, Brec contemplated Honora's tear-stained face, taking in the joy and pleasure she radiated. Anything that made her happy warmed him.

"Are you as pleased as I am, husband?"

"Aye, I am well pleased, wife."

With that admission Brec took Honora's face between his good hand and the injured one and kissed her, unleashing every emotion he had kept from her all these months. He cared nothing for the crowd that turned to gape at them or for the loving spectacle that he and Honora created right there in the Great Hall. The great dark-haired clan chief passionately kissing the lovely, courageous lady of Castle Dunrugis—as he had never done before. Brec cared only that *his wife loved him,* only him, and he loved her—and the devil take wide-eyed villagers.

AUTHOR'S NOTE

Colkitto and his force of Irish and Islemen joined with the Marquis of Montrose in August 1644. They marched forth from Blair to defeat Lord Elcho's forces at Tippermuir on the first of September. During that winter the marquis led a brilliant highland campaign that resulted in huge losses for all: Royalists, Covenantors, and neutrals. He even took Argyll's highland castle and sent the Campbell chief fleeing to the protection of Edinburgh.

A year later Montrose and his forces were surprised and defeated at Philiphaugh near Selkirk by David Leslie, a nephew of Lord Leven. Montrose escaped. He tried in vain to raise the Highlanders once more but was forced to disband his army and sail for Norway in 1646. Colkitto's fearsome sword broke in battle, and he escaped westward to his homeland.

Though Montrose ultimately suffered defeat, he disabled the ambitious Argyll in his bid for supreme Scottish power. Many would no longer support the Campell chief who could not unite the clans.

When Montrose, the cavalier marquis, died beneath the headsman's ax, many Scots mourned. And they were as shocked as all the world when the English executed King Charles. Ironically, in time the Cromwellians lost power and Charles II came to the throne. Then Argyll, the king's Scot foe, also met his death on the block.

By the end of the English Civil War, the Scots had gained little, and the great battle for Scot sovereignty from England was still to be fought a century later at Culloden.

The Duchess

Jude Deveraux

Claire Willoughby, a beautiful young American heiress, had been trained her whole life for one thing— to be an English duchess. But when she travels to Scotland to visit her fiance, Harry Montgomery, the duke of McArran, she finds out his family is more than she'd bargained for. Fascinated by his peculiar family, Claire is most intrigued by Trevelyan Montgomery, Harry's mysterious brilliant cousin who she finds living secretly in an unused part of the estate. As she spends more and more time with the magnetic Trevelyan, Claire finds herself drawn to him against her will, yearning to know everything about him. But if Trevelyan's secret is discovered life at Bramley will never be the same.

AVAILABLE IN HARDCOVER FROM POCKET BOOKS

POCKET
BOOKS